Table of Contents

1 — The Day Before Paulette's Murder......... 1
2 — A Big Butt and a Smile 11
3 — Why You Act So Ugly? 21
4 — Stuck on Stupid... 27
5 — Despicable Me.. 33
6 — Con-vic-tion (Without a Trial) 45
7 — What Happened to My Family? 55
8 — Who Killed My Baby's Momma? 69
9 — The Ride to the Station 83
10 — The Not Guilty Bed 91
11 — Fresh Out.. 127
12 — I See Dead People.................................. 149
13 — Sipping on Some Siz-zyrup.................. 181
14 — The Dope Spot.. 187
15 — My Ghetto Angel.................................... 215
16 — Free at Last 229
17— My First 48 245
18 — Liquidating the Ridgetop..................... 265
About the Author 287

1
The Day Before Paulette's Murder...

THE DAY BEFORE PAULETTE'S MURDER was one of the most blissful days we shared together as a family. I was her lover and her friend. It was Friday night and I was going to pop the question to my Boo during dinner at The Outback Restaurant. I had bought a ring that took me forever to pick out. After visiting every major jewelry store between The Town and Seattle, I finally picked out one. It set me back a little more than I expected, but I knew it was the right one to express the joy of loving her.

The ring was diamond-studded with yellow-rose-gold diamonds set in the shape of a rose in the center of a white gold band. When I picked up the ring on Valentine's Day and saw how the diamonds sparkled, I felt like a proud newlywed husband celebrating his first anniversary with a diamond ring. After only a few seconds, I asked the clerk to gift-wrap it for my Boo. She wrapped it in a red box with yellow and red ribbons. On the way home that day, I drove the entire distance without turning on music or answering my phone. I was anxiously anticipating popping the question during dinner.

As I drove, I imagined what our lives would be like once we were finally married, which left a permanent smile on my face during the whole way home.

I made dinner reservations for six p.m., unheard of on Valentine's Day. Earlier I had called a homeboy Roger, the head chef for the Outback. Only during special occasions did I call upon his services. The last time we were there, his fiancée Sherrie hooked us up with a very nice table for three in a closed section of the restaurant where Baby Riesha was able to cut up and howl as loudly as she wanted. There, she was able to fling food onto the floor without disturbing other patrons.

Roger asked me if I was still with Paulette? I answered ecstatically because he was the first person to know I was going to ask Paulette to marry me. He asked if little Riesha was coming to dinner as well, adding that Sherrie would be upset if we didn't bring her "little Baby Booboo". When I said that Riesha was coming, he said, "Can't wait to see your little girl!" with enthusiasm. Roger suggested we be at the restaurant by five-thirty, saying he'd have our table set up real nice for my family.

When we arrived, the waiting line extended into the parking lot. Paulette felt bad because every time we went there, we walked straight past the entire line to find Sherrie writing down the names of the approaching guest. After seating us ahead of the others, who appeared frustrated, Sherrie said nonchalantly, "Don't pay any attention to those people; they're the same ones the owner calls me to place at the beginning of the line. I'm not tripping." Running the front-end of the restaurant, she acted as if she didn't care if anyone noticed what she did, wishing somebody would say something about reserving seats for her friends so she could curse them out.

When Sherrie pulled out Paulette's chair, I couldn't help but notice her scar. It resembled a thick earthworm that seemed to be crawling from underneath her chin to her right ear, a lifetime reminder of the days when she used to sell her body so she and Roger could get high. Their addiction to crack cocaine almost ended their lives, their relationship, and their freedom.

Sherrie walked with a remarkable strut, swinging her hips from left to right. If you didn't know her past, you'd think she mastered her strut as a runway model, rather than gaining it through years of walking up and down Pacific Avenue. The ho-stroll where she gallivanted was less then a mile from the main gate of two military posts, McCord Air Force Base and Fort Lewis Army Base. Roger acted as her pimp, targeting desperate lonely military men, both greenhorns and retirees, hustling them out of their paychecks just to get a sniff or a taste of her poonani. Her poignant magnetism became her weapon of choice, as her trusted followers never settled for just any prostitute off the stroll. Men were spotted sleeping in their cars overnight to be first in line to be aroused by Ms. Sherrie. If one of her loyal customers spotted her getting arrested, her bail was paid by the time she was done with fingerprinting. If she allowed her tricks to have sex without a prophylactic, they paid her three hundred dollars an hour, triple the normal asking price.

I tried not to stare at the scar, but when Sherrie handed Paulette a menu, Little Riesha reached out and touched it saying, "Ow-ee!"

"Ya, baby, ow-ee."

Paulette pulled the baby's hand away from Sherrie's face, saying, "I am so sorry."

"No worries girl, she just thinks it's a ow-ee; it's okay. When we get our income taxes back this year, we gonna get it covered up."

"That's good," replied Paulette.

"Ya girl, they gonna take some skin off my ass and put it over the scar. Isn't that incredible, girl! I got the scar from selling my ass; now I'm going to use a part of my ass to cover it up. Girl, God is good, God is good!" Sherrie took Riesha from my arms, kissing her on her left cheek and telling her how much she looked like her momma. Little Riesha took the chance to rub the thick wormy scar.

"Wasn't it your birthday the last time y'all were here?" asked Sherrie.

Paulette, never one to turn down a compliment, smiled, showing off her freshly bleached white teeth and the lonely dimple that protrudes from her left cheek when she smiles. "Ya, last September, and my man had bought me this ring!" Paulette showed Sherrie the ring I gave her last fall.

"Damn girl, your man must love you!"

Little did either of them know I bought that ring off a homey for twenty bucks. And here I just paid three racks ($3,000) for the ring I was about to give my love. Don't get it twisted; the first ring was at least a carat. I don't know much about diamonds, but it was a big one, but not as big as the one I had in my coat pocket. I kept my Boo all blinged up. I liked to see her in gold necklaces and diamond rings.

Next it was Sherrie's turn to show off the ring that Roger gave her. "You see my engagement ring my man gave me?" It was gorgeous with a fairly large rock on top, surrounded by diamonds shaped like the letter "S".

"Oh! I can't imagine Roger picking out a ring. I didn't think he knew anything about them, let alone engagement rings," I said.

"Can I see? That's lovely, girl, what you doing to him? You got him working a real job and now this, you go, girl."

Quickly Sherrie corrected me, mentioning they've been clean and sober for over two years.

"That's good, Miss Lady. I knew the two of you were good for each other a long time ago."

Our special table was centrally located in front of a dimly lit fireplace with a big bouquet of red roses in the middle. A young woman appeared with a highchair. Each of her forearms bore tattoos; one said *Queen* and the other read *Bitch*. As she left, Sherrie told her, "Thank you very much, Lacey." Lacey left behind a little teddy bear for Baby Riesha to play with until our appetizers arrived. Sherrie became our waitperson taking our orders, bringing us our drinks and starter salads.

For appetizers, the baby nibbled on some complimentary table bread, while Paulette and I split a Caesar salad. (We knew how big the salads were so we always split them.) As soon as we finished the last piece of sourdough bread, Lacey brought our entrees. I ordered my usual Alaskan king crab and top sirloin medium-well, and my Boo ordered the king crab with roasted garlic chicken and roasted red potatoes.

The wait staff treated us like royalty from Timbuktu. In between the shell cracking and the lip smacking, Lacey kept our table fully stocked with napkins, hot butter to dip our crab in, and fresh hot bread with lots of those little butters on the side. All of the empty crab legs were removed before Paulette or I had cracked open another crab shell. As we finished throwing down our food, I introduced Paulette to the beauty of watching the sun set over the Puget Sound and The Olympic Mountains. There wasn't any greater scene than watching the sun go down over the water. Snow topped the jagged edges of the Olympic Mountains, making way for the light from the reddish-orange ball of fire to bounce rays off the mountaintops. The gleaming sunrays glistened off the motionless water beneath, making the Sound appear lifeless and dreamlike.

"By the time you finish that crab leg, the sun will have vanished, disappeared," I said to my soon-to-be wife.

She glanced to the glass French doors that led out to the deck and said, "Shut up! No way! The sun is going down!" Paulette pretended to be pleasantly shocked, but not too mystified. Nothing could take her attention off the lonely crab leg on my plate that she eyeballed, knowing I didn't want to eat it. One of the things I loved about her was how she knew her way around the kitchen, and still kept a body that looked like she was a personal trainer.

She didn't waste any time turning her attention back on the last enormous king crab leg, "Are you gonna eat that, Ceeze?"

"No, go ahead Boo, knock yourself out!" I replied.

"I have never seen anything like that before. So where does the sun go?" she said so innocently that I wanted to embrace the moment by pulling her close to me, never wanting to let go.

While Paulette waited for me to explain where the sun went, I watched in awe, mesmerizing the way she cautiously fed our baby. The care and attention she used to exchange bits of crabmeat from her mouth to our baby's mouth, reassured me that she was the one I wanted to spend the rest of my natural life with. Just watching the harmony between the two made me feel like I was put here on this earth to protect the two of them. And that was what I planned on doing for the rest of my life. At that very moment I thought about popping the question, but I felt it would be more memorable to wait until we were done with our food. I didn't want Paulette to get her crabby-paddy fingers all over the ring. Instead I settled for a kiss by sliding my chair out a bit and extending my entire upper body over the top of the table to get a kiss from my Boo.

"Give me a kiss girl! I love you so much that it's crazy!" I could taste the crabmeat, butter, and roasted potatoes from her mouth as she stuck her tongue into mine for just a quick second. (She could never give me a kiss without sticking her tongue in my mouth; even in the morning before we brushed our teeth.)

Once Paulette finished the last crab leg, I pushed the fingerbowl filled with water and lemon juice toward her. "I got something for you, baby, but you have to wash off your crabby paddy fingers first," I said. Paulette slowly dipped her fingers in and out of the cleansing bowl; my heart began to pitter-patter. I felt a trace of sweat drip down the side of my head from beneath my brand new personalized lime green Seattle Seahawk hat. I bought it from the Seahawks Home Page just for this special occasion, to match my new lime green Converse. This was a special night.

I was moments away from making the biggest decision in my life and anyone could tell I was slightly nervous. I held my right hand out in front of us to see if it was shaking; Paulette noticed it was shaking too. "Boo, what's wrong?" she asked. "And why is your hand shaking? Why are you sweating, Ceeze, you all right?"

Just like the nurturing mother she was, Paulette took her napkin from her lap to wipe the sweat from the side of my face. *The time has come!* I said to myself.

"Waiter, can I order a Remy Mar, please? VSOP!" Not that cheap shit from the bottom shelf!"

"You don't need a drink, Boo. What is it you want to tell me?" said Paulette.

Before the young brotha could get too far from the table, I yelled out, "Yo, little ice, my man!" Then I yelled back again, "Hey man, make it a double with no ice, and I won't bother you any more."

Working like a bulletproof vest, the Demon God tried to lower my self-esteem to prevent me from moving forward with God's plan to become a unit through the eyes of Christ. I became very judgmental. Negative thoughts raced through my mind. Humiliated and defeated is how I felt all of a sudden. *Am I worthy enough to be her husband?* Before God could answer, the demon sitting on my right shoulder answered, "You're an insensible piece of shit. You don't deserve this beautiful woman. The only thing you're going to do is bring her down if you marry her. You owe it to your baby not to destroy her mother's life by marrying her."

"Yo, waiter! Where's my drink, Cuzzo!"

I wasn't going to allow the devil to hold me hostage another moment. I had made up my mind that Paulette was my soul mate flown down from the heavens above. I asked God to rid the negative thoughts immediately so I could let my wife know that I wanted to spend the rest of my life with her. I knew it was evident I was battling it out with the devil, and I hoped Paulette could tell by the look on my face that God once again prevailed. My life wasn't the same since we became parents and moved in together. She had become more than just my baby's mother. I thought of her as an ambassador sent from God to show me how to live a successful and fruitful life.

My father once said to me, a woman falls in love with what a man has on the inside, whereas a man falls in love with what a women has on the outside. I wanted Paulette as my wife because of the beautiful person that she was both inside and out. I prayed that Paulette could see past all of the turmoil I had previously put her through. I prayed that Paulette would see that I had truly fallen in love with her and that I will become the man she envisioned spending the rest of her life with.

When she finished dipping her fingers in and out of the finger bowl, I pulled out the box from my coat pocket and dropped it on the table in front of her saying, "Bang Bang! Open it up!"

When I threw it on the table, baby Riesha grabbed it and began to pull off the bow.

"What did you buy me?"

"Open it up." I was beginning to get overly excited just anticipating the look on her face. "Let Mommy see it," I directed Riesha.

Paulette pulled off the bow and opened the box. The look on her face was what I anticipated. Her mouth opened and her jaw almost hit the table. She covered her mouth, stood up, and reached over the table, kissing and hugging me saying, "Oh, baby, I always knew you loved me, but damn, baby, this ring is beautiful!"

"Will you be my wifey?" I asked her.

"Yes, baby, just let me know the date, time, and place, and I'm all yours, baby?"

When she said yes, the air around me felt crisp, fresh, and clean. I took a deep breath to ease the stress, opening my lungs, allowing me to breathe fine air again. At that moment I felt like I had just wakened on a houseboat that sat stationary on Chambers Bay.

On the way home, Paulette talked endlessly about how she didn't want a white wedding. In fact, she wanted an all-brown wedding, calling it her chocolate wedding. She wanted to get married in August, because in the state of Washington, August is the only time of the year that rain is left out of weather forecasts. She insisted on getting married outside, at Point Defiance Park on the second weekend of August, in front of the Solarium while the flowers were still in blossom. It all sounded good to me and I was down for it all. Whatever my Boo wanted for her wedding, I was going to provide.

When we arrived on our block, Paulette sprung on me that she and the baby were supposed to stay the night over at her home girl's house on the west side of town. I asked why she waited until we got all the way home to let me know this. She said she was overwhelmed by our engagement and forgot to tell me. I asked if they could stay the night tomorrow instead of tonight? She informed me that her home girl was having some personal issues with her boyfriend and didn't want to be alone, and she was worried that she might do something crazy, like blow his head off or slash his tires or something worse, like committing suicide.

I wasn't too happy, nor did I want to sound vain or start an argument with her either. I even had my cousin Tatiana waiting at the house to scoop up little Riesha so her mother and I could spend the night alone; I envisioned us making love throughout the night after popping the question. And I didn't want to spend the night without her.

I tried to come up with an excuse: I didn't have my strap (gun) on me and didn't want to be caught on the Westside without my gun. Those Bloods tried to ride on me and my homeboys just the other day. I said, "Baby I can't take you over on the Westside because I don't have my pistol!"

Even though Paulette knew that riding on the Westside without my strap on a Friday night was like committing suicide, that excuse didn't work. Besides, she knew I always kept one in the trunk.

"Don't even play like that, baby; you never leave home without it. You can pick us up early in the morning, I promise."

2
A Big Butt and a Smile

THE FIRST TIME I SAW PAULETTE, my breath stopped. Paulette was the kind of girl that shook you up inside just looking at her. Light, bright, almost white skin held together the most beautiful woman I had ever seen, a tall thick tender in her twenties, red-boned with long curly shiny light brown hair. She appeared to be white, but later I found out that both of her parents were mixed black and white.

Wannabe pimp aspirations infused with marijuana laced with embalming fluid had broken my spirit. I had been feeding it by exchanging body fluids with women who also had low self-esteem. Ultimately this kept me in a toxic and volatile off-and-on again relationship with ex-girlfriends.

I met Paulette on the Westside where I bought my weed. Jake the Snake was my supplier of the kush weed that I sold. I made the forbidden trip across enemy lines from the Ridgetop to the Westside of The Town once a month to buy two ounces of weed.

That day, there she was, sitting so proper-like, back straight, no slouching, on Jake's couch, smoking weed from the two-foot-long bong that Jake kept fully stocked for his customers. I was instantly attracted to her; nothing turned me on more then a woman smoking weed, and so elegantly at that. She had the lungs of a professional weed smoker. I could tell she smoked a lot of weed from the way the bong water boiled as she sucked profusely, filling her lungs with white and green marijuana smoke.

Jake harvested medical marijuana for the government; only a person who smoked a lot of weed could take such a major hit of the stuff without choking. I sat down next to her on the sofa, its stuffing coming out of the cushions. As I sat down, the couch levitated off the ground forcing the water from the bong to tip over and spill out on her leg. With a half-baked smile on her face, the witty Paulette said loudly enough for everyone in the apartment to hear, "Ah fuck! You know this shit is gonna stink! Bong water smells worse than chitlins!"

My eyes followed her every move as she rose from the couch and headed straight towards the kitchen to refill the bong. I watched her run her hand over the backside of her tight white jeans. This gesture alone was another turn-on for me especially coming from a woman with such a colossal ass. Paulette had one of the best pear-shaped assess I had ever seen. She knew I was watching as she swiped her backside again, as if she was wiping something off that was not there. I could tell she had practiced this act. I instantly felt arousal from within my left pants pocket. No doubt! I was sprung like a rubber band. I quivered, forcing every hair follicle on my body to rise up and salute, placing goose bumps on my forearms while turning pimples into hard rock blackheads.

When Paulette sat back down again next to me, her side of the couch hit the soiled floor and my side of the couch levitated. She moved closer to me to level the couch so she wouldn't spill any more of the bong water. She reached over me to reach the bowl of weed in the center of the table, samples to try before purchasing. I didn't have to sample Jake's weed; I was always okay with the five-second rule: take a pinch off the weed, place it up on the wall like a thumb tack, and count to five using the one-thousand-number method — one one-thousand, two one-thousand, three one-thousand…. If the weed fell off the wall before your count reached five one thousand, the weed wasn't the sticky-icky-icky. This meant the weed was harvested too early and didn't reach its full potency before it was plucked. To keep from falling over, Paulette placed her hand on my knee saying, "I am so high right now, I don't need any more weed. I've been smoking since noon."

I asked, "That's kind of early to be smoking, isn't it?"

She almost fell over in my lap, as she used my shoulders for leverage, I stuck my nose in between her neck cavity and her chin. She smelled like a crate of freshly picked green apples from Big Momma's back yard.

"Shit, nigga, I used to start smoking at eleven when 'One Life to Live' came on. Now I wait until 'All My Children' starts at twelve. As long as it's after noon, I don't give a fuck!" Without hesitation, Paulette loaded more weed into the bong and began to smoke. Smoke flowed from her mouth and she coughed, almost choking. "Here try this shit; this shit is the bomb, my nigga!" When she passed the bong to me, I noticed she had well-manicured nails, each one painted blood red with little gold hoops on the tips. She had a gold ring on each finger, including her thumbs.

My interest was sparked. She appeared to be a classy heifer with enough ghetto swag to keep me preoccupied for a few years. I used to like fabulous ghetto women who drove Cadillacs, stayed draped in gold from neck to toes, and brandished one gold tooth right in the front. To accent her perfect ears, Paulette wore big dangling gold earrings. I counted ten gold necklaces with various pendants hanging around her neck. A tattoo on her neck read, *Sexy Bone*. I read the signals: because of the red fingernails and the B pendant, it was safe to assume she had some Piru Blood gang affiliation. The gold glimmering off her golden skin enhanced her flawless cover girl skin tone. (Although it was forbidden in my subculture, I wanted to tell her how beautiful her skin looked. By doing so, I would have exposed my vulnerable side to a woman who I didn't even know.)

When I was buying weed from Jake, the Demon God was running amok within me. As usual, Jake's weed had me stuck on stupid, which caused my eyes to fill up with red cobwebs. The very first sight of Paulette's silky shimmering skin made my toes curl up in my original gangster Nikes. I thought she was so damn sexy I would have attempted to climb Mt. St. Helens while it was erupting if she asked me to meet her there for some Ash-Tea.

When "Jake the Snake" brought out my weed, he noticed she had smoked up most of the customer weed on the table. "Damn girl, you gonna stop coming over here smoking up all of my weed without paying!"

"You know the only thing I have to do is flash one of my boobs and you'll throw a sack my way, Jake, so don't start fronting just because your homeboy is here!" Her sassy smart-ass mouth completed the turn-on for me.

I pulled out four hundred and fifty dollars from underneath my nut sack and tossed it to Jake. He quickly tossed it to Paulette and asked her to put the cash bundle in the freezer. "And bring back two Mayo jars from the fridge. Grab the ones from the top shelf." The jars were packed to the rim with bluish-green marijuana that had what looked like freshly fallen snow flakes sprinkled all over several of the male buds that were the size of large jalapeños. Jake stopped me as I headed towards the front door. "Be careful, youngun. She could convince the Pope to let her borrow his ring for her daughter's show-and-tell!"

"I m no dummy, I can spot bullshit a mile away, Cuzzo! You know your boy can handle his. I'm not tripping off her shit! She can't trick a playa, playa!"

"Watch your back cousin; watch your back, I'm telling you this because I know how she gets down." After the brief yet decisive conversation with Jake-the-Snake, I headed out, only to be stopped at the door by Paulette.

"What, you the police now? You gonna arrest me or something?" Paulette said, "When can I expect a call?"

I quickly replied, "I don't have your number!"

She extended her hand to me, resting all of her fingers on my chest as though she was going to keep me from leaving the apartment. She reached around to her back pocket with her other hand and pulled out a piece of paper and said, "You ain't ready for me!" Her nails left imprints on my chest. I asked her if she could remove her fingers so I could leave. "Why you in a hurry, Nigga? You got a hot date or something?"

Quickly I discovered that she was better at the pimp game than I was. Manipulation was her profession. I could tell she used her seductive personality to lure people into her Charlotte's Web where her vagina worked like a straw to suck out all the goodness and common sense that any man possessed. I soon found out after one night with her what it felt like to be raped. Pints of free-flowing spirits gushed from the tiny slit within her clitoris, sending unwanted spirits from her into my urethra. She was so nasty in bed that after I ejaculated in her, I was left feeling victimized and morally stripped, as if my mother had watched the entire escapade go down.

Overnight I became addicted to the tricks she had mastered in the bedroom. Paulette held my penis captive as she squeezed the inside of her vagina walls when we made love. I was hooked on her ability to work her vagina muscles as if she had been exercising this area for the purpose of making me reach my peak. Even if I begged her to let go, she wouldn't unless she watched my body shake unequivocally. The more we exchanged body fluids, the more I felt compelled to remain locked in this subdued zombie-like trance, led by her pretty face and her big voluptuous butt.

A criminal background check is required when anyone applies for an apartment. Although I thought my hustle game was tight, I usually listed some reasons why my arrest record was so lengthy. I presented reference letters from previous landlords, along with a fabricated story, so I didn't have to tell the landlord all of my personal business. As diabolical as it may sound, I had to come up with a motivating, influential story that persuaded many a biased racist to accept me into their world. I had marijuana possession on my record, despite the fact that the amount I was caught with was minuscule, and the fact that I was sentenced only to outpatient drug and alcohol treatment for three months. I had more then a few misdemeanors, which most apartment managers viewed as life lessons learned.

But when the domestic violence charge popped up, I had a whole lot of explaining to do. The Domestic Violence (DV) stemmed from an abusive relationship I was in before I settled down and began to live a productive life. Though I presented a DV completion certificate, I was always asked the big question: "What happened?"

That's when I hit them with my truth, stating, "The domestic violence counseling lifted the cobwebs out of my eyes, giving me a greater perspective on how God viewed me once I asked him for forgiveness." I left it at that. What I didn't tell them was that, in a crazy roundabout way, Paulette was my ghetto angel. If it weren't for her ghetto ass tactics and my inability to trust anyone and control my temper during our relationship, I would not have received the spiritual guidance that I obtained through Domestic Violence Counseling. The side effects from smoking marijuana every day, all day, limited my ability to convey my true feelings. The mixture of what I thought was good sex and hard liquor disabled my aptitude to allow my inner voice to guide me.

My inner voice was God trying to inform me that Paulette and I were not equally yoked. The THC in marijuana drained the necessary coping skills I needed to acknowledge my girlfriend's drug addiction, which was subsequently as lethal as my inability to see clearly. As long as I was smoking weed and drinking liquor, the symptoms of her addiction were not obvious to me. But as she sobered up, her ability to act normal became quite unbearable, while my ability to ignore the true signs of her addiction to hard-core drugs became imperfect.

As the meth vacated Paulette's body, she became very manic, overwhelmed with anxiety, almost psychotic. She fabricated stories of people around her trying to kill her or take away her children. During these episodes, I became frustrated. The woman I had fallen in love with was not the woman I had gotten to know. At first we had marijuana in common, along with the desire to have sex all the time. But once Paulette switched from smoking weed to smoking meth, I realized I couldn't function normally throughout the day without a cocktail of weed and malt liquor, which was the only commonality we had shared.

Once I rose from self-medicating off the weed, I was left feeling like I was a worthless piece of shit for falling in love with a meth head. Accepting her addiction made me feel less of a man. Feeling less of a man destroyed my ability to strive in any which way. When I was around her, the only thing I wanted to do was smoke weed, drink beer, smoke cigarettes, and trip over her heels as I attempted to make love to her.

I was tripping over her heels to the point where I couldn't even perform the simplest tasks, like shaving or showering or washing my clothes, or cooking. Instead, I frequented the local corner barbershop twice a week at twenty dollars a pop to allow someone else to take care of me. Instead of cleaning my own clothes, I would simply drop them off at the dry cleaners to have them do it for me. I had a businessman mentality, setting aside two hundred dollars a month in order to look good, thinking if I stayed looking fresh Paulette would desire me more than she desired Methamphetamines.

The cleaner I looked, the more money I made. Mr. Lee, who owned the Ridgetop Cleaners, made sure that the starch I requested for my jeans was laid on heavy. The straighter the crease, the more street credibility I gained. Only dudes that made lots of money in the streets could afford to take their clothes to the cleaners. It was imperative that my attire was funky fresh every day all day, yet my classiness wasn't enough to keep Paulette attracted to me; she was more attracted to the pleasure she obtained from using meth.

I was hoodwinked into love simply by the smell of the Bed Bath and Beyond body lotion that she doused over herself after every shower, making her smell like a field full of lavender and freshly squeezed oranges. My life was in such disarray after meeting her that I was at the point where I acted ugly because of the demons that had infiltrated my thoughts. I became disengaged from reality, which led me to believe that I wasn't accountable for my actions. I enabled Paulette by allowing her charismatic appeal to fill my eyes with cobwebs. I became disabled to the point where I couldn't see past her brilliant smile, her petite size seven and her perfectly pear-shaped ass which sat atop her track-star legs that were thicker than a snicker.

It wasn't her fault that I fell for the oaky-doke. My heart was opened and left open when I took my first hit of weed at the age of thirteen. With my heart left open, I became vulnerable and easily led astray by getting drunk and high on a regular basis. Unaware of my family's history of addiction, the first puff of weed and first swallow of thunderbird formed unbreakable cobwebs in my eyes, creating a film of dead flies, blinding me to the point I was unable to see through Paulette's solid rattlesnake skin.

Paulette was bitter towards her father for leaving her at a very young age, replacing his love with abusing her body with drugs, alcohol, and jumping into bed with men before getting to know them. Her mother forced her father out the house when Paulette was a pre-teen, a stage in a young woman's life when she needed her father to tell her how special she is and how he loved her more than all the grains of sand on the sea shores across the world.

Paulette's hatred and disrespect for men was a learned experience. Her mother was bitter towards her own father, who had left Paulette's grandmother for the housekeeper when she too was in her pre-teens. The women in Paulette's family had a generational curse hanging over their heads. Though her mother and father rekindled their relationship, Paulette never forgave her father for cheating on her mother. Their relationship was severed, and the two of them didn't speak again until Paulette had her first child. It seemed inevitable for her not to pass down that trait to her own daughter if she didn't learn how to love and respect herself before making any more attempts to love another man. Her mother cheated on her father with the milkman and was impregnated with Paulette's brother. Paulette sabotaged her successful relationship with her baby's father by cheating on him with the little sister's basketball coach. After her father left, her mother never again expressed any feelings of love and joy with her or her brother. This created a cell of self-hatred that flowed painfully through her blood stream, forming a negative disregard for any man who expressed love and joy towards her and her own children.

Paulette tried to convince herself that someone could actually love her for what she had on the inside rather than how she looked on the outside. When she birthed her first child, she tried to convince herself that the love she had for her child would take the place of the love she wished her daddy and her baby's daddy had expressed towards her.

However, no one around her could tell she loved her children by the way she shuffled them around from one extended family member's house to another. As one returned from an aunt's house, Paulette already had confirmed a drop-off time at a cousin's house. And when they returned, one of her girlfriends was awaiting their arrival, so the kids could get a good home-cooked meal, a bath, and spend the next couple of days living among a circular family where the kids would be treated like royalty.

Paulette chose to spend more time with the men she was taking advantage of, rather than taking advantage of the free love that her kids were trying to share with her.

3
Why You Act So Ugly?

A CONFUSED BEING IS AN UNCARING BEING that believes everything must evolve around him. Ultimately that being concludes that he doesn't care about how his life style has a negative impact on his community, his family or his offspring. I must be one of those confused beings, if you look at where I came from.

I know there's a Demon God that takes advantage of people like me — people who feel there is no hope. I roam city streets throughout the ghetto, searching for my next high or next victim to have sex with. I awaken the next morning in a narcotic state, my body laid limp-butt naked on the cold linoleum floor in the bathroom, wedged between the bathtub and the porcelain God that I clung to for dear life throughout the night.

My morning is spent cleaning up trails of vomit sprawled from the front door to the bathroom, defecation that lies in piles on the floor beneath my undergarments. I spend the next two hours trying to figure out what made me act so damn ugly.

Throughout the day I avoid phone calls and neglect all responsibilities. I'm too sick to pick up the phone to let my boss know that I'm not coming in.

After hours of praying to the porcelain God, I'm startled by a shadow of an unknown naked body silhouetted at the bathroom door watching me. Before I can say good morning or good-bye, the body without a face has grabbed all of its personal belongings and made a b-line for the front door. Shame takes over, because I can't remember a thing about this person with whom I undoubtedly exchanged bodily fluids during the night. My head pounds as if someone hit it with an aluminum bat and split it wide open. I suffer hours and hours of vomiting and dry heaving until my dead body feels like I'd drunk ammonia, had a broken rib and emphysema — all at the same time. I crawl on my knees to the bedroom and miraculously find enough strength to launch myself into bed.

Throughout the day I avoid mirrors, fearing to see the shocked, bewildered, and mortified image of an evil twin glaring back.

Once the drugs and alcohol from yesterday's juncture begin to dissolve, I need something to deaden the pain and take one more bump from the cocaine already aligned on the mirror resting on the floor next to my bed.

When abusing drugs, the act of using takes the place of the things that you used to enjoy doing. Fun things like reading the comics at the breakfast table while my father reads the local section. His direction: "You got to keep up with the goings-on in your community, boy." And playing catch in the back yard with the neighbor boy, Bad-Breath Scottie, who never brushed his teeth, rationalizing, "I brush my teeth at night so I don't have to worry about brushing them in the morning!"

I used to ride my bike from Lakewood to the Ridgetop, which was way across town, to Auntie's house just to have her fry me up some bird. "Boy, if you hungry, ride your bike to the *Mini-Mart* and get some chicken thighs and Crisco!" And playing basketball in *Whomper-Stomper* boots in the rain for hours every day — until the basketball court turned into the place to get high.

The fun things in my life transcended into watching my homeboy roll marijuana in *Zig Zag* rolling paper. Instead of going fishing with Uncle Al, my pastime turned to passing a joint around to see who could hold in the most smoke for the longest time without choking: "one-one-thousand, two-one-thousand, three-one-thousand!" The longer I held it in, the longer the weed replaced the air in my lungs, cutting off air needed to breathe. As the weed floated around my brain, the chemicals circumvented normal brain and muscle activity, making me light-headed, dumb as an ox.

I never picked up a newspaper unless it was to see who got arrested or to see if anyone I knew was dead. If you asked me about something other than "who got shot last week?" or "how can I make 100 dollars out of 50 bucks?" I didn't have a clue, nor did I care. For years I ran around town with thugs victimized by societal restraints and environmental shackles that left us all confused and depressed. Until I became one myself.

I became a young thug who believed possessing pimp-like characteristics was a gift from God. I was told I had the gift of gab. I possessed the ability to manipulate people into doing what I wanted them to do. I took advantage of weaknesses by simply uttering the right words smoothly, articulating each syllable with perfection. I was able to revel in my gifts. During such time I wasn't close to God; I truly believed I was put on this earth to pimp women like big-time pimps from around my neighborhood.

As we got older, I went from smoking weed at the basketball court to relieving my frustrations at a local watering hole called Uncle Toms Juke Joint, which we called home, "a place where everybody knew our names". We sacrificed spending intimate moments with our families in exchange for hanging out with the homeys.

We were plagued by the "Cheers" TV show mentality. Talking down to each other became a form of brotherly love. Shooting down each others dreams and talking about each others flaws became a form of breaking bread. However, cutting down one another broke our spirits, confusing us.

To help us embrace our manhood and to save face as we played the dozens, we masked our pain and dejection with double shots of whiskey and bottom shelf tequila, all the while confusing insults with love, honor, and respect for each other.

Statistics: One percent of my childhood friends went to college after high school. One out of 500 became big-time dope dealers. The rest of us were in and out of jail for petty misdemeanors throughout our entire adult lives. Those smart enough not to get caught selling drugs or who weren't arrested for looking like a gang member, or actually being in a gang, became low-end hustlers selling dope to neighbors. We sold weed and stolen merchandise to our cousins and closest friends.

I belonged to that group and associated with individuals who believed they were predestined to fail. Spending a week or a month in Juvenile Detention seemingly became a part of growing up in The Town. By the age of fourteen, our mothers couldn't keep us from being kicked out of school for fighting, skipping class, or just for being deviants.

My friends and I were inseparable; no one could pull us apart. If we weren't in juvenile detention together, we were at each others house. Every member of the subculture that I belonged to grew up in a fatherless house except for me. My father worked hard and worked so many double shifts I never saw him until Saturday mornings when he appeared from the back of the house, toting a beer in one hand and a broom in the other. The broom represented my chores for the next two hours if I wanted to leave the house. My job was to sweep the entire house, even the carpets since we didn't own a vacuum.

Our mothers grew up together and were considered go hard girls: women from the neighborhood who had survived rough years. They were teenage mothers who endured nights without heat, days without running water, and years without lying in the arms of a strong man.

My mother left the house at around five-thirty each morning; she was a secretary during the day for a rude old rich white doctor who wore polyester pants with no belt loops or front pockets. He called her *sweetie* and patted her on the ass after doing what he considered a good job. She was a part-time mother in the evening, for about two hours. Her third job as a janitor on the military base started at six p.m. and ended at 10. Again my father worked hard as a longshoreman, where the average shift was no less than sixteen hours. I was left to fend for myself.

My mother's friends became my aunts and cousins; we were a circular family. After church on Sundays, our mothers pitched in twenty dollars each to make sure our entire households had enough food to support the pack of crumb snatchers — us cousins who were constantly in each others kitchens. Our mothers made sure that we never lacked for food, our favorite hot dogs, banana pudding, and cereal. But they couldn't prevent us from running amok.

I'm from a generation of black men who knew how to ask questions but chose to dumb-down, playing the buffoon so we could continue to be ruthless and rugged. I chose not to ask why all of the brown children were allowed to play the dozens, shoot dice, and toss quarters in the back of the classroom. I became part of an entire generation of late bloomers, dedicated to running the streets, smoking weed, and drinking liquor until we passed out. Instead of reading books, I played basketball from sunup to sundown. Instead of studying for a test, I spent hours memorizing the lyrics of thuggish rap artists who spewed out words of degradation, convincing us that we were destined to spend the rest of our lives in prison.

It was at this point, I began living by our rule: I don't have to work hard in order to succeed, just hustle money by stealing, fencing stolen property, selling drugs, or taking money from naive women.

4
Stuck on Stupid

As the closing credits to "The Young and The Restless" scrolled down the screen, the lines formed at the mailboxes in front of our building used as low-income apartments. The neighbors plagued with the welfare syndrome waited for Mr. Postman to arrive with their government assistance checks. Although Mother's Day occurred only once a year, a celebration on the first of every month was known as Mothers' Week, and lasted for a minimum of seven days. During this week, instead of spending allocated food stamp money on a month's supply of groceries, many used their stamps to buy expensive items such as Alaskan king crab for $18.99 a pound or a six-pound Saluki Salmon for $33.

There are three main elements that kept people around my way oppressed and illiterate — fried food, drugs, and sex. The first of the month meant it was time to party like a rap star. Every house had a party theme; mine was always fried something, but chicken was my forte. Nobody around my way knew how to make fried chicken taste as favorable as I did. My fried chicken let families relish the taste rather than be consumed by the fear of high cholesterol. I fried mine in a blend of olive oil and vegetable oil.

The reality of not having enough food to feed the family for the rest of the month disrupted the joy of Mothers' Week. In order to make ends meet, sending neighborhood children scurrying across town to their grandparents became the norm. The grandparents watched the kids so Mommy and Daddy could spend a few days trying to get their hustle on. By the end of the week those mothers who harbored young adults over the age of eighteen, had to make a drastic decision. Kick them out or lose public assistance. These young folk were adversely affected by the welfare system, kicked into the real world without any formal training to help them succeed in life. They left the nest as strong ambitious young adults eager to unite Africa, only to return as dope fiends, junkies who enjoyed smoking wet sticks mixed with weed and crack kibbles sprinkled on top. They returned to the nest in the middle of the night like a cat burglar. Only this thief was there to steal a leftover meatloaf sandwich, a tall glass of Kool-aid, a warm fuzzy blanket, and a few ZZ's.

In the Ridgetop High School graduating class of 1985, all but three African American men had tried crack, and a substantial number continued the ongoing battle against the demon. Excessive spending to feed the demon affected a family's ability to survive for the rest of the month. Poor, discouraged, and depressed individuals took their frustrations out on each other for allowing the Demon to control their lives and their spending. Roaring sirens and barking police dogs were a part of the scene throughout the subdivision where I laid my head. All of the thugs lived on the west-end of the building. Weed smoke filled the hallways like fog resting over Puget Sound on a brisk October morning. Domino tournaments and weed sessions took place there and became the source of most of the trouble after folks had been up for two to three days popping skittles while snorting lines of cocaine mixed with crystal methamphetamines. One out of three tenants had been issued warrants, and one out of four carried guns or illegal drugs; so it wasn't unusual to witness five to ten people escorted to jail by the end of the second Sunday.

I capitalized off of the downfall of those around me. The role I played in my village was that of a pawnbroker. I was a walking pawnshop. I made illegal money off the buying and selling of stolen property. I was the best marketer around my way. I had a 24-hour return policy. If any of my products stopped working, the next time you bought something from me it was fifty percent off.

My goal was Big Pimping. I took the pimp game mentality seriously. Mind games became mind control, leaving victims feeling powerless when I stepped into the room. I learned early on that verbal abuse was the best way to make a person submit, leaving scars on the brain where branches of happiness once grew.

People who also identified with the pimp way of thinking led me down the wrong path. Breaking bread consisted of sharing knowledge on how to break down the mental stability of a woman. Once you mastered it, you were able to use that knowledge on people who were not hip to the pimping game. Over a blunt and a fifth of Grey Goose, I learned how to be discrete yet deceitful. I also learned how to manipulate those around me to do what I wanted them to do: I had become a little pimp.

My walk was a pimp-ish walk mastered throughout the years of emulating pimps whose names reigned over the city streets of San Francisco, Las Vegas, and Tacoma. My stroll appeared as if I had a handicap or tendonitis in my left knee. My right arm was used as a sway bar for balance, the very same way a pit bull uses its tail for stability during a dogfight. With just the right limp, mixed with a smooth and easy swing of my right arm behind my back, I gallivanted down the ho-stroll, showing off my pimp-like swagger. The work I put into my strut made my walk look flawless, which enhanced my parade. This influenced my pack of thieves, which made me look more like a homegrown pimp from The Town. The way I pronounced my words further enabled the pimp-like characteristics, belittling a less street-credible person after a brief yet meaningful conversation. I purposefully wanted every person around me to feel they were at a disadvantage when I stepped into their personal space.

Every evening a pimp by the name of Dollar Bill, who was known for paying out his hoes with dollar bills after a long night of earning thousands of dollars for himself, gave us an assignment to watch the 1973 black exploitation film about the pimp game, called "*The Mack*". Dollar Bill made sure that each one of us was given a specific scene to memorize so we too could master the pimp game.

We were to pay close attention to facial expressions, hand gestures, and the way the pimps de-humanized and demoralized their hoes — all the way down to the way "The Mack" opened and closed the door to his Cadillac.

I was to concentrate on the way Pretty Tony counted his money after his hoes gave him all their residuals — faces up, starting with the biggest bills down to the smallest, a ten dollar bill, nothing less. "Dollar Bill" kept fives in his left pocket and ones in his right pocket to tip the doorman or valet at the hotel. Pimps loved to brag about how much money they had.

We were told to press "pause" and "rewind" to practice the way the pimps in the movie walked and pronounced their names. We were stuck on *stupid* — huddled around the television, smoking weed rolled up in tobacco paper mixed with the tobacco from a Newport or Kool menthol cigarette. For hours we focused steadfastly on the movie the same way "Rocky Horror" film buffs memorized and acted out each and every scene of the epic movie.

A pimp transplant from Florida who called himself PT, short for our icon Pretty Tony, lived with Dollar. He informed us wannabe pimps never to sleep with our hoes. Mixing feelings with business was bad for business. Nonetheless, we didn't listen to him, and we never made the right decisions. We were unable to realize that pimping was a form of slavery; our brains were fogged up with smoke left behind from smoking pounds of marijuana that was secretly crystallized with Angel Dust and PCP.

Some of my homeys became victims of their own hustle; many developed feelings and made babies with women who they once pimped out for twenty bucks to rival gang members. These were the women who were looking for someone to take care of them. These were women who drove two-toned, oil dripping, dented Cadillacs that missed three hubcaps. These girls bore professionally sculpted hairstyles and always had freshly manicured fingernails. They spent more time at the mirror taking care of their hair, nails, and feet than they did getting their children's hair combed, faces washed, teeth brushed, and bathed.

They became nasty-ass tramps with no class at all. The kind of girls that belched and farted in public saying "oops my bad" instead of *excuse me* or *pardon me*, who spit on the sidewalk and smoked mild black cigars. They became spiteful heifers after dealing with men who used them. They were tricked out in front of homeless shelters on the first of the month when the men received their social security checks. Their "death row" became the hoe stroll to trick off their bodies to groups of five for nothing less than fifty bucks.

It was common for a pimp to have his hoe tattoo his name on her body. Tanisha, my ex, had my name tatted in the center of her lower back, in big cursive lettering reading "Ceeze Bitch". This was done to inform anyone who came after me that she was once mine. However Tanisha was not a prostitute, although I tried to convince her in a roundabout way that hoeing would make us both lots of money. Nonetheless, she left me shortly thereafter.

My mother once told me she could tell the difference between a sickly skinny person and a naturally thin person. Well I was sickly skinny with a face full of pimples to prove I was eating pure junk and neglecting my temple by indulging in an unhealthy lifestyle. The mixture of alcohol and weed did all kinds of obvious things to my body. The weed smoke hacked my nervous system creating a virus that targeted all of the normal brain functions, forcing it to work in over-load mode as it tried to find ways to improve the situation it had fallen victim to.

I could have run my Cadillac off the ethanol spewing from my sweat glands. I walked around smelling like a freshly brewed keg of Old English 900 Malt Liquor beer. The Demon within me kept me pumped up full of weed, liquor, and tobacco. I became reliant on the minimum dosage of a 22-ounce beer and a blunt to get me motivated in the morning, just so I could check the mail or take a shower.

When I was high on weed, I turned into my alter ego *Billie Bernstein*, i.e. tough guy, wannabe pimp daddy *Iceberg Slim*. While high and drunk off of the yak (Hennessey), I could approach any girl who glanced in my direction. I could talk the biggest shit, shoot the best pool, and dance the best dance moves. When the weed was wearing off, all my insecurities emerged twofold. After years of abusing marijuana, I became depressed. I used it to stimulate the neurons in my brain to take away the pain. The downfall, or as major drug reps explain, the "side effects" from abusing marijuana kept me from being a worthwhile person.

Without weed in my system I walked around with a black hood draped over my head, hiding my face, even in 80-degree weather. I was self conscious of the dreadful person that I had become — a person addicted to marijuana. When I couldn't find my black-hooded sweater, I wore a Seattle Mariners hat, the navy blue one with the blue "S" in the middle, pulled down to my eyebrows. I didn't want people outside of my circle to see my bloodshot red eyes because they were a dead giveaway I was abusing my body. When I entered a dark room, I kept my hood and sunglasses on because I was too embarrassed of the dark circles, a direct result of abusing drugs. The marijuana and cigarette smoke had smoked the insides of my body the same way my father used a smoker to prepare a duck and a turkey on Turkey Day. I slept with sunglasses on, too ashamed of the dreaded textbook villain that I'd become. When I used the restroom, I was petrified to look at the real me as I passed the tell-all-truth bathroom mirror. I had become the dreaded villain, the black boy who was shown on the news, the one who used drugs and alcohol to mask the pain associated with his reality — the reality of success not being an option.

5
Despicable Me

I BECAME A MEMBER OF THE REVOLVING DOOR OF MEN, an exclusive club for men who were able to taste Paulette's pussy for two months to see if they could put up with her bullshit. No matter how many men she already had slept with, she still carried herself as if her father was showing her off to his colleagues at a fancy Washington Congressional dinner for the very first time.

This sassy heifer had a distinctive stallion walk. When she entered a room, her stature demanded attention. Paulette kept her left hand upright and her right hand glued to her hip to assure that every person around her was fixated on her practiced red-carpet strut. Her index finger pointed directly to the sky, ready to get sassy with anyone on any given topic. Paulette was under the impression that the louder she spoke, and the more excited she became, the more attention she would receive from men. She needed the attention she lost when her father left her mother for another women.

She used lying as a mechanism to meet her needs. A boldface lie grew into a screenplay full of crocodile tears mixed with snot running down her face. Her bottom lip drooped, but not before she made sure it was glossy wet. The sad baby-possum glare emerged once she created a smile that would convince a drug counselor that the reason she carried a syringe in her purse was to administer insulin to her dead grandmother at the morgue. When Paulette was actively smoking meth, the chemicals from the drug kept her from laughing at her daughter's attention-getting jokes, which were more cute than funny. The time I surprised Paulette on her birthday with breakfast in bed, she couldn't force a smile on her face, as if she was on her twelfth day of constipation. She chose not to do laundry, wash dishes, or clean up the kids' room.

Right around eight-thirty, Paulette often became restless, pacing about from the kitchen to the living room, in and out of the refrigerator and pantry, in search of something to deaden the pain. Pain was associated with her body's desire to get high. I could hear her opening the vegetable crispers where she kept a plentiful stash of grapes to fulfill her inner need to be pleasurably satisfied. The grapes were second best to her favorite snack items of all time, Milk Duds. To keep her chocolate Milk Duds from getting completely infested by baby roaches, she kept them in the freezer.

After she remembered she had devoured her secret stash the night before, she slammed the refrigerator door closed and turned her attention towards the contents in the pantry. The pantry is where I kept most of my snacks to satisfy my munchies after smoking weed. She started on the cereal boxes, sticking her nasty unwashed hands in and out of each half-empty box (she hardly ever washed her hands after using the bathroom). When she found the milk was spoiled, she focused on the cabinet next to the pantry where I kept more of the goodies to satisfy my cravings. She grabbed a handful of roasted almonds from the freshly opened container and headed back to the living room, dropping an occasional almond on the soiled kitchen floor. She never picked up anything she dropped; her reasoning was that she was leaving them for the family of mice that occupied the kitchen at night.

"We need some milk, fuck!" she shouted, as if I were the one who was supposed to cater to her needs. I would be okay with that if she respected me instead of treating me like a servant. I was aware of the game she was playing; she wanted me to leave so she could get high or score some crank.

I knew her next move better than she did. First, she'd start with the remote control, surfing through 300-plus channels without focusing on any network long enough to catch a glimpse of the program; this usually lasted about five minutes. Once I asked for the remote control, she'd start in on me, insinuating I was trying to control her. Then she'd storm out of the room. After the word *control* rolled off her lips, she retreated to the back of the apartment where she paced the rooms and hallways. She'd go through every room, opening and closing drawers along the way, flip through papers and restack them neatly on the floor. Then she'd attack her closet as if she was going to clean it out or rearrange her things, throwing everything out into the middle of the bedroom floor, again making several piles. Ten minutes later she'd return to the living room to say that someone had to go pick up laundry soap so she could do the laundry. Once she noticed I wasn't falling for the oaky-doke, she'd then plop down on the couch next to me and chew on her fingernails, leaving no nail unbitten. She knew how much that bothered me.

During these bouts of restlessness, Paulette abandoned all responsibilities at home, including cooking. At this stage, the corner store became my kitchen. In place of grits and toast, the kids and I ate fried gizzards drenched in Tabasco sauce. I added a bag of pork-grinds for myself and a bag of spicy Doritos for the kids.

Lunch was equally fast and non-nutritious for the kids and me. We spent the afternoons watching dumb TV shows. But without a pint of VSOP, Sponge Bob and Jerry Springer weren't the same. Nachos worked well to keep the crumb snatchers pre-occupied while I smoked on a blunt in the kitchen. After Oprah, it was time for some of Mr. Lee's special fried chicken from the corner store. We called it special because all of his chicken pieces looked like they were pumped up on steroids.

Right at five, Paulette would walk in with her face looking as if she was extremely terrified. Whenever she became aware that I noticed something was wrong, she'd inform me she had somewhere to go. She chose from a list of regular excuses: we need toilet paper, milk, and laundry soap, bread. All of which I knew was bullshit. After she left, I'd find the items she said we needed. I never let on that I knew where her hiding spot was, behind the headboard.

Next to follow is what I referred to as "her disappearing act". She'd be gone for hours and sometimes she wouldn't come back until the next day, leaving me with her kids. She was a messy person, but when she started disappearing, she became a nasty slob. The apartment complex was infested with rodents and insects. Once it was evident she wasn't going to clean up any more, I stopped cleaning too. When we both gave up, the place became so filthy that red ants and baby roaches they both fought for their rights to get their grub on. If you slightly bumped the countertop you could hear the hard shells of adult roaches hitting dirty dishes and glasses as they all came tumbling down from the mile-high stack of grimy dishes.

When Paulette started disappearing, her body started losing fat, as if she was taking the best fat burners money could buy. Her friends started wondering if she was on a new diet or if I was abusing her. At first she chose to say she was working out, until she was unable to explain the painful expression that remained painted on her face. She quietly started telling friends that their assumption of me stressing her out was in fact correct. This is when I was coined the abusive boyfriend from the dreaded Ridgetop Crip Gang.

As the methamphetamines invaded her body, she wasn't capable of functioning without smoking more of the intrusive-yet-atrocious man-made drug. Negative self-hate images turned her into a manic-depressive bitch. Nothing could get her out of bed. The kids never had breakfast, yet they ate a minimum of seven bowls of cereal a day. She kept three dirty bowls and three filthy disgusting spoons in a Payless shoebox on the nightstand next to a box of chocolate Pebbles cereal. Because she was lactose intolerant, she could drink only rice milk, which she forced on her kids whenever she was hung over. The effect of the drug was clearly beginning to destroy her face, forming dark circles and air-like pockets beneath her eyes, reconstructing her outward appearance into an anorexic shell. Her eyes sank in; her skin stretched out, appearing as though her skin was falling off her cheekbones. Her muscles fell from her bones, and her beautiful robust ass dropped from her back and hung off her tailbone.

Paulette tried reluctantly to take her mind off of the ultimate high that she obtained from smoking meth; she was haunted by the utopia that she attained every time the cloudy white smoke intruded on her brain cells. The drug forced her to lead a secretive life. She didn't want anyone close to know that she was addicted to such a nasty decomposing drug. She feared once anyone knew that she was addicted, she wouldn't be able to blame others for her problems and she'd have to deal with the addict in the mirror. She knew deep down inside that she would never stop smoking meth unless she was dead. She tried to take the attention off the obvious — that she was an addict — by placing the blame on me so that she could claim empathy. After many attempts to destroy my character, she became distant, self centered, and couldn't look me in the eyes anymore. Yet I felt sorry for her when I read the look on her face that said, "I wanna kill myself for smoking up the rent money."

She walked around the apartment with her head hanging so far down that her bottom lip could touch the floor. The drug is so mind-altering that one-minute she yearned for help and the next minute she created an argument so she could leave to get high.

I didn't consider myself a victim, but she treated me like I was a trick off the street. It started with a smirk, then that evil stare, as if she caught me stealing a gold ring off her dead grandfather's finger as he lay in his casket.

"Why are you giving me an evil look?" I asked, sending her into a frenzy, cursing me out, calling me a low-life piece of shit. Our relationship had become grounded in hatred and overwhelmed by demonic values. When her addictive behavior surfaced, she chose to attack the only person she knew she couldn't fool — me. After her first hit of meth, she turned into an intolerable, malnourished, cruel-hearted fiend.

She was faced with a conundrum. Without the drugs in her system she felt incomplete and this compelled her to get high. Yet once she smoked what she had in front of her, she felt despicably dirty and abandoned. She became overwhelmed with disbelief in her propensity to move beyond obstacles. Choosing to get high instead of seeking therapeutic help to overcome her addiction was not on her radar.

To her dismay, once the drugs wore off, usually a couple days later, depending on whether or not she continued to use or took a break. Once she had gone two to three days without getting high, she quickly crashed. The crash was as traumatic for her as if she were thrown into a tree from the back of a crotch-rocket going 130 miles per. When she was recovering, her thought process became unclear, forcing her to stammer — a dead giveaway of meth abuse. She was unable to hold a conversation, her thought process was breached, and she was unable to materialize an answer. It would take her five minutes to respond to a simple question, such as "where's the remote control?" She'd stare up at the ceiling as if she was watching a cockroach dance.

In the attempt to answer any question thrown her way, she hesitantly answered with a question. "Did you check the mailbox?" Her speech was slow; her answers were more like presumptuous metaphors flowing freely from the lips of a flower child high off acid and tie-weed. On one occasion when she was attempting to feed the kids, she mistook a can of dog food for a can of chili. "Hey kids, Mommy made your favorite chili!"

The drugs washed out the stored dopamine in her brain so that she could not fake contentment. On Christmas day, the kids burst into the bedroom yelling "Merry Christmas, Mommy, Merry Christmas!"

"Mommy doesn't feel good, call Nana and tell her to come get you guys," she responded.

In order to remain on an even keel, she used the electric, laundry, and cable bill money to get high. When she realized her pockets were tapped dry, she attacked me, blaming me for not having enough money to pay her rent and her bills.

Her manipulation skills were exquisite and could have earned her a Ghetto Fabulous award. The award is only given to dope fiends for their incredible *mackadocious* skills and lack of compassion trying to swindle a bounty out of someone. Before approaching her friends or family for money, she rehearsed at the bathroom mirror and in front of her kids who became her captive audience. With the saddest puppy face look on her face, she stared endlessly at her kids' faces while saying "Do you have some money to buy some milk?"

Her daughter's response was always the same. "That was better than great mommy, that was excellent!"

With no regard for the big blue elephant in the room — me — she simply brought out her little black book and began calling those impressionable people she had fooled in the past. She came up with a fictitious story about how I spent all of her money on weed and lap dances at the local nudie bar. Within an hour she had enough money to pay her rent and all of her bills. She even paid my bills by using me as a scapegoat. I didn't care as long as I was also getting my needs met.

I was a confused young man. Some would say I was uncaring and believed everything must revolve around me. At one time I was into breaking bitches for all they had. However Paulette had me so damn pussy-whipped it was ridiculous. This made me not even want to take advantage of her, which was a first for me. Because of my past, which many in her inner circle knew about, her glorified narrative of me taking all of her money to satisfy my needs was believable.

Like Paulette, I too blamed those around me for creating havoc, causing grief, destruction, and sadness in my life. My reality became a game I played to avoid the truth, the truth that Paulette didn't like me as much as I thought she did. I had fallen into lust with a woman who was openly cheating on me with her lover, Mr. Methamphetamines.

After one such award winning performance from Paulette, using my name to get our needs met, I became particularly depressed. Part was due to the chemicals from smoking weed; how each of weed's elements depressed me after the high was long gone. Nevertheless, once my phone bill was paid, the reality of being used besieged me.

To escape that feeling, I tried to use the weed Paulette purchased to appease me, so that I too could escape our reality. Nonetheless, after the weed wore off, I became an enemy to myself; I dreaded seeing the person I had become staring back at me from the mirror.

I felt like a sucker for allowing her to use my name to depict me as a textbook villain. I began to question the morality of it all. How could I be so damned ignorant for being okay with anyone using my name to destroy my character? And for what? Just to have my phone bill paid? And for her to buy drugs?

"Damn, Ceeze, you are a major fuckup!" I could no longer look at Paulette.

Overwhelmed by feelings of regret and mistrust, I retreated to my apartment to mourn all by my lonesome. Once alone in my apartment, away from her, I began to plot ways to uplift myself from the pit I had fallen into. In other words I could use my own remedies to take my mind off the obvious: I was being pimped.

Alcohol made me feel manly again, giving me power to strike down any bad thoughts that filtered through my head. I was able to seek out immorality in more ways than one. Once full off the yac juice and a couple of blunts stuffed with Humble County weed, I turned into another alter-ego, the richest drug dealer in The Town, who started off as a pimp, who became the wealthiest, most hood-rich rap artist in town. I became *Pimp OG Mack Daddy*.

After a long night of smoking large quantities of marijuana and drinking to the point where I couldn't hold down my liquor, I fell into the arms of women who were also in search of hope in the form of hood potions that only lead to promiscuity. A quick booty call worked temporarily to empower me, since the girl of my dreams was having a secret love affair with Mr. Meth.

With no one telling me right from wrong, or leading me to Christ, my powerless efforts to strengthen me were ultimately reached in the form of companionship. I had countless women at my beck and call to fulfill my pointless desires. My warped thinking compelled me to believe that being promiscuous was okay because Paulette was also cheating on me.

Before the break of day, I cleaned myself up and returned to the one person that I felt duty-bound to share my personal space with. As sinister as it may sound, I rushed back into the arms of Paulette for comfort and for her to console me. "Ceeze! It's okay, Booboo; Mommy loves you."

When I returned to her after a night of immorality, drinking and drugging, I looked horrid. Even so, I used my translucent demeanor to my advantage by turning up the sad puppy-dog look as I walked into her room. It was my turn to get my needs met. Paulette took one look at me and said, "You look like shit!"

Whenever Paulette told me that, I knew she really meant, "Ceeze, I feel your pain." And I knew what was to follow — some nasty, hot, sensual, make-up sex. At times we played this game of break-up-to-make-up just to satisfy each others sick, deceitful, self-centered desires. We both knew that we used sex as a mechanism to satisfy the void of happiness in our lives.

Yet the fact that both of us enjoyed having sex together was not a far-fetched notion either. At times, when she was down and out or just horny, she used me to satisfy her. To add to our sexual desires, the fulfillment of having make-up sex intensified the more we stayed apart. And the moment I entered her house looking like a vagabond, my penis became instantly hard.

The first time we had sex, I was taken back by her quivering vagina muscles. Taken back in the sense of "what the hell kind of move is this heifer using to trick me into doing whatever the fuck she asked me to do?" She could make her hooch shutter like humming bird wings. She used her talents to make me bust-a-nut quickly so she could go back to sleep when she didn't feel like being bothered. However, during our make-up sex, she used her skills to keep me aloft for as long as she wanted me.

When it was time, she broke out the Cinnamon-Spice lubricant to add a certain zest to the moment. The more I stroked her, the more friction the spice produced. The Cinnamon-Spice turned hot in and around our pleasure points. Her walls heated up my dong, making me long and hard for hours. The taste of hot cinnamon made licking her clit much, much more pleasurable, even if she didn't have time to wash up before we began.

After the first point of entry, she gripped me around both forearms until I was all the way up in her. Her nails dug into my muscles, tearing my skin and leaving behind her signature fingernail scratches. The scratches were located on my arms just beneath the horseshoe 'U' on each sculptured bicep.

I was always more than eager to make love with her, even months and months after the so-called *honeymoon period* was over. At the beginning of our lovemaking sessions, we started off slow and sensual. Her vagina walls cupped my pole, while quivering and fluttering about. During such time I found her moans were moans of pleasure. She would say to me "Go easy, Ceeze, go easy!" She knew I was impatient to get the party started.

Nonetheless I took it easy and slowed down to just a slight thrust. This was when I put my back in-to-it so that my thrusts were unhurried. Her hips pushed up against me, making our bodies levitate off the bed. With her lips resting on mine, our tongues were able to sit back and relax, waiting the right moment to take off. We breathed through our mouths, forcing air in and out of each others bodies; we were each others oxygen. Because of the cinnamon body gel, our saliva tasted like Big Red chewing gum, which turned me into a vampire as I tried endlessly to suck all of the nutrients from her mouth. We did this thing with our front teeth slightly touching. This was a skill that had to be mastered; one false move and teeth could chip. Our tongues converged once I felt a burst of air beckon from her mouth into mine. This was when I knew it was time for me to dig deeper and deeper into her pelvis so that she could feel the entire me and I could feel her entirely.

Our moans and groans transcended into rhythmic motions, making way for the abandoned emotions we chose not to show to implode in the form of orgasms. She cried tears of fulfillment; I stuck my tongue deep into her ear and whispered, "Damn girl, your pussy is so good!" As I shifted my body to the left for deeper penetration, Paulette swayed her body to the right so she too could put her back into it. I gripped the back of her head with my entire hand, running my fingers through her hair for more intimate touching. She trusted me to take her flimsy neck in the palm of my hand, where I was able to slowly guide her closely against my body. Our tongues became tongue-tied, and our chests became stuck together by perspiration. I could feel her heart racing through my body all the way down to the tips of my knee caps, and at the same time Paulette was finally able to confirm what I always told her — my heart skipped a beat when we made love.

The best part of our lovemaking was when our hips conjoined belly to belly. It was as if we were playing strip Twister without a referee. We squeezed each other ever so tightly to the point where we became one. Air bubbles emerged in the form of sound waves. Our legs became entangled and our toes played pussyfoot underneath mucky wet sheets. When we made love it was evident that Paulette and I became two entirely different people. We were successful in allowing ourselves to escape the pain and mental anguish associated with being controlled by a drug addiction.

For that brief implausible yet remarkable moment, we became clear-headed adults having consensual sex. We were not selfish in any way. We were able to feel the power of gratitude for someone other than ourselves. Nor was it Christmas time, no matter how we rendered our bodies over to one another as secret Santa gifts.

I knew she was just as messed up psychologically as I, which I used to stay in our turbulent courtship. I wanted to save her. I knew that she was a good person, and I truly believed that once I saved her she would be the woman of my dreams. And for that colossal crisp moment when we reached that orgasmic plateau, I felt I was able to overcome all obstacles that the devil threw our way in an attempt to break us up.

My friends and family claimed I was pussy-whipped, whereas I felt I had merely fallen in love with the woman sent down to me from heaven. The sex was so immaculate that for several days after we made love, I was tormented by vivid thoughts of attempting to reach that very same pleasurable point I had reached only a few days prior. These 3D visuals infiltrated my mind so badly I had to pleasure myself if she wasn't willing to share some of that fluttering hummingbird twat. Once I was done, I was left feeling like a born-again sinner.

6
Con-vic-tion

The lead story read: "Boyfriend arrested on probation violation and is a person of interest in the abduction of his daughter Riesha Jenkins Lewis and for the murder of his ex-girlfriend Paulette Jenkins. At this time no charges have been filed. —*Tacoma Herald* Chief Field Reporter Henry Livingston"

What the fuck! In the eyes of those who had access to my criminal record and who knew about my affiliation with gangs and the pimp/hustle game, the statement "has not been charged yet" meant "that sorry-ass motha-fuckin-trifling-ass-nigga killed his baby's momma and kidnapped their daughter". Residents of The Town convicted me way before I was even arrested.

Livingston, editor of the *Tacoma Herald*, a local news source responsible for the dissemination of half-truths throughout my community, was informed by the chief of police that I was a drug-dealing, gang-banger who tried to recruit the mother of his child to join the notorious Ridgetop Crips (RTC). It was simple for the editor (and lone reporter) to develop a scandalous story about me. All he had to do was copy and paste implications from previous articles written about "the deceptive, misguided, colored boys that were terrorizing the city streets throughout The Town". His articles suggested African American men between 12 and 27 were "vicious criminals".

He used slapstick words to best describe his racist view of black people, hoping to impact the mindset of his readers. According to Livingston's articles, *black gang members were taking over the city*.

The Ridgetop Crips had become the largest Crip gang outside Los Angeles. At one time the estimated number of Crips in The Town reached an overwhelming 500. Most, if not all of the members resided in a small 10-mile radius in and around the Ridgetop. Competition with other L.A. gangs only heated up the crimes in The Town, further heightening Livingston's garbage.

The destruction of Ridgetop gangs became the number-one priority for the Police Department, city officials, and neighborhood coalitions. Government funds allocated millions of dollars towards developing drug and gang task forces, disbursed through collaborative efforts of such task forces alongside the development of community outreach organizations and block watch programs. However these programs were all designed to rid the entire Ridgetop community of most, if not all, black men associated with any gang.

The spiteful police chief and his officers convincingly slandered my name in public and in the local newspaper, making me a victim of circumstance. The chief stated that their investigation had led them to me. I knew there wasn't any supportive evidence to link me to the murder or the abduction because I did not do it!

The police reported, "At this time we are not able to find a motive why someone would want to harm the deceased or kidnap the victim's daughter other than her ex-boyfriend, the father of their child, Brandon Lewis aka Ceeze Green, one of the original leaders of the violent street gang, the notorious Ridgetop Crips. Because of their rocky relationship, he is the only person who would possibly commit such a heinous crime against Paulette Jenkins and their child."

The investigation into Paulette's murder and the abduction of my daughter was spearheaded by Chief David Doyle. He was hurled through police ranks for his ruthless attacks against gang violence. It was evident that the chief and city officials worked side-by-side with representatives from the *Herald* to develop a scare tactic to manipulate the delicate minds of longtime residents of The Town. Deception at its finest began to manifest through the community, tricking people into believing all young black men were heathens, gang members who carried guns and sold dope.

It appeared to me that the chief had tainted the picture of black men in general and me in particular to divert attention from reports that were surfacing about the chief's physical abuse of his wife. He was a volatile sadistic man whose sick state of mind surfaced during Paulette's murder investigation. An intern who was working for the police department came forward accusing the chief of rape. Later on that day, his wife called 911 to report the chief was physically abusing her. The heat came down instantly on City Attorney Lou Helen Chow. She was responsible for the chief's swift surge through the ranks to become chief. So what did the city attorney and the chief come up with to take the attention off them? When in doubt, paint a tainted picture of a black man and blame an unsolved murder and child abduction on him. And it was working.

Meet Troy White, big city television reporter who often portrayed blacks in a negative light. And note that the television station also owned the *Tacoma Herald*.

Reports indicated the police had strong evidence linking me to the murder, which I knew wasn't possible. I also knew how the crooked-ass police operated; falsifying half-ass evidence was not out of the ordinary.

Here is the story they concocted: My wallet was found in Riesha's baby bag that Paulette had with her when I dropped them off last night at what turned into a murder scene. Field Reporter White reported that the evidence was strong enough to have me arrested. I supposedly had found out that Paulette was having an affair with another man. Furthermore, White interviewed the chief, who made it appear as if I was present when Paulette was murdered and when my daughter was abducted. "Several witnesses at the address where Ms. Jenkins was murdered said they heard a couple arguing and spotted Brandon Lewis driving a blue car leaving the murder scene at the time Ms. Jenkins was killed and their daughter was kidnapped."

White went on to hint that I was hiding my daughter's body where no one would find her. "A confidential informant informed the chief that Lewis, aka Ceeze Green, may have left his poor neglected, innocent child in the care of a crack addict who resided in one of the many abandoned buildings used by fellow gang members as crack houses." He went on to accuse me of placing my daughter in harms way by attempting to hide her in a stash house, a place where the Ridgetop Crips stashed their drug supply.

The sinister chief confirmed everything White suggested. "These crack houses are used as brothels where pimps force women to sell their bodies in order to pay off drug debts, a place where no little girl should be left alone. Mr. Lewis could have owed money and was using his daughter to pay off his debts. This is why we're looking forward to speaking with Mr. Lewis upon his arrival." Oh yes, they had reported I was about to turn myself in for questioning.

Though my child was missing, no child abduction alert was announced. In fact, the media focused more on accusing me of the murder than trying to find my daughter. Questions ran through my head in a constant stream: How could a child just up and vanish? Why aren't the police and White showing concern for Paulette's family? How come a picture of my baby girl hasn't been released to the public so they would know what she looked like, what she was wearing, and who they could call if anyone had witnessed anything that would help the case?

The viciousness of Paulette's murder and my criminal background made it feasible for the chief and the media to use me as a scapegoat to ease attention off the police department and the city attorney's office. I was being used to clear the chief's own deeds and as a reason to fear black men, all the while making it practical for the police to continue to go on harassing every black man and child living in and around the Ridgetop.

Very soon the people who I considered supporters, and those who considered me a close friend acted as if they didn't know me. Guys from my childhood who often frequented my house — the ones who ate up my family's food and who sold Kool-aid with me at the end of the street — didn't have any comforting words to help me understand what I was going through. These were the friends I would have given the last piece of fried chicken. Even my favorite aunts had no encouraging words to help uplift my spirits. My name was thrown around on the party line as all of my relatives talked about me like a dog, insinuating what I was experiencing is exactly what I deserved for living such a menacing life style.

As I walked towards the chair of my personal barber Ralph Sr., he stopped me in my tracks to inform me someone else was next. Ralph has cut my hair every since I was three years old. "This is my last cut for the day, Mr. Lewis," he said. He never called me by my last name.

"I only need a shape-up, sir." I smiled broadly at him and said, "Come on, sir, you know it will only take five minutes."

"Try back tomorrow. After this one, I'm going home for the day, Brandon." He hadn't called me Brandon since I was in the tenth grade.

My favorite teacher, Mr. Stewart, had always allowed me to stay after class to finish a quiz because he knew my brain processed information a little slower than others. When I saw him at the filling station, he looked the other way.

According to people around me, I had become a hazardous waste of space. The entire community that I had dedicated my life to was out to hang me for a crime that I didn't commit. Paulette didn't deserve to die. Nonetheless, many people wanted me dead, and word on the street suggested a bounty had been placed on my head — $5,000 to the first cat that killed me.

PAULETTE WAS A DEDICATED MOTHER to our baby Riesha, and had stuck by my side through all of the bullshit I had put her through. Riesha is my only daughter, and I cherished every moment when she was next to me. Before she was born I didn't know my purpose in life. When I tied up with her mother, I thought my purpose in life was to become the best hustler in my neighborhood. That purpose did a one-eighty as I witnessed the heavenly spectacle of the birth of my child.

After twenty-three hours of labor, my little girl was pulled from my woman's womb during an emergency C-section. Paulette couldn't dilate enough. All bloody, frail, and lifeless, Riesha was immediately taken to a large sink where the doctor shoved a large tube down her throat to clear a passage so she could breathe. She had defecated inside of the placenta, and the doctor feared that Riesha had swallowed some of her own feces. The tube was pulled out as abruptly as it had been shoved down her throat. This was my first glimpse into my daughter's life.

As I watched this painful moment, I made a promise to both God and Paulette that I would protect Riesha with all my heart. There is no way I would kidnap my own daughter or kill her mother. After the successful birth, I understood what my purpose in life really is: to protect and provide for Riesha and Paulette, to help my daughter recognize what her purpose in life is, and to teach my daughter how to honor and respect her mother.

Although I knew my life purpose on the day my daughter was born, I still didn't know how to deal and cope with my reality. I didn't know anything about living a clean life. I knew it was possible because I watched Paulette switch from a whore to a housewife in a matter of nine months. The reality of providing for my family without hustling was nowhere on my radar. For the next three weeks after Riesha's birth, I hit the streets trying to find a job to support my family without having to hustle someone out of a jig (five dollars).

Aunt Helen advised me never to smoke weed or drink alcohol the night before I looked for a job. "Drugs and alcohol make you tired, which may keep you from making attempts, or you'd cut your day short after filling out one application," she said. She also suggested I prepare a nice lunch, iron my clothes, and have them laid out and coordinated all the way down to the socks the day before. "Don't leave the house with your pants sagging," she added. Auntie provided me with a briefcase, the same one my father and Uncle Jimmy used when they too went looking for a job. She said it was very important to walk into a business place looking distinguished, like a gentlemen wearing a shirt and tie, dress shoes, and carrying a briefcase, even if you're applying for a warehouse job or one unloading boxes off of UPS trailer. My aunt made sure that I knew what to say and how to say it: "My name is Brandon Lewis and I am here for the open position of…"

When Riesha was born, my downfall was that I was still considered a hood figga — inches away from becoming the number one stunner in my neighborhood. I possessed all the attributes attached to being a thug. My motto was MCM — making cash money — what I did best. The fast money I got off the streets had catapulted me to another level of respect in the hood. And when I added the little bit of money I was getting from work to my hustle game, I started making money hand over fist and returned to the streets to roam among the other hood figgaz.

Because I worked long hours and partied in the streets, my body quickly shut down. Without proper nutrition from Paulette's home cooking and without proper sleep, I couldn't get up on time to go to work. I eventually lost my warehouse job after three write-ups in just four months. For the next couple of months, I pretended I was going to work, but I returned to hustling in the streets.

Once Paulette caught wind of my ruse, she gave me an ultimatum: get a job or she and the baby were leaving. I wasn't going to lose my family. The very next day I went out and got a job working for Surreal, an Arab friend who I used to buy stolen big screen televisions from. Surreal owned several 7-Eleven stores in The Town. I worked at the one down the street from Aunty Helen's house. Surreal asked me what shift I wanted to work, and I chose the graveyard shift, 11 p.m. to 7 a.m. The graveyard shift allowed me to get my hustle on, selling ten-dollar white-girls-joints, fifteen-dollar blunts, and twenty-five-dollar sacks of weed. I sold an array of pills, ecstasy, mollies, Percocets, Oxycontins, and cigarettes dipped in PCP. I even sold bootleg DVDs to customers straight at the register without being bothered. Although I was still hustling at work, when my paychecks started rolling in my priorities gradually shifted to home. Instead of doubling up (purchasing a substantial amount of drugs to sell at a 100 percent profit) I handed my checks over to Paulette for her to buy groceries, things for the baby, get her hair and nails done, and to pay the bills.

Before my daughter's kidnapping and Paulette's murder, it was evident to everyone that Paulette and my little girl Riesha were transforming me into a family man. I went from having aspirations of winning the lotto player's ball to working towards winning the title of Father of the Year. Paulette led me to church, and we even had Riesha baptized. My father once told me, "Behind every strong black man and his family, there's a strong black woman keeping the family together." Overnight Paulette became that strong black woman, showing the inherent motherly instincts that her mother imbedded in her at a very young age.

During those heady days, I entered our apartment after work each morning to be embraced by the warmth of the apartment, all of the windows fogged up. Steam seeped from beneath the bathroom door where Paulette and Riesha were just finishing up their lukewarm bath. The smell of warm pancakes, scrambled eggs, and crispy bacon sent me straight to the kitchen sink to wash my hands, then directly to the dining room table where Paulette had my grand-slam breakfast waiting. As I finished spreading butter and syrup on my pancakes, my girls joyfully greeted me with huge smiles as though I had just returned home from an extended vacation. Riesha was glued to Paulette's hip, and the two of them wore semi-wet bath towels while smothering me with wet kisses. This gesture clearly made me feel like a proud father and a blessed husband.

Immediately after breakfast I changed out of my work clothes, fed little Riesha some grits and toast, read her one of her favorite stories and, before finishing the book, the two of us fell fast asleep. Paulette, still wearing her bath towel, would grab the baby and put her in her crib and then slide underneath the bed sheets, where we practiced baby-making moves.

The more I held the two of them close to my heart, remembering, the more I felt the streets slipping from beneath me. Nobody around me believed that Ceeze could change from being a common street thug to a loving and caring father. Most importantly, I knew Paulette believed in me. During such time, my homeys stopped calling me, and I stopped calling them, which made me feel like a boy leaving the family nest for the very first time.

7
What Happened to My Family?

THE NEXT MORNING I WOKE UP ON THE LIVING ROOM FLOOR, naked with the most excruciating headache ever. I assumed I had blacked out after another long night of binge drinking and smoking weed. I couldn't remember a thing about how I got there. Before getting up, I looked around for some clue to bring back my memory. My pants were sprawled over the back of the couch like a throw blanket; my shirt lay on the kitchen counter with ketchup and mayonnaise covering most of the Mariners logo; I wore only one shoe; my keys lay next to my gun on the dining room table.

An unopened bag of weed and a half-smoked blunt unearthed a memory of buying some weed in front of the liquor store last night, but I still couldn't remember what had happened after that. When I arose, I stumbled against the wall; my head banged. I yelled for Paulette, but there wasn't an answer. Once I regained my equilibrium, I headed to the bedroom. The bed was still made. "Fuck! Where is my family?"

Still naked, I sat down on the bed and tried to think. I noticed my phone on the bedroom dresser and I quickly went to check if I had any missed calls. A text message read, "I'm on my way." The name *Iron Lungs* immediately sparked my memory. Iron Lungs is the nickname for a long-time childhood friend named Bernard, the nickname a direct derivative of his ability to expand his lungs when he smoked weed. I remembered Bernard offering to follow me this morning so I could drop off my car at my mechanic's house; I had a standing appointment with John (Junior) Rob to get my brakes checked and to install a stereo in my Nova. I also remembered that

Bernard and I were out late last night in Seattle at an after-hours club, gambling and playing pool. I remembered coming home, but leaving again. I checked the 7-11 receipts next to the phone. I purchased a pack of Newport's at four a.m. from the corner store on the Ridgetop, where my Arab homeys sold me liquor after two a.m. I always bought two 22-ounce bottles of Mickey's Malt liquor and four single Newport cigarettes (I rarely bought a full pack because I was trying to quit.) I found one bottle, half empty, next to my keys and identification.

    Immediately I took a long gulp of the warm beer and sat back down on the bed with the bottle. With another hurried gulp, the beer spilled over my bare chest all the way down past my belly. I saw a spot of beer beneath me on the sheets, which looked more like I had wet the bed. Sitting there, still butt naked, I remembered dropping off both Paulette and Riesha at her home-girl's house after proposing marriage to her. A spontaneous smile surfaced on my face; I took another long sip of the warm beer to ease my worries. Yet I was still ridiculously baffled at what could have transpired to find me waking up naked in the middle of the living room floor.

    Just as I finished with the three S's — shit, shower, and shave — Bernard knocked on the door and walked right in before I opened it. I had a freshly rolled blunt dangling from my lips, and Bernard reached for it before I could offer him a pull. His reaction when he opened the door was classic. "Yea, I'm right on time!" He was always *just arriving* when I was *just beginning* to smoke. The aroma from the strawberry swisher I used to rap my weed formed small clouds of thick white smoke that levitated in mid-air throughout the apartment. Circles of smoke shaped like donuts floated throughout the kitchen towards the window that I had cracked slightly open, clouds so thick you could use a spoon to eat the smoke vapors and still get high. As soon as we finished the blunt, Bernard followed me over to Junior's house to drop off my car.

When we arrived, one of my homeboys, Mack Money, was dropping off his car. As we exited our vehicles we said, "What-up, Cuzz?" to one another and shook hands. I asked him what's he getting done and he replied brakes. "Me too." From under the hood of one of many old school Jeep Wagoneers he collected, Junior shouted, "Leave the keys in the ignition."

"How long?"

"Come back in two hours," which was his usual response, regardless of the work.

Bernard and I followed Mack Money over to Uncle Tom's Juke Joint where fish, grits, and eggs are the daily special. Before going in, we smoked another blunt. This time Mack shared one with us. The higher we got, the more we laughed, bragged, and boasted about the good-old-days, and the not-so-good-old-days. We had a long history, reaching back to middle school. We remembered the school bullies, and we shared a few quiet moments remembering dead homeys shot in the line of fire as we defended our hood.

Bernard and I met when my family moved here; I was thirteen. He and I quickly discovered our ties; we both loved making money, any way we could. Bernard honed his pool skills and became a champ. I hadn't played in a while. That day he rejoiced as I continued to miss shots and he continued to make them. After the first three games and three beers I regained my confidence and redeemed myself by beating him two games in a row.

As I put the pool stick back in the rack, I noticed the light flashing on my phone. It appeared I had several missed calls from Paulette's friend's phone number. I hit the Call Back button and received no answer the first time. I tried again. Still no answer; I left a message on her voice mail to have Paulette call me. I hadn't heard from Paulette since dropping off her and the baby last night.

This wasn't like her; we usually talked every couple of hours when she was away from home. Paulette would call to let me know what time to pick her up or just to let me know she and the baby were thinking about me. I usually didn't call over there unless I knew her best friend wasn't home. Best Friend and I didn't get along at all.

Paulette's Best Friend didn't like me, nor did I like her. Over time I changed my ways, but to Best Friend I was still a rogue, a pimp, and a gang-banger from the dreaded Ridgetop. She knew about my gang involvement and how I dreaded driving on the Westside to drop off my family. I was placing my family in her building that housed the Westside Bloods, the largest Piru gang in The Town.

My phone rang again, but only this time from a blocked number, which I usually didn't answer. This time I answered, thinking it could be Paulette. "Ya!"

"I need you to come over to my house right now!" said Paulette's Best Friend. From the tone of her voice, I assumed she and Paulette might have exchanged words. The last time Paulette stayed over night, the two of them had a heated argument about my involvement with the Crips. Regardless of how much Paulette tried to paint a perfect picture regarding my fatherhood, I still wasn't good enough in the eyes of Best Friend. My ability to work and pay the bills made no difference; in her eyes, I was a ghetto bastard.

Before she could get a word in edgewise, I told her I was on my way to pick up my car and that I would be there within the hour to pick up my family. When I asked to speak to Paulette, her response was, "What you need to do is get over here immediately!"

We left the pub and headed straight over to Junior's house. As we pulled up, he was slowly letting down the jack underneath my car. After paying Junior, I handed Bernard my last blunt and told him he would have to spark it by himself because I had to get Paulette and the baby. Bernard looked at his phone and noticed he had twenty-two missed calls from his mother, "Look Cuzz, Mom's called me twenty-two times. I hope nothing's wrong!"

"After you talk to her, call me, let me know what she wanted" I replied.

Once I got in my car, I made a B-line for the Westside wondering what the fuck was going on. My mind raced in directions I didn't want to go. I thought something must be wrong, because her Best friend never called me for anything, and I couldn't remember a time when we said more than hello or goodbye to one another.

"Something just isn't right about this." I didn't know what came over me, and I knew I was supposed to be heading towards the Westside, but I found myself making a whole bunch of left turns towards my pad, in the opposite direction. My mind began to drift. I saw flashes of Paulette holding our baby, the three of us sharing intimate moments. Then my mind went blank. When I arrived at my apartment building, I didn't know why I was there. A paranormal moment struck fear in me: a young girl's voice whispered, "Hide your gun, Daddy." My body jumped awake and quivered before I could make a move. The last time I heard voices was when I heard Papa Dukes yelling "Get up, my son, get up! They're coming back to kill you." That was when I had fought with some Seattle Bloods and was left for dead after being knocked out. My grandfather's voice saved my life then, so I wasn't about to waste time by ignoring the young girl's voice now.

Who was this telling me to hide my gun? Wow, what the hell is going on? I'm really tripping now. Instead of heading for my apartment door, I headed towards the back of the building to hide my pistol. Immediately I broke out in a sweat, trembling as I scrambled through Old Man Henry's junk underneath the building's back porch. I stashed it underneath a pile of old broken-down beat-up furniture, a good hiding spot where no one could find it. There wasn't any need for me to go back to our apartment, so I returned to my car and headed back towards the Westside.

I made it three blocks from my house before my phone rang. Ecstatic that it wasn't a blocked number, the caller ID said "Bernard". Maybe he could help me understand what I had just experienced. Before Bernard could get a word in, I shouted into the phone, "Cuzz, I think something bad happened to Paulette or the baby, Cuzz! Cuzz, I'm scared as a motha-fucka, Cuzz…"

Whenever I was nervous or felt threatened, the term "Cuzz" flowed freely from my mouth, with the same vernacular as a sailor's curse words. Before I could finish my sentence, I found out that it actually was Bernard's mother on the phone. She interrupted me to inquire whether or not I was sitting down. My mind raced. I thought one of the Piru niggaz shot up Paulette's home girl's house thinking I was in there. Or maybe there was an accident and the baby fell and bumped her head. Paulette had threatened to haul off and whoop her homegirl's ass if she said one more negative thing about me, her fiancé. Now that we are getting married, Paulette probably isn't going to let anyone talk bad about me. "You go girl!" Ya, that must be it. Paulette done kicked that girl's ass and got arrested for it too. Good for her. Now it'll be my turn to bail her out of jail. Ya! That has to be the reason why Bernard's mother is calling me.

Now with a smile plastered on my face, I silently giggled inside. For a brief moment I was compelled to answer Bernard's mother. With a lackadaisical approach to her question I replied, "Yes I'm sitting down. What's up?"

Ms. Williams asked, "Have you heard the news?"

Though I was still flabbergasted inside thinking that Paulette beat-up her home girl, there was still an inkling of doubt that made my stomach turn. My heart began to beat profusely, forcing my shirt to rise off my chest. I didn't want to hear the real answer, but I asked, "What news?"

After a moment of silence that seemed to last a few hours, I repeated, "What happened?" adding, "Are you still on the phone?" Maybe Bernard got in a car accident on his way home or one of the homeys was shot or killed. This would have been the third one this month. The once normal road ahead of me turned into a tunnel, creating tunnel vision as I waited for Ms. Williams to drop the news on me.

In the next moment I connected Paulette's Best Friend calling with the difficulty Ms. Williams was having telling me what transpired. I clutched the steering wheel harder and harder, perspiration forming between my fingers.

"Paulette is dead, baby. Paulette is dead, and someone kidnapped your daughter!" said Ms. Williams.

Effervescent flashes of Paulette and Riesha and me walking at the waterfront on a sweltering August evening replaced my eyesight for an instant. Cherished moments of the three of us having a picnic on the water's edge, eating crab legs and corn-on-the-cob just last week infused my body and spirit like peppermint tea. Imaginative life-sized images of my girls filled my mind. Paulette's beautiful face stared endlessly into little Riesha's magnetic eyes, as her mother held her up to the sky. Riesha was laughing and giggling abundantly as her mother spun her around and around. Their images engulfed the entire tunnel before me, then their faces hastily circulated around and around my car. Paulette's enchanting smile and Riesha's dazzling marble russet eyes replaced the light in front of me.

That's when my world came to a complete stop. I felt as if I had just experienced life after death. The word 'dead' killed me faster than a bullet from a self-inflicted Magnum 44 gunshot to the right temple. Yet I was still here. It was as if I was the only one at my own funeral, lying in a glass casket waiting for someone to attend before I could be lowered into the ground.

Did I hear correctly? My wife is dead and my baby daughter missing? I must be dead now! I just knew I was in a car accident, and now I was living in the afterlife, which simultaneously became my hell. Although I was still driving, I felt trapped, strapped in a speedboat during the hydroplane races gliding me over Lake Union at 170 mph. So this is what it feels like to be dead! Trapped in a body that was still able to see three feet ahead.

I knew then it was Paulette telling me to hide my gun. Now I know why; if I had it on me when I heard Bernard's mother utter "Paulette is dead" and "Riesha is missing", I probably would either have killed myself or murked somebody. I couldn't think straight, nor could I feel my body. I felt as lonesome and bewildered as if my parents had left me on the steps of a Mormon church in Utah during a snowstorm on Christmas day. I was filled with the rage of five preteen slave children sickened by the sight and sounds of their mother being raped by a gang of sheriffs, employed by Mr. Charlie to oversee his stock of African slaves and Native Americans.

There was no way that I heard Ms. Williams correctly. I asked her again, "I'm sorry, Ms. Williams, I couldn't hear you. Can you repeat that please?" Only this time when I said *please* she couldn't hear me because she was crying profusely. "Sweetie, your Paulette is gone, baby, and they can't find Riesha."

I pulled over on the side of the road and, before the car stopped, threw the gearshift into Park, forcing the car to abruptly jerk forward and then backward. I jumped out of the car as it was still moving and started stomping up and down, stomping on the pavement hard while yelling and screaming, "Paulette is dead, Paulette is dead!" My feet and legs turned numb and ached as I stomped again and again uncontrollably. I went back to the car and reached in through the window for my phone and asked calmly, "Hello, Ms. Williams, are you there still?"

"Yes, baby, I'm still here. I'm still here, baby."

I needed one more confirmation from her. Again I asked, "Is Paulette really dead and my daughter really missing?"

"Yes, baby, she's dead, and they can't find Riesha. Baby, I'm sorry."

I threw the phone back in the car and went back to my rampage yelling, "My Boo is dead, my Boo is dead, and they can't find my baby, they can't find my baby!" Passing drivers looked at me, but I couldn't understand why they were staring because I felt I was dead, a ghost stuck on earth having to experience the pain associated with losing a loved one. I jumped up on top of my car and continued my tirade, taking out my pain on the hood. I jumped back down and started running in and out of traffic, yelling, "Someone killed my wife, and my daughter is missing."

I looked as if I was high on PCP; I tried to stop any car approaching to see if someone would wake me from this horrible dream. I continued on my tirade until I reached the car of a sister-girl. The familiar face glared at me through the window, giving me a blank yet warm expression. She rolled down the window and asked, "Brandon! Are you okay?"

I looked at her and said, "Someone killed Paulette, and my daughter is missing!"

"Paulette Jenkins?" said the familiar face. I then started crying and sat down in the middle of the street. She parked, got out of her car, and came over to me and placed her arm around my shoulders. "I just heard the news on the radio, but they didn't say her name. The news just said…" She stopped before finishing what the news said. "I went to school with Paulette," she said, rubbing my back and shoulders, providing me with the needed touch of an angel to calm me. She was brave and caring and proved to be a part of my Ghetto Angel crew sent down from heaven to ensure my safety. "Its gonna be okay, Slim. God will help you through all of this. Know that your woman is looking at you right now, praying for God to strengthen you." Her warm embrace did calm me down, allowing me to breathe again. The reality was just coming over me. My daughter was really missing and her mother was gone forever.

Sistagirl helped me to my feet and walked me over to my car. She waved traffic by and stopped the oncoming traffic so we could walk safely towards our cars. Once we reached my car, she said to me, "Let's pray for a safe return of your daughter right now." She took my hand in hers and placed it in her lap. She then took her left arm and wrapped it around me and continued to pray over me: "Dear Lord, I ask that you watch over this young man next to me and shield him with the blood of Jesus Christ, and shield his daughter with the blood that Jesus Christ shed on the cross for our sins. I ask that you return Brandon's daughter to him, dear Lord, and you continue to bless the two of them. Accept his woman, your daughter, and my sister in Christ, dear Lord, into your heaven with open arms. Dear Lord, I ask that you guide and protect this young man from evil and help him cope with his new reality, in the name of Jesus Christ, dear Lord, our savior, amen! Amen, amen."

She turned to me and asked me if I would be okay to drive home. I informed her I would be okay. Once she noticed that I was calming down, she asked me again, adding, "I don't want to read about you in the paper after the police have to subdue you because you're out of control on the side of the highway. So please, my brotha, take care of yourself, please." Her considerable kind-heartedness provided me with enough strength to regain my courage to go on living. She informed me that she does hair and owns a shop over on South Homer. Her name is Antonia, an Afro-Panamanian sister that use to date one of my homeboys back in the day. I distinctly remembered her because my homeboy David was sprung on her. Antonia informed me that once my daughter is returned to my side, I could bring her to her shop and she will do her hair for free. She gave me her card, hugged me, and added, "Please give me a call later so I know you are okay."

"I will," I replied. She went on her way.

I needed to keep my head on straight for the sake of my daughter, so I could find her. I had no time for remorse. It was time to be the diligent father that both God and Paulette knew I would be during her absence. Once I got back in my car, my belly began to twist and turn. I had the bubble guts, but nothing I ate earlier was causing the unfathomable unrest in my belly. Piercing bolts blasted through my intestines, making me feel like explosive diarrhea was just about to make matters worse. Backward gas bubbles surfaced quickly, forcing me to pass gas, smelling up my car with the smell of burnt rice and cow manure. "I think I shit on myself!"

It didn't hit me right away that Riesha was abducted. I was in shock and wasn't thinking clearly at all. However, I did assume an alert was made and by now my daughter was returned. I just knew that the person that killed Paulette was surely caught by now. I picked up the phone to find Ms. Williams still on the other end, sniffling as if she'd been crying for quite some time.

I was waiting for Ms. Williams to utter the words, *they found the killer and your daughter is okay*. I never heard those words.

"The police are searching door-to-door right now, looking for Riesha," said Ms. Williams. I didn't respond. Nor did I place any value to what she was saying. I was surely convinced that there just wasn't any way someone could kill my woman and snatch my kid. My brain couldn't process the two incidents. I could deal with only one. I completely focused my grief on the loss of Paulette. Daddy's little Baby-Boo could not be missing, and that was that.

Like most insecure perplexed boys who were never taught how to grieve without being ridiculed for crying, my homeys and I used drugs and alcohol to permit us to feel remorseful, but in a drunken manly kind of way. We replaced our sorrows with drunkenness and foolishness. We drank and smoked weed until we passed out, or until someone said something stupid and a fight broke out and one of us was hauled off to jail.

I was more than ready to get high so I could begin the grieving process, but I didn't have any weed on me. I wished I hadn't given away my last blunt to Bernard. I couldn't handle the pain. I was being forced to deal with it sober, without the mean-green I desired to help alleviate my pain.

I had promised Paulette I would never pick up our daughter when I was high or under the influence of any drugs. Still, I couldn't envision living day to day without getting high or sipping on alcohol. How was I going to deal with this tragedy and take care of my daughter sober? The thought of having to pick up my little girl was making me nauseous because I was just too bewildered to accept the things that I couldn't change. I would do anything for a freshly rolled vanilla cigarillo (tobacco leaf used to roll marijuana or tobacco) dipped in Remy Martin, stuffed with weed and recently pulled fresh from the toaster oven. Just the thought of the burning leaf mixed with weed just a little damp touching my lips and hitting my lungs gave me symptomatic signs of being high — for just a brief moment, allowing me to escape momentarily. If I did have the opportunity to smoke, I would graciously allow myself to escape from reality for just a brief two minutes. Two minutes is all I needed, because I knew once the high was gone, the problems I had before I got high would return with vengeance.

Aw hell, I needed a blunt just to motivate me to take care of the three S's in the morning. So how was I supposed to take care of my baby girl without smoking weed? Overtaken by the need to remain sober for life now that my Boo was gone, I quickly began to lose my breath and my mind. Damn, I wanted to get high. This was the worst feeling ever. I was consumed by the thought that most of my free time would be spent tending to my daughter rather than getting high with my homeboys. This was a bittersweet moment in my life. I've always loved my daughter and being a father. However, I didn't have to parent Riesha on my own... until now!

When I came home from work, high as hell, or when Riesha woke up screaming for a bottle in the middle of the night, Paulette took care of us. Who prepared Riesha's dinner, washed and ironed her clothes, bathed her, combed her hair, cut her fingernails, cleaned her ears, put baby oil on her, matched her socks, held her when she got shots? Paulette did. Again I felt nauseous. Only this time I couldn't control what happened; I threw up in my own lap, profusely as if I were an addict jonesing for more methadone after finding out my drug dealing doctor lost his license and now he wouldn't be able to prescribe me any more synthetic heroin.

Over and over again I heard a voice telling me *Paulette is dead* and now my baby didn't have her mother. Nevertheless, I didn't know if I was responsible for her death. Was she strangled? Was Daddy's little girl a witness to her mother's death? I tried to answer the voices in my head although I wasn't successful in providing concrete answers. There's only *one* thing that I did think caused her death, more than anything else — my gang affiliation. Deep thoughts rolled around in my head, formulating feelings making my belly knot up like the best Boys Scout knot one could tie. I always figured my gang banging would get me killed. Never did I imagine it would lead to the demise of my entire family. I kept asking myself over and over again, who would hate me so much to kill my Paulette. Maybe it was one of those suck-ass niggaz from Steilacoom that I robbed of their weed last year? No! They don't know Paulette or where her best friend lived. Hell they didn't even see my face. The only thing they knew was that I was some Crip from the dreaded Ridgetop. Plus, I wore a ski mask the whole time anyways.

I felt a teardrop tumble down the side of my face, resting beneath my goatee. At that moment it finally hit me that someone murdered my Boo. Damn! Damn! Damn! My Boo gone? Who do I cry to now? Paulette was the only person that I felt close enough to, to express my feelings openly. She wiped the cobwebs from my eyes when I was confused about what my purpose in life was. Now she is gone. I felt hopelessly abandoned, frightened, lonely, and depressed, baffled, and defeated. Who would kill my baby's momma?

Is the killer or killers holding my baby for ransom? Are they going to kill me? Instantly I had to convince myself not to entertain such thoughts? Why would Paulette tell me to hide my gun? Where is Daddy's baby Riesha?

As I was exiting the highway towards Paulette's Best Friend's house the estranged thought again arose. I couldn't stop my mind from attempting to fathom the thought of daddy's little girl being in the presence of the person who killed her mother. Does she have her sippy cup? I knew she would be going bananas without it! Is she in a diaper or training pants? Paulette bought Riesha some training pants just a few days ago. Do they have enough sense to feed her and change her diaper? I know she's frightened, and I hope she's not shivering from being in a wet diaper all day long. I know she's hungry because Paulette is the only person that could get our baby to eat anything. Oh no! She doesn't have her little black Barbie doll to hold when she falls asleep. My baby must be raising hell for her abductor. How are they going to deal with my baby screaming? "Oh my God, dear Lord, what has happened to my family? What has happened to my family?"

8
Who Killed My Baby's Momma?

WHEN I PULLED ONTO THE STREET where Paulette's homegirl lived, I couldn't help but notice all the local news trailers posted next to the entrance of each building. They were interviewing people and taking pictures of what I assumed was the murder scene. It appeared as though the entire apartment community was waiting for my arrival. An abundance of police cruisers were parked alongside several unmarked cars with no hubcaps, just black rims, long antennas, and dark tinted windows.

As I pulled onto Swan Drive, I felt swarms of evil glares beckoning for my attention. It appeared as though the residents of Creek Apartments knew I was on my way and knew what kind of car I drove. Watchful eyes tried to belittle me and, for the first time in years, it was working. As if I really had done something wrong, the evil-eyed stares turned uglier as I continued to drive slowly, acknowledging the "Deaf Child Area" painted beneath the numbers.

The complex was full of speed bumps; the bouncing started an eruption of gastric acid that erupted like a volcano out of my mouth, landing all over the dashboard. I felt and smelled like shit on a stick. I pulled in front of the complex where her home-girl lived and thought it was ironic to find an empty parking stall where there usually wasn't one. I needed to take time to get myself together for what I was about to bear witness to. I had some mouthwash in my glove compartment next to some *Clear Eye* and a bottle of dollar store cologne for emergency purposes. I took a sip of the mouthwash and doused my white-T with cologne that smelt like mountain fresh soap, hoping to kill the embarrassing odor of throw-up that surely nothing could cover up. I wasn't ready to deal with what had really happened to my Boo. Like pandemonium, thoughts of how I could avoid this encounter with the police filtered through my mind, turning me into a motionless zombie stuck like chuck, in the driver's seat of my car. I sat for about three minutes before police poked their heads out the front door to see what was taking me so long.

"Boom, Boom, Boom!" A young brotha wearing all green banged on my window. I read his lips, "You alright blood. You lost or something?" This boy looked like he was around thirteen years old and weighed all of sixty-five pounds soaking wet. His demeanor was innocent; I didn't feel threatened. To Young Blood I appeared as though I was stuck on stupid, ignorant to the fact that I could be shot on 'gp' (i.e. general purpose) for being an e-ricket (Crip) in slob (Blood / Piru) territory. Like a lion on the prowl, the blue '72 Chevy Nova I drove, known to be driven by predominately Crips, was a dead giveaway. My car let all the Bloods in the apartment complex know that the dreaded enemy was on their turf. Although Young Blood came across as if he was concerned about my welfare, I was still hesitant to trust any Blood. His mere presence woke me up out of the zombie-like state of mind that had forsaken me.

As I exited my car, someone yelled, "Dead e-ricket walking!" Then, I noticed three slobs approaching me. I wasn't concerned about them shooting me or trying to hood-bang on me because I felt I was ready to die anyway. The three were joined by another group of three wearing their colors. I stood my ground and kept my head up high, my chin in the air, as they approached. Once at arms length, I sized them up and knew I could handle just about all of them at once. It wouldn't be the first time I had to fight more than one person. One of them began to muster up spit, then others spit at me, messing my T-shirt. They're catcalls were standard gang threats. I wished one of them did have the balls to throw a punch at me. I felt like I should of fought back after they spat on me, but my mind was on Paulette and my baby.

I removed my T-shirt and threw it to the ground, not giving a fuck about what had just happened. This was a ritual that normally took place at funerals when a relative attending the funeral was from a different gang. I continued to walk down the sidewalk that led to the murder scene, feeling like my shoes had gum plastered on the soles, forcing me to try harder and harder to lift my feet. The normally short-distance walk from my car to the apartment turned out to be a long distance journey to Hells kitchen.

That journey had me remembering all the confrontations I had ever had with enemy gangs. And a recurring dream I had about being nailed in a coffin and falling, falling, wondering how it would feel to hit the ground. Now I knew. The coffin crashed to the ground at speeds too high to record, throwing me out of the box as it shattered in the foothills of the members to the city's largest gang — The Town's Original Gangsters, The T-Town Police Department.

A voice that sounded like my grandfather Rob, an ex drill-sergeant for the United States Marine Corps for thirty-two years, yelled out a deep boisterous command, "Shut those fucking mutts up! As a matter of fact, take them loud ass bitches out back until we get done in here!" Although I was familiar with the game — good cop / bad cop — to manipulate me into believing that the police department cared about my feelings, the voice didn't comfort me at all. "Come in, Mr. Lewis. The door to the apartment is open." He sounded like a preacher at the end of a sermon informing the congregation that the doors of the church were open and now its time to confess your sins. I thought, *Shit, I haven't got anything to confess to these fucking bastards. They need to confess to me why the fuck they want to hang me for a crime that I did not commit.*

The front door was riddled with spots in a kind of collage of blood and buckshot that resembled spattered blackberries. Each spot had a thick black circle around it that was recent; the aroma from the sharpie pen sent vapors off the door, landing on my upper lip and postponing any additional fragrances from entering my body through my nose. I tried not to touch any of the spots willingly, I didn't want to give the forensic team any evidence to set myself up, or to make their attempt to frame me any easier. The door was slightly open already, just like the drill sergeant stated. As soon as I heard barks echoing from the backyard, I entered, using my right Chuck Taylor to slowly open the door. Then I began to move towards the inevitable. My anxiety sent overwhelming sharp, razor-like pains through both shoulders and up my spine to my brain. I softly squeezed my head trying to subdue the unlawful pain. I anticipated a surprise beat-down and was eager to find out what and who was on the other side. I used my index finger to push open the door. As soon as I peered into the apartment, someone grabbed the back of my neck and pulled the rest of my body inward throwing me to the ground and scaring the Holy Ghost out of me. There, I realized my face lay in the blood of my loved one, my fiancée, my Boo, my baby's momma, my Paulette.

The officer who threw me to the ground wore gloves to protect himself from her blood. I couldn't tell if he was black or white. As though I was resisting, he began to frisk me, using bodily force.

"What the fuck is going on? Why am I being arrested?" As the officer continued to frisk and prong me, his boney knee sat firm in between my spinal cord and my upper shoulder, sending my headache into an oppressive state of mind and silencing me. Repressed memories of being beaten by the police a few years earlier surfaced, making me wiggle and resist even more then he could handle. Another police officer jumped on my back, taking over what the weak frail rookie could not handle. This is the bullshit I could never get used to. Being helplessly pronged and poked. Having to submit to the oppressor for no other reason than being a part-time hustler and a full-time black man in a racist city where police brutality and police corruption was prevalent. City and state officials had fabricated policies and laws made behind closed doors to protect their own; I knew I was up shit-creek.

A familiar cry momentarily deadened my pain. The cry came from a toy baby doll, the one my daughter never left home without. One of the punk police stepped on it as he passed by me, still laying face down in Paulette's blood.

"Where is my baby?" I pleaded, still in shock, unwilling to accept my daughter was abducted. I thought maybe she was watching this incident go down, which belittled me even more. I couldn't take my mind off of where she was or whom she was with.

"He's clean, sir." The frisking stopped.

"Now get him off the fucking ground and bring him to me."

My assumption was correct. The controlling voice was surely in charge. As the officer helped me to my feet, I noticed my attire was smothered in my woman's blood. There was so much blood all over me it wouldn't have made any difference if I tried to wipe off any of it. A horrific stench of slop infiltrated my nostrils, rising from my clothes and beneath my feet. This forced me to cover my nose, blocking out the unforgettable stench of death.

I tried to put pep in my step as I made my way down the home stretch of what seemed like a quarter of a mile from the front door to the kitchen, but my Chucks kept slowing me down. Dried up puddles of vomit mixed with blood covered most of the rug, my all-blue Chucks turned purple as the contents seeped through the thin fabric of the soles of my shoes. For each step I took, I felt like I was stepping on Paulette's body. Everywhere I looked were blood spatters, chunks of vomit, each circled with a black marker. To the left of me were splats of blood all over the pictures of her homegirl's family that lined the wall leading to the living room, and on pictures of Paulette and of my daughter when she was first born. I tried not to stare at the stomach contents on the floor, but I couldn't help noticing a few little white rocks within the spew. My instincts suggested that they were either pills or crack rocks. The last time I saw little rocks was when Paulette vomited after ingesting Oxy pills and 'E' pills at the same time. I was stuck for a second trying to get a better look at the white pill substance, but was abruptly poked in the back with a nightstick. I didn't pay Mr. Policeman any mind; I was still tripping off of what could possibly be the substance on the floor in front of me? *Crack! Ah shit, don't tell me my Boo relapsed! But what could have caused all the blood?* Most of it rested on a glass showcase wall unit full of collectable black baby dolls neatly arranged by size and color of clothing.

    There was a horror about the dolls and how the blood was magnified off the mirrored shelving case, suggesting that the murder was vicious and sinister, almost helter-skelter. I tried to hold up my head, but I couldn't bear the pain any longer, nor could I keep myself from getting teary-eyed as I began to break down and cry like a little boy shedding black permanent tattoo tears.

    I felt my stomach stir again at the very sight of more vomit, only this time my reaction set in motion my own stomach contents. Instead of spitting it out, I swallowed it to save face in front of the TPD gang members. The HNIC (Head Nigga In Charge) asked the officer to bring me to him. I was finally able to see the face of the officer that frisked me. He was a young brotha who looked like he was fresh out of the police academy. Had he arrested me before or did I go to school with him? "Right this way, Ceeze," he whispered as though he was ashamed for calling me by the name most white people had a hard time articulating. How did he know me? I told the young brotha that he didn't have to stick his knee in my back the way that he did. He hesitated for a moment then said, "Just doing my job, C. I didn't know if you was strapped or not."

    I followed the barks of the commanding officer's voice that bounced off the kitchen walls. My heart was beating a mile a minute, making me feel like I was riding the boat (East coast term used to describe the high associated with smoking marijuana laced with Angel Dust) and about to have a heart attack. I seriously felt like someone needed to call the paramedics, but I was too proud to beg for attention. I didn't know if the weed from earlier was making me paranoid, or if I was full of apprehension surrounding the death of my baby's mother and the kidnapping of my daughter.

I didn't have a clue how Paulette was killed yet, when she was killed, or where my daughter was. I prayed to God that the white substance I saw wasn't a drug. I wanted to know why there was still blood all over the place. A detective walked out from the kitchen, holding a manila folder. Once he noticed I saw him viewing the contents, he closed it. He made it apparent to me that he was done taking notes as he exited the kitchen, pushing the top of the ballpoint pen to insinuate he had everything he came for.

Paulette's homegirl was in the kitchen holding my baby's favorite doll. That's when it hit me that my little Riesha was missing. She wouldn't be caught without holding her favorite dolly. This was a sign that wherever Riesha was, she was unhappy, which made me even more manic. I needed to stop all of this bullshit so I could find my daughter. For some reason the homegirl refused to look me in the eyes, as though I did something wrong. It was then I knew the police thought I murdered Paulette and had something to do with Riesha's abduction.

"Search him," the head detective said to a uniformed officer. "Put your hands on the table over here please, Mr. Lewis."

"Youngun just searched me when I came in the apartment. You think I picked up something on the way down the hallway?" The officer placed my hands on the counter where there were bloody hand prints resembling Paulette's. I turned my head towards the homegirl, asking what is going on here and added, "Do they think I killed Paulette?"

She turned her head away from me as she walked past, holding my baby's Barbie doll tightly against her chest. The homegirl's body language suggested she couldn't talk to me because she was the one hiding something. I instantly felt she informed the police I had something to do with my Boo 's murder and abduction.

"This bitch is trying to set me up!" I said to myself, but loud enough for everyone around me to hear. Once the officer was done frisking me, he turned to the chief and said, "He's clean, sir."

"Is someone gonna tell me where my daughter is and what happened to Paulette?"

"You need to stop playing games and tell me where the gun is and where you're hiding your daughter?"

"What gun? And I don't have my daughter!"

"The gun you used to kill your girlfriend, you fucking bastard!"

Then a second officer in the room looked dead at me and shook his head from side to side saying, "So why did you stuff twelve crack rocks down her throat? What was the significance of doing that? Wasn't shooting her in the fucking head good enough for you?"

An earthquake hit my chest and quickly gave me an upper cut to my chin, knocking me cold the fuck out. For the next five minutes, everything the punk police were saying became a blur. I was concentrating on figuring out why someone would want to kill Paulette and snatch my child. I was stuck on believing that the accomplices to her murder were the Bloods, probably the ones trying to hood-bang on me when I first arrived. Why aren't the police questioning them? Everyone knows that the killer usually hangs around the murder scene to watch the reaction of the police. The police witnessed the Piru Niggaz spitting and fronting on me outside. What the fuck!

The punk police were convinced I was the one who stuffed twelve crack rocks down her throat and shot her in the head. I had become the killer who returned to the murder scene. "This was a set-up, all the way down to Paulette's homegirl informing me to get over here quickly. The only thing they were looking for was the murder weapon, my daughter, and a confession. The police continued to twist my words as they persistently tried to get me to say I murdered my Boo and was hiding Riesha somewhere close by.

"Is your daughter in the trunk of your car? Give me permission to check your car so we could still save her life, Mr. Lewis. Do it for her mother if you can't do it for yourself." I began to tune out their imperious voices. I wasn't afraid of the punk TPD, never have been and I wasn't surely going to start fearing them now.

How often had I seen the way the media had painted blacks and minorities from the inner city in negative ways? How often had I been pulled over because… well, they quoted strange laws I had broken and terrorist crimes I had committed and made-up "obstructions of justice" they interpreted in a thousand-and-one ways. And mostly quotations of the growing wars between the Crips and the Bloods in Ridgetop or Westside of town — all made by the stern looking chief of police — or the mayor?

The head Nigga in charge (HNIC) was furious at me because I wouldn't confess to a murder I didn't commit or the abduction of my daughter. For the next twenty minutes the HNIC sat inches from my face, so close I could make out the brand of Starbucks latte he was sipping on —vanilla nutmeg. His coffee breath was mixed with Marlboro red cigarettes, a deadly combination, which caused little poisonous gas spit balls that shot towards my face. As I tried to explain my whereabouts, some of these gas bubbles landed in my mouth. My assumption was wrong; he was drinking Seattle's Best Coffee, nonfat milk, with a hint of nutmeg and *Sweet and Low* Sugar.

The detective who took charge of the way the questions flowed called me a coward for killing Paulette.

"What the fuck you say to me?"

"You heard me, Cuzz, you coward! Instead of working out your problems with your girlfriend, you went the punk way out and stuffed twelve crack rocks down her throat and then shot her in the head, you sorry son-of-a-bitch!"

That was the first time someone told me how she was killed.

"So what happened, Ceeze? You came home from work to find one of your homeboys from the hood getting it on with your old lady?" The police officer and his buddies began laughing and giggling freely. The officer with jokes became the center of attention briefly as his peers gave him high fives and solid closed handed pounds to one another. "Is that why you murdered her in front of your daughter? Is that why you snatched up your daughter, killed her too, and now you're hiding the body somewhere so we can't find her?"

"You are a ruthless sick bastard." Mr. Officer was going in on me. He lunged at me as if he was going to try to take my head off. I wasn't moved by his awkward shenanigans. The HNIC had to hold him back, before he could reach me. Either way I wasn't worried.

At that moment, my life as I knew it changed emphatically. I felt I didn't have anything else to live for. Paulette's homegirl came walking down the stairs holding my daughter's little Barbie doll asking the HNIC how long they were going to be. No matter the situation, my skin chilled at the first sight of that heifer. I never liked this ho.

Whenever I was around Paulette and her, I knew she was unreal. Yes, I was jealous of the relationship she and Paulette developed; however I was torn between being unsure whether or not jealousy could have been misconstrued for the intuition rumbling within my belly, which undoubting was telling me that this heifer was un-trustworthy and bad company.

"Why am I being arrested?" I asked the officer who was attempting to torment me.

"For not cooperating with the authorities. You are on probation right?"

"Yes, but I don't have anything to tell you because I didn't kill her!"

"Since you won't cooperate with us, I'll just take your ass to jail for interfering with a police officer's business! Now get his ass out of here!" The arresting officer put the handcuffs on me so tight I couldn't even turn my wrist. Without circulation, my hands went numb and cold. No room to maneuver around the excruciating pain. I wasn't going to play the handcuffs-too tight game with Mr. Top Cop either.

"Try not to resist, Ceeze!" the young brotha with the familiar face said to me. I relaxed my arms. I didn't want him to think he controlled my thoughts. Making the handcuffs exceptionally tight was a tactic that was used to make the victim submit to the person inflicting the pain, a tactic passed down from the original *sheriffs* — plantation overseers who ensured slaves were where they were suppose to be. I'd been in this situation many times before and had learned how to deal with the pain on my own. But this time it was more then just physical pain. I felt the pain my Paulette went through. Gunshots rang in my head over and over while visions of a person without a face jamming a bag full of crack rocks down her throat. Boom! Boom! Boom! The gun kept going off in my head.

Determined to control my pain and my fears, I knew how to keep my wrists straight enough so the handcuffs wouldn't faze me. I just needed to relax my body, and my wrist would simultaneously contour to the position of my wrists within the cuffs. I slowly closed my eyes and took three deep breaths. This allowed my heart rate to mellow out. With my hands behind my back, the officer held the cuffs downward using his strength to direct me towards the front. Similar to a person directing a horse with the reins, I followed. As I approached the living room, I noticed Paulette's homegirl walking up the stairs holding Riesha's doll, as if the doll replaced my daughter against her bosom. Again, she wouldn't look me in the eyes. Instead she took Riesha's Barbie Doll by the hair and headed back up the stairs allowing the doll to hit every rail as she proceeded to the top.

    The crowd began to clap as the police escorted me from the murder scene; all I could remember was seeing a bunch of young black males and Asians boys wearing red, green, brown and burgundy. The only conclusion I could reach for someone wanting to kill my Boo was thinking that one of those motha-fuckas saw me slide through here last night and thought I was still in there when they shot my woman instead. But what was the deal with the dozen crack rocks?

    The front porch became center stage where the cops showcased me. I felt like I was on the auction block for all of the slave owners to view the mighty strong, fit, and broad-shouldered boy that would make a good field nigger to work from dusk to dawn. The newscaster from KTOY was the auctioneer: "Strong young buck from Ridgetop for sale. Once ran with a gang of village Mangalore's called the Ridgetop Crips. This young stud has fathered one fine young heifer. The mother, no longer with us, had childbearing hips, and the daughter is surely likely to follow. Do I have a bid?"

    I never had experienced death to this degree. I had lost my parents, a few relatives and many close friends and associates from gang banging and police brutality. However, grieving for them at home or at a friend's house after the funeral was completely different from grieving for the mother of my child, my soul mate for life in the back seat of a police car after being accused of the murder. Thoughts of spending the rest of my life in jail blocked my ability to grieve like a man should. Any and all spare thoughts were steadfast on the whereabouts of my daughter.

As the officer sat me in the back seat, I looked up at the apartment to see Paulette's homegirl in the window staring down at me, as she held my baby's doll tight to her chest, brushing her hair with one of those little pink plastic brushes that came with the doll. As soon as we made eye contact, she quickly closed the blinds. "That bitch," I said, loud enough for Mr. Officer to hear me. "Where the fuck is my daughter?" I yelled out towards the window. Instead of opening the blinds, she put her hand in between two slats and turned her middle finger up at me. "I know she didn't just do that!" I said to the officer. He smiled and laughed in my face.

The agony attached to stripping a man of his dignity made me feel like a buffoon. It was as if I was being used to amuse the police department as the chief's jester. I had finally lived up to the label of being the town's fool. "The joke is on you, jack!" said the cop.

9
The Ride to the Station

AS USUAL, THE POLICE HAD THE HANDCUFFS WAY TOO TIGHT, forcing me to sit upright in the back seat of the police car and digging the handcuffs deeper into my boney wrists.

"Sit your ass down and shut the fuck up," I heard for the second time.

"Is that all you punk police know what to say?"

Mr. Hook-my-ass-up didn't respond as he wrapped the seatbelt around me. I didn't want him in my personal space, so close I smelled his cheap cologne, Grey Flannel. I used to steal that stuff from K-Mart when I was a teenager to hide the weed and cigarette smell from my parents, I thought.

"Ah, sit back and relax, you fucking murderer." He wanted me to lash out at him again, resist arrest, or kick the windows out and spit in his face. I wasn't going to allow insecurities to destroy any chance to see the daylight again.

After his unsuccessful attempt to frustrate me anymore, we started off. ."Where are we going?" I asked when I noticed us heading in the opposite direction of the jailhouse.

The Korean Officer answered with an unauthentic yet flawless white vernacular, sounding like a white boy from the Peninsula. "Just sit back and enjoy the ride; it'll be your last one for a while." He accentuated his pronunciation to convince me he was superior. I wasn't going to let him take away my power and the peace that I was searching for.

The officer might be right; this could be my last ride through the city for quite some time. I swear, every time I'm taken to jail, the driver makes like a taxi cab driver and takes the longest route through the city. I was not only uncomfortable with the hard plastic seats and handcuffs, it was knowing that I'd be subjected to the strenuous drawn-out process to prove my innocence to a bunch of racist, manipulative, insensitive white detectives. Their inherited white-man complex convinced them they were on this earth to rule and control it; I am greater than thou and emancipation was a farce. Thinking about the manipulative tactics momentarily discombobulated me.

I wasn't in a hurry to get to the county jail, to be reunited with fake-ass pimps, wannabe gangsters and jive-ass Niggaz who believed jail hours counted towards college credits in place of a law degree. Many felt that they were lawyers, but never picked up a case study out of any law library. They fed off telling other lost souls what they should do in order to get out of jail, even though they'd been going to jail three times a year for the last two decades. Some truly believed they possessed the same knowledge and experience as any lawyer fresh out of law school.

Sitting there, I appeared wide open to the onlookers breaking their necks to make out what a real thug looked like as the police car passed. Little white children stared at me from the back seats of their mother's SUV, asking, "Mother is that a gang member?" Being seen riding in the backseat of a police car is the equivalent of a public hanging. Fuck it! I didn't care anymore.

My head sank further into my chest as I thought about the number of years I was looking at for murder and kidnapping. My white counterparts might look at a minimum of thirty years. My fate as a gangbanging black man in the state of Washington had me looking at death by lethal injection.

My mind was jolted with the sudden thought, *what the fuck did I do last night anyways? I did experience a blackout from consuming an overwhelming amount of drugs and alcohol.* To top off everything, I felt like I had ants forming colonies inside my bone marrow. I don't know what it is, but whenever I found myself in the back seat of a police car, my right foot itched. Could the police have something on me that would tie me to the murder last night, something I don't remember?

My head sank even further just thinking I may have something to do with the murder. The undeniable itch scurried through my body, beckoning me to greet it. I tried to shake it off but there wasn't much room to work with. Overwhelmed, I needed to take a leak.

My foot begged for a sharp object to satisfy the itch, and I felt a dribble of urine seep out. I had to get at the itch, though the bathroom would have to wait. With my hands handcuffed behind my back, I felt defeated, as if I was in a dream. I wished my momma could waken me from this one. She was the only one who could successfully waken me from a horrible dream.

I tried stomping my foot, then I tried rubbing it on top of my left shoe. Nothing alleviated the burning deep down itch. The burning continued to creep up my leg until it rested in my shin. I was overtaken by an urge to kick out the window to stop the pain. '*Boom, boom.*'

"What the fuck is wrong with you, mister?" '*Boom, Boom*' I did it again, but only this time, I lost control over the amount of force. Still, the window didn't shatter. Momentarily, I allowed the officer and the onlookers to steal my power right from beneath my feet; I was out of control.

All the pain and frustration of last night's blackout, my Paulette, and my Baby Booboo Riesha surfaced. I felt like an outcast on the way to a public stoning for a murder I did not commit. I stomped my feet, one at a time, as I ranted uncontrollably, screaming obscenities as spit streamed from my mouth. The plastic seats became my therapeutic couch; the windows I tried so hard to break embraced me as I tried to bust them into pieces. My pain was surging through my legs. I felt like I was handcuffed in a coffin, on my way to my own burial, to be buried alive. Stomping feet and yelling momentarily satisfied my urge to beat on someone or something. Throwing myself up against the doors and backseat of the car also helped.

The confused officer pulled over on the side of the road and threw the car in park, hopping out before the cruiser came to a complete stop. He called for backup on his shoulder two-way radio.

I couldn't stop carrying on like a demented thug. I needed my mom to hold me, to comfort me. I needed Paulette to tell me to settle down and that everything was going to be all right. I began to sing the lyrics to the Al Greene song as I continued to try to smash through the back windows to freedom. "Ev-ver-thing is gonna be all right, it's over now, like you said it would." Though I couldn't remember all the words, the song comforted me. The cop watched franticly with his hand on his gun, glaring at the psychotic gang-banger in the backseat of his cruiser.

I called this outburst a *panic attack*; the police called it *resisting arrest*.

"Fuck you, Mr. Kor-re-an po-lice. I don't give a fuck what you motha-fuckas do to me now! I've already lost my girl and not one of you punk police will tell me where my daughter is, so I don't want to live anymore!"

He swung his baton through the window, hitting my head hard. As I fell over to the other side of the police cruiser, dazed, I rested there with my eyes wide open. Slowly, I focused on a bag of weed tucked underneath the passengers seat; someone didn't want to get caught with a marijuana charge. Though I was almost comatose, I was thinking about who really killed my Boo and where my little girl could be. And I wished I could smoke the weed lying on the floor and flee from the truth for as long as it would take to get to the station.

When the back-up officers arrived, they stood outside pointing and laughing at me. I heard one say, "The little nigger looks like he's settled down now!"

The other one responded, "Looks like you won't be needing these!" He pointed down to the tazer attached to his belt.

There, in the back of the police coffin, I felt trapped inside a huge cobweb. For the first time in many years I was afraid and couldn't mask these feelings with drugs or alcohol. I was worried I wouldn't make it out of the coffin alive this time. My misery delivered self-hate to the point where I contemplated suicide and knew it wouldn't be hard at all to persuade those punk-ass police to shoot me dead. The only thing I had to do was lunge at the Korean and his scary ass would surely shoot to kill me. That's what they were taught in the police academy: shoot a nigga first and explain later.

With my chin tucked tight, my father's face appeared inside my forehead informing me, "Didn't I tell you to always keep your head up regardless of the situation?" Aloud but with my head still down, I answered, "Yes you did sir."

"Then lift your head up, boy" My daddy used the word *boy* when I was to respond quickly without question. His voice continued, "Did you kill your baby's momma?"

"No sir!" I answered as though my dad was in front of me.

"Did you snatch your only daughter, kill her, and hide her in the woods some damn where so that the police can't find her?"

"No sir!"

"Who you talking to?" the Asian man-child asked from the front seat of the police cruiser.

"Not you," I replied. My father's voice continued. "Lift your head up, boy, and start talking to the Lord."

Another Ghetto Angel came to light in that lonely back seat. This time it was the voice of Granddaddy Rob preaching, "Boy, if you running around worrying about shit, that shows God you don't believe in him!"

That is what I needed to take with me as we pulled into the stall at the county-city building where the jail awaited. His remark taught me how to trust God through any situation. I lifted my head and said aloud but with my eyes closed, "I trust God, not the system."

All of the pain that ran through my body up until that point exited right then and there. "Man up, Ceeze, man up," said Poppa Dukes.

While the officer held a short conversation with the dispatcher, I envisioned walking alongside Paulette, clenching her left hand as we walked through an ominous tunnel of darkness, and transporting me to a place where memories replaced time. I sat in the back seat rocking from side to side, all along asking the Lord to forgive me for my sins, asking God to look over Riesha and keep her safe, healthy, and happy. I asked God to let my Boo know that she will always weigh heavy on my heart, and that I look forward to the days when we are reunited.

I wasn't in a hurry to be reunited with cats I grew up with whose claims to fame was purse snatching and selling nickel bags of fake weed. I didn't miss reminiscing with broke-ass thugs who hustled to support their drug habits.

The first thing that usually pops in my head as I enter into the county jail is "this can't be happening to me!" Immediately followed by, "I wanna go home!" Again I started to slip into depression. My thoughts ran amok, taking me to a place where I didn't want to go. Like a scared little boy, I wanted the comfort of

Paulette's arms convincing me that it will be *greater later*. When Paulette mentioned she wanted me to drop her off at her homegirl's house I should've been more assertive and told her that she and the baby were coming home with me. I never wanted Paulette to feel like I was trying to control her. Now I felt like it was my fault that she was dead. I had been more concerned about making it home so I could smoke a blunt in peace without Paulette bugging me because I was high. I didn't want them with me.

Them fucking niggaz over there were always trying to hood-bang me whenever I drove up to her homegirl's house. I just assumed one of them cats was responsible for killing my baby's momma. Let there be one in the county jail; it's on! The first one I see, I'm going in on him — a combination of upper cuts, left then right so all his teeth are broken. Then I'm gonna back up and kick him in the nut-sack, followed by a right jab to the eye and a left jab to his throat.

My spirits broke in waves, up and down, one minute planning revenge, and the next minute wishing somebody would kill me. And in between, all I wanted was to find my Baby Boo and grieve for her mother, my sweet Paulette.

Incarceration occurs in steps. The first attempt is the Waiting Game, being held in solitary confinement with no phone, no eye contact, and no one to speak to. This usually lasts two to three hours, but no more than five. I liked to ask the guard how much longer I would be held without making my phone call. The reply? "Sit down and shut the fuck up."

Next comes the Moping Mode, where my sorrows make my chin sink deep into my chest for hours on end as the result of hearing my criminal record used to manipulate facts, truth, my words, and my whereabouts.

With my head still dangling above my lap, my father's thick scratchy baritone voice returned. "Boy, don't question authority.

You just do as they say and lift your head up. What the hell you moping for? You don't have the time to mope. This isn't about you. This is about my little grandbaby and her mother, and what you have to do to raise your daughter alone."

10
The *Not Guilty* Bed

"It's your lucky day, killa!" the guard sneered as he lowered his head to peek at his clipboard. "You're assigned to bed number seven — the Not Guilty bed."

"The not-guilty bed?"

"Yes, the… the… the Not Guilty bed, motha-fucka. Did I stutter? These Uncle Tom negroes around here say the bed has special powers."

I let out a sigh, but almost immediately shook it off. *Was this the Demon God?* I began to rub the cobwebs out of my eyes. The death of my Boo had made me see clearer. No longer was I able to be drawn into the Demon God's trickery masked by superstition. I stopped the Demon from entering my body by acknowledging, "Not the stars, nor the moon, nor some mystical bed could set me free." And I added, "No one can foresee my future except God."

I wasn't yet aware how the devil used fear to create stagnancy in my life by controlling my every step. Many people fall victim to this as setbacks create cobwebs in their eyes. Magical hexes and root evils consume the mind, the heart, and soul. These same superstitions are used eloquently by the devil to justify another's misguided downfall. Astrology takes the place of Bible verses, desperately seeking a sign or a conviction to send a message, which states, "It will be greater later." Sometimes a doorknob or a screwdriver is used as a metaphor for a higher power. Once all of the attention is taken off God, the Demon's mystical powers surface like dead flounder rising in algae-infested Chesapeake Bay.

With the Demon God imbedded in a your life, ghosts and goblins run amok through the house, scaring the be-Jesus out of you and your children. The Demon God pollutes minds with visions of monsters attacking Mommy and Little Johnny at night. You find yourself trying to convince yourself and your family that seeing, hearing, and talking to evil spirits is the norm. Trusting in God slowly disappears and becomes a rare glimpse of your past.

I wasn't sure of this; but I was feeling it now through the memory of my heritage combined with the trauma of losing my family.

"You can't be superstitious and believe in God at the same time," I said without stammering so that the guard would know I was confident in what I believed.

"Shit! I'm not superstitious either," he returned. "If it's not God's way, it's no way." His face suddenly appeared Christian-like. The brief silence that followed confirmed he too was a true believer. In my mind, I said *Amen*, but out loud I said, "You got that right!"

"You still want bunk number seven? I could give you bunk number five, but you would have to share bunks with OG Skitzo," said the guard.

"Crazy-ass Skitzo up in here?" We both knew Skitzo and were aware that everything about him was monkey-shit. He was one of the original boys who arrived from South Central Los Angeles back in the summer of '85. He was among hundreds of go-hard gang members from California who introduced crack cocaine and gang life to The Town. Sean Watson, aka Skitzo was once a local legend for being a flamboyant drug dealer and part time pimp. His main whore usually drove him around town in his fancy cars. He simply referred to her as My Chicken-head. "Chicken-head, buy me a 64-ounce of Mickey's!" Or "Chicken-head, pump my gas!" Or "Chicken-head, light me a cigarette!"

Skitzo once had three houses. At one point he was one of the most powerful gang member-drug-dealing-pimps in Washington State. Now he was known around town as the neighborhood slapstick comedian who knew how to tell convincing sidewalk stories to earn enough money to buy a bottle of Night Train.

Reminiscing about Skitzo and his comedic past freed my mind. I even got a couple chuckles, which allowed me to briefly escape from reality. But the more I tried to smile, the more Riesha's face appeared in front of me, her face covered in tears. She had the sniffles and was shaking from the tears that soaked her shirt. She was trying to say Daddy, but the sniffles made it hard for her to get any word out. I saw her arms stretched, trying to get to me. I couldn't make out who was holding her, but I knew it was a woman.

Talking about Skitzo allowed the guard and me to chuckle simultaneously. For just a moment our enormous egos conjoined culturally, fusing us spiritually, making way for the Holy Spirit to strengthen our souls indefinitely.

With a smile on my face, I said, "I'll take the not-guilty bed, bro! I don't want to spend five minutes listening to Skitzo tell his lies and try to monkey-shit me." It was hard for me to enjoy the laughter, to let it flow freely through my body. Within moments, I started to feel guilty for laughing, as if I had something to do with the abduction of my daughter and the murder of her mother.

"I'll place you in bunk number seven," the guard repeated.

Negative thoughts began to race through my mind. *Is she dead? Did she watch the killer murder her mother?* I slipped up, saying aloud, "Fuck! Where is my daughter?" I looked at the guard. "For the record, I didn't kill my baby's momma, and I don't know who snatched my daughter."

"Were you read your rights?" asked the guard.

"Cuzz! Nah, they didn't tell me shit! I didn't even get to use the phone."

"Keep your mouth shut, and don't say a fucking word to any of these snitch-ass bitches in here. Ya dig what I'm saying, Buzz?"

"Ya, no doubt. I'm not saying anything in here."

"Watch your back, Buzz. Watch your back!" said the guard. His use of the word *Buzz* threw me off for a split second. The first time I heard the word, it was used by a Piru gang member from Logan Heights, a small neighborhood in Southeast San Diego; his name was Bee, and he was a booster homey who supplied me with brand-new everything: clothes, flat screen TVs in the box, rims and tires, and sometimes a whole car. I never knew his name, but I did know that when somebody used a name with a single letter, you didn't ask questions. I did know that Bee was a hustler who dealt with a lot of people from different sets across the nation and used *Buzz* to let people know who he was. Whether they were Crips from Tacoma or a BGD (Black Gangster Disciple) from Minneapolis, saying *Buzz* became his unorthodox way of saying "though we are from different sides of the track, I come in peace; I am here to do business with you."

When the guard said *Buzz* to me, I took it to mean he was saying, "I no longer gang bang, and I feel your pain." Although he was from the opposite sides of the tracks, I could tell he was concerned about my safety and my freedom.

All business again, he said, "Follow the yellow line to the next counter where you pick up your slippers and mattress, and don't talk to anyone. You feel me, Cousin!"

"I feel you, Dog, I feel you." At that moment he became my Ghetto Angel.

There wasn't time for small talk anymore with smooth Blood. I could tell he didn't want his colleagues to see him acting kindhearted towards the neighborhood villain. Our silence represented our farewells. I was on my own again, thrown to the coyotes, disguised as a hood figga in a pink pajama suit with PCJ (Pierce County Jail) stamped on the back.

Ah shit! Ain't this a bitch? I didn't want to deal with the prick of a guard leaning over the next counter with his hands folded like he was trying to impress his kindergarten teacher. He had been the neighborhood smelly kid, and now he was a Pierce County Sheriff. I mumbled to myself the name *James Bond*.

He read my lips. "Who said you could speak to me as if I was one of your Crip home-boys from the neighborhood, mother-fucker?" His pronunciation of the "er" at the end of both *mother* and *fucker*, convinced me he didn't use the words often unless he was trying to make an impression on someone. It didn't impress me at all; in fact, it made me feel sorry that he felt the need to impress me. This man who became a police officer was named for his mother's favorite British special agent, James Bond, which gave all of us neighborhood kids something to tease him about. I never really disliked the poor kid, nor did we have anything in common, so we never spoke to one another; yet we lived on the same block. Although he was always a nerd, I still felt sorry for his punk ass.

"I heard the conversation you was having with Mr. Friendly over there. Was it God that told you to shoot that girl in her face and stuff dope down her throat the way you did, you sorry ass mother-fucker?"

I couldn't resist; I had to say something about how he pronounced motha-fucka the second time around. "That's a-bit better. You remember how to pronounce motha-fucka. I was worried about you the first time, Cuzz! You sounded like a white boy." I laughed.

"Don't call me *Cuzz*! I hate you good-for-nothing niggers from the neighborhood who used to run around town talking about how you guys were gangsters and big pimps. That big-pimping shit landed all of you mother-fuckers in here." He smiled from ear to ear, while shaking his head from side to side as he continued to lean over the counter. This time he leaned closer towards me so that he could whisper, "You all used to talk bad about me in school and now look who's laughing! I got a Mercedes and a boat, a house and a condo. Every time I see you wannabe gangster-ass niggers come through here all high off of PCP, lying about where you've been and why you up in here, my dick gets hard. Now, look at you. I hope they find you guilty and stick your arms up with poison very slowly." He rose up from over the counter and it was at that moment when I had remembered the nickname we called him, Bullet head. His head was shaped like a bullet, which coincided with his special agent name, Special Agent Bullet Head.

I didn't have time to think about whether or not he was making any sense. One thing that he did say which caught my attention was that I might be sent to death row and for a crime I didn't commit. My head briefly sagged again hitting my chest as Bullet Head continued to taunt and harass me for the next several seconds.

"That's enough, Bullet!" Smooth Blood yelled out from his checkpoint.

"They still call you Bullet? They must think you used to shoot up folks or something around here. They don't know where the name came from, do they Bond?"

Hesitating for a moment, he looked in my direction not saying a word with an evil look on his face that read, *I'm gonna get you, sucka*. He then reached underneath the counter and grabbed a pair of slippers that had a number eight stamped in red on them and threw them on the counter in front of me.

"I haven't wore size 8 since Junior high school."

"Did I ask you what size you wore, Cuzz?"

Next, he walked over to the wall and pulled out a ladder that was stuffed beneath the counter and set it up so he could pull down a dusty old mattress from the top of the shelf that surely contained bed bugs. When he pulled it down, dust particles filled the air, forcing him to sneeze. I had to gasp for air. After coughing and clearing his throat, Bullet said, "Punk-ass wife beater, take bunk seven, Ya Bitch-ass nigger." He continued to taunt me and I almost kurked (suddenly explode, go off) out on him: I was fixed to bust out all of his teeth, but I was interrupted by his rude interrogating antics. "Why don't you just tell me where you hid your daughter's body and I will see if I could get some time taken off of your sentence for cooperating?"

Again my head hit my chest. Before you know it, Smooth Blood came over and stopped Bullet Head from saying any more damaging remarks to me. "Say Blood, didn't I ask you nicely to stop harassing this dude?"

I didn't have to acknowledge Young Bleezy, he simply informed me to grab my shit and follow the blue line. "Can I get my blanket?" I asked Smooth Blood.

"Bullet, where's his blanket, Cuzz?" said Blood. From the way the two of them used the words *Cuzz* and *Blood*, I assumed they were aware they came from different sides of the tracks. Though Bullet Head never gang banged, he was still from the Ridgetop, which meant he acknowledged his neighborhood affiliation.

"Murderers don't get blankets nor do child abductors. Not on my watch. Here is your pee-stained mattress; have fun, and good night!"

"Damn Bullet, why you got to be so damn cold, Cuzz? Damn!" said Smooth Blood. He then reached over and under the counter himself and grabbed a blanket for me and tossed it to me saying, "Follow the blue line, Buzz."

"Good looking out, Blood!" I replied.

In a deep boisterous voice, James Bond yelled, "Bitch beater on deck!" Again he yelled, "Bitch Beater on deck!" The whole entire community of felons, convicts, and guards looked my way. I followed the blue line towards the bunks that were numbered sequentially. As I approached bunk number seven, I noticed someone on the bottom bunk writing on the wall. Once he noticed I was going to be his *celli* (a person who shared a cell or bunk with another inmate) he quickly hopped to his feet. The occupant jumped to the top bunk and claimed it by lying down and squeezing out a humungous fart. Acting as though his sleep was not interrupted whatsoever, he laid back down and commenced to snore. I was close enough to make out what he had for dinner that night — tacos.

I spread the mattress across the bottom bunk and ran the palm of my hand across the entire bed to make sure nothing was poking out. Many inmates hid fake knives made from toothbrushes, spoons, and hairbrush handles between the mattress and the thin layer of plastic that covered the bed. The plastic was used to keep the bed bugs from invading your privacy at night. The mattress had debris all over it from sitting on the top shelf for years on end. I looked down at my hand to find a thick layer of fiberglass shingles and dead bed bugs, along with lifeless red ants.

After I felt it was safe, I took a moment to get on my hands and knees to pray. My momma always said, "When you struggling or in desperate need for God to make an immediate change in your life, take it to the Lord on your knees."

Who do I cry to you, Dear Lord? It is you that I cry to with silent tears. Please, dear Lord, forgive me for my sins. I thank you for bringing me this far, and I know that you will carry me even further. I ask that you bless my family. I ask that you welcome my Boo in your heaven. I ask that you watch over my daughter and keep her safe and bring her home safely. I ask that you bring those who murdered my Boo forward so they are charged with murder and I am set free. I ask that you continue to watch over my daughter and me.

When I am in the weakest state from all of the torture and turmoil that I may be up against, I ask that you enter my body and fill me with your Holy Spirit. I ask that you come into the hearts of those that have arrested me on false pretenses. I ask that you place me in the footsteps that you lay out in front of me for me to follow.

I come to you, dear Lord, on my knees, asking you to answer these prayers and walk in front of me as we head back on the right path of fatherhood, manhood, and cohesiveness among the many who follow you. I ask that you shield my body with your Holy Spirit and protect me from my enemies. I am aware that what I am going through is nothing compared to what Jesus went through as he died on the cross for all of us to be forgiven for all of our sins. I ask that you use the blood of your only son as a weapon to keep my enemies from persecuting me anymore. I ask that you continue to instill faith in me and keep me safe, healthy, and blessed. I am not going to ask why did my Boo have to be taken from me, but what I will acknowledge is the need for the Holy Spirit to strengthen me so I can continue to be a father to my child upon her return. Dear Lord I ask that you bring my daughter home quickly. I ask that you fill the hearts of Paulette's family and friends with picturesque memories of happy times. I ask that you instill in me the Hope of Glory that I am having a hard time seeing. One thing that I know for certain is that you will prevail. This I ask in Jesus name, Amen.

As I arose from my knees I could see scores of roaches fleeing in the opposite direction of Bunk Number Seven. The last time I left the county jail, I went home with the *e-bee-gee-bees* i.e., scabies. I later found out that scabies are worse then bed bugs or crabs because you cannot see them but you know they are there. At first, scabies surface as little red bumps all over you that itch a little. They look like you may have come in contact with poison ivy or you just discovered that you're allergic to Dollar Store detergent. A couple days later the itch intensifies as the micro-sized bugs are trying to work their way out of your skin. The itch turns into a burning pathway throughout your entire first layer of skin. As the hours pass, the itch starts to increase, which hurts like hell. The intensity of the itch gets worse and worse and becomes a nonstop fire-burning itch. Falling asleep with the e-bee-gee-bees is impossible. You think taking a shower would help cure them, but the water only makes them more active.

    I felt compelled to stay awake. The thought of having mites and bed bugs eat at my skin as I slept convinced me to sit upright at the end of my bed until the break of daylight. I was hopeful; if I stayed awake, praying with my eyes wide shut, the pain and agony attached to the suffering of losing my beloved soul mate and having my daughter snatched out of my life would soon vanish, disintegrate as if this were all a dream. Four hours in, I was reluctant to make any attempt to close my eyes. Even when I attempted to get some sleep, the blackness within my eyelids turned into bright specks of shining stars with the faces of both Paulette and Riesha on each star. Magnified spotlights lit up my eye sockets turning the murder scene into the biggest drive-in movie theater ever, playing back dramatic scenes where Paulette's dead cold body lay limp while my daughter is swooped up and carried away by her abductor — a white-girl wearing a bright red sundress and dark shades.

    I had a hard time spending the next six hours with my eyes closed, dwelling on the blood and gore associated to the grueling murder scene. I couldn't get past the thought of someone stuffing Paulette's throat with dope and then shooting her in the head. I tried to set my thoughts on my little baby girl, envisioning her pretty little smile and her tiny chunky legs. I tried to sense her smell, but it was impossible because of the substandard aroma of spoiled broccoli, filthy dirty-ass and smelly feet that hadn't been washed in many moons, all fermenting through the entire pod where I was stuck. The insufferable stench filled my entire two feet of private space, making it impossible to envision little Riesha's first tooth.

    Somehow, I convinced myself to make viable attempts to picture glorious moments of the three of us spending happy time together. I envisioned us on the shores of Sunset Beach eating barbeque King Crab and pulled pork sandwiches. We laughed and giggled while feeding each other chocolate-covered strawberries. We spent endless moments searching for flathead rocks to throw against the still surface of the clear blue lake. I smiled thinking about how we searched and searched for the perfect rock, and, once we found it, took pride in examining each others rock. We were delighted to seek each others approval as to whether or not the rock would glide over the surface of the sea.

    Paulette always asked the same question jokingly, as if I were an expert in selecting flathead rocks, "Mr. Lewis, sir! Is this rock flat enough to float?" I remembered easily. The surface of the lake was calm, pleasant and so lifeless. With watchful eyes, we focused all of our attention on one another as we took turns tossing each perfect flat rock, measuring with watchful eyes the distance that each rock traveled, both Paulette and I bragging about whose rocks sailed the farthest downstream. Just the three of us, there sitting on the rocky, pebbled seashore, lifting large boulders to see if we could catch a glimpse of the tiny dark red crabs that rested beneath the rocks undisturbed. Watching as the three of us awakened them as we counted out loud before turning over the massive black boulders, "One, two, and three!" We lifted the rock as fast as we could to find the startled crabs scurrying off in several different directions, just like tiny startled roaches during a feeding frenzy in the middle of the night.

    The thoughts were so vivid that as I sat there on the end of the not guilty bed, I visualized Paulette and me walking down the shore with our baby between the two of us. We played the lifting game, swinging baby Riri in the air: "On the count of three. Ready?

One-two-three-lift!" I remembered vividly the first time she told me we had to turn the rocks back over after we disturbed the crab family so that the nasty, dreaded seagulls didn't eat them. She hated the birds with a passion after witnessing a flock tormenting an injured one of their own, all along taking turns plucking and pulling at the feathers of the wounded bird to expose the flesh so that each member of the same flock could tear apart the exposed flesh while the injured bird fought for its life.

There, sitting in the county jail not knowing my faith, not knowing the whereabouts of my daughter, I felt like the injured seagull facing the judicial system, and my dreaded background tearing me apart piece by piece.

What am I to do without my best friend, my wife, my Boo? Where is Baby Riri and why did someone snatch her? What did I do before blacking out last night? These thoughts quickly turned into unlawful acts of violence in my head, appearing as a scene from a movie: a doorbell ringing, my Boo answering, and an unknown gunman with no visible facial features appearing, holding a chrome cannon 357 Magnum. Suddenly the shooter pulled out a bag full of crack and ordered Paulette to smoke all of it; when she refused, he stuffed the entire baggy down her throat. Next he pointed the cannon at my Boo and pulled the trigger. When the gunman pulled the trigger, both of our heads exploded, awakening me instantly. A dry sweat surfaced beneath my skin, producing invisible icicles in the form of sleeping volcanoes all over my body. *Say it isn't so, dear lord! Say it isn't so!* I cried.

ALTHOUGH I FINALLY HAD GOTTEN SOME SHUT-EYE, my body felt like I had drank a pint of Ever Clear (99% pure alcohol) and had smoked three dippers (three cigarettes dipped in PCP). I awoke out of a deep sleep because of the horrific stench that filtered through the top bunk mattress. The smell was that of fermenting cabbage mixed with stale old socks and Bruit Aftershave Cologne. A smelly old homeless bum slept in the top bunk. The person with the horrific smell was known around The Town as Professor X. I knew it was he on account of the gibberish he disgorged as he lay in the bunk talking to himself and answering his own questions. The word around town was the Professor had many degrees, one being a PhD but from what college, no one knew. Those who spoke to him and saw him daily disrespected and mistreated him as if he was placed on earth only to amuse people. He was a heroin head and a late-stage alcoholic who would rather piss and shit on himself than miss out on the opportunity to shoot black tar heroin into his veins or satisfy his taste buds with vodka or Milwaukee's Best.

    It was evident from the aroma that drifted out of the Professor's personal space that he had gone several months without showering. His nickname was derived from his claim to fame as a great debater. Professor X earned money for his beer and heroin by debating anyone on his favorite topic, "Who was a better leader in the black community — Malcolm X or Dr. Martin Luther King, Jr.?" The people with whom he debated consisted of the slickest pimps, the most profitable drug dealers, and the highest paid prostitutes who shared the same street corners as he.

    The professor debated against anyone who passed by 27th and D street that would lend him their ear, "Who was a greater leader for the black community, Malcolm X or Dr. Martin Luther King, Jr.?" asked the Professor. At the end of each debate, the Professor let you know who he believed won the debate by simply reciting either Dr. King's famous "free-at-last speech" or by acting out Denzel Washington's effective and convincing portrayal of Malcolm X's famous speech in Spike Lee's movie *Malcolm X*, "You've been bamboozled, led astray." I couldn't recall the Professor smelling as bad as he did this day. I had to turn towards the wall on my right side to position my body closer to the partition, in hopes of using the wall and my forearm as a shield to keep the smell from entering my nose.

I tried to focus my mind on something else, whereas my mind was running amok on account of the disgusting odor that was invading my private space. As I lay there quietly not speaking, not thinking, and trying not to breathe, I couldn't help but notice some chicken-scratch words all over the wall, regardless of the direction I fixed my eyes. I moved my eyes down the wall and noticed whole entire sentences start to unravel. This wasn't jailhouse jargon from jailhouse lawyers that presumed they knew everything. The sentences actually made sense. As I started to read what seemed to be poetic, some influential words with true meanings popped out at me. I started to see what Smooth Blood meant when he told me I was getting the not guilty bed.

The words: *"Now that you think jail is not so bad, partaking in illegal activity to make ends meet sounds like the right thing to do. Fast money equals long-term jail sentences, which leaves fatherless children. Living the Thug Life requires you to be stripped of all your dignity. Replacing love, honor, and admiration with greed, dysfunction, and self-pity causing a ripple affect of dysfunction within the family structure. Without parental advisories in your life, many are misguided into believing smoking weed, doing jail time, or playing video games all day instead of working or going to school is exactly how black boys are supposed to live. This metaphoric do-as-others-do kind of stinking thinking is what black boys have accepted as the true way they are supposed to transition from boys to men: Thug Life mentality has become a part of black culture, which has kept black men subdued into believing all black men are bred to hustle, become good thieves, pimp, and sell dope. For every minute you have spent getting high or rolling a blunt or chasing pussy or plotting to break into a sporting goods store, the time lost should have been spent teaching every young black child how to become a proud black father of many young black children who are living lives free of illegal drug and criminal activity. Black men were once considered leaders to young men in their community, showing children how to open doors for strangers and say hello to people that pass by. Proud powerful Men of God, teaching those in need of extra support how to grow closer and closer in their faith and how to trust God and believe in his promises. Black men, be down for yours; don't be embarrassed to show the world how much you care about your future. Express the love you have for your family and be a witness unconditionally for the supernatural blessings that God has given you. You were given this bunk for one purpose, to spread the word when you are set free. You are not guilty. You are not guilty. You are set free."*

I felt as if I had been stuck between a hard rock and a turtle shell — my spirit being the metaphor for the turtle shell, hard as a rock, yet easily broken. The rock represented the four corner walls of the cell that I sat in as they slowly closed in around me. Being stuck between a rock and a turtle shell meant my spirit is vulnerable.

The only thing I could do now was dumb down by acting as if I didn't know anything about the waiting game that the police played. This could be a long game because, technically, I hadn't been arrested yet. The only thing I could do was wait it out, here on the edge of my bed.

The pay phone was kitty-corner from where I was sitting. I pondered calling someone but I had no one to call. The only people who came to my rescue when I needed to be bailed out were my mother and Paulette. Now that the two of them were gone, I felt like I didn't have anyone to cry out to.

The phone sat next to one of three very skinny windows only large enough to see out of with one eye. The gap was roughly a foot long and four inches wide. It was made out of some sort of thick Plexiglas to ensure no convicts attempted a Houdini-escape through the thin portal.

As I sat staring out of the window for hours on end, I played the guessing game of who was going to pick me up. Would it be my

Paulette or would it be my mother? This time it would be neither. I was stuck there, watching convicts exiting the jail who were supposed to go straight to their probation officer, but who would end up going to buy drugs.

Mr. Fresh-out (a person just released) held a large yellow envelope given by Smooth Blood after collecting his valuables and being released from jail. In his pocket is a check for $1.75 for him to use to catch the bus home or to make a phone call for a ride. Other contents in the envelope were his belongings, a prepaid cell phone, gold plated ring, a lighter, and a pack of cigarettes.

Those who had just got out of jail and were determined to stay out walked with conviction, heading towards the six-point star corner. The first point within the two-block radius of the jail is where the probation offices sit. Many are ordered to show up there immediately after being released from jail. Some are required to obtain an ankle bracelet to monitor their every move, while others are simply supposed to check in, provide a urinalysis or set a schedule for when they are required to return.

The second point is the public defenders office, where many are recommended to set the earliest appointment available to speak with a court appointed lawyer to discuss their case. If you slipped up and procrastinated going to the public defender's office until a few days before your court appearance, you would inevitably be assed-the-fuck out. In other words even though the odds were already against you, you allowed the system to fail you even more after having an opportunity to have a lawyer represent you for free. I always learned that the earlier I showed up, the better chance I had to actually meet with a lawyer, rather than meeting to discuss my case three minutes before trial. But in the past, when I was fresh out of the county, the only thing on my mind was to get smoked out immediately, instead of taking an hour out of my busy day to speak to a lawyer regarding my case.

The third point is located in the same building just three doors down from the public defenders office — the Victims Adversary Commission. This is the place to go to set up either a schedule to pay your victims for a crime you were found guilty of, or where you find out how much money you are able to obtain for being shot or harmed in any way during a crime that was committed against you.

The fourth point is the bail bond office. For many, this stop was just as obligatory as checking in with the probation officer. The bail bond agent either acted like a runaway slave driver or more like your sponsor, checking in on you periodically to make sure you were on the right track. My bail bondsmen, Walter Mason, came to court with me on several occasions to inform the judge that I was taking care of my business. Mr. Mason even came to the hospital the day after Riesha was born.

After the cons spent about an hour at the bail bond office, they would head to cash their check at Orlando's Pizzeria, located on the same side of the street as the jail. They call this block the fifth point because you could almost make out a five-point star as your watching the cons travel point to point. In the back of the store, Mr. Orlando has a check cashing business, which caters to those just released from jail. You didn't need any identification to cash a check there if the check had Pierce County Jail stamped on the front.

As I looked out the window, I could tell who was on a mission to take care of business. They wouldn't acknowledge the bum's begging, "Mister, you got some spare change?" as they so patiently waited for the cons to exit the pizza joint. It was only obvious which ones were heading home or heading to the sixth and final point.

Most convicts went straight to Mickey D's (McDonald's) after the fifth point. Subsequently, this is when it gets tricky. I watched many relapse as soon as they exited McDonalds and headed towards the sixth and final point located in the alley right across from Mickey D's. The final point is where many from jail got high before going home to deal with the same bullshit that they got locked up for. Once they crossed the street from McDonalds they wouldn't be seen again.

Those who took their addictions for granted exposed symptoms of crack use way before buying any drugs. Money and freedom triggered receptors in the brain, which left behind a desire to reach the euphoric sensation that was permanently planted in their memory bank just after the very first experience when they tried crack. When the con sensed he would soon be free, the brain honed in on both the experience and the chemical, which induced the sensation that he obtained the very last time he got high. Emotions that produced a smile or happiness in the past were high- jacked by the crack demon.

The addict believes that happiness can only be conquered during the process of seeking, buying, and finally getting high. Getting high is the only way the con can feel good about anything. The very thought of obtaining crack sends bursts of electrolytes down the spinal cord, forcing an addict to walk faster and faster. His strut is called the crack-head shuffle. The crack takes over the addict's nervous system as he loses control of his body. His body gyrates uncontrollably from side to side; as the arms are swung so low his knuckles scrape the ground. If you stood in front of a person high on crack and accidentally dropped a quarter, dime or nickel, it would be picked up by the addict faster than you could say son-of-a-bitch, or kibbles and bits.

Normally when I got to *general pop* (the area in the county jail where most of the jail inmates come together to socialize when opportunity is granted) my first instinct is to call my momma in hopes she would pick up the phone before my father. No matter what the charge, my father would let me marinate in jail until he felt it was time for me to come out. To offset the shame and embarrassment associated with me being arrested, my mother and I had a secret code; I would let the phone ring two times then hang up, and then wait for thirty seconds and call back. My mother kept five hundred bucks in a separate bank account just for my bail money. Once Paulette took over as the hierarchy member in my circular family, my mother made sure that Paulette knew all about the bank account.

The last time I was in jail, my father picked up the phone before Momma did, and it wasn't pretty. I couldn't get a word in to explain the circumstances to my arrest. The only thing he heard was, "This is a collect call from the Pierce County Jail. Inmate Brandon Lewis is calling collect. Will you accept the charges?" He always said yes to let me know that he was acknowledging me. Then he hit me with the "you sorry son-of-a-bitch" line followed by a rhetorical question, "What you done did now boy?" Before I could answer he always said the same thing, "Excuses are like assholes; everybody has one!" Then he would hang up on me and I wouldn't know whether or not he was coming to get me out until I was either summoned or released on bail after being seen by the magistrate.

Sometimes he came the next morning; other times he didn't come at all. At times when I was brought up from the jail for court, I was reluctant to look who was in the courtroom. I never could forget how disappointed both my parents looked while sitting in the courtroom waiting for the judge to throw the book at me. My mother could never carry stress well; her face aged ten-plus years overnight after receiving the first collect call. My father had asthma, and when the stress of my fate wearied my mother, his asthma worsened. I could hear him gasping for air and breathing heavily from the first step I took into the courtroom. The embarrassment of being shackled at the ankles and handcuffed around the wrist with eight other cons in the presence of my parents made me feel like a complete letdown and a royal piece of shit.

Throughout the night, the Professor jerked his chicken in search of a chance to feel good again. He was convinced that a climax would make the heroin spew out of his body. In search of some form of pleasure to replace the gratification of injecting himself with the black tar substance known as Black Smack, the heroin destroyed the area in his brain where the sentiment of pleasure was stored. Without more of the devil delicacy, absolutely nothing could make his body settle down. The Heroin Devil received its pleasure from the agony of pain, which defeated the Professor. The Professor hummed like he was having convulsions while trying to have sex at the same time. The grunts and moans were in synch with the squeaking of the bed as he continued masturbating, disturbing everyone's sleep. He caused himself excruciating pain after hours of squeezing his urethra as hard as he could. The Professor tried endlessly to reach that plateau, which seemed unattainable. He already smelled like a peppermill; after hours of attempting to ejaculate, he perspired heavily, stinking up our area even more. When was he going to give it up? I heard someone yell from across the ward, "Hurry up and get a nut Blood! Fuck!" It had to have been swollen up to the size of a large bumpy yellow squash by the way he was going at it for hours. He never stopped jacking off until the guard yelled, "Breakfast!" and then only long enough for onlookers to pass by without disturbing his concentration. The grumble quickly returned, only this time sounding similar to a litter of meowing alley kittens crying out for their mother. I couldn't sit in my bed much longer not knowing what he was going to do with his spew once he finally reached his climax.

I wasn't hungry; instead, I took refuge across from the eating area in a chair next to the phone. A *Seattle Times* newspaper lay crumbled up under the chair. The headlines read, "Boyfriend Arrested on Suspicion of Murder! Whereabouts of daughter unknown!" *Ain't-this-a-bitch! What am I going to do now? Will I ever get to see my little girl again? Is my daughter dead or alive?* Damn, I felt helpless as though the world was against me.

"My nigga! What up wit you, Dog?"

"I'm not in the mood for small talk, Cuzz! I just want to do my time in peace, you feel me? Dog!" Back in the day while under the influence of whatever substance came to pass, I would have socked him in his jaw for referring to me as a blood, but that was then and this is now and I don't have time for that bullshit anymore. I referred to him as "dog", which suggested that I knew he was a blood. Just to keep the peace, I said to the familiar face, "I'll get at you later, my nig." I couldn't recall where I knew him from or what his name was. Nor did I care if he was offended by my reaction to his hood greeting. I took what Smooth Blood said to me very seriously. I was determined to keep my ear close to the ground (listen out for important information to help me stay safe and focused) to see if I could overhear someone talking about the murder and kidnapping, and keep my mouth shut while I was in jail. I wasn't there to reunite with friends or to reminisce about old times. I was in mourning and wanted to mourn all to myself without some crack-heads trying to befriend me.

Breakfast was scrambled eggs, one Texas-style toast still half frozen, a fat sausage link, one generic brand package of ketchup, and a miniature tobacco package. I had a choice of instant powdered apple juice or instant powdered orange drink. I always chose the orange because it tasted more like orange Kool-Aid, but without sugar.

There is a jailhouse code of ethics that people stuck to regarding who I was and why I was there. In most scenarios, there is an unspoken jailhouse rule: *when you're in the county and someone is brought in for murder, people usually stayed away.* They are the ones wearing the pink suits as opposed to the normal gray jumpsuits. To deal with the reality of going to prison for the rest of their lives, having that final peace of mind is extremely important.

During breakfast, not one person spoke to me, and I was cool with that. I also could tell that most figured out I didn't want to converse or shoot the shit with them. I was left alone to mourn all by myself as I wished.

The aroma of pork sausage, eggs, and toast reminded me that my mother's cousin, Fredrick Tucker, was the head chef here at the Pierce County jail. I worked for him in the past as a caterer, so I knew how important hygiene was to him. Although he couldn't prevent everyone in his kitchen from spreading germs, I knew that the food would at least be edible.

I was so hungry that my stomach felt like it was going to punch its way out of my back. I was beyond hungry, misguided by a broken spirit that prevented me from picking up a fork to feed my face. My mind was playing tricks on me, trying to convince me that I wasn't worthy enough to eat anything. I sat staring at the food on my plate. My eyes, steadfast in a trance, gazed deep into the eggs and sausage. The sausage transcended visuals of Baby Riri happily playing in the living room banging on pots and pans with a wooden spoon. The happy thoughts were quickly bombarded by thoughts of Riesha yanked and swiftly torn away from her mother's arms by a woman wearing a gray three-piece suit. I couldn't understand why someone would want to snatch my daughter. Thoughts about my little girl growing up without a mother plagued me, forcing acidic fluids to clog my throat. I felt as if I couldn't breathe. I became faint, yet my chest kept expanding. I began to panic as I realized my daughter needed me now more than ever before. I felt trapped inside of a body that was without spirit or blood.

If I had the chance to smoke some goop, I would surely have taken the offer. The high from smoking PCP left my body feeling as if the entire jail was resting on my forehead, disabling me from moving or seeing anything three feet in front of me. I was left to fend for myself, solely dependent on the hallucinations going on in my mind. I wouldn't have to think about, or make any attempt to keep my mind from running amok concerning the whereabouts of my daughter or who killed my baby's momma. I would simply be stuck on stupid, which inevitably I would have rather been during this juncture in my life, so I didn't have to deal with the realism of my family being destroyed.

"It's time to man up, Nigga!" I said out loud, not caring who could hear me. Now I was able to see hope in glory as I began to shake my head from side to side, thinking about how much I didn't truly want to be high anymore. I must have looked like some crazed man, smiling and clapping my hands while sitting in front of the payphone. Thoughts of handling my parental duties produced solitude in the form of hope. This allowed me to envision glorious pictorial moments of me holding Riri's hand as she grew into a beautiful and proactive woman.

Paulette was always the one to bear witness to any painful acts administered on our daughter. It wasn't because I had more important things to do; it was because I had a hard time watching someone inflict pain on my little baby-Booboo. When it was time to administer her shots, I was good for slipping out to hit a blunt to keep my mind off the pain that Daddy's Little Girl was about to endure. Now that Paulette was gone, no longer could I excuse myself from Riri's doctor's visits or dentist appointments. This is a task that I was not looking forward to and dreaded.

I remember when Paulette was having our baby and the doctor had to put his hands up my woman's v-jay, I was ready to knock his lips off. I was there to witness the pain she was going through as the doctor shoved most of his arm into her to feel our baby's head. Again, I removed myself from the ceremonious scene to administer my own version of self-medication. I used a fat white girl (twenty grams of marijuana rolled up in white tobacco paper. Other street names; fat-ass baseball bat, Mary Jane, or joint) to set my nerves straight, although the injurious affect of smoking weed caused me to become even more intolerable at the same time I had calmed the fuck down.

I will be the one to attend all of her school functions, teacher conferences, and orchestra concerts in hopes that she plays the cello just like her father did. I have to become her personal trainer looking out for her health. How am I going tell her how to use a tampon? How am I going to explain to her why she was bleeding down there for the first time? I thought that would be her mother's responsibility. I thought I could just agree with what Paulette was doing and that would be it. I am supposed to ward off the bad guys and show her how to defend herself, how to dribble a ball, and how to hold a bat. I always thought that her mother's job was to teach her how to carry herself like a lady. Paulette was supposed to teach her how to spit without being seen, and how to fart without being heard. I had to prepare myself for the task; I couldn't do it in jail. I needed to get out of here so I could find her.

I was caught up in my own sorrows and I was trying hard not to get sucked into my own fears, the fear of going to prison for the rest of my life. While thinking it was all about me, I had forgotten about Paulette's family and their feelings. Just the thought of the Jenkins family believing the propaganda that I killed their daughter and kidnapped my own daughter made me contemplate suicide. If I did that, many would assume I could do such heinous crimes, and I would be remembered as a thug, and that was not happening. Before the murder, Paulette's family was beginning to trust me. I had progressed from being thought of as *the foul thug who stole their precious daughter*, to being invited over for dinner several times a month as a future son-in-law type of guy. Mr. and Mrs. Jenkins trusted me. I was the go-to guy who used to drop them off at the airport as they traveled to and from their hometown in rural Virginia.

Paulette's parents grew up as true black hillbillies from the Blue Ridge Mountains, eating and growing everything on the land. I was called upon so often that I had my own opener to their garage door. They knew of my ambition to become their son-in-law. Her parents had waited until they were both in their early forties and set in their careers before having Paulette. Her father was a retired Boeings machinist, a reserved type of guy who only spoke when spoken to. Not because he was rude, or felt oppressed, he just didn't speak much unless he felt the need to do so. He enjoyed a good German beer twice a week, a habit he picked up when he was stationed in Germany. On Tuesdays and Thursdays after his dinner he sat down on his front porch, rain or snow, to drink one bottle and smoke one cowboy, a Marlboro Red cigarette.

Mrs. Jenkins' only vice was working late hours towards improving her business, a workforce agency where ex-felons could receive much needed support obtaining a job and housing once they were off paper (not required to check in with the department of corrections). Mrs. Jenkins insured that her under represented clients had the opportunity to become productive citizens and rebuild their careers after paying their debt to society. Paulette was their golden child and spoiled rotten. She and little Riri had everything they ever needed and more.

With no one to call, I decided to take a leap of faith and call the Jenkinses after breakfast. I had convinced myself I would call them to clear my name and to set the record straight — that I did not kill their precious daughter, the mother of my child, my soul mate, my mentor, my Boo. Nor did I have anything to do with the abduction of my sweet innocent child.

The decision to call someone to speak my piece helped me gain some type of empathy for my situation that I so desperately needed. I was okay acknowledging the need for someone to be sympathetic towards me. *It's going to be okay, Ceeze. It's gonna be okay once the Jenkinses find out that I didn't murder their daughter or snatch baby Riesha. I will finally be able to mourn the lost of my woman, my baby's momma, my Boo and their God-sent daughter Paulette.*

I began to eat as though there was no tomorrow, feeding my face as if I hadn't eaten for days if not weeks. After eating it all, I convinced the inmate sitting across from me that I was a member of the notorious Ridgetop Crips. Once I was finished showing off some of my exposed tattoos, he flaunted his own tats, which signified that he too was a Crip from the town. Once he figured out that I was triple OG from the hood, he gave me his entire breakfast. With my belly knotted, upset from the dairy products my uncle used to stretch the powered eggs in order to feed the masses, I was able to organize my thoughts and words that would best represent my feelings.

Immediately following my pig-out session, the after effects made my stomach tremble uncontrollably, due to the whole milk used to stretch the eggs. The food tasted good going down, but was something afoul coming out. The government sharp cheese made my gastrointestinal track weak, causing arsenic gas bubbles to form in my stomach. Unwillingly, I squeezed out my ass colossal sweltering fumes of burning sagebrush mixed with a fresh batch of pickled pigs feet. My intestines weren't able to break down the sugar in cow milk. I wasn't alone; jailhouse food usually made most of the black inmates spew out chemicals in the form of invisible poisonous gas bubbles. After dinner the entire blue unit smelt like burnt boiled eggs.

I returned to my bed, bent over holding my belly. I was hopeful that the Professor was finished taking care of his personal business. As I approached, I didn't hear sounds of kittens crying; The Professor must have got his nut. He was knocked out and snoring abruptly to match his comatose state. He sounded like his tongue was stuck in his throat causing his breathing to lapse, which made me uncomfortable; I actually hoped he was choking. The noise persisted, making sounds similar to the gobbles made from a male turkey trying to attract a hen. I wouldn't be able to sleep now anyway, knowing that his spew (semen) could be resting around where I laid my head.

The acid in my stomach arose to the middle of my chest, creating brutal heartburn. Piercing pains filled the center of my breastplate. The cover to my heart was withering away. My heart, already heavy from the pain of losing my Boo and not knowing where my daughter was, felt like an 80-pound weight. Agonizing acid flowed like a river of fire swiftly through my throat where it materialized into rocks of vomit, forcing me to choke while spewing up Ink's powdered eggs.

I found myself in bad shape and I missed my Boo. She knew what to do when my stomach filled up with exploding gas bubbles and backward farts. Along with the acidic stomach pains came migraines the size of a .45 bullet traveling straight, then side-to-side, zigzagging as if it were a .22 bullet. With the pain I became vulnerable. I headed straight to the bathroom to regain some solitude to wash away the vomit that rested beneath my bottom lip. The guards made you mop the entire wing if they found out who was responsible for spreading infectious bodily fluids throughout the area. Before I could reach the bathroom, diarrhea slowly crept through my engrossed butt cheeks to rest within my drawers.

Three oval steel pots cemented and screwed to the wall, the centers removed, were meant to simulate toilets. In actuality they were the same buckets for the inmates to either piss or shit in. The way they sat lonely in the middle of the floor reminded me of the first time I went down south to Stratton, Virginia to my uncle's house; he didn't have indoor plumbing. The very first time I entered their house, Aunt Wanda handed me a large bowl of steaming hot water and a bar of soap, along with a hand towel, saying, "Now I know you had a long bus ride from DC, so go on upstairs and get right for dinner." After washing up, my Auntie checked behind my ears and said, "Next time wash behind your ears; you don't wanna leave soap behind there because you'll wake up with half your ear hanging off!"

That was when she took me straight to the girls' washroom. There were four white buckets aligned in the middle of the floor with names on them — Stephanie, Ruth, Jade, and Naomi. She informed me that the buckets are for the women of the house. If I had to use the bathroom in the middle of the night for emergency purpose only, I could use that one over there, she pointed, saying, "your uncle's bucket, but don't go number two in there; your uncle don't like smelling someone else's *stank* in his bucket." There was a lonely bucket way over in the far corner of the room with no name on it. Auntie pointed at it and said, "Now that one is mine, you can go number two in mine, only if it's an emergency; you just make sure you take it out in the morning before I wake up, you hear me boy?"

If I needed to use the bathroom during the day, I was supposed to use the outhouse. Most outhouses were located in a small shed out back, just big enough to hold one person. It had a door that opened with a string, no light, just a wooden box with the center opened in the floor for all of your business to flow through. Once a month my Uncle and I pulled the porcelain four-claw bathtub out from under the outhouse that was used to catch the entire mess. We carried the tub three feet behind the shed and dumped it in a huge whole. The bathtub was heavy and full of shit and piss. As we carried it, the contents spilled all over my hands, arms and feet. My shoes were soaked with human dung and urine; I could feel it squishing between my toes. Unc acted like the fluids didn't bother him as it spilt on him too. Once all of the contents were in the hole, Unc poured kerosene over it and set it ablaze.

The jailhouse toilets were these provisional urinals with barely enough water to flush away your business. I could hardly hold back anymore, so I quickly glanced over the entire restroom trying to find some toilet paper or paper towels to place over the seat before sitting down on the icy cold metal. The overseers insured that a full bottle of green disinfectant spray sat next to every toilet for you to spray on or around the bucket. What was I supposed to wipe the seats with? I looked around the bathroom for something to wipe my ass with, but there wasn't anything. So I looked around some more and found an old wrinkled up newspaper and picked it up. I walked swiftly to the nearest toilet before I had an accident in my pants. Squeezing my butt cheeks tightly so nothing could leak out, I grabbed one of the spray bottles and sprayed the green stuff down and around the toilet. I swiftly tore off a bit of newspaper and wiped off the seat and immediately plopped down on the icy cold mischief toilet. Because I am lactic, I easily relieved myself in no more then a minute and half. I took the newspaper and began to look over it making sure there weren't any infectious particles lying about. Next I rubbed the newspaper together, thanking Auntie Wanda at the same time for sharing the old school secret: how to wipe your ass when you don't have any toilet paper. The trick was to rub the paper together until it eventually became soft enough to use to wipe. Though it wasn't sanitary the newspaper trick worked.

As I washed my hands, I glanced at the image looking back at me. I was not aware of how much stress had aged me overnight. I looked horrible; my face was showing how much the death of Miss Paulette affected me. Steadfastly, I took the attention off myself as I pondered who was watching our baby Riri. I was hoping that she wasn't with Paulette's homegirl. I prayed that she had enough sense to call Paulette's parents for them to come and pick her up.

I kept repeating to myself while staring in the makeshift mirror, "Damn, I look old!" My face appeared ghostly, dry like I couldn't afford lotion for years. Stress formed in dime-size dry white blotches and hives all over my face. Along with the stress came rows of pimples all throughout my forehead, which lowered my self-esteem even more.

Once Paulette and I moved in together, she made me drink a cup of green tea every evening after dinner. Her dad had taught her that the tea helped extract toxins from our bodies. Before bed, she cut up a grapefruit and sprinkled a little sugar on top, saying that the grapefruit would help me with my occasional constipation and would break down the fatty acids found in the foods we just ate for dinner. Her parents taught her well. After rehab, Paulette went back to her home training and was very conscious of what foods we were consuming in our bodies. She made it clear that her responsibility was to keep our fridge fully stocked with fresh oranges, grapes, lettuce, and carrots to snack on. She yelled at me when she caught me eating chips instead of fresh fruit and vegetables. She did this because she watched both of her grandfathers die painful deaths from colon cancer. She educated me on how hazardous all of the chemicals I consumed daily from nicotine, weed, and liquor, caused me to look old and worn out. The worsening affect, Paulette explained, was how the harsh chemicals destroyed my physical and mental state. She had a bird's eye view of the harmful items that inflicted severe emotional yet invisible pain on me. The cleansing had my skin looking and feeling vibrant, silky ebony, reddish like, emphasizing my Ethiopian heritage.

    I missed my Baby Riri, who use to rub the back of her hand over my forearm as she laid in her favorite position, her back on my chest while she sucked on a warm fresh bottle of Rice milk mixed with just a little rice cereal.

    I looked at myself in the busted, scratched-up mirror riddled with gang graffiti, and saw a face plastered with ridicule, pain, and frustration. The man in the mirror resembled a scrawny old man with a five o'clock shadow, bearing wrinkly old elastic skin destroying the mythical belief that black doesn't crack. It appeared as if I had been drinking dandelion moonshine for breakfast, lunch, and dinner since I was eight years old. Damn, I looked old! For a year prior to my arrest, I had rubbed coca butter around my eyes every night trying to rid my eyes of dark circles. Paulette read somewhere that coca butter erased the dark circles. The article didn't specify that you were also suppose to stop abusing drugs and alcohol, in addition to getting at least seven hours of sleep each night. My addiction was a direct result of not getting adequate sleep. Once I stopped parading the streets and cut back on the weed and alcohol consumption, the dark circles diminished. Yet overnight the black circles resurfaced, only this time they filled up the entire eyeball area. My eyes looked lost, sickened, as if I was forced to work like a slave on a tobacco field from sun up to sun down on a plantation in Maryland. Damn, I looked old!

After staring in the mirror at that unfamiliar being, I decided it was time to face the music. I headed straight to the phone to call the Jenkinses. I owed it to Paulette's family to speak the truth because I knew by then that rumors were floating around about me killing their daughter and kidnapping their grandchild.

I opted to use 1-800-collect, a service that used a polite recorded voice with a southern swirl that said, "Hello" before asking you to accept a collect call, tricking the most impolite individuals into replying, "Hello to you too" even though they already knew they are talking to a machine — clever choice of words mixed with a seductive voice that inflicts connotations and pronunciations to convince you to say yes. This way whoever you're calling wouldn't know you're locked up unless you tell them. The service offered by Pierce County Jail is that of a rude, uncomforting, robotic recording that has given some mothers mild to severe heart attacks after hearing the recorded voice of the phone operator say, "Will you accept a collect call from an inmate of the Pierce County Jail?"

Paulette's grandmother, acting as their housekeeper during the day, answered the phone and accepted my call. This comforted me for a spell, which lasted all of thirty seconds. She occupied the mother-in-law apartment at the back of the house above the pool. Below her home, she kept a garden full of fresh herbs and native vegetables, claiming they had kept her free of sickness and pain while growing up in the deep woods of North Carolina. Granny was raised on the Black Foot Cherokee Indian reservation; her mother was Native American and her father was a descendant of freed slaves. She's a sweet, round lady who forced her employers to eat her homeland food for dinner three times a week, claiming that the herbs and traditional food she prepared kept Mr. Jenkins' diabetes in check.

Ms. Connie, short for Consuelo, claimed to be pushing ninety years of age. She informed us that ninety was the new sixty. She carried herself sophisticatedly to back her claim to fame as the sexiest looking grandmother over seventy years old.

To my disappointment, the family wasn't home. My head again hit my chin. To my surprise, Ms. Connie informed me to be patient because the Jenkinses were on their way to break me out of jail. She added, "We know you wouldn't hurt my sweet Paulette. We know you wouldn't kidnap your own daughter. Be patient and don't say a word to anybody in there, you hear me?"

"Yes Granny!" I replied.

"YOU'RE FREE TO GO, CEEZE," said Smooth Blood who greeted me once I reached my bunk. I gave him a head nod and that was it. I had so much on my mind I didn't have time to get friendly with anybody. I was ready to deal with whatever was coming my way because Paulette and my parents taught me how to trust God. I knew that God wouldn't place me in any position I couldn't handle.

"Just show me the door, playa, I'm ready to get the fuck out of here."

"I feel that, Buzz. Sign for your shit and you free to go." Youngblood pointed over to where Bullet-head was posted. He was dangling over the counter holding the yellow envelope, which contained all of my personal items I came in with. "I got to deal with this motha-fucka again Cuzz?

"You know what? Hold on!" Smooth Blood walked over to Bullet-head and signed something on a clipboard. He then grabbed my shit and brought it back to me. "Here you go, Ceeze." He placed the envelope underneath my armpit and said, "I got to cuff you, Cousin."

After entering the elevator, Smooth Blood un-cuffed me, saying, "The camera's stopped working in here a long time ago." He added, "I read your record, and you don't have any crimes that would convince me that you would do what you're being accused of."

"What you going to school to be a lawyer?" I said to the intuitive man-child.

"As a matter of fact I am," he chuckled. "I'm going to Seattle U. at night."

"No doubt, are you gonna be the first Blood lawyer?"

"Naw, I got a Blood homey from Pasadena and he's the DA there; cool ass cat, cooler than the other side of the pillow!"

As the elevator doors began to open, I turned to Smooth Blood and informed him to get at me if he ever sees me in traffic. Smiling, he extended his hand while placing the other on my shoulder, and said, "You are a cool cat to be an E-ricket and all." We both laughed.

"Oh now you wanna hood-bang now that I'm leaving. I see how you slob ass niggaz are." We laughed again.

"Naw, I'm just trying to shed some light on your situation, that's all," said my brotha in faith.

Before exiting the elevator, we shook hands and I said, "Peace-out. Get at me, Young Bleezy!"

His response was, "No doubt, Cuzz, I'll see you in traffic."

The elevator doors opened up and the Jenkinses were standing there with my cousin Titi. Everyone wore blank expressions on their faces. I didn't know how to react or how to greet any of them. My cousin had her back against the wall. She wore a red Seattle Mariners hat and shorts that looked more like over-sized jeans; she never wore jeans and or skirts; she always wore long shorts that hung to her ankles. The Mariners hat she wore was tilted to the right side, which, tilted to the right side represented Blood gang affiliation. Tilted to the left represented Crip gang affiliation. She was puffing on a Black and Mild cigar, with one leg bent at the knee, her black and red Jordan shoes resting against the brick wall. Mr. Jenkins looked lonely, scared, and disconnected.

Still poised, though you could see stress in her eyes, Mrs. Jenkins stood tall, looking eloquent in a solid gray business suit. Her hair was pulled back in a bun, uncommon for her; her hair was usually straightened, flowing down past her shoulders with a slight bump on the ends. The jewels she wore gleamed off her gray suit as she held her hands across her chest. Her white silk shirt slightly exposed her breast. I don't think she knew her shirt was unbuttoned as far as it was, exposing her white bra — very unlike her. Though she stood strong, her face appeared weathered. With nobody approaching me, I headed in the direction of Titi, who held her hand out for a handshake, pulling me in close to her chest. Her muscular arms were decorated with neighborhood tattoos: faces of clowns and skulls smoking on what presumably were blunts, surrounded by dark shades of smoke protruding from the end of the blunt.

She placed an arm around me and whispered in my ear, "You all right, Cuzzo?" Bloods and Crips with kinfolk from the opposite side of the fence intermixed each others gang related slang to justify favor.

"Not really. I can't really describe what I am feeling." As I caught eye contact with the Jenkinses, I sensed a stammer about to rise off my lips as I beckoned for the word *hello* to come out. Out of respect for Mr. Jenkins, I acknowledged him first by thanking him for breaking me out of jail. No words came from his mouth, nor a handshake, or a smile. He began to come towards me, and I was thinking he was going to throw a punch to the middle of my face. I tightened up to take one, hoping I would have the opportunity to explain to him later that I didn't kill "daddy's little girl". Instead he embraced me and, at the same time, he cried liberally, like a man who just found out his daughter had been killed. I embraced him. Mrs. Jenkins embraced the two of us, and she too began to cry abundantly.

Mrs. Jenkins uttered, "We know you wouldn't have killed our baby. We know how much she meant to you. They're gonna find the killer and we're gonna get through this together like a family." More cobwebs poured out of my eyes, rolling down my cheeks, creating white tracks from the salt infused minerals found in tears. Mrs. Jenkins wrapped her soft hands around my face and wiped away my tears with her thumbs.

As we continued to cry on each others shoulders, Mr. Jenkins said to Titi, "Come on over here, girl. You family too." He used his hands signaling for the masculine Titi to come over and join in on the group hug. I could tell she was hesitant. She never shed tears in front of people who weren't kin to her, nor did she give hugs during moments of sadness. I was waiting to see how she was going to handle Mr. Jenkins' request. Titi nonchalantly approached the circle of love and joined in. I continued shedding cobweb tears while trying to formulate some words over the continuous yelps and stammering cries that were long overdue.

I tried hard to explain to my family how much I loved my Boo, saying, "I don't know what I'm gonna do without her by my side. I had just asked her to marry me, just yesterday."

"She told me," said Mrs. Jenkins, and kept repeating, "We must stick together, we must stick together!" Mrs. Jenkins added that collective prayers would bring the assailant forward.

Once we were done embracing, I noticed Smooth Blood was still there watching us all. I felt a bit vulnerable, as if I just lost my hood stripes for crying like a poo-butt. He waited for us to release each other and then greeted Titi with a Piru handshake — a conjoining of two hands that formed the OK sign, which also represented Piru gang affiliation. The two of them unlocked the upside down letter 'P' in order to conjoin in the middle, solidifying unity as Piru Blood brothers.

"I should've known you knew my cousin," I said to young Blood.

"This your cousin? This is my big homey!" Youngun then turned to the Jenkinses and confessed his greatest sympathy stating, "My condolences go out to you and your family. I will keep my ear to the ground and let you all know if I hear anything about the killer and the whereabouts of your daughter."

In a soft but hood/street vernacular, Titi said, "What up Youngun?"

"I'm all right. I just wanted to tell all of you that I too would say a prayer."

"No doubt, get at me, Dog," said Titi.

I added, "Thanks bra; get at me, my nig!"

Ms. Jenkins then asked, "Please let Titi know if you hear anything."

11
Fresh Out

"Watch this, Buzz!" Tatiana pushed the red button on the remote control attached to her key chain. The initial start up roared like two lions fighting over the queen lioness and her entire pen. Veroom! barked the 1982 Buick Regal, Grand National. Again she pushed the red button and the car went veroom-veroom. She paid $10,000 cash the day I drove with her down south to Olympia where she purchased the classic car from a widow whose husband was killed serving in the Iraq Bush War.

Titi was willing to pay the original asking price of $30,000, although she brought forty-five stacks in case the lady wanted to up the price. Titi and I sensed that the widow wanted to get rid of the car when she informed us that it reminded her too much of her late husband. Price was not an issue after she stated, "The government is paying me ten thousand a month for the rest of my life," and added, "I really don't need the money. If you ask me, I think it's an eyesore."

"Feels good to be free!" I said to my cousin as we walked through the parking lot towards her Regal. Though I was free, I still felt enslaved in my shell of a body. I felt light on my feet, like I was floating through the parking lot on air pockets. My feet rested on the assumption that Paulette and Riesha were peering right around the next corner, anxiously waiting to jump out and yell, "Surprise!" with their faces full of great big smiles. My heart started pounding at just the thought of seeing the two of them.

However, my inside voice told me different. "*She's gone, Brandon; she's gone forever and Riesha is still missing!*"

"Where is my baby?" I asked the silent voice in me. To my dismay, the voice with all the answers never responded. Damn! I wish I could smoke a blunt right now. Just a couple of puffs are all I need to escape to a private place where my inner voice and me could kick back and relax. I would like to go somewhere secretive so that I could have some peace. My mind desperately needed a break from the torturous thoughts that were successfully obstructing any and all peek-a-boo thoughts of my family returning.

The weed sensors in my big nose honed in on the aroma of the top-grade weed that was increasingly getting stronger and stronger as we approached her car. She smoked only the best of the best of the best high-grade weed. My symptoms arose quickly, making way for my taste buds to react. I envisioned a nice white-girl joint stuck between my lips, resting there waiting to be sparked. I could smell the sulfur burning from the matches. As I lit the joint, a bit of the burning sulfur crept into my nose. I was a master at sucking in the weed smoke and exhaling through my nose, blowing out the matches. My mouth trembled and felt parched; I needed a Gatorade to quench my thirst.

As soon as I placed my hand on the door handle, I jokingly asked if she hit a skunk on the way to the jailhouse. The lingering smell signified that my assumption was right; she had copped some of that hydro-killa weed that got you so high it made you want to eat a whole smoked pig. The skunk fragrance drifted from inside the car. Any cop on a bike passing by would surely be waiting for the owner to return so that he could get high too.

"Can you smell the weed or am I tripping?" I asked. Instead of an answer, she gave me her signature grin, a smile pasted down by all of the women in our family. When Tatiana laughed or smiled, a little bit of the sweet innocent child that was left in her appeared. "You know when you smile, you look just like my momma!" I told her.

"I know. Your auntie tells me that every time I crack a grin. Your momma was so sweet and beautiful," said Titi.

"I think about her every day."

"I could feel her smiling and grinning down on us right now."

I didn't look forward to breaking the news to Titi that I had decided to stop smoking weed, because at this point I truly didn't know if I could turn some down. Even though we are cousins, I was more or less worried about how it would affect our kinship. Would it end now that I have given up smoking weed? We've smoked together almost every day for the past ten years. During which time the weed sessions allowed us to be serious and share intimate tear-jerking conversations with one another. While we were high, we talked about our past, our future, our mistakes, and our goals. When we shared intimate moments together getting high, the weed permitted us to divulge our innermost personal feelings. We gossiped just like our mothers did as they cooked dinner together after church on a rainy Sunday afternoon. Discussing family secrets and problems that we dared not discuss outside of our weed sessions became our form of intimacy. Things like, "Brandon, is Uncle Al your real dad?"

The two of us knew we had a problem with weed as early as the tenth grade, though we started smoking weed when we were fourteen. No matter the cost, no matter how many Saturday schools and in-house suspensions or phone calls home to our parents informing them that we were caught smoking weed in the bathroom, we remained focused and determined to get high. No matter how much our attention span was confiscated in class, we sacrificed grades and dignity to get high. We became a big disappointment to our teachers, to our family, and to ourselves when we traded in our honor roll status to become classroom idiots.

Because of Tatiana's power in the underground drug world, she had the freedom to hand pick specific weed that would provide the kind of pleasure desired. Weed grown specifically to make you wish, ponder, and dream was called Indian Dream Catcher. When we smoked it, we road our bikes around, looking at expensive houses in forbidden neighborhoods frequented only by those who lived there. We rode our bikes up to the most expensive car lots talking about what cars we're going to buy when we get out of college.

Marijuana grown specifically to make us sit still on the couch was called Man Down. When we smoked it, we usually stayed in the house, stuck chilling on the couch, staring at whatever channel we were watching before we got high. The weed she usually purchased was called Muscle Head, which made us feel strong and invincible when we smoked it. Muscle Head made me feel like I had special powers, giving me the confidence and security I needed to travel down the rough, tough, dangerous streets of The Town. When we first started smoking Muscle Head, Tatiana was able to act out and be as masculine as she wanted to be.

To belittle our addiction, we conversed about the downfalls of our peers who were also addicts but were strung out on much harder drugs like crack cocaine, dippers, and heroin. We felt the need to talk down to members of our subculture who wasted money on a new outfit every Friday night, but whose driver's license was suspended for not paying child support. We talked down to chicken heads in our community who were spending more time in the mirror primping and ironing their two-hundred-dollar weaves than they spent preparing their children's school clothes or making their kids' breakfast, lunch or dinner.

I sold weed periodically, just to support my habit, but even when I didn't have any weed, I never had to buy any because Titi always had it. Over the years when I tried to quit, she became my trigger. When Titi called me, I could smell the weed through the phone lines. Every time I looked at my family portraits that lined the wall to the front door in my apartment, I thought about calling her to get high. And now that I had decided to stop smoking weed, the devil was trying to convince me that I could smoke just one last blunt with my favorite cousin Titi, and then I would quit.

Like a good cup of Seattle's Best Coffee, in order to function normally, my body relied on weed to give me that extra jump kick-start to my day. The chemicals were just as important to my brain as the blood that flowed through my veins to keep my heart pumping. I knew this moment was coming, the moment when I had to acknowledge that the cause and effect induced by the *Mary Jane* (marijuana) had a hold on me like a true addict. I didn't smoke crack or shoot heroin; I smoked weed. But my body was trying to convince me, "Motha-fucka, you need some weed right now, shit!" And when I first saw my cousin as the elevator doors from the jail opened up, I became instantly overwhelmed by the symptoms relating to my biggest trigger, who was standing right in front of me. I coughed as if I just hit some weed, then my mouth dried up like a bag of rotten oranges, my head began to throb, and my stomach muscles impulsively tightened up.

There wasn't any way on God's planet that I could survive without weed. There was just no way; or at least I thought. Right then and there I had to confront my addiction. My taste buds started quivering. I could smell and taste the powerful unseen hallucinogen as vapors bounced off Titi's clothing. I envisioned a thick whitish-gray cloud of smoke penetrate all the way through my mouth, tasting like a fresh piece of apple sour Bubble Yum.

Before leaving the parking lot, T reached underneath her seat and pulled out a small cigar box filled with her own personal stash of the Washington grown skunk weed. She had the kind that was only available to drug dealers, like a gift, an incentive to keep Titi coming back for more. The main distributor threw in a little "Thank you for spending your money with me" gift bag full of the private stock weed, a couple hundred pills of the latest exotic ecstasy, and usually an 8-ball of methamphetamines or heroin, depending on the current trend. Titi reached into her glove compartment and pulled out a Grape Swisher Sweet and threw it on my lap. "Break that up for me, Blood." While T commenced to pull marijuana off the stems, I gracefully ran my thumbnail atop the cigar and carefully removed the tobacco so she could refill it with her weed.

"Damn! Damn! Damn!" I was saying to myself as she began to light the blunt with a torch that resembled a .22-caliber pistol. Face it, I didn't want to get high anymore, but the skunk aroma was enabling me to say yes instead of no. I felt like the Demon God masked himself as weed smoke and attempted to destroy me nonchalantly. My body craved the smooth tasting illicit drug so badly I just wanted to take a pinch of the weed and stick it underneath my tongue so the taste could stay there all day.

The usual routine following being sprung from jail was to fire up a fat blunt that was dipped in Hennessey and slowly baked in honey. Most, if not all, of my days began with a blunt. This was the custom within my subculture. I smoked at least five large blunts per day, so my body and mind were begging for a hit. How was I supposed to wake up in the morning without smoking some weed?

How was I supposed to take a dump in the morning without the weed smoke in my body to help relax me so I could take a dump smoothly? I couldn't recall a time since I was fourteen when I didn't have weed in my system. Weed gave me the munchies, which enhanced my appetite. My body had become used to smoking weed before a meal and after.

The conundrum that I faced was that I knew I needed to sober up from now on to deal with reality, but the reality of all of this was making me want to smoke weed. Either way I was screwed! The death of my Boo had manifested into a metaphoric tool that severely impacted my need to remain drug free. Her death and becoming a single parent overnight to a little girl that has gone missing, vehemently forced me to sober up. I had become involuntarily committed to sobriety, even though my brain struggled to send the memo to the rest of my body.

Representing thug life, all the way down to the M.O.B. (Money Over Bitches) tattooed on my stomach, best described who I was and what I didn't want to represent anymore. Paulette hated the tattoo and what it represented — fast money by way of hustling and the importance of building a bankroll of cash before tending to any woman. And after a long hard day, week, month, or year of running around in the streets making money, it was okay to return to the nest to buy your children a few things, or pay your baby's mother's rent for a couple of months.

Once I got to know my Boo, all of that thug life bullshit was not a part of me anymore. Taking care of my family was and still is the most important thing in my life.

I was ready to get married because I moved beyond the point of courting a different woman every day of the week. Once Paulette influenced me to live a purpose driven life, I no longer needed confirmation from low self-esteem, insecure women to make me feel masculine. I changed from living solely for myself to being accountable for my family's climb towards upward mobility.

When I entered the apartment, the sight of Paulette holding Riesha on the couch, both snoring thunderously, formed chemicals in my brain giving me that ultimate natural high. Once I got into the routine of going straight home after work, the sight of my family resting on the sofa as I entered replaced the oxytocin that I once obtained after making love to multiple women. The natural restoration of dopamine in my brain was begging to waiver; I didn't need to be high all the time any more, once I realized I could get high naturally by acknowledging my role as a father. Endorphines rushed through my body as I developed more of a profound safe haven for my family, filled with love, honesty and hope. I was determined to live the lifestyle that both Paulette and my mother knew I was destined to live. But now, with no woman walking alongside me and Daddy's little girl missing, I needed to use self-control to work even harder to keep my thoughts and my emotions in check. I didn't want my own thoughts to destroy me. When I smoked weed I sometimes focused on what made me sad, what obstacles were hindering me, and why it is I couldn't overcome the fear of succeeding. The more and more I mixed weed with alcohol, the more I continued to lose my train of thought by focusing on what made me happy as opposed to what it took to earn respect from my entire family.

As Titi continued to take long pulls from the freshly rolled blunt, I couldn't help but notice how my seat felt like it was one of those relaxing massage chairs you find at the mall. The roaring tail pipes found underneath Tatiana's Grand National barked echoes of an awakening Grizzly bear on the first day of spring. The after-market Flowmaster mufflers pulsated in my body through the customized rally sport racing seats to the point where I had to hold onto the door handle to keep my body from levitating.

"Damn, Cuzz! When did you get the automatic start and the pipes put on?"

"The same day I brought her home from Olympia. After I dropped you off, I went straight over to the muffler shop and had them put on."

Usually, when she was showing off her latest toys, I was there pumping her head up to make her feel like she was truly something like a pimp. "Yo! That joint nice, Cuzz!" I said to my proud cousin.

"Ya! It sounds real nice, Cuzzo." As Titi continued to boast about her new car and items that she loaded onto it, I quickly became agitated as she searched deep for verbs and adjectives that would best describe how she used dope money to acquire the expensive classic car. "I'm not talking about the automatic start,

Buzz; I'm talking about my new cracks!" She pushed another button on her remote control as I turned my ear towards the direction of the stereo. I played along with her so she could see I was somewhat interested in her exclusive audio system. I could hear the sounds of Chuck Brown and The Soul Searchers "Run-Joe" thumping from the door speakers, making the concrete beneath our feet shake and rattle, producing enough tremors to match the equivalence of a 2.0 magnitude earth-quake.

As Titi and I grew up being bad in the city streets of The Town, our parents got rid of us every summer and sent us to our relatives in the other Washington, better known as Chocolate City; the Nation's Capital, DC. "Since you two wannabe Billy Bad-asses, taking little kids' popsicles and shit, we'll see how tough you guys are with your cousins in Uptown, DC."

Titi and I were up for the challenge every summer. Our parents' logic backfired, and each and every summer we returned even more street smarter than when we left. We had the flavor of the East coast, the swagger of the West coast, and the knowledge from all people from the streets of Washington state and Washington DC. By the time we were sixteen, we became young educated hood figgaz, known around DC as those badass kids from Seattle.

Titi lived the life of a gangster, learned by watching her daddy and his friends as they provided lavish life styles for their families through the distribution of illegal drugs, until he went to prison for selling cocaine and died there from untreated syphilis. She was openly gay and enjoyed the company of many women. She was known to have a man in the freezer chilling, waiting for the right moment so that she could be held and pleased by someone more masculine than she.

Mother and Aunt Helen tried endlessly on several occasions to alter her viewpoint on selling drugs. But her answer was, "My daddy was a dope dealer, and the only thing he taught me was how to sell dope. The only thing that I'm good at is selling dope. So why would I stop getting money?"

Titi was given an honorary gangster degree from some Original Gangsters, from Englewood, California. Once the LA Crips left town, LA Bloods came to The Town to set up shop right where the Crips left off. Titi was the person who made it happen for them. By doing so, she became well known throughout the tight-knit community of drug dealers as "that one-Blood-bitch that gets money."

She's a gangster bitch who sold dope, weed, crank, ecstasy, Molly, Stewie, Percocet, Oxycontin, Vicodin, blue dolphins, Bart Simpsons, cocaine, stupid, crack, Love Boat, Reefer, white girl, china white, Mexican black heroin, Hash, Viagra, Hawaiian Purple, UW Medicine weed, Humble County Marijuana, Portland Indonesian, Canadian Red, and California Kush and Scramble. She even got a date rape drug called Blow Job for girls to use on men. She had a special drug called "Smacked Up" for pimps to convince their women to continue working for free.

Tatiana's boasting about items she had gained from selling dope didn't enthuse me anymore. My view of Titi went from envying her and her worldly possessions to feeling sorry for her because she didn't understand the damage of what selling drugs does to our people. It was like Malcolm X's blood was flowing through my system; I was a changed man. I never felt this way before. Since learning that Paulette was found with twelve crack rocks stuffed in her throat, selling dope wasn't making any sense to me at this point.

The two tragedies stayed locked deep in a vault in my mind. I couldn't stop from wandering back to the gruesome scene that I walked in on at Paulette's homegirl's house. I tried continuously to take my mind off the tragedy, but I couldn't. Knowing that the killer remained out there was driving me quietly insane. And knowing that my daughter could still be with the killer was making me want to hurt somebody.

I had to come up with a way to take my mind off of the murder scene without smoking weed. The face of Daddy's little girl stayed plastered in the cornea within my eyes. Though I was staring at Titi and listening to her talk about her car, everywhere I looked, Riesha's face somehow conjoined with all of the images that were before me. If I didn't find an outlet to escape, I knew I would do something that would land me not in jail again, but definitely in prison this time.

For starters I convinced myself that it wasn't all about me and my sorrows or the pain I have endured. Courageously I shifted my thoughts as I tried endlessly to imagine how the Jenkinses must feel after losing their only child. I remembered how emotional Paulette's mom was when she found out her brother had been killed in a car accident. We were eating Thanksgiving dinner when the phone rang and Mrs. Jenkins rose to answer it in the kitchen. We heard the phone shatter as it hit the floor. Moments later, we heard Mrs. Jenkins whimpering, then loud bursts of uncontrollable moans and volatile cries bellowed from her lungs. Once Paulette reached her and found out her uncle had been killed, the two of them were overtaken by involuntary screams. "No dear Lord! No! Not my baby brother! Why did you take my baby brother, dear Lord? Why did it have to be him? Take me, dear Lord, take me!"

Now that they have lost their one and only daughter, I could only imagine what Mrs. Jenkins was experiencing. I needed to speak to them again. My phone was dead, so I reached for Titi's charger in the cigarette lighter. "That charger only works for my new phone, Cuzzo," she said with a big smile on her face that showed her three gold teeth. She pulled a brand new phone out of the front pocket of her red hooded-sweater and handed it to me in a red case full of pink rhinestones and crystals. I had no idea how to dial a number because it was so high tech.

"Here, give me the phone, country-ass-bama shit!" she laughed while snatching the phone from me. "You open it like this, Cuzzo!" I wasn't impressed. She was waiting for a response from me but I wasn't willing to blow her head up any bigger than what it was already.

After the first few rings, my stomach twisted in knots as if I did something wrong. The knotted feelings reminded me of being informed by the principal that my father was on his way to pick me up from school, after he was notified I had been suspended for getting into another fight. Knowing that my father would have to take off from work to deal with my ignorant acting self, I knew it wasn't going to be pleasant when he arrived. Whenever Pops took off from work to tend to my stupidity, he would ask the principal to use his office in order to tear me another asshole.

I tried again and again, but still no answer. Since the Jenkinses weren't answering the phone, I started to think that they didn't want to talk to me again. Suddenly I became a paranoid schizophrenic. I took to not answering the phone, suspecting it was a formality to show me they have Riesha. I dreaded to think they would attempt to replace their daughter with my daughter through the judicial system. I don't have any money to fight for custody; they would win without a doubt because they have enough money to hire the best lawyer in town, and the judge would take one look at my criminal record and turn over custody to the Jenkinses, before the ink dried on the court order.

The guilt consumed my mind, making way for unwanted guests from my past to return. These visitors didn't have names or faces, just baritone voices that besieged me. The voices without faces had a way of over-staying their welcome. Every time the voices popped up in my head, they brought turmoil and drama with them too. This time wasn't any different.

"Just think, Ceeze, if it was Little Riri who caught the bullet." I didn't want this thought in my mind. Why would I even entertain those images of Riesha catching a bullet? Once this thought popped up, I knew these weren't normal thoughts. Then I realized the voices were the same voices from yesterday's past. It had been a hot minute since I was under attack by the invisible man. I became exceedingly petrified. I felt violated by images of Little Riri being shot. These depressing thoughts exasperated my ability to comprehend what was going on in front of me. I fought with these voices throughout a good portion of my teenage years. During which time, I never told a soul until I was around sixteen when Titi caught me responding to the internal voices.

Instantly, I began to speak to the voices telling them to *cease and desist* from my mind, but I knew that it wouldn't be that easy. This was bad timing for me to have to deal with the voices. I was already having a difficult time putting to rest the vivid images that remained locked in my brain from the murder scene.

Next, the voices said the most terrifying and damaging statement thus far. "You know Ceeze, they could have killed your daughter and were hiding her body from the police, and you'll never know whether or not she was alive or dead."

"Woe-hoe, you ain't gonna get me this time! My Riesha is still alive and I'm gonna find her." It was happening again, I was talking to the voices out loud.

Titi noticed. "Brandon! You okay, son?" She only called me by my birth name and referred to me as *son* when she was extremely worried about me. "Son" is a DC expression used by both men and women to confide trust in one another.

The voices had returned with great vengeance. I knew once they embarked on me that it would be a very long time before my mind would allow my body to rest. The doctor once told me that the voices only attacked me when I was overly nervous, frantic, or incredibly scared about something, especially something I wasn't willing to deal with. I later found out that the voices also returned when I used marijuana nonstop for weeks, if not months at a time. It all makes sense. "I'm stressed the fuck out!"

During the onset of the voices, I had a recurring dream at night about a deprived, illegitimate little boy desperate for affection. I could never tell if this was me. Regardless, there was a little boy sitting on a cold yellow linoleum floor shivering, his little body tensed up tight to endure physical pain. A giant monster of a man without a face inflicted the pain. The little boy in me sat there on the cold floor with his hands folded up tight on top of his knees, which were pulled up close against his chest. He squeezed his knees so tightly together that no light could get in between his knuckles. His chin rested in the tiny space between both of his knees. He was starving, hadn't eaten in a week. He was without parent and protection from the giant monster-like man with no face that kicked, stomped and punched him. The creature relentlessly shouted degrading overtones to the point where the boy was discombobulated, forced to the ground where he laid helplessly in despair as the same faceless man was joined by other faceless people who mercilessly kicked and kneed him for hours on end, constantly telling him he's a worthless piece of shit. The beating would always end with the giant monster-like man informing the little boy the world would be a better place if he were never born.

It seemed that the goals of the faceless man were to belittle me over and over again. Every step I took, the voices besieged me. He called me a coward, a fagot, and a punk, making me feel like I was a failure and a poor excuse for a son, telling me that I was a low life in society, a buffoon, and a dark dummy.

These malicious remarks kept me mulling over the way Paulette was killed. The voices remained unfaltering in the effort to destroy me slowly but surely, implying that it was my fault that Paulette was killed and it was my fault that Riesha was missing. The comments turned into unbearable images of me wearing a black hooded sweater while carrying the gun that killed Paulette. I became the shooter who killed Paulette and the thief who kidnapped Riesha.

As I sat there in Titi's car, I tried to tune out the tormenting voices by bobbing my head endlessly to the thumping beats that rattled from the back of her car. For a few minutes I was able to escape from reality. Only this time it would be without smoking any weed or drinking any liquor. I began to drift off with my eyes wide shut, allowing the sounds of the go-go band *treble funk* to soothe and relax my mind and body. My mouth slumbered, forcing saliva to seep out on its own while my head dangled along with the Ken Griffey, Jr. bobble-head doll that sat on Titi's dashboard.

For the first time since my girls were taken from me, someone who cared about me noticed the pain I was going through. "Keep your head up, Youngun. We going to get my little cousin, but first we going to find that motha-fucka who killed your girl! Don't worry, baby-boy, the word is out. We gonna find that motha-fucka and kurk-out on his punk ass!" Titi patted me on my back. Although my cousin felt my pain, I still couldn't move beyond misery. I felt that the Demon God himself defeated me. "Tell them voices to leave you the fuck alone, son! Tell them they're not welcome in my car!" said Titi. She knew me all too well.

The voices and the ever so tragic memory of the murder scene momentarily paralyzed my thought process. One minute I was normal, not quite happy-go-lucky, but dealing with the murder; the next minute I was distraught over panoramic images of a man without a face snatching my daughter from the frightful murder scene.

Titi tried to free my mind from the turmoil when she noticed what I was going through by switching the program. She chose a topic she was very familiar with, which possibly could kidnap my thoughts for just a spell. Titi went back to bragging about her car. "Wait until you see the glass pipes I put on this bitch, Blood!" she laughed as she placed her fist up to her mouth as if she was about to cough. Instead of laughing she made an enormous chuckle. "Owee! And I dueled her out too with the Flowmasters on both sides, Buzz, listen to this!" She turned down the music and pushed the gas. The car tore down the block roaring like a 767 Airbus.

Yet, I wasn't one bit impressed. I was unable to escape the vivid 3-D pics that kept on resurfacing every time I tried to listen to what Tatiana was saying. My mind remained unwavering, focusing solely on the haunting memories of the puddles of blood that lay on the floor throughout Paulette's homegirl's apartment.

With smoke exiting from her mouth, Tatiana coughed out the words, "Hit this shit dog-blood!" A string of saliva landed on her lap from the thick gray smoke, forcing her to cough more and more. She took another pull from the blunt, then again, and then again. After the third pull, she coughed abundantly again, then tried to pass the blunt to me, saying, "Hit this OG purple Kush, Cuzzo!" Although the weed smelled better than a fat eighteen-pound turkey in a smoker on Thanksgiving at Big Momma's house, I had to stick to my resolutions to Paulette.

"Naw girl, I stopped smoking everything! No weed, no Newports. I'm done with all that shit!"

I didn't want her to feel slighted, but that's exactly how I started abusing drugs, through peer pressure. In order for me to be successful at fatherhood and sobriety, I had to move beyond her feelings in order to protect me from abusing my mind and body any further.

With no vengeance in her voice, Tatiana said to me, "You know I support anything my cousin wants to accomplish." I didn't know how to respond. "This would be a good time for you to just concentrate on you and my little cousin." Then, to my surprise, she put out the blunt in the ashtray and turned up her music as if we didn't even have this conversation. I didn't want to ruin the moment, so I didn't say a word.

Titi possessed the swagger of a street hustler and the instinct of a mother, which gave her the edge on the boys with whom she did daily business. She remained active in the street game, always on a paper chase at any given time. The rule of thumb is when riding with any drug dealer, you're operating on "DDT" i.e., drug dealer time. If you found yourself in Titi's car, you had to kick back, relax, smoke a blunt, sip on something cold, and listen to some good music because she was on the clock. And she worked for herself, so the hours she spent trying to make some money varied. Titi wouldn't give you any set or agreed time to return you to wherever she picked you up. Her time was money. I knew what I was getting myself into when I first saw her face as I exited the elevator doors of the jail.

My patience was running thin with my cousin, the drug dealer. I was more than ready to get home so I could find out where and when Daddy's little girl was coming home. What was preventing me from getting there quickly was Tatiana's greed to constantly make money. I knew when I got in the car with her that I would be stuck-like-Chuck, rolling around The Town until she finished doing what she needed to do in order to sustain the stack of hundred-dollar bills she kept in her glove box. There really wasn't any reason to try to convince her I would just like to be dropped off at my house. I knew that wherever we went, no matter what side of town, or where she was heading, she always had to settle up with folks.

She didn't have time for sympathy, although Paulette was like a sister to her. When you are in the dope game like she was, having a friend or associate die violently wasn't anything out of the ordinary. It was similar to pancakes, butter, and syrup. You can't be a drug dealer and not lose money, go to jail, or have associates die. Both Tatiana and I had lost many close friends violently during the onset of gang banging in The Town. We became passive aggressors towards death, shedding cobwebs in the form of tears at the funeral, and on the way to the burial site smoking two blunts while drinking some brown liquor. Since high school we attended at least a dozen or so funerals per year. Losing someone to a violent crime was both horrible and very ceremonious. Death transcended into just an average uneventful passing of a friend, a friend who we were expecting to die anyway.

Tatiana was acting dispassionately as if she wasn't fazed by the death of my Boo or Riesha's abduction. Her impassionate disposition didn't offend me because I knew how much Riesha and Paulette meant to her. I assumed Tatiana was acting coldly to save face. She wasn't good at expressing herself unless she was either super high, or supper drunk. She was predisposed to losing a family member to life imprisonment first, and then death, like her father. When she said her business would only take five minutes, I knew what she really meant; it would take at least an hour to settle up with her business partners.

I wasn't trying to see her blood brothers. The only reason why they speak to me is because their leader is my cousin. I didn't have a problem with them except for the fact that they were Bloods, and I believed one of them might have killed my Boo. "Ya let's go," I told Titi. "Fuck it! I want to go over to the *weak side* so I can start chin-checking these niggaz to see which one killed my girl."

"Slow down, Cousin. I already been checking around on the strong side and nobody knows who done it. Trust me, Buzz, I went out last night ready to catch a nigga slipping trust! I already put the word out, that $10,000 goes to whoever can lead me to her killer, Cuzzo, for real. That's on Blood, Brandon! I'm gonna slowly kill the motha-fucka that killed Paulette, and when I find out who snatched my little cousin Riri, Owee! I feel sorry for that motha-fucka Blood! I'm gonna slowly cut his dick off and make him suck on it with ice in his mouth, for real, son!"

Damn! She was animated as hell. She continued to tell me that she was going to murk the motha-fucka that killed my Boo. "Look in the backseat, Nigga, under the towel," said Titi. I reached in the back seat and raised the towel to find a .22 semiautomatic rifle, the kind the militia in central Africa used to fight the LRA. "Be careful, Nigga, it's loaded." She was really ready to do some hood banging on the one responsible for Paulette's death. Her boisterous attitude turned me into a ticking time bomb ready to blow the fuck up. Now I was on some oh-hoo-banging shit too.

"Where you get that machine gun, Cuzz?"

"I got it from one of my African homeys, from the Congo! This crazy ass nigga said he used it to kill several Arrow-boys that attacked his village and killed his entire family!"

Shit, after seeing the rifle in the back seat, I was ready to relapse, smoke a blunt, and murk somebody for real.

"Don't let me find out who killed my Boo. I am gonna kill a motha-fucka slowly, Cuzz! I mean it, straight the fuck-up, Cuzz! And don't let me find the one who snatched my daughter, Cuzz! I want to find the nearest Popeye's and fry that motha-fucka for real and make his ass eat his own damn fingers, Cousin, for real! You feel me, dog?"

As we pulled up to the shop, Titi said to me, "When we get inside, don't start wilding out on anybody. This is my place of business, son, and right now you're hot as a motha-fucka. I don't need any attention to my joint. You understand the words coming out of my mouth, Brandon?"

Again, there she goes trying to chin check me. When is she going to understand that I am a grown-ass man who knows how to handle himself? She always got to say, "Brandon" when she wanted me to act right. I asked, "Why you got to go there, Cuzz? Damn!"

"If you start acting stupid in my place of business, it could have a bad affect on my life, Negro! That's why!"

Tatiana is a barber by trade and a hustler by conviction. She hustled straight out of the barbershop that she owned. Without anyone to tell her how to run her business, she had created a laid-back comfortable environment for herself and for her patrons. It was an atmosphere that was consistent to her lifestyle. Her shop was the only place on the Westside that I could walk around and not be harassed when I'm dressed in my favorite true blue attire that is synonymous with the Crip gang culture that I stayed true to. She was running shit on this part of town and had all of her little Blood homeys walking behind her so close that they were tripping over her heels wherever she went.

If you entered from the front of the building through the barbershop, you could get a fresh haircut while smoking a blunt, and get a shave while you re-up (buy more product, mainly cocaine, marijuana, pills and scramble). When you entered from the back of the building and owned a platinum membership card that read, "Titi's", you would be escorted downstairs to the basement of her shop where she operated an illegal gambling joint as well as a stripper joint all under the assumed front, Westside Burger Joint. She owned the only restaurant where you could play pool, throw darts, and shoot craps on a real casino table, while being served by bouncing beauties that just finished hugging a stripper pole butt naked.

When we pulled up to her shop, she said she would only be a few minutes. I was cool with that.

At times, I wished that I had some of Titi's unique bravado. She exhibited the characteristics of a great leader just like her daddy. When she spoke, those around her stopped what they were doing to hear exactly what she had to say. Her crew of outlaws sold umbrellas downtown on rainy days, and ran three hotdog stands, which were best known for having the juiciest sausage links and the beefiest hotdogs in The Town.

She possessed so much originality that she had her soldiers selling crack in the bottom of rose stems across the street from Mexicans selling oranges and apples, on the busiest intersections in

The Town. In order to get a twenty-dollar crack rock, you had to first buy a rose for five bucks.

A pimp once told me, "Sometimes you're up and sometimes you're down." But for Titi, she was always up. Whenever I rolled with her, I never had to pay for anything, no matter how much money I had in my pocket. Watching her perform her role as the HBIC (Head Bitch In Charge) reminded me of how much she and Paulette shared some of the same leadership qualities.

Titi's intrinsic authoritative presence shone as she entered a room, solidifying the power African American women held within the black community. The way Titi was in control of her family of thieves reminded me of the strength Paulette possessed which was leading me to Christ.

As I sat there in Titi's Buick waiting for her to settle up with her people, I felt Paulette's spirit warm up the car, shining as bright as the sun settling over the apple orchards of Yakima Valley in mid July. I sat blissfully watching her luminous spirit travel through the car and finally come to rest on my face, blinding me momentarily. Her presence heated the car the way the oven heat spewed through the house the times we kept the oven door open, using the broiler as a heater when I forgot to pay the electric bill. Paulette's life force kept me complacent, making way for my body to finally take a break.

I was comfortable in my faith in God, knowing that my little girl would return home soon. I fell fast asleep. I was the only Crip in The Town that could take a nap on the Westside in the parking lot where known Blood gang members roamed. I trusted God as I felt myself slipping into a deep slumber, so deep to the point where I started to snore. Paulette's life force quickly vanished when Titi opened the car door, waking me abruptly. I asked her how long had I slept. "I was only in there for five minutes," replied Titi.

With Titi in the front seat, her homeboy approached the passenger side of the car and knocked on the window for me to roll it down. Titi rolled the window down from her side before I could. As if I wasn't even there, the two of them exchanged money and a bag of light blue pills, which appeared to be ecstasy. A few fell out of the bag onto my lap. I picked them up and noticed it had a picture of Bart Simpson on both sides. I attempted to hand it back to the young brotha, but he insisted that I keep them. Though I never tried ecstasy before, the way I was feeling I was truly tempted. On the other hand though, I was already aware of the addictive power that the little blue pill held over those who tried it for the first time. Little did people know that the little blue pills were packed with heroin, meth, rat poison, Drano, and PCP. I had no intention of turning into a pill popper. My brain was already fried from all of the weed and alcohol I consumed over the years. Instead I tossed the pills on Titi's lap. She threw one in her mouth and quickly swallowed it. She then tossed the other in the ashtray.

Usually, she sold the little blue pills in bulks of 1000, yet this bag looked more like it had nothing less than 5,000. Once they were done settling up, the roughneck brotha dressed in all green, including the Celtics hat pulled down over his forehead, patted me on my upper right shoulder and said, "My condolences to you and your family, my-nig." Before I could say thank you, he stepped back and pulled up his shirt to show me his pistol, saying, "I got something for the motha-fucka that did that shit. We don't play that '80s gang banging shit around here, buzz. We about our paper. Ask your cuzzin; she'll tell you. We gonna murk that boward when we find out who billed your girl; that's on Blood." (*Boward, coward*; *billed, killed*. Each word is absent the letter C and K to signify the Piru Blood gang affiliation.) "You feel me, Dog?"

"Ya, I feel you, ma nigga, right-on."

"Back atcha, playa!"

12
I See Dead People

THE FIRST THING I NOTICED AS WE GOT NEARER to my apartment was that my porch light was off. I started leaving the light on after my brief stint as a cat burglar. I had learned to avoid houses that were well lit or had a barking dog. A sign from an alarm company posted in the yard or on the windows also deterred me.

I waved goodbye to Tatiana and went to the porch, where I turned the bulb back and forth, in case it was loose. When I shook the bulb, I didn't hear the thingamajig inside; it was still intact. Then I noticed the apartment was silent; I had left the radio on, blaring Christian music to warn off thieves. As I replaced the bulb, the streetlight in front of my building turned on. *What the fuck is going on?* I wanted to scream but realized that blowing up wouldn't do me any justice; in fact it just might land me back in jail.

"What good would that do now?" said a voice in the back of my mind. "There's no need to lose your temper and cause a scene out here in front of the apartment where your family lives!"

I answered the voice back without questioning whose voice was speaking. "Yep you right, fuck that shit, Cuzz! I'm not going back to jail!"

For a brief moment I stood in front of the door scratching my head, attempting to make sense out of all of this. I convinced myself that if I scratched my head long enough, an answer would eventually pop out.

No electricity! Damn! Damn! Damn! That meant all of the food in the fridge was spoiled, which also meant that when I open the front door, the apartment would smell like a sea of decaying salmon. When I looked around at the neighboring apartment buildings, I noticed that their lights were still on. Nonetheless, all of the lights within my building were shut off. "Why are all the lights off in our building?"

The apartment was fabulous and the rent included all utilities. We paid six-fifty a month for a two-bedroom apartment, exposed air ducts and brick, along with a wood burning stove that we used religiously. We didn't even pay for cable, thanks to my homeboy Vic who climbed an eighteen-foot pole at night to turn on our bootleg cable for a small cost of forty bucks — in a pouring rainstorm at that. Jammed behind the screen door was an embarrassing bright orange flyer from the Light Company. When I opened the screen door, another flyer fell on top of the soiled welcoming floor mat that read "Trust God". The color was lime green from the Gas Company. Damn, what a welcome home! No utilities!

I then found the letter that explained it all. The letter explained that the building is deemed uninhabitable because of the lack of running water, heat, or working electricity. The owner, Mr. Paul Foster had three business days to pay eight months of utility bills. If the bills were not paid within the allotted time, all occupants will be forced to evacuate, and the building would be boarded up. I should have known! We were allowed to move in with no references or credit report and a smaller-than-required deposit. Oh damn! We got hustled! Now I have to find a new place.

Just as I thought, when I opened the door, a wicked odor engulfed my entire upper respiratory system, smelling like a honey bucket full of putrid human dung. In addition, the apartment was considerably colder inside than it was outside. The thermostat read 38 degrees making way for the brisk wintry air to bellow from the loins of Jack Frost.

I suddenly felt abandoned, which sparked a panic attack that had been brewing deep down inside me. I was consumed again by my fears. When a panic attack hit me during the day, I became very volatile. It was like I was in a nightmare with my eyes wide open. I remained cognizant, although my body felt like I was falling rapidly from outer space. Wherever I was when this occurred, the space around me compressed to the size of a coffin. Subsequently the floor beneath my feet swiftly vanished. The familiarity was like a ride at the County Fair as the room spun counter clockwise. Every step I took for the next thirty minutes felt more like three days; the room got smaller and smaller until the walls eventually closed in around me. The feeling of being trapped inside a coffin felt like I was descending rapidly into a sea of blackness. Whenever I was caught up in this unstable situation, I found myself fighting for my freedom to gain back my equilibrium.

I sought refuge in the safe zone, which became the middle of the living room. After the last panic attack, Paulette estimated the farthest circumference point in the apartment was from the dining room table to the middle of the living room. Once there, I was able to rest without tipping over. If Paulette came home and found me sitting in the middle of the living room with my legs crossed, rocking back and forth, she presumed that I had retreated there for stability.

With tears gushing from my eyes, I made several attempts to regain my balance, unsuccessfully. After the last attempt, I fell back to the floor kicking everything in sight while screaming like a deranged psychotic mad man. No matter how hard I tried, I couldn't regain my equilibrium, even though I was sitting in the safe zone. I began rocking back and forth and chanting, "My Boo is dead. My Boo is dead!"

I ripped my shirt off as if I were Superman, tearfully yelling, "Where the fuck is my little girl?" I knew I was out of control, yelling so loud I felt my voice crack as it echoed throughout the dreadfully cold, empty apartment. Unable to control my own body and not having any supernatural ability to bring back Paulette and Riesha, I was taking out my frustrations on the apartment. Since I couldn't stand up on my own, I lunged forward, grabbed the lamp on the end table, and flung it across the room. The force that I put into throwing it caused me to fall over and hit my head on the hardwood floor.

The lamp shattered the green and blue vase that Paulette and I picked out from a thrift store the first week we moved into our apartment. I tried again to acquire my equilibrium by hazardously tipping over the dining room table as I yelled, "Who killed my baby's momma?" This time my body rocked in the opposite direction, knocking me to the floor again; only this time I wasn't able to lift myself up. I lay on my side, noticing how all the pictures on the wall were gradually turning from counter clockwise to clockwise, and then to a complete standstill.

Once I realized that the house had stopped spinning, I said, "Thank you, dear Lord Jesus! Thank you!" I arose from the freezing floor and wiped the tears beneath my eyes. Thinking I was sane enough to rise to my feet, I sprinted to the front door to get some fresh air. Once on the terrace, I discovered I was still somewhat delusional and demented. Again I fought for control over my own two feet and, more importantly, my mind. I had been forsaken again by an unforgiving panic attack. No matter how hard I tried to ward off expressing my true feelings, my mind was determined to express itself without any effort of my own. No longer could I control my frustrations. Wholeheartedly I yelled, "Which one of you motha-fuckaz snatched my daughter!"

A passing onlooker with a familiar face was startled by my outward offensive remark and replied, "Yo, Ceeze, you okay, Cuzz?"

I flung the words back. "I didn't kill my baby's momma, Cuzz! I didn't kill my baby's momma, Cuzz!"

My life seemed closer to the end and I found myself contemplating suicide again. My gun would do the trick; one shot to the temple. Except I worried about surviving the gunshot wound. And if I did, I could become a paraplegic or blind, and still have to do the time for a murder that I did not commit. The thought of Riesha losing both her parents convinced me to keep praying for hope and guidance. It was time for the tirades to end. I had to let it go, sincerely give it to God, and let him help me live respectfully.

I felt compelled to focus on the murder and the whereabouts of Riesha. I had to take my mind off of the grueling events before I ended up going quietly insane. I once lived my life according to how the media portrayed African American men — an oppressive lifestyle surrounded by illiterate boys and girls who also had fallen victim to their own circumstances. I used any uneventful moment as an excuse to get wasted, taking shots of Patron Silver, followed by two Newport cigarettes back to back, along with a fat-ass baseball bat full of purple-gurple UW indo smoke to take the edge off reality. This cocktail of substances made me feel ten feet tall and bullet proof.

The reality: I have to deal with the villain in the mirror. This was the beginning of an end, and I must tackle my addiction while coping with the death of my Boo. I will no longer use weed and malt liquor to keep me disheartened, disenfranchised, oppressed, and illiterate.

I turned my attention to locating the ungodly stench of road kill that engulfed the apartment. First on my agenda was the fridge. Anticipating a whiff of funk to knock me out when I opened the door, I was surprised that the worst smell I could find was from leftover fried-green tomatoes that I brought home three days ago from a local watering hole that served slave food to white folks to keep their business afloat. Old broccoli and a bag of seasoned snow crabs topped off the garbage truck aroma that followed from the bottom of the fridge.

Because the aromas coming from the refrigerator weren't enough to make me nauseous, I kept searching. "Follow my nose!" was a method I used on account of my nostrils being the size of two large green grapes, like the large grapes found on Auntie Stella's grapevine down south in Greensboro, North Carolina. My large sniffer gave me the capability to sniff out just about any smell that I focused on within 30 feet of my face. I referred to this solitaire game as the Superman sniff game.

I opened the freezer and the stench smacked me upside the head. Paulette went shopping the day before she was murdered. Here were two packs of ground turkey, one whole chicken, and a pack of meaty-sized pork chops that looked more like London broil steaks. All of which had gone bad. A toxic gas was created from the mixture of raw pork and poultry blood mixed up in a sea of defrosting ice that seeped through the crevices of the freezer and onto the linoleum floor.

Still, the uninviting funk lingering from the fridge wasn't the stench of decaying muskrat that was funking up the apartment. Once a field mouse was caught in between the fridge and the wall and died, which made the hunt for funk an unpleasant memorable moment that Paulette and I shared. I went straight to the side of the fridge where we had found it before. I found nothing there. Following my nose, I pulled out the stove and sho-nuff, there it was. Only this time, it was an adult mouse longer than the palm of my hand and covered in maggots popping out of the dead carcass. It was wedged between the stove and the wall.

I didn't want to deal with a dead mouse full of maggots and spoiled rotten food, although it needed to get done. Between the murder scene, the jailhouse, and now my apartment, I just about had enough of odors associated with death. Yet I still had to get the apartment clean for my daughter's journey home. I closed my eyes, praying for the return of my child, to show the Lord Jesus Christ that I have faith: "Thank you, Jesus, for returning my child. She is not in my presence right now, but I am preparing for her safe return. Again, Dear Lord, I sincerely thank you."

I felt joy in hope and glory for the first time since the tragic death of my Boo, knowing that my faith in God will return my child safely. This newly found hope gave me strength to carry on and do what I had to. Removing all of the items kept me busy, kept my mind off the unknown.

The battery to my cell phone was dead and, with no electricity, I couldn't charge it. My car charger was in my car, which I hoped was still at Paulette's homegirl's house. That is, unless the police towed it, in search of forensic evidence. I didn't know what people were saying about the murder, nor was I in a hurry to find out. I wasn't ready to cope with the reality of an entire community whispering behind my back. I needed to be alone for a couple more hours to get a grip on what's really going on around me.

Trust in the Lord vanished at the very sight of Riesha's little dolly lying on her toddler bed with her hair in a twist. Paulette spent time trying to comb Riesha's favorite doll's hair, so that it could match little Riesha's hair. Paulette took pride in her black doll collection and, at times, Paulette purchased clothes for her dolls to match both her and Riesha's outfits. Just the thought of my two darlings missing from my life incited a revolt within me. All of my insecurities surfaced.

I didn't want to admit it, but I was committing blasphemy against my Lord Jesus, although I was not happy about it. Before I could allow myself to continue to question God's plan, out of nowhere came a prayer that flowed freely and elegantly out of my mouth as if I were the long lost son of a preacher. "God, please renew my spirit, give me the hope, guidance, and the encouragement I need to trust in you. Help me find the killer and find daddy's Baby Booboo Riesha."

If I allowed myself to fall into the trap of questioning God, then I wouldn't be able to take the time to clear my head. I asked God to keep my Riri safe, healthy, and happy, which allowed me to remain in the safety net of my own home. Knowing that God and Paulette are watching over little Riri gave me strength. I didn't have time to second-guess God's plan, and I refused to let the devil steal the little rumble of hope that I possessed inside.

Even though I had just been released from the germ infested county jail and had just removed a dead mouse from the kitchen, I didn't have enough strength to change out of my clothes to take a shower. Instead I chose to collect some blankets from our bed so I could wrap myself up in them. I heard one of the bed boards break as I flopped down on the bed. I was so exhausted that I passed out the instant my head hit the pillow.

AFTER WHAT SEEMED LIKE 14 HOURS of undisturbed sleep, I was awakened by the persistent soft knock belonging to the hungry little ones from next door. I could tell the boys were starving from the urgency attached to each long drawn-out knock. They only took a small break that lasted all of ten seconds to switch hands in order to rest their boney bare knuckles. The longer I took to reach the front door, the more the boys persevered.

Usually the youngest child knocked first. If you listened closely you could hear the oldest sibling whispering, trying to convince the youngest one to do his dirty work for him. The oldest boy felt his little brother wasn't knocking hard or loud enough. So big brother emulated the way the police knocked — an overtly authoritative solid bang, followed by a closed fist pounding. Little man learned this from tolerating the police beating on their door once, if not twice, a week. In a soft precarious voice, the older boy said, "See, you got to knock like you the hook (police) so that they get up thinking the hook is gonna kick in the door like they did our door, remember? And when you hear footsteps coming, you say in a deep voice, "Open up, Ms. Paulette, we know you're in there!" The two boys giggled.

Ever-so-promptly, right around seven a.m., when "Sponge Bob Square Pants" was just beginning to air on the Nickelodeon channel, the knocking abruptly awakened me. The ladies of the house were always up, waiting for Riri's special friends to arrive. "It's Rayrae and Daydae, Ms. Paulette! Can we come in?"

A smile appeared on my face as I quickly rose to my feet while reminiscing about happier times when Riesha was ecstatic to hear her playmates knocking at the front door. In a spiritual way, hearing the neighbors' kids at my door enlightened me, whereas some other people would have been annoyed by the troublesome crumb snatchers' persistent knocking so early in the morning.

On the way to the door, I turned on the living room TV; I knew the boys would like to watch Sponge Bob, which had just started three minutes ago. Oh damn! No electricity! With the second smile on my face since this tragic episode in my life, I said to myself, "My little homies are here." At times I felt like their uncle or, better yet, their father. Paulette's voice said to me on the way to the door, "You need to call Child Protective Services on her trifling ass like I told you to do a long time ago, Brandon!"

I answered back like I always did in the past, "I know, Boo, I know." Paulette felt since I knew her first, I should be the one to call. But there was one crucial thing that prevented me from calling CPS. I thought I owed Billie Jean something. And that something pertained to the secret I kept hidden from Paulette during our whole relationship; the oldest boy, Raymond, is my son. Billie Jean and I had a one-night stand many moons ago. It was when I was out there doing the club scene, tricking my dick off. During our one-night escapade, the condom broke and I didn't stop.

Billie Jean surprised me in passing one-day, simply saying with no regard for how I would react to this newfound information, "Yo, Brandon, the boy is yours." Ugh, I was disgusted, not at the fact of having a child, but for having the mind set to have slept with her. Looking at her now and placing me in the bed with her while sharing saliva and body fluids was repulsive and repugnant.

Each time I heard the first knock on my door, the Holly Spirit overwhelmed me, and today wasn't any different. I felt the spirit of God rush through me as if a gust of wind came roaring through the apartment. It was at that moment when I concluded, once my name is cleared for not killing my baby's momma, I will pursue custody, not only for Little Rayrae, but for his little brother Daydae too.

"What y'all want?" I jokingly asked with a big happy grin on my face as I quickly flung open the door, startling the oldest boy and making Daydae's smile shine bright.

"You scared, Rayrae?"

Little Rayrae did most of the talking as he held Daydae's hand. "Is Ms. Paulette home, Ceeze? We hungry. Y'all got anything to eat in there?" The boy's asking if she made any breakfast told me he didn't know what happened to Paulette yet.

"Where's your momma?" I asked.

"My momma been asleep for the past two days."

"Where's your dad?"

Little Rayrae answered that one. My dad called our house from jail last night…"

"Collect," added Daydae.

"…and he won't get out until next Tuesday when the magistrate comes back from vacation," Rayrae concluded.

This boy knows way too much to be only seven years old. I was the same way when I was his age, very intuitive and nosey. My mother told me I was always in grown folks' business.

"Okay. Come on in and sit down at the table."

"Oh you slept with that bitch too?" Paulette had asked. "Damn, Ceeze! You really was down for these nasty ass chickenheads, weren't you?" I felt so small when Paulette met women from my past who were days away from being actual prostitutes.

"Yes, Paulette! A long, long, time ago." Paulette slapped me upside of my head saying, "And now you got me living next to that nasty ratchet ass bitch!" Paulette was mad for about four minutes. After that conversation, we never talked about my one-night-stand with Billie Jean.

"I am not gonna let you or that heifer steal my thunder. I forgive you, Ceeze, and I suggest you ask God to forgive you too."

"I already did, baby. You know you're the only one I have my eyes on now." Paulette was a very secure woman who feared God, not women from my past, and that is why I loved her so much.

As time progressed, Paulette tended to Billie Jean's kids as if they were her own kinfolk. Most of the time Paulette made extra food for the two of them just in case they smelled some of Paulette's griddle brewing from across the way. Sometimes their dinner plates were ready before mine. In the morning she set out two extra bowls full of cereal; they weren't picky eaters. Whatever the brand or the type of cereal we had, the boys were grateful.

Every time the boys came over, the first thing Little Rayrae asked me was, "Yo, Ceeze, y'all got any more of that spaghetti?" The boys really liked my spaghetti, so I tried to keep some left over, frozen just for when they came over. Little Rayrae pulled out from under his jacket a package of hamburger patties. "My momma told me to give this to you." Rayrae handed over to me a warm and smelly pound of spoiled bright red hamburger meat still dripping blood from the sides. I ran out of insulting things to say about Billie Jean right after we first moved in, but there was one thing I did know for sure, she is a trifling heifer.

Now she was trying to test my fatherly duties, which was clearly telling me to call the authorities on her trifling ass. The pound of spoiled rotten hamburger meat smelled like it was left out on the counter for no less than four days max. The nerve of this heifer!

"Mommy said you could use this to make some spaghetti," said Daydae. I felt so sorry for my boys; the only thing I wanted to do was to prevent the two of them from going back to their mommy's home, thinking that if I just acknowledged Rayrae as my own, I could provide them with a better life.

They were in luck; I previously took out leftover spaghetti from the freezer, which was already thawing on the kitchen counter. By the time I had grabbed some plates from the cupboard, Rayrae and Daydae were already sitting on the floor in front of the couch with their legs crossed, staring at a TV with no sound, asking if they could watch Sponge Bob Square pants torment Mr. Squidward.

"Sorry boys the TV won't turn on because the electricity is off." Neither one of them seemed to be bothered by the power not working.

"Ours is out too. Didn't Paulette pay the bill, Ceeze?" asked Rayrae.

Whenever they ate over, I allowed them to eat on trays in the living room. Once Rayrae noticed me carrying two full bowls of spaghetti, he quickly rushed over to the space in between the fridge and the pantry to grab the trays. He opened one and eloquently wiped off the top of it with his shirt for his little brother. Rayrae then opened his own tray and placed it next to his brother's. Next, Rayrae went into the kitchen, pulled out little Riesha's stool, and placed it in front of the kitchen counter so he could use it to get their favorite plastic cups. Little Rayrae liked to use my Seattle Seahawks cup, even though I always had to tell him to get a different cup because that one is mine.

"Ceeze, can I use your cup?" he asked right on cue.

But on this day, I allowed him to use it, and added, "That one is yours now. I'm getting a new one." He was ecstatic.

His brother liked to use Riesha's sippie cup, and it was his lucky day as well. "Can my brother use Riri's sippie cup?" Again I just couldn't say no.

This was the first meal I made for Paulette, and she was sprung ever since then. Watching my little boy and his sibling eat my food eased the pain that I was experiencing from losing someone who made me feel as appreciated as my parents made me feel. The joy of knowing that these kids will have a full belly by the time they leave worked like a prescribed narcotic, removing all of the suicidal ideas that previously infiltrated my mind.

As the two boys were scraping off their plates, I took one look at their nappy heads and told the two of them to sit back down. "I can't send you guys home with your heads looking like that! Rayrae! Go in the bathroom and get the clippers from under the sink. Daydae, you first."

The last time they had a haircut was when I cut it about three months ago. I felt as though I was neglecting them for not cutting their hair more often. The two of them looked like two poor neglected nappy-headed mixed children whose mother didn't know anything about black hair and whose father was nowhere to be found. As I was cutting Rayrae's head, I started to doze off. Instead of giving him a complete haircut, I just gave him a shape up and sent the two back home. I was too tired and too drained to go on caring for the boys. "Y'all go on home and come back tomorrow."

"Wake up, Ceeze, wake up!" whispered Paulette as she sat on the edge of the bed doing a crossword puzzle. Every morning she sat in the very same spot, patiently waiting for me to wake up. Again she was wearing my favorite T-shirt, the old Seattle Super Sonics shirt, green with gold and burgundy accents — the one with Sasquatch, the Super Sonics mascot on the front, spinning a basketball atop a miniaturized Seattle Space Needle.

    I had cut off the sleeves, as I do with all my tees, to expose my sculpted biceps and forearms, making my neighborhood tattoos stand out. The tat on my left arm above my elbow read "253" in block letters. On my right forearm was, "Ridgetop till I die".

    I knew Paulette's appearance was a ghost, but I still had to sneak a peek at her breast dangling from the side of the shirt. My lady had the nicest breasts I've had the opportunity to squeeze. That old torn-up T-shirt she wore made me horny as hell when she was breathing; now half asleep, the sight of her nipples bursting through the shirt made me blush as if I was seeing them for the very first time. I said aloud, "Please forgive me, Dear Lord." I smiled as one lonely teardrop dripped down from my left eye.

    Before the tear reached my chin, I was out of bed standing over her lustrous body. "You and those crossword puzzles, girl!" I said as I leaned forward to give her a kiss. With a bright smile, she used her pointer finger to push in her left cheek, forming the lonely dimple that made me melt like real butter. When I tried to kiss her, it was like I was eating a double-decker club sandwich in my sleep; hollow unfulfilling. She then faded away, leaving behind the same pencil and puzzle book she was writing in, neatly stacked at the edge of the bed undisturbed.

    I didn't feel strange hearing voices or seeing dead people. My mother and father never appeared after their deaths; however, on several occasions I was awakened by their voices. I heard my mother's voice during times when I needed that extra edge-like caffeine to get up out of bed after a night of drinking and smoking weed. This always happened at times when I was running late for a job interview, or needed to be up on time for an important court appearance. I heard my mother yell to my father, "Make sure your son is up, so he don't be late!" When my father was alive and my mother asked him to wake me up, his response was always the same. In his loud boisterous voice, he yelled loud enough for me to hear him, "How is he gonna become a man if we keep waking him up every time he is supposed to be somewhere on time?"

I remembered one time in particular when I caught myself turning down the TV to answer my mother's ploy. When she needed me to do something for her immediately, she called my name, adding an extra long reverberation of the first two letters of my name, "Brrrandon!"

Another time I heard my father's voice; I went as far as setting down the beer that I was sipping when I heard him yell, "Come here, Brandon!"

I answered the same way I was taught, "Yes, here I come." I actually got up out of my man-chair for a split second and laughed as I sat back down. I smiled as I answered, as if he were there. "You got me that time, Pops!"

Once Paulette heard me answer the invisible voices, I was no longer able to hide the fact I was talking to dead people. She was aware of these illustrious moments because I had explained them to her. Her response was, "Ceeze, you some kind of crazy!"

WITHOUT ELECTRICITY, OLD MAN WINTER'S first cousin Jack Frost engulfed my bedroom with a brisk and cold embrace. I grew up stacking and splitting wood every winter with my father, so I knew how to keep the house warm without using the heater. I kept a small stack of split wood next to our wood stove, where I had to rely upon my ability to make a fire to heat up the apartment. Paulette would get after me, like my father did, if I allowed the fire to go out. It was my responsibility to place a log in the fire before going to bed. If the thermostat on the wall read less than seventy-four degrees, Paulette wouldn't give me any nookie until the fire was lit and the thermostat was above seventy-eight degrees.

While igniting the fire, I felt my stomach churn, which reinforced the need to prepare a toilet. I went out back where the landlord kept old paint buckets, grabbed one and went next door where the water was still working. I turned on the waterspout and filled up the bucket so I could refill the toilet after the first few flushes. I knew that the water tank to the apartment building held a certain amount of water and after the water is turned off, there is still a little left in the tank. And I also knew that once the tank is empty, I could fill it up to full capacity with water after relieving myself, and it would flush on its own. This would have to work until I could find another place to live.

As I was carrying the bucket full of water, a weather-beaten white lady holding a pack of Salem cigarettes approached me. Dangling from her lips was an old crusty cigarette, which looked like it had fallen into a puddle of water. She said to me with a country drawl, "Is y'all's water turned off over dur?"

I replied, "Ya!"

With no hesitation, she informed me she knew how to turn on the water for the entire building. I asked if I needed a special tool? "Ya, a crow bar." She then told me that she would come over and turn it on for me for twenty bucks. "However," she added, "if somebody ask who turned the water back on, don't tell 'em it was me. I got two warrants out right now and I ain't trying to go back to jail."

I informed her that I just got out too, and her reply was, "Ya, I know. I saw you get out of the car holding that yellow just-released-from-jail envelope." She chuckled then and continued, saying, "I saw you on the news just two minutes ago."

"What did they say about me?"

"They said you killed your baby's momma, but I said to myself, I know that boy didn't kill his baby's momma. I've seen y'all walking around here strolling with the baby and all. I used to tell my old man how much y'all made a handsome couple."

As we approached the water main, I handed her the twenty bucks she requested. Just as she placed it in her bra, a man wearing a light blue work shirt and dark blue trousers approached us. "I wouldn't do that if I were you!" said the workingman. The neighbor lady carrying the crow bar dropped it and scurried off like a frightened white-tailed doe. The workingman laughed as he shook his head from side to side.

"You come to turn the water back on?" I asked.

"Na, I'm from the light company. I came to turn the electricity back on; the owner finally paid the bill. The only thing I know is there was a work order to come turn the lights back on, and here I am. The owner is out front if you want to talk to him."

By the time I got to the front, the owner was talking to a person from the water company while showing him where the water main was located. As I approached the owner, I stopped in my tracks when I noticed the police car pull up behind the water truck, blocking it in. I didn't have anything to be scared of because I didn't kill my baby's momma.

But then it dawned on me, "Oh, shit!" I remembered I had hid my gun out back just inches away from the water main. I turned around and walked back to where the guy from the light company was finishing up. I waited frantically for him to walk back around front so I could do something with my gun. I only had a matter of seconds to get it before the worker from the water company would find it. I went directly to where I hid the gun and scrambled through the old two-by-four floor boards and rubbish left behind by old tenants. I grabbed it, turned, and chucked it over the barbwire fence that separated our apartment building from the greenbelt used as a wild life reserve.

I headed back around to my apartment with my heart pounding. The owner was talking with a detective while pointing in the direction of my apartment. I shrugged my shoulders with no regard to what I was witnessing. I didn't care, nor was I intimidated by the presence of the police. Thinking about what could have happened if they found my gun, made my heart jump from my chest to my stomach.

"Mr. Brandon!" yelled the police officer. I acted like I didn't hear him right away.

Seconds later I acknowledged the officer by saying, "I go by Ceeze Green." I didn't take well to being chastised by police officers that bullied anyone who had the courage to walk in their path.

I was just inches from the entrance to my apartment when I heard Mr. Foster's voice, "Hey-a, Ceeze, I need to speak to you about that five hundred dollar deposit! Do you have a moment?"

I played like I didn't hear him either as I opened my apartment door. I had planned on paying the man the next time I saw him. I went straight towards the bedroom and lifted up the mattress to find hundreds of dollars scattered around underneath. We had over two thousand dollars saved up for the rent, his deposit, and for our special nights out that we enjoyed as a family. I counted out five-hundred for the deposit and six-fifty for the rent. Now that the lights and water were working again, I didn't want to worry about having to pay the rent next month. This would be one thing I didn't have to worry about for thirty more days.

I remembered that my cousin and her Blood homey gave me money towards the funeral. This would be a good time to count what Titi gave me. I pulled out the wad and began counting. Five-hundred dollars. With the amount her Blood brother gave me, I had eleven-fifty I could still use towards the funeral. I wrapped up eleven-fifty in a rubber band and walked out in front of my apartment and yelled, "Mr. Foster, here's your deposit money and the rent!"

Once he looked my way, I threw it in his direction. The money landed at his feet. I waited for a moment for him to count it. Once he figured out it was all there, he gave me a head nod and said, "Thanks, Ceeze, I'll send you a receipt in the mail."

I didn't respond to him or to the detectives who yelled out, "We'll be back with a search warrant for the murder weapon; I promise you that!"

The Chief added, "I'll bring your receipt to you when you're behind bars for murdering your baby's momma." I closed the door before the detective could finish running his mouth. *I ain't got time to pay attention to the rhetoric spewing out of it.*

"Wowzers!" With the lights on, I could see the damage I had caused throughout our apartment. The destruction was worse than I remembered. If the police were to see the apartment like this, they would surely have probable cause to arrest me. They would envision us having a fight before the murder and kidnapping. If I wanted to remain on the outs, I needed to get busy cleaning. I believed the detective when he said he was going to return with a search warrant, so I found myself racing against time.

As I began cleaning, I noticed some belongings of Paulette's that were significant to her, personal effects she cherished which I didn't pay much attention to unless Riri and I broke one by accident. She collected lots of little trinkets, most of which were elephants in various colors and sizes. Some were made out of ivory, heavy but small. For Christmas last year, Mrs. Jenkins gave her a herd of five, each connected by the tails made out of dark mahogany wood that lined the windowpane in our master bedroom.

Paulette also enjoyed collecting portraits of slaves living on master's plantation. One was a picture of four little slave boys sitting on a log chewing on what we always presumed were tobacco leaves. Two of the little boys sat smiling for the camera while the other two looked abused and abandoned. The boys with bare chests also bore blank looks on their faces and wore shredded pants, which were clearly hand-me-downs, cut off just below the knees and used as shorts. Their exposed legs were severely battered, riddled with large boils and insect bites of some sort. The shirtless two didn't have shoes on. Their feet appeared decrepit and weather beaten, whereas the other two boys wore shoes. The boys wearing shirts also bore large smiles sprawled across their faces. My Boo and I spent a lot of time speculating as to why they looked so happy. Were they showing gratitude for having the privilege of owning over-sized leather shoes to cover up their tattered feet? Or was it because they wore pants that somewhat fit, hanging from their shoulders by a single suspender? Or were the boys just ecstatic from beating the other two boys in a game of kick-the-can? I remembered how much of an impact this picture made on Paulette as she walked by it daily. At times I caught her staring endlessly at the little boys' feet, obviously torn and severely moved by their besieged experience.

This picture allowed Paulette and me to convey our own personal feelings and viewpoints respectfully to each other. Paulette was from a black aristocratic family and reared with private schools and private tutors, where I was raised in The Town's public school system during the time when teachers didn't flunk you. Instead, they moved you from grade to grade in order to appease themselves; *no teacher wanted to deal with my black, rambunctious ass two years in a row.*

At times when we had small arguments over whether or not I could leave the house to run the streets with my homeboys, she would find me rocking in the black rocking chair Mr. Jenkins made for his daughter when she was pregnant, resting my eyes on this picture of the four little slave boys. The picture worked better than a marriage therapist for me. I knew Paulette wanted me to stay home, not because she didn't trust me, but because she wanted me to comfort her and our daughter. While gazing at the portrait we felt immediately bound together, as if we've been married for sixty-five years. We spent hours on end conversing and philosophizing as we tried to conclude presumptuously, why the pairs of slave boys were so outwardly dissimilar.

When there was a camera around, Paulette was in front of it. She loved to have her picture taken. Everyone around her knew she was photogenic. No matter what she wore or how bad the lighting was, her face was a gift to the lens. When Riri was big enough to say "cheese", she too became a favorite for the slew of aunts, uncles, cousins, and grandparents who made up the family paparazzi. Although I was supposed to be cleaning, I spent the next several hours laughing and crying while staring at our family portraits that lined our apartment walls. Most of the captured memories were pictures of Paulette and our daughter. I didn't realize until then that I was absent in most of the pictures.

I did however come across one family portrait taken by this dude who I knew from high school who claimed he was a photographer. He took our money and made us wait almost three months before we could get our pictures back from him. In it, our family was dressed in all white linen. We took four pictures in the same attire with three different poses. One was the traditional family portrait of the three of us, Paulette and me sitting close together while she held Riesha. In another portrait I held Riesha while Paulette stood next to the two of us. I preferred the one with the two of us staring adoringly at our newborn baby girl. Paulette's favorite was the picture of the two of us shirtless, separated by Riesha's naked body. Riesha was positioned so that her naked body shielded Paulette's breasts as I held the two of them as close as I could without suffocating our child.

We also had one family portrait with the Jenkinses. The picture was taken atop of the Seattle Space Needle on Riri's first birthday. A memorable day, cloudy as ever; it had rained nonstop for three weeks straight. We ate at the restaurant on top of the Needle as it spun around in slow motion. After we finished eating, Paulette said she wasn't feeling well and threw up everything she had just eaten under the table where we were sitting. I had just purchased a fresh pair of white Reeboks and Mr. Jenkins wore a pair of camel Stacy Adams. Both of us looked down at our shoes before tending to Paulette. Mrs. Jenkins noticed and commented, "You two Negros are more worried about y'all's shoes than my baby girl. Y'all should be ashamed of yourselves!"

One wall in our bedroom was the obituary wall, dedicated to those that had passed on, fallen ghetto angels, whose lives were taken way too early by gang violence or from police brutality. The obituary wall also had newspaper articles of some of my homeboys who received double and triple life sentences. Some were justified; others were not. I ended up late for work on numerous occasions because I got caught up in the moment staring at each noteworthy obituary or newspaper article. My focus was captivated on the stories of each victim of street crimes.

I reminisced about the good times and the bad times that I shared with most of the victims. The simple times playing basketball in the rain for hours in Payless boots. Or the time Harold Brown and I got caught stealing penny fish candies from Mr. Lee's corner store; I got away where as HB got caught, pulled by the earlobe as Mr. Lee squeezed so hard HB had a permanent bruise that was still visible in his casket fourteen years later. Or what about the time when Tommy Seal and I ran from pimps every Friday night after harassing their whores as they turned tricks on 14th Street Northwest.

Most if not all of the men and women on the obituary wall were victims of the gangbanging era. A harsh time, an unforgettable era that has slowed down, yet never ended. A time when people only spoke to folks if someone spoke to them first. A time when young boys and girls started selling crack to their mothers and fathers, thinking it was payback time for being mistreated throughout the years. A time when young boys tried to hide being a drug dealer from their girlfriends because their girlfriends would become their number one customer. A time when all black men who wore black hooded sweaters draped over their heads were publicly harassed and treated like villains and second-class citizens.

Now I will have to add Paulette to this wall. Thinking about where I was going to put her obituary made me fall to my knees again, crying uncontrollably. I cried out, "Who killed my baby's momma? Why did she have to be killed, dear Lord? Why?" Unprompted outbursts of weeping melodies beckoned from my loins as I continued to gaze at the memorable moments caught on camera. Infinite tears strolled swiftly down my cheek, forming puddles large enough to make recycled water at my feet.

A hard knock at my door interrupted me. I could tell the knock was a practiced knock, that of a police officer or that of someone coming to serve me papers. The detective said he was going to return with a search warrant, and he did. "Here we go!" I said to myself. After wiping the tears from my face, I gazed outside through the blinds and saw the detective waving what appeared to be a search warrant. I looked further down to see two news vans with high antennas parked comfortably in front of my building. The newscasters stood next to their cameraman watching patiently for something to pop off at my doorstep. "Jesus Christ Lord, have mercy on me!" I wasn't ready for all of this. The entire South Sound was thinking that I killed my baby's momma. I just couldn't believe what I was going through. Me, an outcast of my own community! Damn, damn, damn!

"Mr. Brandon Lewis! I am the chief of police and we have a warrant to search your apartment. Please open up or we will have Mr. Foster open the door for us!" Again I looked out through the blinds and noticed apartment dwellers out in full force to witness the goings-on of a thug being harassed, tried, and convicted for the murder of the mother of my child and for kidnapping my precious daughter.

A pinch on my shoulder followed by, "Open the fucking door, Ceeze, immediately!" convinced me to straighten up. I took the pinch as a sign from Paulette to follow her command.

When I opened the door, the chief greeted me by slamming the warrant against my chest and informing me, "Stay the fuck out of our way Mr. Lewis!" Ten people in suits and others wearing police uniforms bombarded my apartment, pushing me to the side as if I was a spectator. What was the chief doing at my door? I was blown for a moment, ready to kurk-out on any one of the suits who were invading my home. But now wasn't the time; I needed to keep my cool. I knew they weren't going to find anything here.

Without thinking, I left on my own accord and I went to a private place where spectators and media moguls wouldn't think to look, in the laundry room. We weed-heads referred to the laundry room as the smoke-out room, that is, a place where weed smokers who weren't allowed to smoke at home, smoked in private among other weed smokers. This was a place where we got our smoke-on when it was raining too hard to smoke outside. Even if you didn't smoke weed, but smoked cigarettes, the smoke-out room was for you as well. Those who needed a dry, quiet, safe place to smoke whatever they were smoking, could smoke it here.

The laundry room is where I was among people who I felt the most comfortable to be around, a place where I could find people of various ethnicities smoking on some of that bubonic kronic — people who were considered outcasts, who could go unseen and not be missed. Stick-up kids who snatched purses and broke into houses to obtain stolen property to make money to pay rent and buy school clothes for their kids — these were the guys who had bullet holes and tattoos, the ones who sold dope to purchase matching Jordans for their entire family. I referred to these dudes as my blunt homeys, the ones I could rely on for some of that good kronell to smoke on when I was short. The ones that would lend me fifty bucks so I could double up real quick so I could buy a new Dolce and Gabbana handbag for my Boo on her birthday.

    I was hoping somebody was down there smoking on something. The way I felt after watching the police bombard my apartment, I wouldn't have cared if I stumbled on a wet PCP stick. I was willing to take a ride on that love boat (weed dipped in LSC) to have an excuse to kurk-out on the hook up in my apartment.

    Damn! No smoke in the air just smells of lavender and ocean breeze laundry detergent filtering about liberally. The laundry room was vacant and calm. I felt complacent there, unchanged. The only movement around me came from globs of lint flowing freely across the laundry room floor. The police sirens and the news vans must have spooked everyone. In a form of withdrawal, my symptoms arose quickly because no smoke had touched my lungs in over twenty-four hours. I became overtly anxious and began looking underneath all of the washers and dryers for a cigarette or a corner of a blunt to choke on. I know I said I wasn't going to smoke anymore, except I needed something to take the edge off the pain I was experiencing knowing that the hook was seconds away from coming downstairs to take me to jail.

    My body was sending out S.O.S signals for someone to come and save me with a blunt to choke on and an ice cold Blue Bull to sip on. I was dehydrated and couldn't remember the last time I had some water or juice to drink. I was stuck on the reality; my girls were gone. I felt light on my feet with a kind-of hollow emptiness on the inside. I put my hand out in front of me to see if I was shaking, and indeed I was. I went to the vending machine and kicked the machine until a little kid's box of grape juice fell out the bottom. I knew I was being rebellious when I heard Paulette tell me not to do such a thing, adding, "God, don't like ugly, Mr. Ceeze!"

I forced myself to remember how to inhale and exhale in a timely manner by placing something up to my lips to synchronize my breathing. I closed my eyes and told myself to relax. I inhaled deeply while using Paulette's chewed up pencil that I had in my back pocket to simulate a cigarette. I pretended the pencil was a freshly sparked blunt touching my lips first before anyone had a chance to wet it up with their saliva. For the next several seconds, I repeated this simulation of a smoke session until I began breathing on my own again. If I could just make it until tomorrow without smoking on anything I would be able to quit for good.

I prayed that I make it out of this stage without someone showing up at my house with a real blunt or Newport cigarette. I was what you would consider a late stage weed smoker, which meant I had to smoke a lot of weed in one setting in order to get high. To make matters worse, when I couldn't find someone to smoke with, I smoked by myself, leaving me feeling as if I was the dreaded crack head hiding his addiction from the world and specifically his family. Smoking alone signified I was dependent on marijuana, no longer just an abuser who smoked to obtain euphoria. The dependent stage suggested I smoked weed to deal with the agony of feeling defeated and depleted; the pain associated to withdrawal.

I went ham in the laundry room trying to find something to smoke. We normally respected each others private hiding spots, never smoking somebody else's weed. However I was desperately trying to get high, which meant if I did find their weed I would replace it the very first chance I get. The six-by-five foot room reminded me of a jail cell, which I might be in for the rest of my life. The thought of being down for hours in a room the size of the laundry room for the rest of my life instigated a riot within my own flesh.

It was time for me to face the music. I told myself I wasn't going to hide out like some scared little boy while the punk police planted evidence in my apartment. I was determined not to become another statistic. Papa Duke's face appeared in my head informing me, "Come-on-now, Brandon we don't have time for you to wait on someone to pat you on your back to let you know it's gonna be okay, Booboo. You're not a child anymore, son. Pick your lip up off the ground before you trip over it. Your woman is dead, boy! It's time to stop thinking about you. You don't have time to mourn right now. You can mourn after we find the killer. They are trying to pin the murder on you, boy! You better get your ass up them stairs right now! Get your ass upstairs, boy! And I mean it, damn it! Right now!"

The newscaster from Fox, Ms. Tina Lee noticed me as I was exiting the laundry room. "You're Brandon Lewis?"

Here we go again! I said to myself as she tried to seduce her way into my life. Should I answer her or should I ignore her? Her nickname is "the ear hustler". I knew that she had a knack for keeping her ear to the ground and she's from the hood. Her parents owned two convenience stores right in the middle of Ridgetop. She grew up around all black folks and it showed.

Though she is well accepted in mainstream America, she is also capable of finding out what's really going on in the hood. *I am going to steal this opportunity. She has a large following. People tune into her newscast just to get the 411.* The first thing out of my mouth was, "I had nothing to do with her death and yes, I'm Ceeze Green."

The chief was determined to find me guilty. Who could I cry to? My cousin Tatiana was usually my go-to person; nevertheless, I already knew she wasn't going to come anywhere near the apartment while all of the police and TV crews were parked out front.

"Would you like to talk about the death of your baby's mother?" asked Tina Lee.

"You know what, I would like to talk to you, but right now is not the time. I need to go upstairs and make sure that the police don't plant any evidence in my apartment." I then asked, "Do you have a card on you?" Tina reached in her back pocket for a card and handed it to me. I took the card and was heading back toward the apartment when it dawned on me; I could use her to help prove me innocence.

"If you're not busy you could do me a huge favor!"

"What is it?" replied Ms. Lee. I need you to follow me to my apartment and interview me while the police are going through my family's personal belongings!" She looked at me with the sincere camera-ready grin that she was known to use so eloquently right before making a mockery out of the person who she was confronting. She agreed apathetically to escort me into the apartment to have my back.

As we entered the apartment, we caught the attention of Mr. Chief Friendly and his honoree host, the Mayor of The Town, Ms. Juanita Gonzales. The mayor and Ms. Lee's eyes connected, and immediately the mayor whispered something to the chief. A moment later, the chief pointed at Tina and said to his officers, "That bitch can't be in here!"

"This is my apartment and I can have anybody in here that I want!" I announced.

The chief looked at me as if I lost my mind speaking to him in that tone. I didn't stunt his badge nor did his somewhat high-ranking authoritative position intimidate me. I knew that he walked and shit just like I did. I also knew that he was as crooked as One-handed Willie, the biggest con artist from the Ridgetop area.

I owe it all to Paulette for helping me get clean, which cleared the cobwebs out of my eyes. Before I met Paulette, I feared any run-ins with the police. Paulette hated that. Every time a police officer approached me, my whole demeanor changed. I used an entirely different vernacular handed down from my cousin who taught me how to interact with police officers when stopped, harassed, or pulled over. "Yes sir, Mr. Officer. No sir, Mr. Officer. Have a nice day, Mr. Officer!" My cousin Billie also informed me that I wasn't to belittle myself when approached by the hook either, that our family had survived over the years using respectable verbiage to keep us out of jail, b*etter yet alive*. This is the conundrum we faced as black men.

My cousin went on to explain that at times many a black man respected officers more than we respected each other. Why would I pay more respect to a man who felt he was placed on earth to rule over me than I paid to a grown man who resembled me, but who was simply wearing a different color clothing? That is the question that always riddled my mind after being confronted by The Man.

The truth is, deep down inside I feared the police. Grave conditioning has been passed down from my ancestors who ultimately feared being held captive by Mr. Slavemaster and his band of slave drivers, i.e. the sheriff. Even while I walked around my apartment poking my chest out at the hook while they searched for my gun and searched for a perfect place to plant incriminating evidence against me, my twisted mind feared their every move. As sinister and mind boggling as it may seem, it wasn't that I was afraid of a man; it was more or less I feared that man's true conviction. Was it to unlawfully hang a crime against me, or did it pertain to helping me during trying times? I chose the latter. This was hard to accept because many people who could afford a good defense attorney wouldn't be worried about that at all. I knew that the judicial system was designed to keep the black man out of jail. The cops are known for hanging brothas around my way, arresting and harassing us. In fact, it became the norm over time.

The chief was determined to pin the murder on me to show the law-abiding citizens of The Town that he was tough on domestic violence. He was trying to use me as a pawn to help him out of the sticky situation he was having in his personal and professional life. Tina was responsible for bringing to light the complaints against the chief and the department. His own wife came forward and said he beat her on several occasions, and when she called the police, the incident was swept underneath the rug. The chief denied all allegations and needed to prove to the community that he was a man who didn't tolerate crimes against women.

I told the cameraman that if he wanted to interview me that he must keep the camera rolling at all times. He took his eye off the camera lens for a split second and whispered to me, "I'll keep it on, my brother."

I had forgotten how badly I had messed up our apartment previously when I zoned out before the police arrived. Though I had thrown around a few vases, I didn't think it looked as bad as this when I left. Now the apartment looked like someone had ransacked the entire place. Every cabinet door was open; all of the dresser drawers were pulled out, while all of our clothing was strewn across the entire apartment flooring. The police were walking all over our clothes with their dirty shoes with no regard.

Knowing Ms. Tina's in-your-face style of newscast, once the police saw the camera they became attentive. But for some reason she was acting all brand new at broadcasting. I thought she would have been more outspoken, tougher on the police, and wear her press badge around like she had special privileges to be here. I thought she would have used the Fifth Amendment just like press and journalists used on Court TV to protect my rights and hers. Yet she had nothing to say.

I plopped down on the couch and began reading the lonely *Vibe* magazine that survived the entire throwaway cleaning sprees that Paulette went through every Saturday morning. That's one thing about Paulette; she was not a pack rat. She threw away everything that neither one of us had touched since the last time she cleaned. While looking at the pictures, I posed the question to Tina, "So you wanted to ask me some questions?"

"Yes, but its kind of strange being in your apartment while the police are searching for the murder weapon!"

"I didn't kill Paulette. They won't find anything here unless they put it here. Can I give you a call first thing tomorrow?" I asked the city Asian girl.

"Call me at the break of sunlight and I will meet you," said Tina with a city twang.

As she handed me another business card, I said with an overly anxious but bold look on my face, "Are you familiar with Browns?"

"Yes, my mom and dad used to own the corner store across the street. Do you want to meet there tomorrow?"

I didn't want to make small talk with her, although she smiled at me waiting for a reciprocated smile. I didn't have time for games. What I really wanted was for her to take me seriously. Falling for a cute face with a big smile, tactics that she used to persuade folk into telling her things they wouldn't tell others, wasn't going to work on me, though I still wanted her to be the first to hear my side of the story.

"Ya, we can meet there tomorrow, but I will have to get back to you on what time I can meet you."

Once Ms. Tina was out of the apartment, the chief yelled, "Okay gentlemen, you have about fifteen minutes left to find me the murder weapon! Fifteen minutes is all we got, now please somebody find me that murder weapon?"

13
Sipping on some Siz-zyrup

I SLIPPED INTO A DEEP DEPRESSION. I couldn't sleep; instead I took naps that were supposed to provide a moment of silence, which I referred to as *informal meditation*. Theoretically, I lay in my bed with my eyes wide shut. This is how I've always slept when my life felt empty and when I felt alone or betrayed, let down by those who said they'd never leave me.

The last time I felt this empty was when my parents passed away, forcing me to my bed for a week. I pissed in a pickle jar, too depressed to get out of bed. The only time I got out was when I had to go number two and refill my water jug from the kitchen. They too said they would never leave me. When I woke from that deep slumber, I felt like a simpleton, and not holistic as if I was only worth three-fourths of a mule. I sensed I was vulnerable too, as if anyone could come up to me and knock me the fuck out which made me feel like a punk.

Seemingly I was feeble-minded after my mother passed away. To keep from going quietly insane, I convinced myself that the reason I couldn't sleep was due to a wandering mind. I was simply *meditating*. I spent endless hours in bed drifting to places where time didn't exist.

It wasn't until after years of losing uncompromised moments of time, I was finally able to get a good night sleep — when I met Paulette. Unfortunately, whenever she was away from me for longer than twenty-four hours, the wandering returned. I lost sleep until she returned to my side.

To anyone looking in on me in those days, I looked and acted like Gangster Crankster high on methamphetamines. I stayed up for hours peeping out the window to see if I could spot her return. I was lost and acted erratic. I didn't eat or take a shower; nor did I change my clothes or brush my teeth. I became desolate *and* depressed, the worst combination. To deal with the desolation of feeling abandoned, I self-medicated. I used marijuana and malt liquor to hide the pain in my body and confusion in my mind.

The bad part about smoking weed to self medicate was when I mumbled random thoughts and talked to myself, out loud. Paulette used to ask me, "Ceeze, who are you talking to?" I'd play it off by informing her I was writing a rap song.

In those days, I used the malt liquor to even out the weed that, at the time, I thought relaxed me. I couldn't drink beer or smoke weed without a Newport to keep down the anxiety. The marijuana in my system helped me sleep, which made my wandering mind decrease slowly as the THC (Tetrahydrocannabinol) from the weed kicked in. But all of this was temporary, because as the medication wore off, both the weed and the alcohol increased my anxiety.

Then I was introduced to the purple stuff better known in my culture as the Siz-zyrup. After I drank it the first time it became my only medicine I used to cope with my depression. The purple stuff got rid of the upheaval of feeling alone or deceived.

The Siz-zyrup is a mixture of codeine cough syrup mixed with a pint of Hennessey, a stimulus that momentarily coerced my brain into believing everything was going to be all right. While high off of this deadly cocktail, I became oblivious to reality. Nothing behind me or beside me was important anymore. I focused only on what caught my attention, though my attention span was minimal. If you weren't talking to me about purchasing a stolen item from the trunk of my car or smoking some weed with me, I wasn't interested. I transformed into the dreaded thug and wannabe pimp that I tried endlessly to erase from my image.

No longer did I use proper English. I spoke in Pig Latin, using the *isimz's* and *kisimz's*. Downright dirty hustlers who didn't want anyone outside of their circle to understand what was being translated used this form of communication. If you spoke fluent Pig Latin, you were placed high on an invisible pedestal, seen, heard and understood by triple OG's (Original Gangsters from LA).

After a night of drinking the Siz-zyrup, the codeine floating threw my nervous system made me experience out-of-body experiences. In many cases I took on the characters I was trying to emulate. I became Big Pimpin, trying to see if every girl I spoke to was feeble minded enough to be sold into modern day slavery. I convinced every dope dealer I spoke to, meet up with me later, the kind of meet-up where I made my money.

The day after sipping on some Siz-zyrup, my body felt like it was stuck half way out of a constipated sweaty elephant's ass. My head felt like someone stuck live leeches inside my ears. My eyeballs looked as if they were full of red cobwebs with baby fruit flies scurrying about for dear life. My throat felt like I had spent the entire night sucking on a veteran prostitute's rough Achilles heel for pure enjoyment after she made several attempts to get rid of the dried up skin by soaking her feet in hot mustard and yellow cornmeal.

During the night I became a victim within my own horror movie, unable to control the level of terror that had highjacked my mind. The dreams were comprised of zombies and monsters trying to befriend me just to slowly torture me and then finally kill me. Fearing evil and fearing death momentarily became my only option.

I soon learned that once I was able to arise from the Siz-zyrup hangover induced psychosis, my problems hadn't disappeared at all and, in fact, materialized with great vengeance. I realized that the trickery masked within the stuff didn't help a damn thing. I knew it was going to be tough trying to fool myself into believing I would be able to get some sleep without Paulette and Riri by my side. I was trying to be good, but after the bouts of sleep deprivation, the hood remedy of drinking Siz-zyrup was beginning to take over my thoughts.

In a spurt of reality thinking, I didn't want Riesha to come home and find me lying on the couch, unable to get up to fix her something to eat, or to comb her hair, or give her a bath. It didn't take long to believe I must keep myself sober so that I could raise my child. *I must stay sober, I must stay sober, and I must stay sober. I must stay strong because I am convinced that Daddy's Little Girl would return home soon.*

My mother had convinced me that as long as I relied on substances to make me feel good about being me, I would never get better. She further convinced me that I would have to give myself unto the Lord. "Without God by my side, whatever I set out to do on my own will tumble and fall, but if I place God at the forefront of all my decisions, what I set out to accomplish will prosper and grow."

My father urged me to take all my problems to God, on my knees. So that is what I did. I took to my knees the concerns I had on my mind. After asking God to forgive me for all of my sins, I asked God to throw all of my past indiscretions into the sea of forgiveness. I asked God to keep me safe and sane. I prayed to God, asking Him to protect me with the blood of Jesus Christ who died on the cross for my sins. I asked God to protect my Baby Booboo Riesha, and return her to me unscathed. I prayed for the lost souls who took the life of my Paulette and snatched my daughter. I asked God to bring them to justice quickly so my family could go back to living. I asked God to keep me out of court, jail, and prison. I asked God to help me get some good sleep, to be ready when Riesha returned.

Three minutes after rising from my knees, I laid my head on the pillow Paulette deemed hers. I breathed in deeply the smell left behind from her hair and scarf, the fragrance of apricots and coconut grease infused with the smell of Riesha's spilled rice milk. The fragrances of my two women took me into a deep sleep faster than air exiting four flat tires. I slept throughout the night undisturbed, and seemingly content with my reality.

14
The Dope Spot

"Yo, Brandon, open up; it's an emergency. It's me Karen, your neighbor! From across the street!"

I was in the middle of a dream when I heard someone knocking. I presumed it was the police. I dreamed I approached the door and looked out the peephole to find the chief of police waving a plastic bag with the gun I threw in the blackberry bushes behind my apartment. In his other hand, he held a warrant for my arrest. The chief was laughing, along with other members of the TPD as he repeated, over and over again, "Hay-ah Mr. Brandon Lewis, we know you're in there! We need you to come down to the station to answer some questions about your baby's mother."

The knocking had awakened me from a haunting dream that had plagued me for several hours. Still half asleep, I turned towards the wall that was riddled with lime green *Post-it* stickers from Paulette. She used the green stickers, thinking that since it was my favorite color, I would pay more attention to what she wrote on them. The stickers were reminders for me to take care of my fatherly duties: take out the garbage, take out something for dinner, pay the cable bill, make a doctor appointment for Baby Riri and separate the clothes. She laid them out the day before she was murdered.

I grabbed the one sticker that I hadn't tended to: "Pay the cell phone bill." I searched for the due date on the bill taped to the wall. "Damn, damn, damn! I didn't pay the phone bill!" Paulette's handwriting reminded me of the little girl she had stuck inside of her. Her large lettering writing style mimicked that of a fourth grader who just figured out how to write cursive. All of her letters were capitalized with a swivel and flower on the tip of each letter. This made me smile even more. After seeing the sticky note, I promised to never forget to pay the cell phone bill again. I glanced over at the clock on the wall; it read three a.m. "Where did the night go?"

I let out a chuckle as I grabbed my head with both hands, scratching and laughing, "It has to get better, dear Lord; it has to get better!" I felt like I had fallen asleep only an hour ago. An instant prayer message went out to the Lord wishing, praying, and hoping that whoever was knocking at my door had come to help me, not to break me. Before placing my feet on solid ground, I asked the Lord to protect me with the blood that Jesus Christ shed on the cross for our sins. Then I quickly hopped to my feet, as if I didn't have anything troubling me, only curious to find out who was bold enough to knock on my door at three o'clock in the morning.

Out of habit, I headed towards my closet to grab my pistol, but remembered two things; I had already tossed it behind the apartment, and I just asked the Lord to protect me. "You don't need a gun, my son!"

As I approached the front door the knocking persisted, yet the knock didn't carry any weight behind it — thank God. I was relieved knowing whoever was knocking, it wasn't the police; the police always knocked hard as hell, as if rule number two in the police academy handbook suggested *you must pound on the front door extremely hard.*

I went to the window to see who was responsible for waking me up from the nightmarish unfathomable dream I was trapped in. I found a peephole in the little section where three strings connected to each blind, where I could see who was knocking at my door without being noticed. Sho-nuff! It was Karen, the crazy crack-head from across the way.

What the hell does this lady want at damn near four in the morning? I assumed she was a smoker who wanted either some crack or to borrow an egg, some milk or toilet paper. I regretted befriending her earlier, but I knew now she would bug me for all kinds of shit. I opened the door, still dazed. "What you want, woman? It's damn near four o'clock in the morning?"

A cigarette was stuck between two fingers, and smoke came from her mouth as she leaned forward and whispered, "I thought you might wanna know that the police are behind your building with dogs and flashlights. You didn't tell the police I showed you how to turn the water main back on, did you?"

I didn't even answer her. Instead, I ran through my apartment to the kitchen. Once I was near the back porch, I dropped down to my knees and slowly crawled to the kitchen window where I could get a peek of the field through the window over the sink. To my dismay, there they were, about half a dozen police behind my building with dogs and flashlights, just like Ms. Karen said. I was stuck there for a moment with my back up against the kitchen pantry door, not knowing what my next move should be. I assumed that the police were watching my front door too and knew Ms. Karen had been knocking for quite some time now.

I crawled back towards Ms. Karen who had closed the door after letting herself in. Using my inside voice, I whispered, "Did you see any police out front?"

"No, they're all out back. But I think you'll be safer at my place."

My head lowered. I didn't want to go to this lady's house. But if she had a car for me to get away in, that would entice me to go. I asked her if she had a car.

"Ya. You could use it to get us out of here!"

What the fuck she talking about *us*? This lady is truly crazy!

"But you have to do something for me," she went on.

Was she trying to barter something out of me during this precarious moment I was facing? "What you need lady, quick? We don't have much time!"

"I need to borrow twenty bucks and some toilet paper until my check comes on the first."

"Not a problem, lady. Now, please can we go?"

Her demeanor switched from polite to *give me my money, mothafucka, right now!* She held out her palm, saying, "I need to see the money, sweetie!" Smirking, she added, "Oh and don't forget the toilet paper just in case you need to wipe your ass!"

I ran to the bathroom and tore through the junk underneath the sink and found the last roll of toilet paper. I then rushed to the bedroom to grab my shoes and my red hooded sweater so that I wouldn't look conspicuous. Because of my Crip gang affiliation, the authorities would not expect to see me wearing red. The barking dogs sounded as though they were inches away from my living room.

The notion of dogs on the hot trail of my gun made me contemplate ways I could throw off my scent once they started to hunt me down. During my short stint as a driver for the LA Boys, I was shown how to throw off the scent of police dogs. This involved wrapping little mustard packages around bricks of cocaine and pounds of weed. I pondered the notion of rubbing mustard all over my body. I also pondered using an onion, like many slaves used to successfully escape enslavement.

After grabbing some cash to pay Ms. Karen, I crawled on all fours back to the kitchen where I quickly tore through the fridge looking for onions and mustard. We were out of white onions, which were the strongest. I remembered Paulette didn't buy any the last time we went shopping because they weren't on sale. She did, however, buy a bag of small yellow onions. I grabbed the remaining three, sat on my knees and stuffed one in each back pocket and one in the front pocket. Next, I started looking for the mustard. I remembered I had walked out of Uncle Tom's Juke Joint a couple weeks ago with a bottle of my favorite Heinz mustard. Not because I needed some mustard for the house, but just in case these fools wanted to try me after arguing over a pool game. I was going to use the bottle upside this biker's head if he stepped one foot outside of the main entrance of the building.

    I reminisced briefly about that evening, thanking God for keeping that man in the bar. "Ain't no telling what might have happened, dear Lord. Thank you Jesus!" I found the bottle of mustard in the lazy-Susan pantry, but it was empty. "I can't win for losing!" I ran through most of the cabinets that I could reach, still on my knees. I came across some small packages of mustard in the junk drawer next to the fridge, something I remembered grabbing at the Ethnic Festival last week to spread on the corn dogs I bought for my Riesha and Paulette. "Score!" I stuffed a handful of mustard packages in my front pants pockets and the remaining handful in my right back pocket.

    Ms. Karen and I bolted out of the apartment in the opposite direction of the police cars. I felt as if I was a runaway slave and Ms. Karen was an indentured servant trying to escape enslavement from Master William's plantation. Carlos, the blond blue-eyed devil from Cuba who lived downstairs, spotted us tiptoeing around the last corridor to our freedom. I referred to him as a devil because he could not be trusted. He looked in our direction and said to me in his raspy, hoarse Spanish-accented voice, "Run-nigga-run!"

    I never liked his punk ass. This wasn't the time to joke with me; I was extremely vulnerable and would like to have snapped his fucking neck off for assuming he could use the n-word in my presence, but I didn't have time to deal with his racist ass. Carlos told grandiose stories about how the blood flowing through his body was the blood of slave drivers. He claimed to be a descendant of a secret white-skinned Cuban society whose grandparents told stories of trading niggers for the *Bacardi* root that produced rum.

The parking lot to Ms. Karen's apartment was flooded with at least two feet of run-off water. A flood wasn't abnormal for her complex because of the fresh water stream that ran behind her back porch. Whenever it rained non-stop for more than three days, the entire grounds of the apartment building flooded. Her parking lot became a metaphor for my freedom. And just like a runaway slave, the only thing I had to do was cross the Ohio River to be free.

I sent the white girl, Karen, ahead to make sure there weren't any slave drivers waiting around the edge of the plantation to capture me. If the police found me, I would be accosted, tied and shackled to a tree for a public flogging. Once the police find my gun, I would be cooked, because the gun was the same caliber as the one used to kill Paulette. In order to solve the case, authorities would merely produce evidence to convince the forensic team and the prosecutors that the gun found was indeed used to kill Paulette.

I knew this might be my only chance to remain free. I dashed across the parking lot that resembled a riverbank. "Run Brandon, run! Hurry!" yelled Ms. Karen, loud enough for watchful ears like Carlos' to hear. As I made my way towards her building, I heard echoes of dogs barking and voices responding to calls from police scanners and radios. By the time I reached her apartment door, my whole lower body was soaking wet. The mustard and onions made me smell like a runaway slave that hadn't washed in several months.

"Goddamn Brandon, why do you smell like garlic?" asked Ms. Karen with an ungodly look on her face. The smell was so bad she covered her nose as she reluctantly asked me to come in.

Once inside, I stood momentarily pulling out the mustard packages and onions from my pants pockets. I placed them neatly on the "Welcome" doormat. "These will keep the dogs from finding my scent!"

"How do you know that, Brandon?" asked Karen.

"Didn't you ever watch 'Roots' and 'COPS', girl?" We both smiled for just a moment.

"Have a seat, Brandon, or do you want me to call you, Ceeze?" I was too taken back at the condition of her apartment to respond to her question. Although I was covered with a raunchy odor, I was immediately hit with the stench of stale cigars, ground black pepper, cayenne pepper, and vomit. How could she bring herself to say I smelled if her apartment smelled like a ferocious toxic waste bubble? As I began making my way towards the sitting area, I couldn't help but notice exposed pebbles of rock and concrete all over the floor. I couldn't tell whether or not the floor was once linoleum or gravel. Dirt and cement seeped through the floorboards, which blended directly into the broken up sidewalk just outside of the doorway. Both the sidewalk and her foyer looked as if the maintenance man had been fired midway between fixing both.

"Whatever you want to call me is fine." Right now wasn't the time to be picky. "You could call me Blood for all I care right about now."

"Blood! I thought they called you Ceeze because you're a Crip?" She didn't know I was being facetious. I really didn't have the time to explain the sarcasm to her. *Oh-my-goodness! Poor Ms. Karen.* All of the furniture in the apartment looked like it was either from the dumpster out back or was donated from the church down the street. For pictures or artwork, she used newspaper clippings and cut out magazine pictures still attached to the articles, all poorly glued to homemade picture frames made out of Popsicle sticks. Within the picture frames were clippings of old Elvis and Marilyn Monroe.

"What you know about Elvis, girl?"

"I know more than what you think." She winked and smiled at me, showcasing a dangling old open-faced gold tooth, no longer white, not even yellow, but grey.

Again "Oh my goodness" crept from underneath my lips.

"What you mumbling about over there, Mr. Ceeze?" She must have earned the ear-hustler award last year because I was talking so low to myself that I could barely hear what I was saying.

"Oh, I was just saying how pretty Marilyn Monroe was when she was young; that's all!" I knew what she was intending for me to get from that comment, as if I would be interested in finding out what else she knew. I played it off as if I didn't even hear her say anything.

"I'm just kidding, Brandon. I collect anything with Elvis or Marilyn on it. Usually I get the stuff from thrift stores and antique stores." Her apartment smelled like she smoked at least three packs of cigarettes a day. There was an ashtray built into the arm of the Lazy Boy chair which had the entire cushion torn off, exposing the springs and leftover seat cushion sponge. Next to the chair sat two big lamps with crystal-like ashtrays as the base. Both were filled to the top with old chewed up cigars and cigarette buds. Every cigarette was smoked all the way down to the filter and every cigar was chewed all the way down to the very end. The carpet throughout her apartment was so filthy that the fibers let off an oceanic aroma only akin to a sanitation landfill buried underneath Puget Sound. My shoes protected my feet from the fungus growing within the large black puddles of beer and urine. I couldn't tell whether or not the brown spots all over the carpet were cat poop or human dung. Whichever the case, maybe the spots were toxic.

As I walked further into the apartment, I couldn't help but notice small tubs of curetting cottage cheese with roach butts sticking out. Disgusting. Blocking the entrance to the hallway sat nine beer bottles arranged like bowling pins. The bottles disgorged the stench of urine from beneath the foam floating atop. At least two cases of *Miller Lite* beer cans were mixed in between twenty or so beer bottles. On the window sills sat half empty Budweiser beer bottles also filled to the rim with cigarette buds.

More half-empty beer bottles sat next to a few rows of folding chairs. A small section of the living room resembled a makeshift stage. The chairs were set up right in front of a queen size mattress. It was evident to me that a prostitute or a crack-head set up shop in Ms. Karen's lonely crusty apartment to do strip-tease shows and to turn tricks. The dancers used the chairs to give their patrons lap dances. I could smell the unpleasant odor of fish and pickles rising from the bed, which was surely infested with bed bugs and lice. The distinctive odor arising from the bed without a doubt came from a recent rendezvous between a ratchet prostitute and an unwashed trucker, their body fluids colliding to form the raunchy smell of saliva, salmon, and boiling muskrat.

I shook my head for the next several minutes, as I took baby steps over used condoms and needles with blood still inside. I proceeded cautiously towards the only spot where I felt safe enough to sit. On my way I thanked God for turning my life around, even though I was in a crack house. *"Thank you, Dear Lord for bringing the mother of my child into my life, for I would still be frequenting whore houses, and crack houses, and gambling spots just like this one. Dear Lord, I ask you to guide me through these trenches filled with the spirit of the Demon God where I have landed. I ask you, Dear Lord, to bring to justice those responsible for killing my baby's mother, so that I can return to being the father you have chosen me to be. In God's name I pray, amen."*

Before squatting on the soiled couch, I stood there briefly trying to convince myself that it was safe to sit down. A newspaper lay on the floor next to the couch; I picked it up pretending to read. When Karen turned her back, I dragged the newspaper over the couch to assure nothing would poke me before I sat down. But first I had to remove a plate of chicken bones that looked so old they resembled petrified wood. Then I noticed a regiment of red army ants resting on an old cinnamon bun still in the box. Looking closer, all I could see were roaches fighting for dear life, while other roaches had lost the battle to the much more powerful red ants.

"Can I use your restroom, Ms. Karen?"

"You don't have to ask. It's down the hallway, second door on the left. Do you want something to eat or drink, Mr. Brandon?"

"No thank you, Karen, I just need to use the head."

Oh-my-god! The appalling smell of the room was almost unbearable like a homeless encampment with pounds of dark brown three-day-old grownup dung in the toilet. I held my breath to keep from breathing in the disgusting odor. In the dim light my hands engulfed infectious germs as I rubbed the wall trying to locate the light switch. I finally figured out that the light switch was located in the hallway outside the door. The bathroom looked like a gas station pit stop reserved for tricks and johns, a place where prostitutes turned tricks to make twelve dollars and some change. Now I needed to wash my hands *before* using the toilet. I took one look at the sink and again, "Oh-my-god!" came bursting out of my mouth. Green mold and pinkish mildew engulfed the entire sink resembling the inside of those extra large jawbreakers that Mrs. Lee sold at the corner store, two for a dollar. On and around the faucet knobs rested green slime resembling turnip greens mixed with collards and spinach. What appeared to be snot and saliva seeped out from underneath the faucet knobs.

The toilet was atrocious too, full of rainbow froth that swirled from the top to the bottom of the bowl. By no means was I going to lift the toilet seat. Instead I relied on precision aiming as I urinated right down the center of the toilet. The scum kept growing and growing as it churned out, down and around the entire outside of the toilet. In between the bath tub and sink were three Safeway plastic bags full of empty douche bottles and empty boxes of vaginal fungus killer cream. *She's a whore! Duh! Motha-fucka! Damn, I knew it all along!* Though unfortunate, I wasn't surprised.

I had to wash my hands, but once I saw how Karen lacked cleanliness, I used what little toilet paper she had to turn on and off the water, to keep from touching the germ-infected knobs. I turned the doorknob with the corner of my shirt and left the light on. I wasn't going to touch any one of those infectious disease-carrying things. I headed back down the hallway to the same spot I originally inspected for safe seating.

"If you move to the left a little bit, you could have a clear fix on your apartment," said Karen. I moved just a few inches to the left and, to my dismay I spotted the entire TPD guarding the front door to our flat. Yet, I was more concerned about how she would know my apartment could be watched from this very spot.

"My ex used to date your wife."

What did she just say to me? Now I know this lady is crazy because I know good and damn well Paulette wouldn't have dated any person associated to this ratchet?

"I don't sit here all day watching your apartment; I am not a stalker. Didn't he work on your wife's car once?"

I didn't know what she was talking about, and if he worked on Paulette's car I would have known about it. "I think you're mistaken, lady! Are you a stalker?" I asked with a semi-smile.

"I think he worked on it once or twice after that, didn't he?"

This lady is out of her mind. "Nope, wasn't her car," I replied absently as I watched members of The Town's police department shoot tear gas through my living room window and kick my apartment door off the hinges. I sat impatiently on Ms. Karen's couch picking my nose and biting my nails, waiting for a sign that would tell me I would soon have my life back.

"You hungry?" Ms. Karen asked again.

"No!" I replied emphatically.

"Then why you biting your nails and you digging gold?" I heard her, but I was too engrossed at what was taking place across the street.

"I'm going to prison for the rest of my life!" I said, and then corrected myself. "Naw, man! They gonna make me sit on death row for ten years, then shoot poison in my veins! And watch me die slowly!" My heart began to race as I sat there on her couch.

I watched the police force as they became comfortable walking in and out of my apartment as if they were invited guests. Ever since she asked me if I was hungry I began passing hunger-gas that smelled like tacos, thinking the gas would simply blend right in with the hideous aromas around me. I was at the lowest point of my life; my spirit was poverty stricken. I became more noxious at the first sight of the chief doing an interview with three different news reporters. Ms. Asian Persuasion was not among them.

I was dumbfounded as the police and news crew continued to bombard my apartment. I felt hopeless and bruised just sitting there watching those news reporters persecute me.

"Ceeze, you're on the news right now." I couldn't see anything on her TV. She had plastic wrap over the front, which composed the black and white picture into instant color. Still, the picture was unbecoming. An old large metal antenna stretched out at least five feet, propped up on a chair facing the window for better picture quality.

Karen sat down in the rocking chair across from me and began switching channels with the remote control, never stopping on any channel for more than a split second. She had made herself some coffee and asked if I would like some. I did, although I had major concerns about her cleanliness as well as her ability to wash a cup properly and to make a good cup of joe.

In the Pacific Northwest, people offered you a cup of coffee when you entered their home, similar to the way they offered tea in England. To say no was almost an insult. "Do you like creamer? I got hazelnut and vanilla latte."

Paulette often made me run to the corner store for hazelnut in the middle of a Minneapolis winter just to satisfy her hazelnut fix. "Hazelnut is fine." I replied.

"How much sugar would you like?"

"I'm good, girlfriend. If you have hazelnut, that's all I need." Damn! In an instant I became morbidly depressed and anxious at the same time. I couldn't stop tapping my left foot and shaking my right leg. I felt unconscious and hollow, shallow and bewildered. I was mortified by the chaos taking place across the street. I feared going to jail and losing my daughter to the state and then to her grandparents, the Jenkins. *Ah hell! At least she would have a decent upbringing.*

I spotted a notepad next to a chewed-up pencil with teeth marks all over it. I wasn't too pleased about touching someone else's DNA, but I asked if she minded if I used the paper on the table.

"Go for it, Brandon. What's mine is yours."

With one eye on my apartment, I began to make a list of those who wronged me and who I had wronged in the past. The first person that came to my mind was Tommy Guns, the Columbian who worked for Columbian Charles the HCIC (Head Columbian In Charge). The HCIC was a fat smelly bastard hated by everyone in the dope game. I had robbed Tommy Guns of a few pounds of marijuana one night after he left the gambling spot in Tillicum. I had decided that I was going to take the robbery to my grave;

nobody had a clue about who robbed the Columbian. During the robbery he noticed my shoes. I wore red OG Nikes in order to throw him off and make him believe a Blood gang member robbed him. On Halloween the following year, I came across Tommy Guns in the barbershop getting a shape-up. Again I was dressed up like a rival gang member, a Halloween ritual of mine, again wearing the same red OG Nikes lent to me by my cousin, which I wore during the robbery. Guns tried to confront me while I was waiting to get a shape-up. He said he remembered my shoes and remembered my voice during the robbery, and he tried to punk me into confessing. While there in the barbershop, I took his pistol from him and whipped him with the butt of his own gun. Afterwards, Tommy uttered the words, "You robbed me." If anyone wanted me dead or wanted to harm my family, it could have been Tommy Guns.

    Just when I thought I knew who killed my Boo, I was shaken up over thoughts of Terrance Montgomery. He was a military man who I pissed off a few years back before I started dating Paulette. During my roguish, thuggish wannabe-a-pimp days, I had his soon-to-be ex-wife clean out their bank account every Father's Day (the first and fifteenth of each month). For most of the two years he was in Iraq I took advantage of his woman, using his family's money to buy meaningless items. For an entire year after he got back and found out what I was doing to his wife and his bank account, I watched him watching me. One time I caught him slipping in front of my building. He actually fell asleep in his car waiting for me to get home. I walked up close to his car and yelled out "Boo!" He jumped, hitting his head against the door panel to his SUV. I didn't stick around. Out of the blue, he called me to say he was lying low, hiding in the bushes, waiting for that special moment to kill me. The last time I spoke to GI Joe, at a Burger King, he informed me he was gonna kill me, period, and I believed him; "I'm laying low for you, nigga!"

    Could the Columbian or GI Joe have killed my Boo and kidnapped my daughter? The thoughts didn't improve my situation at all. I sank into an even deeper depression. My legs felt like they were stuffed with feathers and my head felt like it was filled with baby crabs feeding on my brain. I was in bad shape.

Ms. Karen came out of the kitchen toting what looked like a professional sniper's rifle draped over her right shoulder, a cigarette dangling from her mouth. She held a cup of coffee on a saucer at the same time. "What the fuck!" I exploded.

"Don't be frightened! If I wanted you dead, I would've never came and got you. This was my old man's gun. I thought you might need it on account of you going to find who killed your wife and all."

"How you know what I'm about to do?"

"Your paper in front of you says in big bold letters, "Who killed my Baby's Momma?"

"Put the gun away, Karen! I won't need that! Was your old man in the army?"

"He was a member of the Dominican Republic Special Forces! How did you know?" asked Ms. Karen.

"You can't own a gun like that and not know how to operate it unless you were in somebody's Special Forces. It looks like a missile launcher!" I took a sip from the Redskins coffee mug and, to my surprise, the coffee tasted great! "Damn girl, you can make some good coffee! Can you cook too?"

"Yes, I can cook: lasagna, fried gizzards, fried chicken, pepper steak, fried fish. My man stayed with me because of two things — I could cook and make money! I know how to keep a man!"

"Well, say dat den sho-da!" (*Say-dat-den* is Ebonics for "I agree".)

"Are you hungry, Ceeze? I could fry up some chicken." She had me thinking twice. By the way she kept her house, she looked like the type who wouldn't wash her hands or rinse off the chicken before cooking. I envisioned her scratching her trick box while cooking and using year-old lard to fry the chicken.

"No thank you, Ms. Karen, I don't have much of an appetite."

"It took you too long to answer, Mr. Ceeze. I can tell you're hungry. You probably ain't eaten in days."

Damn! She's right. Though I didn't have an appetite, I realized *ain't no telling when I'd be eating again, so I might as well eat.* I tried emphatically to convince myself, *I'd be all right as long as I bless my food.* I was hungrier than a broke dick dog. Three minutes in, the smell of Johnny's Seasoning Salt and grease frying filtered through the apartment deadening the ghastly smell of the seashore at my feet.

I sat tapping my leg up and down anxiously waiting for the morning news to come on the TV. Many of my neighbors began to gather in front of my apartment to watch the local television crews set up shop. From the chaos going on across the street, it was evident that my life as I knew it would never be the same. Without my old lady by my side, I began to doubt my future.

As I sat there all alone with a broken spirit, on Ms. Karen's filthy old couch, I heard a voice say unto me, "Pray up, young man. You have to stay prayed up." This stern yet gentle voice from my past brought back vivid memories of the person who was the most influential in uplifting my spirits, my grandfather. Granddaddy Brown wasn't my real granddaddy, though we were part of the same circular family from DC. He had the body of a dwarf, but stood five feet eight inches. He used his overly large hands to hold an ax to cut down trees and split wood. He wore size sixteen shoes, which made him wobble from side to side when he walked. As long as I knew him, he owned only two pairs of shoes. He wore one pair of work boots in the yard and one pair of shiny black boots for church, funerals, and weddings. His nostrils were the size of two purple plums, and his ears could be mistaken for chinchilla ear mittens.

If you asked him if he had any money, his response was always the same, "I got two pockets, don't I?" He never had less than three hundred dollars in his pants pocket at all times. Granddaddy Brown was the one responsible for showing me how to keep my money rolled up. "You see, Youngblood, you have to keep the small bills on the bottom so that when you reach in your pocket for money you know what to pull out. You don't want everyone around you to know how much money you have."

The memories of Granddaddy Brown mystically created the smell of apple tobacco burning all around me. He always had a pipe full burning. I wished he were next to me to lift me out of the rut where I had fallen. He was a quiet man who only spoke when spoken to. He used only a few good words to explain himself, never big words that had to be broken down three minutes after he used them. He could be in a room full of people conversing and philosophizing and not say one word. But when he *did* speak, he spoke powerfully, sharing words of wisdom while reciting biblical verses. The last conversation we had, he said to me, "With God on your side, who could be against you? My hope is built on nothing else but Jesus' blood and his holy righteousness, so stop pouting and take your problems to the Lord on your knees!"

Ms. Karen was smoking a tobacco pipe, the same one Granddaddy Brown used. She even smoked the same apple tobacco. When I noticed her smoking, I said, "Girl, you is country as all outdoors, ain'tcha, girl?"

"I sure am — country as lemonade and vodka on a hot Sunday morning!"

She flipped over a few pieces of fried chicken with her bare fingers and held onto the pipe with her other hand. I didn't even take the conversation any further; there just wasn't any need to do so. I was dealing with true white trash. The relationship between black folk and white trash had evolved from two groups of people fighting over land and jobs to a group of people working and living seemingly and somewhat sanely as neighbors here in the Pacific Northwest.

The shit that I was watching unfold across the street was mind-blowing in the worst way and would make the average person go quietly insane. However Ms. Karen's amusement kept my spirits up. The devil will have his way with children of God only when one is not prayed up. I needed to stay prayed up. There was just way too much doubt flowing through my body; I didn't doubt God, so something had to give. Though Karen's carpet was atrocious, nevertheless I had to take it to the Lord on my knees. *"Dear Lord, forgive me for my sins, and restore me with faith and I ask that a supernatural occurrence come over me with great vengeance. In Jesus name, amen!"* Straight and to the point!

I could hear the crackling of chicken, and with it arose the aroma of well-seasoned chicken. As crazy as it may seem, I knew that the kitchen was unsanitary, yet I knew any hungry black man wouldn't pass up fresh fried chicken. Even if the chicken was fried at a gas station or a funeral home, some cats I know will eat it. My homeboy Freddie Baxter's mother was blind, had one leg, and only three fingers on each hand, and could fry up a bird better than me. That's saying a whole lot, because I feel I am the best bird frying Negro west of the Rocky Mountains. I was looking forward to what smelled so good.

I was praying she might have washed her hands or at least used some Tabasco or some red-hot sauce to kill some of the unwanted germs. Every time I looked out the window and saw the police and the news vans along with all of the people gathering, I would lose my appetite. Swiftly thereafter, as the familiar aroma of fried chicken infiltrated my nose, my appetite recaptured its position deep, deep down south within my belly. I was raised to follow my gut instincts, but it was hard for me to decipher between gut feelings and hunger pains.

Knowing that I had made a conscious decision to eat her food, I knew something seriously was wrong with me. I concluded that I better say a good blessing over the food before ingesting infectious disease particles. *"Dear Lord, I would like to thank you for allowing me to have this deliciously smelling food to eat. I ask that you remove all germs from the food so that my body isn't harmed in any way. Amen."* I got up off the floor and sat back down on the couch.

I had the feeling I had forgotten something. *I didn't say a prayer for my girls!* I couldn't sit comfortably knowing this, so I hopped off the couch and began praying again for the safe return of my Riesha. *"I thank you for embedding memories of Paulette deep within my mind and soul. I ask that you continue to watch over Riesha and reunite us soon. Dear Lord, I ask that you bless me with the ability to find the person who killed Paulette. I ask that you make this possible so that I can get back to raising Riesha. I am not capable of being the father I need to be if I am behind bars or dead. I am also aware that an unforgiving heart is a broken empty spirit. I ask that you forgive the person responsible for killing Paulette. I ask of you to carry me forward and to continue to bless me with the ability to overcome any and all obstacles that are in my path."*

Right at that moment from beneath the couch, a large mouse came running out. I jumped up off of the floor screaming, *"What the hell, lady!"* Then the rest of the family of mice scurried across the floor in the same direction as the big one.

I had to laugh. Smiling and laughing out loud while my heart pitter-patted two miles a minute, I continued to rejoice in the name of the Lord. The mouse and its family metaphorically represented family and hope for me to be reconnected with my offspring. Ms. Karen heard me yelling and laughing, but she didn't see the tears that came out of nowhere.

"Ceeze, are you okay?"

"God is good, Karen. I'll be just fine."

One of the most important spiritual lessons that Paulette shared with me was trusting God's promise. Having faith through trying times and believing God will see me through all of this gave me hope. While sitting in a crack house I was still able to reminisce about the good times that Paulette, Riesha, and I shared together as one close-knit family. Memories of the good times and the bad times allowed me to rejoice in God's name.

"Would you like some more coffee?" said Ms. Karen as she set a large plate of crispy, golden brown wings still steaming hot on my lap. The plate was wrapped in a black kitchen towel. "I ain't got no napkins," she added. I could tell the towel was actually a kitchen hand towel on account of the flour and seasoning salt all over it, and I deemed it somewhat safe to use as a napkin. When she set the hot plate down on my lap, her hand brushed my jewels; I thought for a moment she did that on purpose but, oh well, I wasn't tripping.

Five wings sat half way over three *Eggo* waffles already buttered and smothered in thick rich syrup. One wing was just a partial wing, and it appeared as though she tore off a part for herself. Ms. Karen came back out of the kitchen chewing on it, a knife and syrup in her other hand. She placed the syrup down on the table next to me saying, "Just in case you need more syrup. Oh, I hope you don't mind, but I stole a piece of your chicken!" She smiled. The syrup was Mrs. Butterworth, the bottle made to resemble a full-figured house slave.

I asked her if she was hungry and added, "I'm not gonna eat all of this, Karen."

"Well I am hungry; can I have just one?"

Before I could hand over the same one she had already picked over, she took it off my plate. I noticed her fingernails were chewed down to the nub, and the fingers that had any nails left were brown and crusty. After seeing her nails, I momentarily contemplated handing her the entire plate, but the chicken was calling my name. Next to the chicken and waffles, lay a glob of yellow scrambled eggs, soft with cheese. She took the Redskins coffee cup into the kitchen with her and came back with it full of an orange substance, along with a spoon click-clacking around. As she walked, she spilled some of the contents all over her hand. When she handed the cup over to me, she said, "Hand me the towel." She took the towel and wiped off the cup before handing it to me. She folded the towel and placed it on my knee.

I looked in the cup and then took a sip. "Damn girl, you country!" I said once I realized what I was drinking. "I haven't had *Tang* since I was twelve, girl. Wow!"

"Oh, I almost forgot!" She ran back to the kitchen and placed something in the microwave. After I heard the chime, she came scurrying back with another coffee mug. Only this time it was the Philadelphia Eagles cup. The cup was full of grits with a slice of cheese atop, along with pepper sprinkled all over and within the mug. "Every black man likes grits right? Don't say you don't like cheesy grits, Mr. Ceeze?"

I looked closer at the grits, and she had added bits of bacon. "Damn, girl! Do you cook like this all the time?" A spontaneous gesture came over me in the form of a smile. With this much-needed smile on my face, I jokingly said to her, "I may have to come around here more often."

She held a cigarette between her index finger and her middle finger while holding a frying pan. She was shaking the skillet with a professional chef's soft touch so that the grease wouldn't escape. With one hand on her hip, Ms. Karen said in a feisty southern belle tone of voice, "I only cook like this for my man!"

No disrespect to Ms. Karen, but I wasn't in the pimping game. I could tell that she was interested in me from the start. I feel that she is a very nice lady, but we don't have anything whatsoever in common. With the family of mice in plain sight, I again blessed my food and then commenced to eat. "I would take another cup of coffee, please. You make a fine cup of joe, Ms. Lady."

Before I could ask for some hot sauce, she had already gone back to the kitchen to retrieve some and brought it back. "Is Tabasco okay?"

"Yes, thank you, Ms. Karen. You're so kind to me." I embraced each bite with the same exhilarating intensity that a child showcased at the dinner table on Thanksgiving Day. I wanted to kidnap each taste that seeped through the tiny taste buds on my tongue so I could experience this brief moment of ecstasy later.

The commotion across the street entertained me for a spell. It was like watching an episode of "Cops" as it was filmed right here in The Town, starring me! As I sat there patiently, the rug beneath my feet began bubbling. *You got to be kidding me!* I knew what could be causing this — a panic attack. *Now? Are you serious?* This was not the time for a panic attack to kick in; the food was way too good. I knew I was tripping out, yet I didn't allow the moment to prevent me from finishing my food. Each bite I took momentarily deadened the symptoms of the oncoming attack. Besides that, I was hungry as hell, and Ms. Karen's fried chicken was off the *chiznain* (chain). I normally didn't eat the gristle, but this time around I did. I didn't want to waste a speck of this perfectly seasoned chicken. I could taste a little cayenne pepper, ground pepper, a dash of seasoning salt and a sprinkle of cinnamon. "Karen!" I yelled from the couch, loud enough for her to hear in the kitchen.

"Yes, Ceeze?"

"What you know about cinnamon on fried chicken, girlfriend?"

I wasn't going to feed into the psychosis by making it any worse than what it truly was. I just started grinning as the floor started to turn into Jurassic Park. All dead species on the surface of the rug came alive and were staring at me. I lifted my feet to prevent anything from crawling on me and placed them on the phone book that was underneath the table. Still, I continued to eat. The ceiling fan was getting lower and lower every time I glanced up. I chuckled, saying, *"This shit is funny! Please, dear Lord, make this go away, I can't handle this right now. Plus the food is really good!"*

Across the street, people began to gather around the corridor that led to my apartment. But I kept eating away, removing all remnants of chicken from each bone. Karen returned with a large glass of orange *Tang*. I was down to my last bite of the waffles thinking out loud how good the entire meal is. I normally don't like blueberry waffles, but these were banging! After finishing the last bite, I said, "Ms. Karen, that was excellent!" But, as I began to drink the *Tang*, I noticed an eyelash floating in it, too light a color to be mine. Instead of getting grossed out, I simply removed it with my fingertip and flicked it on the floor. Knowing that I wasn't superstitious, I said a wish anyway, and smiled. The whole act of feeding my face kept the panic attack at bay. Now that I had completely devoured the food, I needed to come up with a more concrete solution to keep the panic attack from getting worse. Concentrating on my escape should do the trick.

"Ms. Karen, it's time for me to go. Where's your car?" I quickly rose to my feet, but became dizzy again and had to sit right the fuck back down. The after-effects of a panic attack were just that, dizziness. I needed to sit out the rest of this one while Ms. Karen fetched the keys. I began to contemplate where I could hide once I left her apartment. It's almost impossible for me to escape the small cul-de-sac because of the entire police force resting literally fifty yards from where I sat.

"Let me drive you out of here, Ceeze," said Karen. This sounded like a good scheme. "I have an idea. You slip out of the bathroom window; I'll pull my car up to the window and you jump straight into the trunk."

I set my plate on her coffee table to investigate the size of the bathroom window to see if I could easily jump out. I already knew her apartment building faced the alley; I used to break into cars out back when I was a kid. Without a doubt, I didn't have anything else to lose. My freedom rested on the shoulders of my newfound Ghetto Angel.

"This may work!" We began to plot my escape. Karen went out of the front door while I sat in the dreaded bathroom waiting for her signal to jump out of the window. The horn honk twice would be my signal to hop out the window and jump. *Honk*! I opened up the window to find Karen's car backed all the way up against the apartment building. The only thing I had to do was step out of the window into the trunk, a smooth transition.

Once I was inside the trunk, she slammed it down, got in her car, and drove off. Again *"Oh my goodness!"* came out of my mouth. I couldn't see anything in the trunk, and it smelled like the rear end of a sweaty hippopotamus. I still rejoiced in the name of the Lord, and still I prayed, *"Thank you, dear Lord, for allowing me to be alive, safe, and healthy. I will not begin to complain about my situation; I will begin to pray for encouragement to make it through this next passage. Dear Lord, I ask that you carry me emotionally and spiritually. I ask that you give me the wisdom needed to stay strong as I search for the person who killed Paulette. Now get me out of here, Dear Lord!"*

Many hood figgaz from around my way claim not to be threatened by the presence of the police. But I am not ashamed to admit it. When I hear sirens from afar that are getting closer and closer, or see flashing red lights in the rearview mirror, my heart enters my throat. We were only thirty feet down the road when I heard sirens getting closer and closer to Karen's car. Then the sirens stopped. The stench rising from within the trunk smelled like a bag of rotting potatoes mixed with molded yellow onions, which was making me light-headed.

    I began to sweat profusely when Karen's car also came to an abrupt stop. The hook had me shook. To make matters worse, when Karen's car came to a complete standstill, the contents within the bag shifted towards me and my face was up against whatever was creating the ghastly smell. The horrific smell now smelled more like a herd of wild boars grazing in a Texas land field on a hot summer day. I could hear a lazy person's dragging feet, and the clank of keys approaching the left side of her car. The thought of being caught mixed with the unpleasant smell threatened my small intestines.

    The smell engulfed my throat, forming egg-size lumps of mucus resting on and around my Adam's apple. The nervousness from within me created acidity deep within my stomach, which slowly descended upwards through my esophagus where it joined the existing lump of saliva. I needed to clear my throat badly, but I didn't want to get caught. I could hear chattering voices coming from the front of the vehicle. Karen was running her mouth a mile a minute as though she had just took a blast from a glass pipe. Ms. Chatter Box was going to land us both in jail. She tried to explain that her brake light had a short in it. I could see the brake light flickering on and off from inside the trunk. Ms. Karen was pressing on the brakes to show that the brake light worked sometimes. The right brake light lit up the trunk while the other one worked sporadically. I feared that the police officer would turn Good Samaritan by requesting Ms. Karen pop the trunk in order for him to see if the light was just loose. While the police were questioning her, I began fooling with the loose brake light to see if I could possibly get it to work right. The warmth from within me began to surface in the form of fried gristle mixed with tiny bits of waffles. This made my throat sore and painfully irritated. I needed to clear my throat badly, but if I did, the police would surely hear me. I had to man up and literally swallow my pride.

I could hear the two of them holding a conversation, but what they were saying was unclear. At the end of the conversation, I could hear the radio of the officer as he approached the trunk. When I could hear the voices clearly on the radio, I knew the hook would soon be invading my personal space. The officer tapped on the taillight with his nightstick to see whether or not the light would stay on. "Okay miss, tap on your brakes when I say tap. You ready? Okay now!"

After tapping on the brake light a few times, the officer headed back to the front of her car. I heard him ask for her driver's license. I knew once the police ran a check, it would come back with a warrant. Without a doubt, I was becoming overwhelmed by the fear of going to jail. Racing thoughts of being sentenced to death for murdering my Boo besieged me. The very same nightmare that inundated my sleep as a child returned with great vengeance. Immediately I felt like I was in a coffin that was spinning around and around in circles freely. The recurring dream of being locked in a coffin finally came true.

Could this be my destiny? Could this be my end? All of my life I had prepared myself for this terrible death. For the first time, I concluded I didn't have any other choice but to embrace death. I clenched my fist and my body real tight, not knowing when the end was going to come. I squeezed my eyes tight and clenched my teeth waiting for the hard impact to hit me abruptly. The trunk subsequently enclosed firmly around me like a sleeping bag. I kept my eyes shut waiting for the falling to end, but the end was taking too long. The little air that was left in the trunk was fading quickly. Despite the fact that I felt my death was imminent, I was okay with it. I can't face going to trial for a murder that I didn't commit, let alone being tried for the murder of my baby's momma. If I die here in this trunk, then that would mean I wouldn't have to kill myself in a cell with bed sheets tied around my neck.

My fate was approaching rapidly as the air within the tiny space around me thinned, increasing the illusion of me rapidly falling from outer space. Next, the bottom of the trunk evaporated, levitating me off the bed of the trunk. My panic attack rapidly forced out what little air I had saved in my lungs.

I heard the officer inform Ms. Karen to "Get out the car; you're under arrest." Quickly I became frozen in panic mode, facing death around the corner. I heard Ms. Karen crying and pleading to the officer not to arrest her. The thought of not knowing whether or not she was going to tell the hook that I was in the trunk convinced me that it was time for me to check out. The suspense was killing me… literally.

15
My Ghetto Angel

"Ceeze, wake up! Come on, man. Wake the fuck up, C, before the hook come back and hook us both the fuck up, man! Ceeze! Wake up, man!" A hideous looking Caucasian woman stood inches from my face, screaming obscenities while slapping the dog shit out of me. "Get the fuck up, Brandon! Get the fuck up, man!" I tried to rub out the cobwebs from my eyes to see if the ugliness in front of me would magically disappear. "I knew you'd wake up if I called you Brandon like your momma!"

I heard a chuckle and wondered who was talking to me as if they were part of my family. Once the cobwebs were removed, I learned that the repugnant mug in front of me belonged to my Ghetto Angel, Ms. Karen. I too smiled and then immediately fell back asleep.

Suddenly I was fully wakened by a crisp smack against my left cheek. "What the hell, lady!" If I wasn't awake before, I was surely awake then. Her palm reverberated off my face, making the sound of freshly diced romaine lettuce under attack by a greenhorn prep cook using a *Ginsu Knife* for the very first time.

"I'm up, I'm up! What the fuck, Karen!" She held my chin up with her crusty fingertips so I could make out the gruesome visage that was staring back at me.

"Oh now you don't know me, okay. After all that good food I done made you! I see you're one of them niggaz who hit-'em and quit-'em, uh?" She giggled aloud while all along trying not to show her meth mouth, looking like she was chewing on a Tootsie-Roll, the extra large ones that are only sold around Halloween. I could tell she grew up around black folks the way she pronounced *niggaz*. There weren't any misinterpretations from her vernacular that she let it be known she assumed she had a hood-pass to use the n-word so openly and unexpectedly.

    I tried to come to my senses as I felt air entering through the side of my face. That's when I found the long paper cut from where the weather beaten, razor-sharp palm sliced me. Her hands were scruffy, as if she had worked in an apple orchard picking apples most of her life. As she held my face up, I could feel her knife-like fingertips digging through my chin. Her fingertips had dried layers of crusty old skin, resembling burnt *Oscar Meyer* wieners and sharp enough to slice rhubarb pie. Blackened fingertips made it apparent that she preferred to use matches instead of a lighter to ignite her crack. When she used a lighter, it would ruin her high because she became increasingly paranoid not knowing when the fluid would run out. On the other hand, when an addict used matches, the flame went out once it reached their fingertips. On account of her crusty burnt fingertips, it was only evident that she spent many-a-day holding a constant flame ablaze to a crack pipe.

    The light was out in Ms. Karen's trunk, so she struck a match to help me see that it was her slapping me upside the head. The smell of sulfur ablaze triggered her emotions. She was now symptomatic. Her muscles tensed up, her mouth and throat became dry, and I could see her jaw start to sway back and forth as she visualized herself sucking on the glass dick (a metaphor for a glass pipe used for smoking crack). As I came to, I caught her geeking — as many crack heads do after smoking crack, honing in on any little white object that somewhat resembled a crack rock.

    As I slowly regained consciousness, she became irritable and looked more and more confused. Her eyes quickly honed in on its prey, like an owl spotting a white squirrel. She picked up two small objects, one a chewing gum wrapper and the other a dime-sized balled-up piece of paper. The sulfur atop the matchstick was the mechanism that confiscated all of her attention. The very sight of a matchbook transcended her body and mind to a lonely dark dimension where she could only foresee herself getting high on crack. By the look of her fingertips, she barely had any readable DNA left.

Though I was already awake, Karen still tried to awaken me for the next few minutes. She shook me as if I had stolen something from her momma. She clutched both of my shoulders with all of her strength over and over again, trying to lift me out of the rather large trunk of her car. I wasn't budging.

Her voice became very boisterous as she went in on me again, cursing up a new hurricane, "Get the fuck up, man! Shit! Now goddamn it! You ain't gonna get me arrested, motha-fucka! Oh hell no, nigga! I'm not going to jail tonight! Not this bitch! You aren't even my man! Aw hell, Ceeze, get the fuck up, man, please! Shit!"

I rose a bit. Still I wasn't aware of reality. My body felt like I was still falling fast from outer space. As she yelled and shook me, my eyes slowly opened, and were quickly filled with smoke from the cigarette dangling from her dried up iguana lips. She exhaled right into my face, making me choke and gag for much needed air. The smoke convinced me that I was unquestionably in hell. I thought the next thing I was going to see would be fire all around me. Instead, I was greeted by Ms. Karen's weathered face, full of craters the size of mines and topless volcanoes. When I caught the smell of gasoline and saw her cigarette so close to the gas tank, I jumped out of my fetal position and tried to hop out. I bumped my head against the inside of the trunk, making me stumble back in.

At this point, my only concern went from running from the police to learning the whereabouts of baby Riesha. I wasn't fully coherent as yet, but one thing I did know — I missed my little girl more than ever.

Ms. Karen steadily tried to talk to me, though my thoughts were possessed by picturesque references of daddy's little girl showering me with kisses and hugs. Her infamous statement, "Hugs, no drugs", followed memories of Paulette joining Riesha and me in a group hug while exchanging wet kisses! "Right, Ceeze?" During such times, Paulette showcased her genuine smile. It took possession of my newly freed spirit as I sat on the bumper of Ms. Karen's car trying to wake from the deep slumber.

Paulette's genuine smile came with a package. She smiled and said hello to anybody who walked by, even when she wasn't spoken to. After rehab, Paulette returned to being the classy young lady that both of her parents raised her to be. She possessed sex appeal and knew how to dress sexy without showing off too much skin. If she had a problem with someone, she dealt with it without getting loud or acting ghetto. She would pull you aside and simply ask, "Yo, do you have a problem with me?"

Sister-girl took walks in the morning and sometimes in the evenings. She cooked and ate the right foods, and made sure she was in bed by ten. She would say to me, "If you want some nookie, you got to get it now before it's too late. A sista got to get her eight hours of sleep in order to deal with these knuckleheads!"

Damn, I missed my Boo! My body was spent. My head felt like I had been up all night drinking rotgut Night Train mixed with grape Kool-Aid. I had to sit upright for a good five minutes trying to catch my breath to obtain some sort of stability. "I thought I had died!" I said to Ms. Karen.

She giggled. "You were out cold, but still breathing and snoring hard when I got to you." Ms. Karen laughed a silent laugh while using her hand to shield me from her blackened yuck-mouth. The black around her teeth highlighted the barely little white left on each tooth. This created a 3D affect when she spoke, making her teeth protrude outward. The effect made each tooth appear as if it would fall out if she laughed too hard.

"Okay, Ceeze, I know you're still tired and all, but it's time to go, Cuzz!" Ms. Karen continued, "I don't know where you're going, but you could drop me off at my momma's house around the corner and take my car if you still want to."

Now that I was awake, I wondered why Ms. Karen came back for me. She's done a great deal to save my life. Her actions led me to believe that she was once a kind-hearted whore, the kind that did anything and everything, not only for her pimp, but also for her pimps other whores too. I felt sorry for her, knowing that she could have been a great lover and a friend to a man who respected her and wouldn't have taken advantage of her kindness.

"Karen, why are you so kind to me?"

"I wish I could tell you why, but now is not the time. We got to get you up and out of here before the hook comes to hook both of us up."

"Tell me what?" I asked.

"Okay, I am gonna tell you this. I was trying to figure out when it would be a good time. You know, on account of you losing your wife and all. You know I can see everything that goes on around your apartment from my couch, right?" I nodded. I kind of assumed that she was digging me, but I felt that I should save her from embarrassing herself. I didn't know how to tell her that we aren't equally yoked. I could tell that she too was feeling kind of embarrassed as she quickly changed the topic.

"You wouldn't wake up, so I took the stem from the gas can and waived it a few times underneath your nose and you woke the fuck up. Some gas may have spilled on you."

"How long was I out?"

"I've been gone for about twenty minutes. The hook arrested me, but then immediately released me on my own recognizance. I was given two hours to find someone with a license to come and get my car or it was gonna be towed."

"Who did you call?"

"My mom is on the way." She then paused for a few seconds allowing herself to take a deep puff from her cigarette. When she finally let out the smoke, she threw it down on the gravel and stomped on it. She sat down next to me on the bumper, close enough for me to smell the cigarette smoke lingering off her skin and clothes. The cigarette stench made her smell like she smoked one cigarette every seven minutes of her life for the last fifteen years. I could barely breathe as she spoke. The aroma of stale wet cigars bellowed from her mouth nauseating my already feebleminded state. She placed one arm around my shoulder and one arm around my waist in an attempt to help me gain my balance.

As she helped me out of the trunk, I felt compassion resonating in the form of electric energy flowing through her body as if she was a close friend from my past. Our faces met cheek-to-cheek while our bodies conjoined at the hip. Again I could feel her positive energy bouncing off her and flowing through my body, uplifting me and giving me a sense of security and hope. It was obvious that she was a good person underneath the smell of sewage and burnt boiled eggs. Though her mug was raped of any and all natural beauty whatsoever, it was her spirit that dispensed positive energy.

"Brandon, there is something that I need to tell you. I saw…." As soon as I placed both my feet on the pavement to brace myself for whatever Ms. Karen was going to tell me, three police cars swarmed around us. "What the fuck!" yelled Ms. Karen. "How did they know you were in the trunk? I didn't rat you out, Mr. Lewis! I swear I didn't."

She didn't have to say that. I knew that the Anglo Cuban turned us in. Whenever I saw that bastard, I wanted to kick him in the mouth for saying things to me that he thought were funny, although I knew they were racially motivated. I couldn't stand that son-of-a-bitch. The police had all their guns drawn and pointing in our direction. Not one of the officers spoke. It seemed like the officers were stuck on stupid and didn't know what their next move should be. Damn! I was hell-a-nervous. Sweat started dripping from places where I didn't know I could sweat. My left leg began to shake unequivocally, as it would when I was in any situation where I felt my livelihood was in danger. I could feel and hear ever ounce of blood flow to and from my heart. I thought about letting the police know I felt like I was having a heart attack, but I already knew they weren't gonna take me seriously.

There was dead silence between the two of us as we waited emphatically for an officer to say something like, "Ms. Karen, please step away from the vehicle" or "you could put your hands down now." Not one of the officers was brave enough to tell me I was under arrest. Thinking to myself that if I suddenly moved anything other than my eyes, both Karen and I would be shot in the head. Instead, we chilled, using eye contact and facial expressions in search of some sort of message that would prevent the two of us from getting murdered.

Rapidly closing in on us were the sounds of police authorized Michelin tires screeching around nearby street corners. I knew something bad was about to happen. Whoever the police officers were waiting for was not too far from us.

As the sounds of the screeching tires got closer and closer, a helicopter hovering above appeared out of nowhere. Slowly I turned my head towards the sky to get a good look at it. I noticed the *Q13 FOX* insignia plastered on the bottom in large white letters. I wasn't ready to die yet. I glanced over my right shoulder to see if the police were sneaking up behind me and noticed a couple of white news vans waiting for the show to begin.

While I held my hands high in the air, Ms. Karen paced apprehensively back and forth in front of me almost taunting the police, now saying, "So what y'all gonna do, shit? Shoot me, because I got a warrant? What the fuck! Damn, are you gonna arrest me or what the fuck?" A K-9 officer holding one of those out of control barking police dogs approached the officer that was telling Ms. Karen to calm down. The two of them exchanged words, and then the officer holding the dog walked off in the opposite direction.

An officer from the perimeter pointed over to Karen and uttered to the K9 officer, "Use the dogs!" The K-9 Officer laughed and made his dog sit. Once Ms. Karen noticed how big the German Shepard's teeth were, she quickly calmed the fuck down and returned to resting on the bumper of her crusty old Buick. When Ms. Karen sat next to me, I decided to put my arms down. I knew the police were crazy, but they weren't crazy enough to shoot the white girl. It was only evident that Karen took a hit of something. She could only sit still for just a few seconds and she wouldn't stop shaking.

"Hold your hand out, Karen." On command, she held her hand out as if someone had requested this before. She had the hands of an ironworker or a bricklayer. Her shivering hand started to make me nervous. Is this lady high on meth or crack? Shit! Every time I presumed she was abusing one drug, as soon as I turned the other cheek, I thought she was abusing something different. From the way she was acting, I couldn't tell what the hell she was on. What I was for-sure of was that she was high on something. "Look! You have to stop kurking out. The hook ain't here for you! Trust me."

"Oh yes they are! I got three warrants, one in King County, one in Watkins County, and one in Thurston County!"

"For what?"

I could barely make out what she was trying to convey on account of her dry, hoarse voice. "First degree assault in King County, check fraud in Watkins County. And jumping bail in Thurston County."

"The hook want me for murder!" I replied so effortlessly. There was no end in sight as the two of us held our arms as high as we possibly could after one of the rookie officers informed us to put our arms back up. The wind within my private space bellowed the stench of sweating red onions and an old wet stray dog from Karen's direction. She was a hot mess. Her pupils were beyond dilated, blacker than shiny Alaskan muscle shells.

Acting like her AA sponsor, I asked, "Did you get high while you were gone?" Before opening her mouth she cleared her throat and hacked up a large lump of mucus and spit it on the pavement between the two of us. Smoking an abundance of crack usually produced flimflam, which subsequently caused a cracked hoarse voice.

Ms. Karen could barely sound out a word. I managed to understand her pointless plea. "Shush!" she said. "Be quiet; they might have bugged my car."

"Oh-my-god!" I said to myself. Her paranoia and cracked voice confirmed that she was high on crack, yet honestly, I wasn't quite sure. It really didn't matter to me what she was high on. What I did next startled even me. I asked Karen to say a prayer with me. Again, as if I were a drill sergeant, she quickly followed my command by lowering her head and closing her eyes. *"Please, dear Lord, forgive us our sins. I ask that you guide us through this storm. Help us, dear Lord, to see the next day. Help keep the two of us from going to prison. In Jesus name we pray. Amen."*

"That's it?" replied Ms. Karen.

"If you have more to say, then go for it. I'm not stopping you."

"Please, dear Lord, return Brandon's daughter to him safely!" This woman always seemed to amaze me. I appreciated her kind-hearted gesture. My life was resting on her remaining calm, though it seemed as if she was going to break down at any given moment. She was acting more and more belligerent. She leaned over in my direction quickly asking me also to lean towards her so that she could whisper something in my ear. I didn't think this was a good idea on account of having so many guns pointing in our direction.

When I pretended as if I didn't hear her, she became very adamant about me leaning closer to her. She continued to taunt me, almost forcing me to submit to her request. Immediately I could smell her horrific breath as bubbles of spit landed deep, deep inside my ear. She then said to me in her crackled voice, "I'm high as shit!" When she said this to me, the officer holding the dog yelled, "Stand up and stop talking and put your hands back up!" And so we did.

Several moments had passed and my arms were getting way too tired. I told Ms. Karen that I was going to put my arms down regardless of what they were saying. I figured out if they wanted to kill us, they would've done it already. Ah hell, I was going to go for it. The thought of resting my arms made the screeching pain through them even worse. I told Ms. Karen, "On the count of three, I'm gonna put my arms down. If you want to, then follow my lead."

She uttered the word yes, but her voice was so far gone I had to rely on my lip-reading skills.

"On the count of three, follow my lead. You ready?" Ms. Karen shook her head yes informing me that she was all in. "Ready! On the count of three! One! Two! Three!" As soon as we put our arms down, we both collapsed on the back bumper of her car. Our shoulders rested on the others. She took the cigarette from her lips and started taking long hard pulls. There was complete silence for just a spell. Ms. Karen suddenly became cumbersome as if she was content with what cards life had dealt her. I was nervous as shit.

As we waited to be arrested Ms. Karen said to me, "I still have the pipe in my back pocket. That's why I'm so freaking paranoid." Every seven seconds, she took a long drag off the cowboy light 100s that she was so dramatically smoking on. She was acting so skittish that I thought she was going to approach one of the officers to find out why they hadn't made a move yet. Every time she moved to light another cigarette, an officer would shift his position. The arrogance of Ms. Karen to light a cigarette during these trying times when most people would have been too scared to make any sudden moves in front of twelve angry trigger-happy police officers. What was taking them so long to kill me? I wanted all of this to end dramatically so that the community could get what everybody wanted, a public execution.

The officers had their guns drawn on me because they felt threatened by most, if not all, black or brown folk from my neighborhood. The officers that day were from small towns outside of the city limits, small towns such as Black Diamond, Algona, Lynch and Port Orchard, towns where blacks were still viewed as recently freed slaves. The only interactions those officers had with brown folks was when they patrolled the streets of The Town. At work, they became aggressors showcasing the inbred prejudices passed down from the three Ps — parents, peers, and newspapers.

For the first time I was able to capitalize on the fear that drives white America. As soon as an officer felt threatened, one would shoot me, and the rest would follow, ending this madness.

I began contemplating what-if scenarios: What if I pushed Ms. Karen out of the way and ran in the opposite direction, the most threatened officers would send a barrage of bullets after me.

Or what if I start yelling that I have a gun and reach into my pocket? Naw, then Ms. Karen might get shot. I like the former. "This could work," I said out loud.

Ms. Karen asked, "What will work?"

"Nothing." I was just waiting for the right moment to act out. I felt another panic attack ensuing, but I couldn't tell whether or not this one was going to be a full-fledged attack or just a tremor, like after an earthquake. Having an attack in front of all these officers was really bad timing. I didn't know if I could handle that right now. I wanted to go out quickly, but maybe, I would mess around and have a heart attack just waiting for the attack to begin. It was time for me to make my move.

Suddenly, all of my fears of dying exited my body. I went for it and pushed Ms. Karen, using all of the upper body strength mixed with frustration, heartache, and despair, forcing her to fall. I ran in the opposite direction towards the white marsh that lay three feet ahead of me. The police let loose a plethora of bullets, sending them buzzing by both ears, one grazed the back of my head but didn't slow me down. Another one hit my forearm, but that one didn't bother me; I had been shot there before. Then I felt something burning in my right leg, but I was determined not to let it stop me. I felt the same pain in my right shoulder, yet I kept running. All along, I prayed to God to save my soul so that I could be next to Paulette. Then out of nowhere, my good leg buckled, forcing me to the ground.

Once I hit the ground, the panic attack kicked in and I was stuck crawling on all fours until I felt someone kick me in my ribs, yet I still kept crawling. Then, another gang member (police officer) kicked me on the other side, yelling, "And stay down, you fucking wife killer!"

I heard someone yell, "Taze him!" All of a sudden I felt bolts of electricity shooting through my body, paralyzing me from the neck down. The tirade was over; I lay half dead on my back, looking up at the pretty blue sky. An officer with an extremely large boot stomped on my nuts, as if I were an attacking pit-bull. The burning in my shoulder and leg intensified once they figured out where I was shot. I could feel each blow thrown to each specific wound, as I lay helpless on my back.

I heard three voices simultaneously asking me to stop resisting arrest. It was as if they were laughing at me while beating me unconscious, and unconscious is where I was quickly heading. I could feel the heels of their boots digging into my wounds, causing excruciating pain. I tried to scream and kick, but I couldn't get the words out. My eyes began to close slowly as a hoard of fists and nightsticks continued to pound my body.

Before passing out I saw a huge pasture-fed farm boy approaching me fast. Once the gang members realized Big Dog was approaching, the beating gradually decreased. Big Dog placed his head inches away from my face so I could see who it was. "Are you Brandon Lewis, aka Ceeze Green?" I tried to answer, but my lips were fused together with blood, and my vocal cords were bruised and shattered from having a slew of boots planted against my throat. When he noticed that I couldn't answer him, he informed me to move my good eye left for yes and right for no. "Are you Ceeze Green?"

Looking and sounding like the Elephant Man, I managed to utter the words, "Ask your momma!" The big farm boy laughed and called me a smart ass before kicking me in the face and punching me in the throat. As a result I couldn't breathe anymore.

As I gasped for my last breathe, the chief informed me, "You are under arrest for the murder of Paulette Jenkins."

I heard Ms. Karen yell, "He's dying! Someone help him!"

Big Dog's reply was, "Good, let him die!"

16
Free at Last

I WOKE UP IN A BRUTALLY COLD AND GLOOMY STORAGE CLOSET full of shiny silver medical equipment along with two mop buckets smelling of bleach and dirty bong water. As I attempted to rise for a morning yawn, I found my body hog-tied to a steel gurney, my hands handcuffed to the sides of it, my feet shackled to each leg of the table. The steel slab originally used to transport dead bodies had become a makeshift bed prepared for me by the nursing staff.

The duty nurse made sure I had one pillow to lay my weary head on, and for my fatigued body, the hospital staff provided a provisional mattress made up of two stale crusty bath towels snuggled underneath a grimy bed sheet with three very thin pillows on top. The smell of new leather rose from the straps across my chest and forearms.

The police ensured the hospital staff and residents of the Ridgetop General Hospital that they would be safer if they used real cowhide belts to strap me down. To keep me even more submissive under their care, I was given an intoxicating narcotic, morphine, making my body feel like a rattlesnake had bitten me. With this synthetic heroin running through my body, my organs felt as if they'd been hard-boiled for several hours on high.

Whenever I felt weary, weathered, and stressed out, a sleeping giant emerged, called sickle cell anemia. The disease released agonizing pain throughout my body. The simplest task of breathing was excruciating as blood flowed from one blood vessel to another. And when the arctic chill rose from the freezing metal gurney, my stressed-out nervous system went into fight or flight mode.

    I was stricken with hyperthermia. All the skin on my body tightened, clinging to my malnourished boney body. This created a fire-on-ice effect inside as my organs shut down, sending shock waves of ice sickles throughout my body. My breathing was compromised, and my pain level rose to ten. I lost the ability to reopen my good eye. As the pain rose, I came to realize I was breathing through a tube that was deeply rooted in my gut. I lay, lifeless and motionless, my spirit broken, waiting for the pain to subside and for my lungs to expand on their own. I wasn't having any luck. The tube in my stomach made me gag, and no one was coming to my rescue.

    I felt an enormous force squeezing my left shin. As quickly as the tension in my leg subsided, the pressure compressed my right shin. I learned that each shin was covered with a pulsating airbag to prevent blood clots, allowing blood to smoothly circulate through my legs and prevent my toes from curling.

    My conclusion: I had been placed under anesthesia while undergoing some sort of surgery. That must be the reason for the breathing tube in my throat. I mustered up enough strength to open my good eye to find Ms. Karen and a member of the leading most organized crime syndicate in The Town hovering over me. When Ms. Karen noticed, she jumped up and down in place, yelling, "He's awake, he's awake!" I was hoping for Karen to pull the breathing tube out, but her country ass was too excited to realize I was choking to death.

    A rather large blue-black aboriginal nurse with the biggest nose I'd ever seen ran into the room and yanked the breathing tube from my throat and checked my vitals signs. "He's good!" he reported, offering thumbs up to the duty officer. Once the bama and the officer made eye contact, he quietly left the room. But before the door closed behind him, another police officer slipped into the room.

I could hear a slew of reporters waiting outside for a status report on my condition. They bombarded the officer, asking the same questions over and over again, "Is the killer still in critical condition?" "Did Mr. Lewis say where he's hiding his daughter's body?" And finally, "Did he say why he killed his baby's momma?"

Karen and two officers went to the corner of the closet to discuss something in private. At this point, there wasn't anything else I could endure that would break me any more than how I was feeling. She was doing most of the talking with her hands and neck while the younger of the two white officers wrote notes. Though I deemed myself the ear hustler of the family, I couldn't make out much of the conversation between them. I did hear the officer tell Karen, "I need you to take me to the guns right now!"

Ms. Karen didn't hesitate. As she left, she looked over at me. With a half-crocked smile on her weather-beaten face, she uttered, "I'll be right back; I promise!" I wanted to ask her where she was going, but I couldn't get my lips to respond. The morphine they were pumping into me put me in a catatonic zombie-like state. Half dead, I couldn't respond to any questions; at this point, I could have been coerced into signing away my life.

Once Karen left the room, I started to wonder if the cops had me sign a confession. This wouldn't be the first time the police used dubious tactics to close a case. What guns were they talking about? All this skepticism brought on another panic attack, but instead of taking over my entire body, it began down south, just below my abdomen.

I knew it was coming from my growing area, but I couldn't identify it. Still half-dead, I lifted the covers to find a tube covered in dried blood coming out of my penis. I screamed, "What the fuck is that?" and tried to yank the tube out. I was stopped in mid-motion by the tight handcuffs. Again I tried to get a better grip. The catheter went from a 2-milliliter tube to a large jawbreaker. As it reached the exit point, my penis felt like a burning meteor had traveled ablaze from planet Uranus to planet urethra. It was too late to stop; the last yank caused a massive amount of blood and urine to seep out all over me.

My yelling woke the sleeping thug nestled in the Lazy-Boy chair next to a supply cabinet. He rose to his feet, simultaneously grabbing his handgun and nightstick. The nurse bum-rushed the room, followed by a doctor, to find me sitting up on bloody sheets mixed with urine. Ms. Doctor from India asked me in her authentic Indian voice, "What the hell you do, Mr. Lewis?"

Once the catheter was out, all of my senses began to overload, centered on my groin area. Magnetic energy produced agonizing jerks in the form of sharp pains where the catheter once rested. The sting was so severe it took precedence over the fact that I might get the death penalty — lethal injection for a murder I didn't commit.

Just inches away, I could hear a familiar voice, "*What lies are they spreading now?*" As I listened to the voice from the hallway, I heard the reporter use slanderous words — *murderer, cheat, pimp, and woman beater* — to describe me. I tried to keep the negative rhetoric from sealing my eyes with more cobwebs — cobwebs I had been trying to get rid of for the last couple of days. I remained unsuccessful. I had become a product of my environment. Most of my negative self-images had been developed over years of living within the subculture I belonged to.

Spoon-fed images had prepared me for a future of criminal and deviant behavior. My educators were old white wrinkly-faced newscasters who provided me with information that was disconcerting and demented: *I was feared because I was black. Black boys were second-class citizens. I wasn't part of a "traditional" American family.* I had been bombarded with these images even before heading off to school.

In school, I secluded myself, my spirit broken. I was used to sitting quietly in the back row, silent as a church mouse. When I was called on, I broke into a sweat and developed a stutter. I felt stupid and unworthy, and eventually was tossed into a Special Ed classroom, the place where goofball trouble-making brown and black boys were held. Like a juvenile holding tank, Special Ed was used to protect teachers and other students from OC (out of control), ADHD (attention deficit hyperactivity disorder), and AA (Afro-American) bad asses.

The development of Special Ed classrooms initiated opportunities for government funding to be misappropriated through schools without scandal. The realization that black boys needed to be shut away from "normal" kids worked well to lower self-esteem and tempt them to act out the stigma by abusing marijuana and alcohol. While under the influence, I started acting out the role of a degenerate and didn't even know it. The weed kept us in a catatonic state during school hours, handicapped our ability to express emotions, and impeded the learning process. What we learned was preparation for prison: how to be shallow, how to accept being mistreated, how to accept being deprived of an education. I finally accepted the belief I was headed for jail, which is why I was able to accept the fact that now I would be going to jail for a crime I did not commit.

Ms. Asian was holding a live broadcast from the hallway. She announced that the dean of the state's leading forensic school, a Dr. Kinsley, was asked by the chief of police to conduct more tests on the gun used to kill Paulette. The police initially stated it was a handgun. However, Dr. Kinsley, after reenacting the actual murder, reported his team of highly skilled forensic specialists had concluded a high caliber rifle was used in the murder of Paulette Jenkins. Tina added that it was found at a neighbor's house across the street from where the victim lived. To make matters worse, Tina reported that the occupant was also hiding the ex-boyfriend of the deceased and father of the missing little girl.

I remembered Ms. Karen pulling out a rifle she claimed was her ex-boyfriend's. Swiftly I became consumed by the thought I may have touched it. Again my head dropped and my body felt like the hospital was sitting on top of me. Had I fallen for the oaky-doke? Oh my God! She was using me the whole time, but for what? My heart had dropped down to my toes. The impression became clear; the money-earning Dominican Pedro, Paulette's ex-boyfriend, planned the whole thing with Karen.

"What the fuck!" Extremely dumbfounded, all kinds of questions ran through my mind. What was this heifer getting out of setting me up for murder? My mind was racing amok. The Dominicans are known for manipulating women by taking advantage of their weaknesses, capitalizing from the way their father's mistreated them. It was all coming together. Sadly enough, Ms. Karen had all of the markings of being a good whore — brainwashed and beaten into submission. She would do anything for her so-called boyfriend: steal, rob a bank, sell her body, and... kill!

"I've got to get the fuck out of here!" I felt asinine knowing that the killer lived right across the street the entire time. I became stupefied thinking about the way the living room chairs were directed towards our apartment. "This Dominican mutha-fucka was stalking Paulette!"

My heart raced as it all started to unravel. What is he getting out of keeping Riesha? I haven't heard any news reports of a ransom note. I remembered seeing Dominican Pedro in the crowd at the murder scene. And it was Pedro that gave me a jump when my battery was dead. In fact, I remember him knocking on my door asking me if I needed a jump, which is way too peculiar now that I think about it. He had come over to sell me a big screen TV on the same day Paulette was released from drug rehab. This startled me at that time because of his past history with Paulette and the questions surrounding who addicted who to crack cocaine.

When he came over to sell the TV, he stuck his head in the apartment first. I assumed he was looking around to see if we already had a flat screen; now I believe he was looking for my Boo. I never really paid any attention to Pedro because we were so cool. We respected each others space before and during the beginning of my relationship with Paulette. I trusted my old lady, so there wasn't any need for me to think twice about her loyalty to me or her loyalty to her sobriety. That's where I was wrong. Relapse is part of recovery.

On the contrary, I began to think that the two of them were hiding something from me! Could she have relapsed? Was she cheating on me with Pedro?

I clearly remembered seeing Pedro coming from the direction of Ms. Karen's apartment with the jumper cables he used to help me jumpstart my car. Was he watching my every move to get closer to Paulette? Why would he want to kill my Boo? Where is he keeping Riesha? Does Ms. Karen know where Riesha is? I felt dumber than a screen door with no screen.

Then the worst thoughts: Maybe Riesha is not my daughter, and Pedro is her father. This would explain why he kidnapped little Riri! Thinking about how Paulette could have betrayed me made my body perspire faster than four sweaty whores in a beetle-bug on a hot summer day in Bangladesh. My skin turned beet red; my fingernails turned blue; and my eyebrows became permanently strained. I was all fucked up listening to Ms. Asian Persuasion destroy my future. The pain went from my groin area to my heart. My heart felt like it was about to explode. Knowing this information made me feel so low to the point where I didn't want to live another day.

I became unfathomably depressed. I was in a state of nothingness. Immovable. I felt powerless, incapable of breaking free from the shackles around my hands and feet and, quite frankly, I didn't care. Nothing could replenish the emptiness I was feeling. I sensed the feeling was like being trapped on a slave ship lost in the Bermuda Triangle while shackled to four dead rotting bodies for several weeks. The overriding notion of Riesha not being my daughter forced me to stop breathing. I felt there was no need to go on living.

I decided to hold my breath as if I were underwater, thinking I could stop breathing on my own. My eyes became fixed in the rollback position, endlessly staring at red sugar ants just inches away from my face on the wall. At this point all kinds of beeps and warning lights connected to my anguished body started going off. From the sound of it, I knew I was in bad shape. "Momma and Daddy, here I come!"

Boom! Boom! Boom! I could feel a stampede of nurses and doctors rushing down the hallway, forcing their way through the slew of reporters camped outside. In her deep Indian voice, I heard the doctor shout, "Get out the way; move to the side!" The Australian was the first one to reach me. He whispered, "How you feeling, son?"

I replied, "Not too good, boss. I don't want to live to see another day."

Dr. India leaned towards me smelling like curry and burnt toast to say, "I got something for your pain, Mr. Lewis!"

Even in the state I was in, I whispered back, "Yo, doc, I'm drug free now; please no drugs, doc, please!"

The nurse came back in a deep boisterous Australian accent, "You were shot five times, my brother. For now you will be receiving something for your pain."

Hearing this news slightly took my mind off of my reality. Damn, five times, Cuzz! That was the first time I heard this. The only thing I could remember was someone had kicked me in the nut sack, leaving his boot in my ass for safekeeping. "I'm not mad at you, my brotha; do what you need to do. I can't take any more of this pain!" A stream of uncontrollable tears began to flow from both eyes.

The drugs he injected crept into my nervous system quickly. The meds were taking me to places where a blunt and a shot of Paul Masson VSOP could only take me. I drifted off to oblivion where several Ghetto Angels joined me from my past. I wasn't dressed in all-white linen like most would believe. Instead I was dressed in a very nice black suit. I wore a crispy white button-down shirt under my suit jacket and a pair of freshly shined black gators with no socks. The men surrounding me were dressed in the traditional Washingtonian casual wear: sports coat, button-down shirt, jeans, and dress shoes. The women in my dream wore silk lingerie tops, tight jeans, and stiletto shoes.

The first person to greet me was my Uncle Vincent. He was the only friend of my father's who tried to steer me in the right direction when he noticed I was heading down the wrong path. My uncle had a huge dislike for the cockroaches-masked-as-women that I ran around with. Unc informed me to stop running around with those wild women, the ones who only came around after spending their welfare checks on shoes and prepaid cellular phone cards. "They only come over to smoke your weed up and drank your liquor!"

Unc was holding my Cousin Darlene's hand. She educated me on the importance of using a condom. "If she's willing to sleep with you without a condom, imagine how many other boys she's either slept with or was willing to have sex with, using no protection." I can't count how many times her voice ran through my mind before I contemplated having sex without a condom.

Standing next to my family was Old Man Henry, holding the leash of his longtime companion Charlie, an albino Doberman Pinscher. Promptly at 8:30 a.m., Old Man Henry and Charlie took their long stroll through the Ridgetop area, picking up garbage that the "lazy people" dropped. One morning, Old Man Henry caught me opening a pack of Newports and throwing the wrapper on the ground. He told me, "It's because of you people that I stay looking so young and healthy!" He never explained what he meant by that until a few years later when I asked him why he picked up garbage every morning. "It's because I feel sorry for the lazy people who don't have respect for their neighborhood. A real man is dedicated to three things, his family, his community, and God." As he traveled down the rough and tough city streets of Ridgetop picking up garbage, he sang the only two verses that he knew from the spiritual hymn, "I'm going up yon-der-er! To be with my Lord!"

I awakened to the voice of Ms. Tina Lee who was informing the public via satellite from outside my hospital room that "the gun is in the hands of the police department". Yet I heard no mention of Ms. Karen's boyfriend. Though I was still sedated, I was aware that I was still handcuffed. I figured that Ms. Karen was using me to protect Pedro. But why did she lead the police to her house for the rifle that killed my Boo?   Next, I heard Tina say, "Bullets are being tested for ballistics to match the ones found at the murder scene." This made me close my eyes and shake my head back and forth in disgust. Trying to prove my innocence would take more than a wish and a prayer. I'll need Jehovah himself to come back down and handle this one for me.

I had been painted the villain by the media based on two things, my past involvement in gangs and the damaging portrayal of African American men in the media and newspapers for the past 300 years. In order to prove my innocence, there would have to be a rebirth of humankind, repairing the damage of the negative image of blacks. My chances of receiving a fair trial were slim to none.

Every syllable, every pronunciation of each incriminating word Tina used gave me heartburn. My heart pounded in my throat. My legs turned numb, and my fingers and arms tingled. My body felt as if it were falling 35,000 feet per second; yet I was lying on my back, handcuffed to a bed with nowhere to go.

I knew my life was over. I felt sick, as if I was about to throw up. I asked Mr. Night Stick if I could use the bathroom. He acted as if I were bothering him, taking his sweet-slow time. I could smell coffee infused with spit and chewing tobacco as he yawned from across the storage compartment. Slowly, he took the keys from his belt and unhooked the handcuffs and shackles. I got up off the bed slowly, like an old man wearing thirty-five pound steel-toed boots with dried North Carolina red clay affixed to the bottom. I shuffled towards the bathroom, dragging the IV tower alongside me. I felt air flowing freely under my family jewels through the nightgown that exposed my butt. Every step I took made my penis feel like it was full of razor blades. I could feel the police officer's hot breath on my shoulder as he closely escorted me towards the lavatory, holding my cuffed hands behind my back.

"You got to be kidding me!" In the corner next to the supply cabinet sat a grey bucket with white paint stains on the side, along with a lonely toilet seat cushion afloat on top.

"Go ahead, boy, you said you got to piss; don't be shy, Cuzz! You might as well get use to pissing and shitting in front of people because where you going you ain't gonna have any privacy for sixty years!"

Say it isn't so, dear lord, say it isn't so! To make matters worse, the plastic seat cushion was torn, with red blood spots and yellow pee stains covering the entire cushion. The stench of urine and funk burst from the sides as I sat down, making a whistling sound. The beat-down from the hook had left bruises the size of a sweet melons all over my legs, rump, and feet. The toilet seat absorbed my body weight, making me feel at ease for the first time in days. I was able to relax, momentarily taking a load off of my feet. I used my leg to hold up my arm while my chin rested comfortably on the palm of my hand. I did not want to move from this position.

My body was in grave discomfort from being shot and from the brutal beating the gang in blue gave me. I could still feel every spot where the bullets exploded. I could feel the tear where my skin met the muscle where each bullet traveled through. I could feel the area where the bullet ricocheted off my bones and where the bullets that the surgeons couldn't remove rested. I even knew the chief wore a size-twelve boot on account of the pain drifting towards my nut sack, and I could still feel that boot up my ass.

When I looked into the full-length mirror, I caught a glimpse of how this whole ordeal aged me seventeen years in three days. My nose was swollen so bad that my nostrils stretched from cheekbone to cheekbone. I think my jaw was broken from the nightstick assaults. One of my gold fronts was missing, and I could barely open my right eye, which was severely blackened and felt like the eye socket was broken. I counted seven stitches above my left eyelid. I forced my good eye open with my fingers to see what damage was done inside. The inside of my red eye felt as if a tablespoon of pollen floated around. Crusted yellow eye-boogers fell from the corner of my eye as I broke it to search for permanent damage. Both eyes sat way deep in the middle of my cranium, making me look more and more like I hadn't slept in a month.

The pain had destabilized me to the point where my whole body yearned for a big strong squeeze from Big Momma's massive strong tobacco-leaf-carrying arms. My skin looked two shades darker, as if my kidneys had stopped filtering out toxins and urine, making me appear as though leathery raw black cowhide was dangling from my bones. My lips were purple and blue, resembling two grape popsicles without the sticks.

The seat cushion became my sanctuary where all of the pain and suffering I endured was sucked out of me and released into the smelly old pee-stained seat. I passed gas that smelled of sulfur and old rusty nails. I sat there on the bucket, procrastinating, tapping my foot impatiently, trying to make time stand still. But it wasn't working.

"Hurry up, woman killer!" shouted the ruling gang-banger dressed as a peace officer. I squeezed my buttocks to circumvent some of the excruciating pain I knew would follow. I relaxed my testicles, anxiously waiting for the first sprinkle of urine to exit my penis. My family jewel stick had the sniffles; only a couple drops of urine mixed with thick globs of blood dribbled out, accompanied by piercing pain.

As I shook the last bit of drizzle from Mr. Henry, the remaining droplets of urine caused havoc down under forcing me to my tippytoes to help deaden the pain. Before I could finish wiping the blood from my penis, I was overtaken by hoards of acid bubbles rising quickly from my stomach. Without hesitation, I lifted myself from the cushion to turn around and vomit. For the next several minutes I began to dry heave and was stricken by bouts of invisible vomit. My body temperature shivered from hot to cold. I picked up the seat cushion and placed it back down on the bucket; I was not ready to go back to the gurney just yet.

While sitting on the bucket I became extremely paranoid. Terrified thoughts of the possibility that Ms. Karen had set me up to go to jail for the rest of my life or be put to death by lethal amounts of poison overwhelmed me. Agonizing vivid thoughts of poison bubbling beneath my skin took over. *Could there be poison in these tubes right now?* I quickly yanked the IVs out of my arm and crawled for dear life back to the bed. When I lifted myself up onto the bed, I tore two of my wounds wide open.

"Lay your ass back on the gurney, boy, where you belong so I can shackle you back to the bed poles!" My body and mind were now in fight or flight mode as the police officer placed the shackles back around my feet. The room began to spin while my body temperature bounced between sizzling and freezing. I lay there tossing and turning inside as my body lay still. The shackles contained my every move.

I was unsuccessful in trying to keep the entire room from closing in on me. The janitor's closet that shielded my weather-beaten body began to truly resemble a morgue. I felt as if I was lying on a steel slated table waiting for the mortician to slice me open. I tried to break free from the shackles just to stop the room from twisting and turning. The room flipped upside down and then turned horizontally as all four sides of the casket closed in on me.

The fight was over. I was spent, done in like a baby sea lion after hours of torture by two juvenile killer whales. The hookmaster saw that I was suffering and unhooked all the shackles. All of a sudden, he acquired a heart. He checked my pulse on my throat and informed me that he was going to get the nurse to make sure I was okay.

I saw my chance. I decided to end my life while Mr. Policeman was out of the room. I commenced to twist the bed sheets the best way I could while crying profusely, thinking how my baby girl would be without both of her parents. The thought of Riesha not being my child made me twist the knots even faster. Uncontrollable cries made up of sorrow and a broken spirit filled the air around me. My crying went from a soft whisper to a whimpering howl. I could hear Tina outside the door giving another news report.

I had made my way to the top of the bed with the bed sheet in tow. I tossed it over the metal room divider so I could finally hang myself, and all of this would finally be over. Snot poured from my nose as I heard Tina report, "Mr. Lewis's neighbor turned in the gun used to kill Paulette Jenkins." With tears racing down my face, I continued to toss the bed sheet over the divider, but I wasn't having any luck. I was too weak to get it all the way over the pole; the sheet kept hitting me in the face.

As I stood there on the bed with the makeshift rope in my hand, Ms. Karen burst into the room smiling and wiping away tears at the same time. Mr. Policeman rushed in behind her, grabbed her, and forced her against the wall.

"You are under arrest for withholding evidence!" he said, pushing her face against the wall. He frisked her and found her pipe. "Why didn't you tell me you had this pipe?" he shouted, holding it up to her face. The only thing she did was smile. As he held her against the wall, he tilted his face towards the radio on his shoulder to hear the dispatcher recite Ms. Karen's entire police jacket.

"Why didn't you tell me that you had three warrants in three different counties?" he asked, pulling her arms behind her back and cuffing her.

"What the hell is going on?" I asked Ms. Karen, but she just smiled and informed me that her mom will get her out in a couple of hours.

She added, "I'll come over when I get out."

The officer began walking Ms. Karen out in handcuffs, then stopped and turned to say, "You're free to go, Mr. Lewis!"

"What's going on?" I stood dumbfounded on the bed, the twisted sheet still in my arms.

A slew of news reporters pushed and shoved each other to get into the closet. Ms. Asian Persuasion made her way through them without a fight, as if she had major clout. Without hesitation she spoke to me kindly. "Well, Mr. Lewis, now that your neighbor identified her boyfriend as the killer, what are you going to do with yourself?"

I flopped down off the bed, dropping the sheet to the bedside, speechless.

After several minutes, my mind came up with the words of Dr. Martin Luther King Jr.: "Free at last, free at last, thank God almighty, I am free at last."

Then as my brain began to process the situation, I wrapped my aching arms around my aching body and said, "I'm gonna go find my daughter now."

17
My First 48

THE HEATED SUNLIGHT BEAMED THROUGH THE BLINDS of my bedroom window resting beneath my eyebrows. There wasn't any need for an alarm clock during the spring and summer months in the Pacific Northwest. My eyes slowly opened as the morning sun brightened my bedroom, transforming all my morning blues into an eventful awakening.

As usual, my first steps out of bed were to the window where I took advantage of the beauty that surrounded our apartment. While standing there, I asked God, "*Shield me with the blood of Jesus Christ.*" The sun rose from the east behind the majestic Cascade Mountains that exhibited a glimpse of this year's first snowfall. Luminous rays glistened through the blinds that I left open on purpose to allow Gods gift of light to magically awaken the house. Nestled in the Evergreen Fir trees just outside my bedroom window were a pair of squawking blue jays. The tree branch that housed the pair brushed against my window every morning as they began their morning ritual of flirting with one another. First, the male serenaded his lifetime mate with sequential chirps and whistles bellowing from his lungs. Next, to keep her interested, he continued to sing while flashing parts of his black and blue tail feathers. She conceded with a single flap of her wings, exposing the uniformed blue and white stripes on her tail feathers. Now that they had caught each others attention, they snuggled, wedged against each others breastplates feeling the warmth of the brilliant sun as it seeped through their feathers for solace and comfort.

The scene became both surreal and tranquil for me, transcending back to a happier time, a time when I had both of the most special women in my life. A time when Riesha lay between my chest and forearm, sipping on her *Dora The Explorer* sippy cup with her eyes squeezed shut. I could never understand how she could be sound asleep with her lips, mouth, and throat still active. A time when Paulette lay on my right, her head resting on my chest. She used to do this trick with her left arm, wrapping it around my back without making me uncomfortable. Every night she slowly moved her right hand underneath my shirt, resting her palm on the middle of my breastplate where she fiddled with the little bit of chest hair I have.

The harmonious spiritual hymns bellowing from the lungs of the blue jays quickly reminded me that it's okay to be humble for just two minutes. After the jays flew off, I stretched my hands way above my head, saying, "God is Good!" My knuckles scraped the ceiling, forcing popcorn speckles to fall on my face. I was able to close my eyes before any became troublesome. A few managed to land in my mouth as I yawned a morning yearning.

I felt one of my stitches tear when I stretched. To comfort little Henry and to let him know I felt his pain, I placed my hand around my family jewels and held them for just a brief moment. The wounds, still fresh and tender, reminded me of the beating I suffered. The time was etched in my mind for eternity.

I grabbed the remote control from the nightstand and turned on the flat screen that Paulette bought herself to watch her soap operas in peace. She recorded all of her soaps, especially her favorite, *One Life To Live*. Around eight p.m., after giving Riesha a bath and putting her down for the night, Paulette retired to the bedroom to watch her shows without interruption. The DVR warning on the screen reminded me that her soaps were being recorded. I didn't know how to stop the recording; I'll have to deal with this later.

I started surfing through the channels to see what the world thought of me now that I'd been exonerated. On the very first station, I turned to the face of my Ghetto Angel, Ms. Karen, that graced the TV screen. The mystifying Asian persuasion Tina Lee was interviewing her. Though Karen's dome was hideous, I was still grateful, happy to have her face grace my television screen. Because of her swift actions during my interlude with the law, I was freed, and she became apart of my circular family forever.

Karen looked as if she had received a makeover by Tina and her publicist. Both of them sported the same Jackie Kennedy hairstyle, a high bouffant held together by three cans of hairspray and pulled back off their foreheads by scarves that matched their outfits. Karen sported a baby blue scarf, and Ms. Tina wore a white one with a red ribbon dangling from behind each ear. If you were seeing Karen for the first time, you wouldn't know that her face was once full of mini volcanoes. Each crater was filled with the thickest Maybelline cover-up makeup the TV station could afford.

The interview unfolding on TV was taking place at the West entrance of Ms. Karen's apartment building. The two of them were sitting in the stairwell right underneath the awning that read, "Ridgetop Terrace". With one eye on the big screen, I wanted to take a glimpse of the spectacle across the street. Both were sitting overly poised and a bit too eloquent on the concrete steps, as if they rehearsed the whole interview. I knew how ghetto the two of them really were. I wasn't buying the whole approach to show biz they were trying to display — two women sitting out front on the stairs, chatting it up as if they were longtime best friends.

Ms. Lee sat with her back perched in an upright position with her legs crossed. She even had a white prayer napkin draped over her exposed knees to keep away attention. She appeared articulate and charismatic, leaning back on one elbow as if she'd been there before, chilling after church on a warm Sunday afternoon, smoking a cigarette with Ms. Karen while sipping on a fresh cup of Seattle's Best Coffee.

On the other hand, Karen looked as nervous as a fresh con exiting McNeil Island after spending the last thirty-five years locked up. She wouldn't stop twitching. She was perplexed and lacked sophistication. All of her jerking and twitching on live TV was making me feel sorry for her.

Acting like her protector, just as she did for me, I began talking back to the flat screen as if Ms. Karen could hear me. *"Come on, girl, pull it together! Be still; stop twitching and moving around, girl. Damn, Karen, pull yourself together!"* My heart bled for her as I continued to watch the debacle unwind in front of me. She looked pitiful, and I could tell she was high on something. But I was unsure of what that something was. If she's not high on crack, then it has to be methamphetamines, the most addictive drug in the United States.

On national television Ms. Karen said she felt hotter than fish grease on the inside, although the temperature outside was at a comfortable fifty-five degrees. She used a most-wanted flyer with her boyfriend's face on it as a fan, fanning herself rapidly. The twitching, unable to sit still, appearing anxious, her pupils dilated, the zombie-like blank look on her face, the grinding of her teeth, and her blackened teeth were all sure signs of using meth. Although her responses were garbled, Tina continued asking Ms. Karen the basic questions. "How long did you date your ex? When did he tell you that he killed her?"

Karen didn't respond. Her mind was preoccupied with something other than Tina and her questions. Tina tried again, "So what was it like living in fear for your life after finding out your boyfriend was the killer?"

Before Karen could answer, she nodded out while the camera was focused dead center on her. Her eyes flew to the back of her eyelids for five seconds or so, which was a long time on live television. She quickly opened them again when Tina asked abruptly, "Where is he hiding the victim's daughter?"

"I don't know! Hell, I wish I did know so that y'all would stop asking me! Like I said before, I don't know where he took her!" She quickly nodded out again. Falling asleep in mid-conversation was a solid indication of recent heroin use.

A street theologian once told me those who abuse crack and heroin may sometimes do a speedball; those struggling with both heroin and cocaine may combine the narcotic heroin with the stimulant cocaine to produce the most grandiose high. While some may have a preferred drug that they stick to, Ms. Karen was using a plethora of drugs. The cameraman tried to break away from her close-up before her eyes rolled again to the back of her head, but it was too late. Silence is a reporter's worst enemy.

During this brief intermission, the cameraman cut back to Tina. Caught off guard, Tina's mouth uttered the words "What the hell, lady!" Once Tina saw that the camera was on her, she said to Karen in the fake practiced proper voice she used on TV, "Karen, are you still with us?" Tina snapped her fingers in Ms. Karen's face. Although her reaction was severely delayed, she finally snapped out of it.

The first words out of Karen's mouth were, "My mouth is dry." Immediately she turned to the cameraman and calmly asked if she could have a sip from his water bottle. From my window, I watched the cameraman slowly and nonchalantly hand her the water bottle. Without letting go of the camera or taking one eye off the lens, he was assured that the hand-off was as smooth as the passing of a torch during the Olympics. Before he let go of the bottle, she snatched it from his hand, twisted off the cap and downed the entire contents in a matter of seconds. After finishing the water, she turned apologetically towards Tina, adding, "It's been a long forty-eight hours for me, and I haven't got any sleep at all!" She could barely finish her sentence. She was out of breath.

Once Karen awakened from what appeared to be a heroin induced nap, she could only recall and answer one query. It was because her speech had become so slurred that Tina's viewing audience, including me, was unable to make out what she was saying. Ms. Karen became overtly restless and somewhat anxious. For Tina, trying to hold a conversation with her was increasingly becoming impossible. I noticed Tina make the slow-down gesture with her hands, palms up in front of her chest, suggesting that Karen slow down before answering any questions.

"Well, we've known each other for several years, but for the past year or so he's been living here with me." Throughout the interview Karen's jaw swayed uncontrollably, from left to right. This was a symptom of abusing crack cocaine. Karen forgot she was on live TV as she began fiddling with the dead skin on her burnt up fingertips. While the cameras were rolling, she used her teeth to pull off the black foreskin, and then spat out the dead particles on the steps in between the two of them.

Laughing hard, I said, "Karen is ghetto!" She scratched her head moving her wig at the same time, which made me laugh even more.

After all of that, I did a high-five punch with an open fist in the air. By allowing myself to laugh, a tear escaped my renewed eyes. Sobriety had humbled me. And now with all of the cobwebs removed from my eyes, a lonely teardrop was able to escape freely as I jumped up and down in my living room. I was feeling remarkably renewed. I felt both privileged and honored to be free and alive.

It was at this moment God came to me and said, "Riesha is your child, a gift from me and Paulette to you." My soul was replenished with authentic morality in the form of self-spirituality, a gift from God. I appreciated the gift of freedom and the spirit of fatherhood. This was a gift from God, which had led me to believe there is still hope — hope in the form of glory and freedom in the form of building a concrete and profound relationship with my God and with my daughter.

"And besides, do you see how big her nose is?" This was the voice of reason, Granddaddy Rob. I laughed even more as never-ending teardrops rolled down the side of my face. Still crying I fell to my knees thanking God for carrying me throughout this storm. It was at this point when I no longer felt any more pain in my heart. My faith had been restored.

The perception of how folks in my village perceived me had almost killed me, and this must change for the better. One of my top priorities is to have a better working knowledge of why an entire community turned their backs on me and truly believed that I would have done such a heinous crime such as kill my baby's mother and kidnap my own daughter. In order for my daughter to have any chance at upward mobility and have any chance of becoming a genuine person like her mother, I must work on this immediately.

While I was getting dressed I was startled by a knock at the door. I wasn't in the mood to entertain anyone. Nor was I ready to express my *feelings* now that I was exonerated. If they didn't have my daughter in hand, then I didn't want to deal with them. Just the thought of being questioned pissed me off, so I decided to ignore whoever was knocking and returned to trimming my beard.

What if they did have my daughter? The thought flashed through my mind. I didn't take the time to turn off the beard trimmer before I made a mad dash down the hallway towards the front door to the apartment.

"Yo, Ceeze, open up the door, Cuzz! I know you're in there, man, stop playing, Blood!"

An unprompted smile appeared on my face. "Titi! Is that you?"

Her voice was calming. I was acting like a five-year-old who just learned the family is going to McDonalds for lunch. *Ya, Buddy, your cousin is here!*

With the exception of Paulette, Titi was the only person I could relate to and who understood me. It was okay for the two of us to be super-emotional when we were together. Although she is a woman, we were raised like brothers rather than cousins. Damn, it felt good to hear her voice. Her voice made me feel pure, as if I was just baptized in Lake Washington wearing nothing but a wife beater and whitie-tighties.

When I opened the door, we damn near knocked each other over trying to hug. Off the top, I noticed there was something brand new-ish about her. She wasn't high, nor was she bleeding (wearing red clothing items from head to toe) like she normally was. She looked halfway decent, handsome in her own right. Her attire was professional, casual, and dapper. She wore a fresh polo jacket over a green polo shirt with matching polo jeans and a pair of green leather polo boat shoes. Her dreadlocks looked freshly twisted and braided to the back. "Ah girl, I'm so happy to see you, Cuzz, you just don't understand!" I could have cried, but I held back to save face.

"Yo, cousin, you know once I heard about O-boy from across the street killing Paulette I had to come right over here to let you in on something." When I invited Ti to come in, she said, "Hold on for one second, buzz!" She ran back down the stairs. I watched her jet across the street wondering where she was going.

As she rushed through the parking lot in front of Ms. Karen's apartment, Karen noticed me standing in my doorway. She yelled out, "Yo, Ceeze, whenever you want me to cook for you, you come get a sista, ya hear me! You know where I'm at, homey!" Oh my goodness, she didn't just call me homey! And she is not black. Why did she refer to herself as a sista? With a smile on my face I thought, *Wow I wondered if she was trying to sound hard or if she really thinks she's black.*

"I'm getting dressed right now. I'll be down in a hot minute!" I replied.

She signaled and yelled back, "Awright, get a sista, playa!"

Damn she's as trashy as she wants to be. It's almost a cardinal sin to trust a crack head, but Ms. Karen is one crack head I could trust, because she had a hand in saving my life. I just wish she knew where daddy's Baby Booboo is! Damn I miss my little girl!

"Mr. Lewis could I have a word with you too?" Tina called out.

"Give me a second and I'll come down."

When Titi returned, she had Riesha's homegirl Monique with her.

What the Fuck! I couldn't stand that heifer. "Oh no, hell no!" Why did she bring this bitch to my house? She's the one who called me over to the murder scene, that lying scandalous whore. She has an evil spirit dragging behind her and I don't like having it in or around our house. I couldn't stand her! If only she hadn't begged Paulette to come over that night, I'd be standing here looking at Paulette instead of looking at her trifling ass!

When Titi brought her over to our house for the very first time, I was thinking Paulette would've made her out to be a marauder like I did. To my dismay, when Titi introduced the two of them, they instantly became friends. I contested their friendship from the very beginning. There was something awfully wrong about her, which just didn't resonate well within me. During the onset of their friendship, I wasn't sure myself. I had a hard time being comfortable with my women hanging around a stripper who happened to be gay too. It wasn't easy for me to trust her because I was a tramp before we started dating, and all of my previous relationships were with women who were tramps too.

The worst part of trying to trust Monique was I knew how nasty she really was. Titi shared many stories about how she and Monique had sexual encounters with both men and women after getting bumped in all night. I was with Tatiana when she first met Monique. She worked at a strip club called The Aurora Palace. After Titi got hold of her, she took her out of the strip joint and turned her into an escort diva, a professional working girl that you could call for a date.

Tatiana built a stripper pole and full bar in the basement of Monique's house. The stripper pole ran straight down the center of a free spinning table; the bar was kept completely stocked with top shelf liquor. When I voiced my concerns about how much I didn't like Monique hanging around the house or around our child, Paulette always came back with a similar rebuttal, "I don't like any of them nasty-ass niggaz you hang around with!"

Whenever I tried to voice my opinion to Paulette about how much I distrusted Monique, Paulette came up with as many good reasons why she would remain friends with her. When Paulette said to me, "You're trying to control me and who I hang around," I nipped that in the bud right quick, by leaving my pride at the door when I entered our house. From that point on, I kept my feelings about Monique to myself because I didn't want to let them get in the way.

At times I would catch myself trying to make her feel at home, just so she wouldn't have to act so dang-on plastic. Because of her actions, I became standoffish when she came around. If Paulette was at her house and I picked her up, I would go inside to retrieve my family. Once inside, she'd say hello with a big huge fake grin on her face and then franticly begin cleaning, or she would run to the back of the house where she would shout her goodbyes.

Now with Titi by her side, all of a sudden she felt the need to address me by my government name. "I got something to tell you, Brandon," said Monique.

Now what does this bitch got to tell me that is so damn important? She never had more than two words to say to me in the past, what could have changed all of a sudden? *Could it be that she was in love with my girl? Please, dear Lord, please give me the strength to deal with the things* I cannot change! I've been able to handle anything thrown my way, but I don't know if I could handle someone telling me that my woman was having an affair with another woman.

"You might wanna sit down, Cuzz," said Titi.

Before sitting down I assumed the worst. "Look, ya'll need to stop playing with my emotions and tell me what I need to know!" I started to get upset because they were beating around the bush, acting like they didn't want to tell me something that I needed to know. I felt my stomach turning inside letting me know something isn't right with this whole situation. I grabbed my stomach before saying directly to Monique, "Whatever the hell you need to tell me, go-head and say it, please!" My heart was pumping faster and faster while my right leg started shivering.

"I know Pedro," said Monique.

"Who?"

"Pedro The Dominican, from across the street; he was a customer of mine!" Monique flopped down on the couch next to me and looked directly into my eyes and said, "I am so sorry for your loss." The once fake and evasive Monique inexplicably had shed all of the fakeness. Somehow, I sensed she possessed true compassion for Paulette. Her sincere condolences led me to believe that I had been very judgmental towards her in the past. Damn, I felt bad. I was hypocritical, judging her solely based on the life style she had chosen, no better than the life style I was leading.

Monique was turning into a sophisticated woman right before my eyes. I never knew how attractive she really was. I had never sat this close to her before. I couldn't help but notice her flawless dark chocolate skin and her radiant and blemish free face. She filled my personal space with the scent of recently sliced mangos and freshly squeezed grapefruits. Her eyes looked dark brown, but I could still see traces of the black cornea. The lines underneath her eyes suggested that she had little sleep and lived a roguish life style.

Paulette had informed me that Monique was from Chicago, the daughter of a minister and a product of a secret love affair that her mother had when she first arrived from Mississippi. She was always referred to as *the fatherless child* in the church where her mother worked as the church secretary.

Sitting next to me, Monique swallowed up my personal space. Her low cut shirt exposed the massive breast that Titi paid for. On her right breast, she bore a tattoo of a red heart with 'Titi' in the middle. When Monique noticed I had taken a quick glance at it, she said, "I got *Paulette* tatted on my shoulder." She stood up and asked Titi to pull her shirt down low enough so I could see the tattoo. The tattoo was fresh, still covered with plastic wrap over what appeared to be traces of Vaseline. Configured in black ink with old-English lettering read *Paulette*, surrounded by little red hearts aligned by different shapes and sizes.

Monique continued, "One day when Paulette was over at my house, The Dominican came over for his weekly dance like he always did on Tuesday right around four p.m. When he arrived, I was changing Riesha's diaper because Paulette was just finishing cooking our breakfast. So when the doorbell rang, I asked Paulette to get the door and take The Dominican downstairs for me. Both Pedro and Paulette were shocked at seeing each other. It was three years since they had dated. Once downstairs, Paulette told him to have a seat. As I came down the stairs, I saw Paulette playing around on the pole, just like all of the home girls did when they came over. They want to spin around on the pole and try to slide down it. Paulette said to us while twirling around the pole, 'Oh girl, this is easy; I could do this for Ceeze.' After that, Pedro became highly infatuated with her again. Whenever he returned for his weekly dance he couldn't even concentrate on me. Instead he always inquired about the whereabouts of Paulette. He wouldn't stop bugging me about when she was coming back over."

As the details continued to unfold, I felt Monique was being sincere. "Brandon, you're not gonna believe me; that crazy-ass started calling me Paulette when I danced for him. But the most bizarre part happened when he found out he lived across the street from y'all. He became like a stalker. He'd wait for you to leave and for her to come outside. The day she came home after getting out of rehab, Paulette told me that he walked up to her and tried to kiss her. And when she said no, he tried to seduce her with some crack. After that, Paulette said she thought she could feel him watching her in y'all's apartment. She didn't pay it any mind until he knocked on y'all's door."

This is when I almost lost it. I jumped out of my seat and asked, "He was doing what?" I couldn't stop shaking my head from side to side. I paced the room in search of something to smash in. I walked to the window to cool off and spotted Ms. Karen and Tina Lee still sitting on the stairs with cameras and over-head microphones dangling in front of them. Ms. Karen saw me and waved. She then mimicked eating invisible food, making Ms. Lee smile. I put my index finger up to inform Karen I'd be down in a minute. She threw up an OK sign and went back to her interview.

"She was too scared to tell you, Brandon. After several attempts asking her to get high, she finally told him that if she gets high just once, then he will have to stop harassing her. He agreed. They used my basement and got high for about six hours, nonstop."

My renewed spirit vanished in an instant. All of my trust in the Lord crept out the back window of my apartment. The pain I endured over the last few days, that had suddenly vanished, now immediately resurfaced. I didn't know how to react. What was I to do about this information? My *woman relapsed with her killer! What! You can't be serious? Was I hearing this correctly?* I became overwhelmed by hate, anger, and defeat. I felt like the Lord had finally paid me back for all of the dirt I had done unto others — people throughout my life that I had wronged. "*I hope we are even now, dear Lord!*"

    I felt Paulette was being selfish. The idea of choosing to get high to appease another man other than me was absolutely repugnant and absurd.

    My whole thought process took a turn for the worst. Now I was thinking that there could possibly be something sinister about Paulette. How could she tell me she loved me and then turn around and smoke crack with that idiot Pedro. She couldn't be the woman of my dreams. God surely would not have sent down a demonist spiteful selfish being like Paulette. It was hard for me to believe that the women I entrusted with my life and the life of our daughter could make a bargain with the Crack Master Pedro, who ultimately took her life and kidnapped our daughter. Just that brief moment, that one bad decision, destroyed our family forever.

    Again, I was overcome with hatred and grief. Only degrading words could explain how I was feeling about Paulette. "That heartless Bitch!" I yelled from the top of my lungs so that everyone in my apartment and surrounding apartments could hear me. "Ya I said it, that heartless, ruthless, selfish, lying, weak, insecure bitch! Fuck that ho!" *Ya, I said it. Fuck that heifer!*

    I needed to place the blame for Paulette's relapse on someone. Initially, I had placed blame on Monique and wished I'd held my ground and not allowed my family to be involved with her. If Paulette hadn't been at her house the day Pedro came over, none of this would have happened.

I almost lost it when I glanced over at the family portrait on the wall — Riesha, Paulette and me. I had mixed emotions brewing up inside of me. Yet I slowly felt humble, thankful to be alive and truly sorry for Riesha's loss. Although it was painful for me to realize that Pedro could be tormenting my daughter after he tortured my woman. It was even more painful to realize that Paulette didn't tell me he was stalking her. For the next several moments, the pain I felt deep within the walls of my chest plate created a nonstop heart attack. The pain I felt could possibly be compared to giving birth to a child. The pain was a derivative of being betrayed.

At this moment it was hard for me to even mourn Paulette's death. Yet the love I still felt for Paulette was just as intoxicating now as it was after the very first time we made love. I felt more than just compassion for her; I felt admiration, sorrow and dissatisfaction. *How could she betray the only person who respected her wishes and desires? I glorified in having her in my life; I adored her.* How could she not feel the same way? How could she not trust me enough to tell me Pedro was stalking her? I thought we had a permanent bond. I thought we had become one.*

"Why didn't she want to tell me?" I asked Monique who was beginning to change back into the rogue that I presumed she was.

"She thought you would have blamed me!" *Yep, she got that right!* In the middle of her sentence something came over me. The sob story she was telling didn't correlate with being arrested at her place.

"So what was all that about when I came over to your house the other day?" I asked.

"Brandon, I tried to tell the police the truth, that you wouldn't have murdered Paulette. I even tried telling them about The Dominican stalking her. The hook is responsible for coming up with the scenario that you had killed Paulette in a violent rage thinking that she was having an affair. That's where the whole story came from about you being the abusive boyfriend from hell!"

I knew how much the police wanted me to go down for this murder solely based on my previous gang involvement. As it unfolded, I began to believe her spellbinding story.

"During my lap dance performance and after Pedro saw Paulette for the second time, he couldn't perform; he was that fixated on her."

This was way too much information for me to deal with at one time. Though I was trying to remain in a tranquil spot, hearing all of this gave me flashbacks of getting high to alleviate the pain and stress. Monique continued, saying, "Paulette told me it was the very next day when he came over here to help you start your car."

"Dude was overly friendly. He went out of his way to replace my alternator for me. He didn't even charge me. I paid him for the alternator, but that was it."

"What topped it all off, Brandon, was when dude started threatening Paulette."

"Threatening Paulette!" Okay now I've heard enough. I was ready to ask Monique to leave my apartment. I didn't want to hear any more of this monkey-shit.

"Ya, he caught her coming from here, called her a slut and told her that if she didn't give him a dance at my house that he was gonna tell you she was smoking crack again and having an affair with him."

As badly as I wanted to know if she went through with giving him a lap dance, I tried to keep from asking Monique. Still, she hadn't reassured me that it didn't happen.

My insides were boiling in a jealous rage until I couldn't keep quiet. "Well did she give him a dance?"

"Come on now, Ceeze. Of course she didn't!"

Now she wants to call me Ceeze! This is getting bizarre. I tried to keep calm as Monique continued her horror stories about what went wrong and how deeply regretful Paulette became as The Dominican became more and more sinister. I could only fathom what Paulette was going through. I felt her pain as if I was experiencing it for her.

Monique became more and more remorseful as she continued to share her deep sorrow for her part in Paulette's death; while I became speechless.

Titi didn't utter a word throughout the confession. She finally needed to express herself. "Yo Cuzz, when I find him, I'm gonna put two bullets in his forehead; one for Paulette and one for you, Cuzz."

I had never heard Tatiana so animated before. It was obvious from her silence that she regretted introducing Monique to Paulette. To make up for it, I believed she would do that if she found The Dominican before the police did. If that were true, then I'd be out two special women in my life.

"Yo T, I think we gonna let the police handle this one, Youngblood." The only time I called her Youngblood was when I was trying to get my point across. "If you get caught, then Riesha would be out two moms."

"You right, B, you right."

"And what about me?" said Monique. "If you're locked up, Honey Bun, how are we supposed to get married?"

Oh lord, here we go again. The two of them are going to try a relationship again. This would be their fourth or fifth try since they met. Tatiana is the jealous type, always wanting to know where Monique is. In Monique's profession, she deals with men for money. Tatiana usually starts out trying to be more of the pimp than a lover and always ends up being a hands-on pimp who also loves his ho. After Monique returned from doing a bachelor party, it always ended up with Tatiana confronting Monique and putting her hands on her.

"I'm turning my life around, Ceeze. Every since all of this started, Monique and I have been talking about getting back together, starting a family and shit. Get married. Know what I'm saying?"

I'd heard it before, so if they wanted me to jump for joy, that wasn't going to happen. I just smiled and congratulated both of them.

We turned our attention back on the TV interview that was taking place live across the street. Ms. Karen informed T-Lee that she provided the most compelling evidence to the police, which supported her claim that her ex boyfriend Pedro planned to kill Paulette and keep her baby to raise as if she were his own.

The thought of Riesha not being mine popped back in my head. I was hoping that nobody around noticed the distress all over my face. I tried not to let my head hit my chest this time. I figured since the truth was already coming out, maybe this would be the time to inquire if she knew whether or not Riesha was my daughter. I wanted to know so badly that I felt a panic attack boiling up.

Not right now! In the name of Jesus, I ask that you stop this attack from happening, dear Lord! I felt too embarrassed to ask, like in the fourth grade when I had the answers to teacher's questions while none of my classmates knew the answers but me. I was too cool and too embarrassed to raise my hand.

Ms. Tina Lee asked the troubling question for me. "So why did your ex-boyfriend kidnap her daughter?"

Karen replied, "Because he wanted to keep a part of her with him forever."

Before I could react, Monique said, "No, that's not the reason why. It's because Paulette aborted their baby when they were dating and he wanted to keep her only child!" I started to breathe again; I already knew about the abortion and I was relieved to conclude he didn't think Riesha was his child.

Now I could go on trying to figure out where my daughter was being held. Karen stated her ex kept a journal under their bed in a shoebox. She told how he wrote in it for seven minutes when he woke up in the morning and again before he went to bed. She explained he wouldn't let her see what he wrote. If he suspected that she read his journals, he'd beat her to a pulp. Karen stated that on two occasions he beat on her even when she didn't go through his shoebox, telling her the beating was a reminder to obey him. Ms. Karen stated that even when she gave the police the journals, she had never peeked inside.

Tina confirmed that she spoke to sources close to the police department who informed her that the journals contained compelling evidence that suggest The Dominican planned and followed through with the sadistic killing of Paulette. The room became silent as the three of us decided to just kickback and take in the silence, allowing the calm of the room to flow over us.

"Your neighbor on TV?" Titi said, breaking the silence.

"Yep, that's her. That's Ms. Karen's crazy ass."

"Wow, she is ugly as hell!" commented Monique.

Though she was laughing, Titi replied, "That ain't nice, Monique. You know God don't like ugly; you better watch out."

"Y'all ain't right, cuzz, ya'll ain't right," I replied.

"We about to b-out buzz," said Titi.

"Okay, girl, I'll call you."

THEN CAME THE MIRACLE. I heard Ms. Tina interrupt Karen to announce, "My producer reports that the victim's daughter has been brought to the police by a cab driver who claims a guy with a Spanish accent paid him two hundred dollars to drop her off.

"God is good!" replied Ms. Karen as she threw her hands in the air to praise Jesus. My whole body cried tears of joy, tears of relief, tears of release.

The three of us were enthralled at what we were witnessing. Our emotions ran freely. Collectively we rejoiced in the name of the Lord. One at a time, prayers flowed freely as if we each taught Sunday school. Naturally we gravitated to the middle of my living room and formed a prayer circle. Conjoined hand to hand, we each took turns thanking the Lord for Riesha's return. We showered one another with hugs and kisses as the burden of the unknown was lifted from my shoulders. And now I could get back to living.

For the second or third time in my life, I witnessed Tatiana cry. Once her tears surfaced, mine followed. The three of us cried uncontrollably, repeating the words of Ms. Karen, "God is Good!"

When Monique embraced me, I felt her compassion resonating throughout her warm body, comforting me. Now that the grudge against Monique was lifted, I could look forward to developing a profound relationship with her. But about her being Riesha's godmother, I still needed more time. The devil uses guilt as a main dish to eat away at your soul. Once the devil senses your guilt, he regurgitates in you as hopelessness, self-pity, and regret. I didn't want Monique to be consumed by that kind of guilt. I whispered, "I want you to know that I don't believe it was your fault that Paulette was killed."

As soon as the two of them left my apartment, they were bombarded by a torrent of cameras and microphones. It happened so fast they didn't have a chance to break free. I was happy for them because I felt it was important for Monique to tell her story.

18
Liquidating the Ridgetop

BEFORE PAULETTE'S DEATH, we had shared momentous adventures as a family, venturing into the city every weekend. The significance of visiting the city resonated in the quality of time we shared with each individual who we came in contact with throughout the day. We approached our trip as if we were going to a New Years Eve party hosted by Mary J. Blige. Paulette took lead in color coordinating all of our outfits down to our socks, drawers, and shoes. She couldn't stand for my pants to sag; yet when they did sag, she insisted I wear boxers that matched my outfit. Now that she was gone I still approached venturing into the city as if we were going in together.

The day of Paulette's funeral would be special because those who knew me were expecting to see the old me, wearing my hood colors, draped in baby blue from head to toe. Today I wanted people from my community to see me as a man, not an object. I decided to replace wearing my normal funeral attire — a blue button-down, heavily starched 501 Levi jeans and blue Chuck Taylors — with the Easter Sunday outfit my Boo purchased for me last Easter — a Ralph Lauren purple button-up with white stripes, gray pin-stripe slacks, lavender Stacey Adams alligator patterned dress shoes, and gray socks with a gray sweater vest. I didn't have to worry about doing any ironing; I found the Easter Sunday outfit still in the closet underneath the plastic from Ms. Lee's dry cleaners. Paulette insisted that I wear a bow tie, but I couldn't get myself to do it then. Today, in honor of my Boo, I will. The gray pin-stripe slacks she bought me were a bit too snug around my family jewels area when I wore them the last time; now they fit just right on account of losing ten pounds in a short period of time from not eating and stressing over the murder and my missing daughter. Usually I was always in a celebrative mood wearing my lavender gator shoes. I only wore them when I was stepping out on the town to catch a Mike Epps comedy show or a Keith Sweat concert. Nonetheless, wearing the entire Easter outfit suggested this was a new day, a new beginning, the rebirth of Christ arising from the dead to walk within me.

Usually the night before we headed into the city, I was responsible for making coffee while Paulette did all of the ironing. Because of the rain and the need for a quick warm-me-up, a significant number of Washingtonians drink coffee. Similar to the way the Brits are known to drink lots of tea. After the magical age of twelve, it wasn't uncommon to drink coffee along with our parents, as each household member prepared for the next day. In the morning, having a cup of coffee with my pops was a form of breaking bread, not only in my household but for many Washingtonians as well. Over a nice cup of joe we discussed the does and don'ts, the birds and the bees, and the cigarettes and the weed.

Making my Boo's coffee was a task I had to earn, and if I made it just right, sometimes earned me some nookie before heading off to the city. The mixture of caffeine and sugar made Paulette horny as hell, which triggered my hormones in a good way, because I loved it when Paulette drank more than two cups of coffee. She became sexually aggressive with me. A quickie in the morning started the day off just right.

It was my job to make sure that we had enough coffee for our trip to the city while Paulette prepared Riri's sippy cup and enough snacks to last throughout the day. Usually two packs of fruit snacks, some cut-up cantaloupe or apples depending on the season, and some carrots did the trick. She did the baby's hair the night before and wrapped it in a satin scarf to keep her hair from frizzing up overnight. We spent the entire Saturday together as a family unit, sliding by historic businesses that we previously deemed most significant to our past.

Our first stop was K-Mart. Paulette always liked to start off there because by the time we were done visiting friends and family throughout the day, we were either too tired to do any shopping or too broke to pay on our layaway. On the day of Paulette's funeral, I too started off at K-Mart knowing that I must still pay down on our layaway if I wanted to have any fresh clothes for Riesha; she is growing so fast.

After K-Mart, we headed to the Ridgetop Post Office for stamps, lollypops, and to say hello to Paulette's Aunt Lydia. The post office operated from an original cozy one-story brick building built in the 1920s. This historic building was the last of its kind in and the Ridgetop area. Before saying hello to any of the patrons in the post office, Paulette always headed straight for the Life-saver Fruity Rainbow stand. When auntie noticed her niece attacking the suckers, she stopped what she was doing and yelled out in her southern vernacular, "I know that ain't my niece and my great niece over there!"

With one hand on the wrapper and the other on the lollypop stick, Paulette said to the lady behind the counter, "Hey, Auntie, how you doing!" As the two approached each other, Paulette snuck in a few licks off the sucker.

"You and them dang-on-suckers, girl. Your teeth gonna fall out!" said Auntie. As the two hugged, it was evident they were thrilled to see each other. The lollipops still sold for the original price of fifteen cents each, and Paulette never left the post office without buying a dozen, which usually lasted into the following week.

Before we left the post office, we made sure that we picked up some of the latest black heritage stamps for Paulette's stamp collection. She started collecting stamps on the very same day Riesha was born. Paulette was ambitiously awaiting the arrival of the *Slave Revolt* Collection. This selection was a series of stamps dedicated to legendary First Americans and freed black slaves who fought battles and lost their lives together as they helped slaves escape from slave plantations across the South.

After Paulette purchased a book of stamps, we'd say our goodbyes and head down the street and around the corner to the renowned Shrimp Boat, a place where we could kick back and relax. The setting allowed us to shoot the shit with decent old school cats that landed in Washington State by way of the military forty years earlier.

The ambiance was synonymous for the easy laid back lifestyle of its patrons. The owner, Sammy Wilkerson, permitted my family to enter thirty minutes before the rest of his paying customers. Sammy did this because he wanted Paulette to see how fresh the cooking oil was before he prepared our special dishes, two Ridgetop specials. He knew how picky Paulette was about fried foods. She trusted Sammy because she grew up with him, yet she still asked the same question, "When was the last time you changed the oil?"

His answer was always the same, "Last night before I closed up shop. I just turned the grease on. Come take a look at it, girl!"

A Ridgetop special consisted of two King Crab legs, two fried chicken wings, two fried fish fillets, and four jumbo fried shrimp. The food was ridiculously pleasing to our bellies, and the blend of olive oil, vegetable oil and canola oil decreased the chances of Paulette enduring a major acne breakout. For dessert we shared a scrumptious bean pie. The first time I bit into a freshly baked bean pie, I was addicted, comparing the taste to a sweet potato pie mixed with pumpkin pie and filled with maple syrup, nutmeg, gobs of brown sugar and a hint of vanilla. Sammy had a way of knowing just the right amount of time needed to heat the pie to keep the perfect scoop of soy ice cream from melting on top. Next, he drizzled a little bit of caramel syrup on top, making the dessert the most memorable part of our weekend outing.

With our bellies full, we'd head to the hair palace — the beauty shop for Paulette and Riesha, and the barbershop for me. Socializing among friends and family members while eating good food or getting our hair done was a deep-rooted part of our lives. Paulette enjoyed patronizing the salon where her mother took her when her hair started getting thicker at the age of twelve. While there, Paulette caught up on Ridgetop gossip and Ebonic fashion.

When I entered the barbershop on the day of Paulette's funeral, I was greeted with a respectful sound of hands clapping. Every barber left their posts to greet me with a handshake and a pound on the back. Though their faces were emotionally bland, I felt the positive energy seeping from their bodies as we embraced in lieu of a brotherly handshake. Even the little Korean ladies who owned the shop extended their hands to me.

As each little lady shook my hand, she asked if I wanted a haircut. This was a new experience for me. I never had barbers arguing over who would cut my hair. They were even pulling and tugging on me trying to get me to sit in their personal barber chair. However I had to let them down gently, apologizing to each one while informing them that I had a standing appointment for a shape-up with Ralph Junior.

I never had experienced such a display of emotions geared towards me before. In the past, I acted belligerent to a point of insulting many of those present. That day, I stood up and announced, "Today is a new beginning!" Then I apologized to those who I had offended in the past. As I apologized for my trifling past, I felt my eyes begin to water up. I had to catch the tear in my right eye before anyone noticed.

From the flow of positive energy in the room, I felt compelled to change my self-image. On the spur of the moment I decided to cut off my braids. Paulette would be proud of me.

Historically the black barbershop was considered the most powerful and influential center force within the black community. A place where your barber discussed ways for his patrons to attain upward mobility. A place where barbers taught you how to resolve a problem peacefully. Your home away from home, where everybody knows your name and the names of your parents and their occupations.

Although Ralph was my personal barber since I was just a boy, I didn't feel comfortable going to the suburbs to get my haircut. Ralph's grandson followed the family tradition by becoming a professional barber like his grandfather. Unlike his grandfather, RJ made a statement by remaining in the neighborhood. Though he had to rent a booth in the very same shop once owned by his grandfather, now owned by the little Korean ladies, he still held his head high. And by doing so he had taken his grandfather's position as my barber.

He swung a barber cape over my chest and fastened it from behind, snapping it together in the back of my neck, a bit snug, but I didn't say anything. He whispered in my ear, "Before we get started, come to my office, I got something for you." I knew that *something* could be one of two things, a blunt or a shot of Hennessey. I was baffled about how to deal with this situation because it was happening so fast. Turning down drugs and alcohol was new to me. To top it all off, when I entered into the barbershop and saw Ralph Jr., I could already taste the yac. We had been yac partners in the past.

I did want the drink! Hell, I wanted to smoke a blunt too. But I had made a covenant with God and my daughter not to get high anymore. A voice was telling me that it would be okay if I took just one last drink. The same voices tried again to trick me into celebrating one last time for Paulette and for the safe return of my daughter, though I hadn't seen her yet.

By the time we reached the door that led to RJ's office, I realized that the devil is real, and if I took one sip of the yac, I'd be persuaded to smoke a blunt, and it would be like I never stopped smoking and drinking. Yet I found myself following RJ, almost tripping over his heels. RJ grabbed the cognac and a cup, blowing into it. "No matter how hard I try, there's always hair everywhere. Man, I go home with hair in my draws; it's crazy, son!" We both laughed hysterically.

When Junior handed me the cup full of yac, I became discombobulated. The aroma of fresh black licorice, perfectly aged, filled the air around us. The smell gave off a euphoric sensation, forming a haloed effect that had engulfed the air between the two of us. Heated fumes arising from the plastic sincerity cup full of yac consecrated us. The liquid spoke to me saying, "I missed you, little homey! Where have you been?"

RJ tilted his cup towards the ceiling and said, "Saluté!" I followed suit tilting my cup towards his. I didn't know what else to do because part of me wanted to drink and the other part of me didn't want anything to do with it at all.

Before we took a sip, Ralph said to me, "I know this doesn't mean much to you right now, but I knew you didn't kill your baby's momma, and I knew damn well you wouldn't hurt your little girl!" I took the cup and tapped his, confirming that I believed every word he was saying, and then I put the cup in motion to take a sip. I knew that it would be okay for me to enjoy a drink. I placed the cup up to my lips and slowly started to turn the cup upwards so I could swallow every drop.

Before the liquor touched my lips, Junior said to me, "All these fake-ass niggaz around here were saying you killed her. Watch out, Ceeze; you never know who your true friends are until something tragic like this happens. Know what I'm saying?"

His words moved me in the right direction, giving me the specific uplift I needed to prevent myself from drinking. At that very moment Ralph Jr. joined the ranks of many hood figgaz including his grandfather; Ralph became one of my Ghetto Angels. And if I took this sip of poison, I'd go back to my wicked ways in an instant, starting off right where I left off — two blunts and two brews in one hour. In an attempt to destroy my future with my daughter, the devil led me to believe it would be okay to take just one drink. However, it was God placing me in front of my Ghetto Angel to hear the truth so that I would bounce back to reality. My Ghetto Angel Ralph Jr. saved me from continuing to live a dysfunctional life style that would ultimately land me six feet under. I chose to shed my wicked ways so I could fully embrace the glory of God. I feared God now; I was experiencing the presence of his glory and his grace. God said to me, "You don't need that drink, Brandon."

Though Ralph was being considerate by offering me some medicine to help ease my pain, I finally drew enough strength to say, "No thanks. I don't drink anymore."

"Oh, my bad, my nigg! I didn't know you stopped drinking." I handed the cup back to him and watched him pour it into his cup. Ralph pulled out a blunt from his front pocket and said, "I know you didn't give up smoking too!" With a huge smile on his face, he continued saying, "Please tell me you still smoke weed, Cuzz?"

"I'm done, Cuzz; I don't do shit."

"Okay, Cuzz, I'll leave you alone for now, but when you snap out of whatever you going through, you know where to get some of this good shit, homey."

Once Ralph Jr. was done cutting my hair, he handed me a mirror. My head looked smaller without the braids; RJ had given me a skintight fade, high and tight, and I was impressed. I told him my hair looked good and handed the mirror back. Even when RJ told me that this haircut was on him, I still reached into my pocket for some cash to give him for a tip. I never had this type of gratitude thrown my way. "My man!" We shook hands and then did fist pounds to the centers of our back.

"What time is the funeral?" he asked. Before answering, I glanced over my new and improved look again in the extra large mirror. I was really overwhelmed by my new look and wished Paulette could see me.

"One o'clock!"

Every week, after Paulette and I got our hair done up, we went to visit Uncle Howard. Paulette was Unc's favorite niece; he truly had a thing for her. Whenever she was around, my uncle sat upright in his bed and put in his teeth so he could look more presentable. Paulette's presence brightened up his day. At the very first sight of her, he asked me the same two questions, "Brandon, when you gonna marry this pretty young thang, boy?" and "What, she's good enough to sleep with and have your child, but she isn't good enough to marry? What kind of shit is that?" Although we'd both told him how inappropriate the second question was, he still asked. Diabetes stripped him of mobility, leaving him with no legs, cut off just beneath the kneecaps all due to poor eating habits, drinking hard liquor, and smoking two packs of cigarettes a day.

My mother had asked me to take care of her brother after she was gone. That day, I took care of my uncle's leg and tended to his atrocious apartment. Paulette's funeral was in two hours. However, my mother would refuse to acknowledge me once I reached heaven if I left his house looking so hideous.

I rolled down my sleeves, hugged Unc and headed out the door with one thing on my mind, reuniting with my Baby Booboo Riesha. Grateful and thankful for taking the time out of this day to take care of my decrepit Uncle, was a way for me to validate my existence. Doing something positive like cleaning my uncle's roach-infested, mice-cruising abode, and ensuring that his bed sheets, towels, socks and underwear were as clean as his body, provided me with a glimpse of what God has promised me.

Before leaving for the funeral, I glanced back at the apartment and wiped the sweat off of my forehead. Unc got out of his bed and flopped over onto his wheelchair scratching his head. "Your momma would've been proud of you, boy! My place looks brand new; the roaches are gonna have to pack up and find somewhere else to live. Good job, Squeaky!"

THE FUNERAL SERVICE WAS HELD at the Ridgetop Christian Center, formerly known as Ridgetop Baptist Church. It was built in the heart of the bustling Ridgetop community in a section of town called the Emerald District, known for quaint sidewalk cafes and tiny yet eloquent wine bars.

The congregation was composed of the most powerful, influential black leaders of the Ridgetop, most with ties to the community that dated back to the mid- to late-1800s, when the first black settlers arrived in the Pacific Northwest. The pastor was summoned by prominent old money community members to form a coalition to fight crime in and around the district.

As soon as I left Unc's apartment, I was caught up in a rainstorm, which dumped more than eight inches of rain in less than thirty minutes. I couldn't see three feet in front of me because my wiper blades were worn out and now stopped working completely. I had to keep stopping to stretch my arm out the window to wipe off the windshield with the trusty old blue rag that dangled from my rearview mirror. Paulette had begged me to change the wiper blades a long time ago, yet at that time I was more concerned about getting high and hanging out with my homeboys than taking care of something as uncomplicated as changing wiper blades. The defroster wasn't working so good either. The fan blew out cold air, which also meant the radiator was low on coolant or my thermostat wasn't working properly.

Paulette's voice came out of nowhere, softly, simply asking, "Did you take the car for the appointment I set up last week?" My black ass was laughing regretfully for not listening to her.

I couldn't catch a break for nothing; there weren't any parking spaces available within three blocks of the church, which frustrated me even more. I was already stressing because I didn't want to attend Paulette's funeral without having my daughter by my side so she could see her mother for the last time. I was also having a hard time dealing with the notion of being around a church full of people with grandiose attitudes, who had the bravado to smile in my face as if I didn't know most of them initially accused me of killing Paulette. I despised doing things I didn't want to do.

As I drove around the church looking for a place to park, I came to the conclusion that I couldn't put off buying new blades any longer. *Right after the funeral, I'll head straight over to Pep boys to purchase a new pair.*

Sweat began to trickle out from underneath my hat and stocking cap, a sure sign of a panic attack. After shedding the braids, I purchased the stocking cap from the barbershop to see if I could form some waves quickly. I removed both the hat and stocking cap to stop sweating, I ran my hand over my head to see if any waves had formed and all I got was a hand full of hair from my previous haircut; I hadn't had time to wash my hair. I was getting all hot and bothered, as I always do when I begin to stress out. The heavy breathing, my rising body temperature, the defroster not working, and the sweat mixed with hair dripping on my face was making me itch. I decided to pull over and chill out for a brief moment.

Normally this would be a good time for a quick bottle of serum along with a Newport or a fat ass baseball bat, but I had decided to stop destroying my mind and body on the very same day Paulette was found dead. Even though I still struggled, it was unfortunate that the day Paulette's cold body was found, would also be my sobriety date: *Damn, what a crying shame.*

I didn't want to observe Boo's death every year sober; that wasn't how we do it around my way. I wanted to mourn her death the same way I did all of the hundreds of dead homeys.

The thought of dealing with Boo's death and the reality of not knowing if and when my daughter would be returned to me increased the sweat; the windows were beginning to fog up. Which made a great excuse for me to stay right where I was so I could just chill until the rain subsided. I was besieged by uncontrollable urges to get high.

My heart wanted to remain righteous, but my mind and body were used to not dealing with the obvious; I am a drug addict. But in my subculture we never could imagine weed could be labeled addictive. "I just need one pull, just one pull off a blunt, dear Lord, and I'm good!" I've found weed and cigarettes in between the seat cushions and underneath the seats of my car before, so I was hoping that would be the case now. I looked underneath the passenger seat. Nothing there. Then I pulled up the back seat to see if one had fallen behind there. Still nothing. I remembered I had put out a blunt in the ashtray the night before Paulette was murdered, but there wasn't one there now. *Fuck, I wanna smoke on something!* I thought about turning around, going back to the barbershop so I could get high with Ralph Jr., but I was too embarrassed to do so.

I prayed a quick prayer, "*Lord, help me deal with this feeling that is making me want to get high. I'm stressing out, dear Lord! Help keep me focused. I'm trying to be good!*" And I added, "*Please make me stronger so I can be a good father to my little girl Riri, and I ask of you, dear Lord, please bring Daddy's little girl home to me today!*"

I found myself in a crazy mental state. The death of my Boo was finally sinking in. I started crying, hard as hell. I couldn't separate the sweat from the tears flowing across my face. I was really messed up. *Who do I cry to?* Everyone who was special to me, who I could lean on, was gone. I felt vulnerable, as if I had been caught leaking over on the Westside without my strap. Nothing around me could convince me I was supposed to live without Paulette by my side. The thought of Riesha being without her father didn't seem to stop me from feeling like life was worth living. I knew a good family would raise her.

I had spent the last twelve years using drugs and alcohol to control my erratic emotions. Now it was like I was thirteen all over again, having to learn how to manage reality without taking medication. I began to question God's plan to keep me alive as I frantically continued searching through the dirty ashtray for a roach or the corner of an old blunt that was not there. What part of his plan pertained to me having to experience this pain that resonated deep down inside of me. "Fuck this shit, Cuzz!" I said to myself. "I should just check out right now! I could go to the Narrows Bridge, jump, and be dead before I even hit the water."

Still shedding uncontrollable tears I could barely get a grip of the steering wheel. *This isn't how life is supposed to be! How come I just can't smoke one blunt? Dear Lord! Just one blunt and I'll be okay! I can't take this shit. I can't live like this! I'll just hit the blunt one time, and then I'll be done, and I'll stop smoking weed forever.*

The problem was I didn't know how to deal with the rage erupting inside of me. I couldn't remember if I had ever felt this way before. If I did, it didn't last long because Titi always had some weed. I just had to make it across enemy lines to get to her house, but it always was worth the trouble. On the way I could stop off at a liquor store to grab some serum: four shots of Jack Daniels 151, one for the trip there, one each for Titi and me after we smoked a blunt, and one for the trip home. I knew once I reached her house, I was safe and, in a matter of minutes, I'd be high.

This wasn't the way I had planned living my life. I assumed my death would end violently, and Paulette and Riri would have to attend my funeral. Never did I fathom me attending Paulette's funeral without Riesha by my side. I envisioned both Riesha and Paulette wearing black dresses, with black veils pulled over their faces, the two of them chauffeured to and from the funeral home and burial site in a black Lincoln Town car, not a limo. While the two of them rode solo in the back seat, Paulette would rock Riri in her arms as tears streamed down her face. Paulette would be holding Riri close to her chest as the child sipped on her favorite Dora The Explorer sippy cup full of diluted apple juice.

After saying another quick prayer, I started driving around the block several times again looking for a parking space. Reality started to sink in.

I said forget about it, and decided not to attend the funeral after all. The deciding factor didn't pertain to unavailable parking; I refused to attend the ceremony after realizing that I didn't want to be around a bunch of phony ass niggaz trying to smile in my face after I was already publicly stoned and painted as an outcast. Their apologies would mean nothing to me.

The gravesite is where I should be, so I could pay my respects to my baby's mother without being bothered by a bunch of charlatans. I knew that people were expecting me to attend, but I didn't have to go if I didn't want to. This was the first step I took to control the energy around me. I was comfortable with the decision not to attend, which was most important to me at this point.

The burial site sat in the middle of grassy sea-green meadow just inches away from a wild life preserve protected by raccoons the size of a brown bear cub. Possums were on point as well, the kind of possums that never played possum and would charge at you until you were out of range. In order to get to the burial site, I had to park the car at the main gate and walk down an uncouth dirt path that the locals called Death Row.

Regardless of the weather, the journey was dark and gloomy; the *row* was also known for having a haunting revolting aroma that arose from the thin layer of fog that rested just inches off the ground. I walked on my tippie-toes trying not to let the dust ruin my white shoelaces. Since I wasn't going to the funeral, I changed into my OG Nikes. Once the laces got dirty, the shoes would be ruined. I bought these shoes for the special night out when I proposed to Paulette. Now I'm wearing them at her gravesite. My crazy life!

I approached the big rock that stood six feet high and ten feet wide. The rock was used as a message board for gangs and for the dead. The boulder rang out mostly gang-affiliated names, scores of them. Someone already had written "R.I.P. Paulette." on the message board.

I continued toward the only tent with a casket beneath it. There lay my darling Boo. From afar I noticed a man standing alone and holding a child. Could that be? Sho-nuff! Mr. Jenkins was holding my Baby Booboo Riesha. I quickened my walk, never doubting God's will. I knew my baby would be returned to me.

Once I was close enough to see my child's face, our eyes connected and a smile appeared on her face, though she never stopped sucking on the bottle. Her little feet began to kick faster and faster as I got closer. She twirled a finger on her hair in the very same spot she always did. She was developing a bald spot from this, a reason we were trying to take her off the bottle.

Before the murder, Paulette and I had weaned her off the bottle. For only a second, I was disappointed she was back with a bottle; she must have been hollering something awful. Paulette's voice interrupted, saying, "Stop nit-picking and go hold your baby."

Once I was in front of Mr. Jenkins, he immediately handed over my Baby Booboo. "She missed you, son!" said Mr. Jenkins.

I couldn't speak. Nor could I process the way I felt. I was too busy trying to take in all of what was in front of me. In front of me sat a casket with my woman in it. In my arms was my baby who had been taken from me. Now she was safely back in my arms. All of this overwhelmed me. Tears without emotions attached poured like an overflowing ravine from both of my eyes.

Again came Paulette's voice, "Just imagine what Jesus went through." There wasn't very much talking between Mr. Jenkins and me. I focused most of my attention on my baby girl so I didn't have to acknowledge my Boo's casket.

I couldn't stop kissing Daddy's Little Girl. Her face, full of excitement, smelled of freshly squeezed oranges and Neosporin; she must have a diaper rash from sitting in a soaked diaper. But the diaper rash and her sucking on a bottle were the least of my concerns. At that moment, I was as proud to be a father as I was the day she was born.

Daddy's Little Girl continued sucking on her bottle while wiping away my tears with her right hand. I tried to take the bottle out of her mouth but she wouldn't let me. Without letting loose of the strong hold she had on her bottle, she let me kiss her on the side of her mouth as she continued to suckle away. I pulled up her pants leg, searching for visible marks, scrapes or bruises. I pulled up the front of her shirt, then the back, again checking for marks or cigarette burns. I found no visible signs of abuse.

"Did you check her private area?" I asked Mr. Jenkins.

"The hospital doctor gave her a complete physical. Everything came back normal."

As I continued to give Riesha a once-over, Mr. Jenkins stood quietly in front of the casket, staring at the box where his little girl rested. In a way, I felt his pain. For just a brief forty-eight hours I too had lost my only daughter. Yet, I didn't have any comforting words to share with him, nothing to help alleviate an ounce of the pain he surely was feeling. I stood quietly holding my daughter who had just been returned to me, both of us feeling the deep agony attached to being defeated. I made a silent promise that his daughter would always live within his granddaughter and me, and that I would never keep Riesha from her grandparents.

I felt I needed to whisper, "Mr. Jenkins, I want you to know that you and Mrs. J. can come and get Riri anytime you want."

In a quiet soft murmur, without looking up, he said, "You know she was a good momma who loved both of you very dearly. You two reminded me of Paulette's mom and me when we first met, except you had enough sense to stop running the streets way before I did." Then he turned to me and said, "I have a little money stashed away for Paulette and Little Riri; now, it's yours. You're gonna need a fresh start after all of this is over and done with."

Then he asked, "Weren't you and Paulette thinking about moving to DC?"

"Ya, we talked about it. She wanted to go to Howard to study law." As soon as I finished saying the word *law*, I was inundated with tears, disobedient animated tears. Mr. Jenkins pulled out a handkerchief from his back pocket and handed it to me as he took the baby from me. I succumbed to a barrage of unwavering sobs.

I fell to my knees, weeping copiously, letting my sorrow flow like crystal clear Mount Rainier spring water. There I sat, wishing my Boo would pop out of the casket alive. I lunged towards the casket, trying to open it. Mr. Jenkins calmly placed Riri in one of the fold-up chairs that faced the casket and pried me off her casket before I could open the hatch.

He pulled me in close to his chest, squeezed me with his powerful Virginia Blue Ridge Mountain wood-splitting arms and said, "Get a grip on yourself, son. You have a little girl to raise. Your daddy didn't raise a fool, boy. Now step up your game and tend to your daughter. Look at her over there crying, boy. Go get her and do what you have to in order to make a good home for her. Mrs. Jenkins and I got your back, son. So whatever you need, you come see me."

Mr. Jenkins instructed me to tend to my baby, and so I did. I wiped off the tears and picked up my Baby Booboo and headed away from the gravesite. Riesha acted like nothing was wrong until we began to leave. She dropped her bottle and stopped twisting her hair long enough to point at the casket to say, "Mommy?"

"Yes, Mommy."

Surprisingly she then said, "Mommy gone bye-bye?"

"Yes, Mommy gone bye-bye." Before the murder, Daddy's Little Girl didn't speak that clearly. I realized how much Riri had grown in just the short period of time she was gone from me.

As we were leaving, the caravan of on-lookers from the church was approaching. It was good timing for me, because I wasn't in the mood to speak to those phony-ass people. Instead of sticking around, I wanted to take my baby to our family spot; our family's little getaway, Foss Waterway, the waterfront.

On the way, I stopped to purchase a fake beer and two single cigarettes. Though I decided to give up self-medicating and getting drunk and high, I still craved the taste of beer. For what it's worth, I figured I could wean myself off cigarettes as long as I had a plan. A single cigarette to go along with the near beer sounded real chill.

Mrs. Lee informed me that they no longer sold single cigarettes. She didn't give any explanation, just pointed over to the Newport's behind her saying, "Two for one." Damn, I didn't want two packs, but I decided to buy them and give away the second pack to one of the cats begging for a cigarette in front of the store.

The waterfront is where cultures from all over the world merged to enjoy the company of others. A place where people said hello just because they wanted to be friendly. A place where childhood friends reminisced with long lost best friends. A place where ex-cons fresh out showcased their jailhouse stature and prison tattoos. A place where church folk came to flaunt their Sunday best, taking in the breathtaking views of sailboats on Commencement Bay. It was the sight of the pretty blue skies that rested above us which kept us coming back.

I pulled over in my favorite parking spot where I was able to see all the way across the Sound to the humongous houses that sat alongside Sandy Rock Seashore. Whenever I was there, the same white couple, appearing to be in their late 70s, was always chilling too.

They appeared never to say a word to each other, both staring out the front windshield, taking in the panoramic views of the waters of God's country. He drove a cocaine-white Fleetwood Brougham with sparkling white Vogues that he kept crispy clean, gleaming brighter than the North Star from up above. We all sat peacefully and quietly watching the motionless, undisturbed emerald green waters at rest.

My baby girl had fallen asleep in the back seat. I contemplated smoking a cigarette, although Paulette would knock me upside my forehead if she caught me smoking while Riri was in the car. Instead, I turned the pack over to the opposite end so that the tobacco could ascend towards the filter. I hit the pack on the palm of my hand ten times. I believed that the mint freshness taste forced out the mighty power of the deadly chemicals, a procedure that provided a full-fledged nicotine fix. My lips became numb as the chemicals sifted through the dry crusty cracks on my lips, lingered in my mouth, and produced a nicotine-high, even without lighting the cigarette.

    I lit the cigarette, then twisted the cap off the St. Paul Girl Non-Alcoholic Beer and tilted it up to my mouth. I held the cancer stick outside the window and turned my head towards the sky to assure none of the smoke reached Riesha. The old man acknowledged me by giving me a two-finger salute atop his forehead without turning towards me or looking in my direction at all. I gave him back the same.

    Though the beer didn't contain alcohol, I still poured some of it in an old Styrofoam cup I found on the floor. I set the half-empty bottle back down on the floor and glanced at the old man to see if he was watching me watch him; he too was drinking from a white Styrofoam cup. Raising it in the air, the old man saluted me, and I did the same. The old lady in the passenger seat leaned forward and acknowledged me by saying, "Let us know if you see the hook and we will do the same."

    "Not a problem," I said, the cigarette dangling between my lips.

THE WARM AIR MIXED WITH THE COOL BREEZE that drifted off the coldest body of water on the west coast worked better than a good cup of sleepy tea. I leaned over the back seat to be sure Riesha was fast asleep so I could catch a quick catnap while she was resting. I wanted to make sure Riesha had her sippy cup in her lap for safekeeping. Knowing that Riesha was safe and secure, after making sure all the doors were locked and the windows were rolled up half way, I folded my arms across my chest. In a matter of seconds I was completely out.

Shortly thereafter, I woke up when Riesha dropped her sippy cup and shifted in her car seat. While she was still sleeping, I reached back and unbuckled her from the car seat and took her in my arms. I pushed the entire front seat back so I could comfortably hold my baby against my chest as she continued to sleep so innocently; I wanted to hear and feel her breath vibrate off my chest. After just one exhausted exhale from my baby's lungs, my spirit was converted from somewhat hopeful to grateful, pleased, and sanctified. I felt so blessed to be able to hold my daughter again, so thankful with Riesha lying against me. I ran the back of my hand over her baby hair, soft yet a bit nappy because no one had combed it over the last couple days. With Riesha lying against my chest, I felt capable of accomplishing all tasks set before me. Her breath smelled of tainted crushed apples, which transcended into encouragement, giving me even more hope and joy.

With my little girl snoring on my chest and the brisk sea air slowly and quietly drifting through the car, I too started to drift off again. Knowing the old man and his wife were watching my back like they always did, I began to nod off quickly. Moments later I awakened to see Paulette sitting in the front seat of my Nova, chilling. She too was taking a catnap. When I dozed off, our daughter was fast asleep in my arms. Now she was awake and sipping on her cup. I had left it in the back seat when I took her out of the baby seat; Paulette must have given it to her.

My Paulette was the prettiest when she was asleep. The way her eyelids lay over her eyes, her eyelashes long and lustrous... oh-my-goodness, she was such a beautiful work of art. She looked as if she was in a deep, deep sleep, at peace with herself and her surroundings. I sat there staring at my Boo, my hand lightly running over her black, silky hair, looking as if she had just flat-ironed it. (She usually flat-ironed it every two weeks or so, or after we had an argument over something petty, in an attempt to keep me from straying away from home.)

She appeared so picturesque sitting there, calm and tranquil. Her lips still shimmered as if she wore the best lip gloss heaven could afford. Rays of the sun bounced off her glistening bronze, almost crystal-like, skin. As my Paulette sat there peacefully with her head tilted back, I touched her sparkling lips with the tip of my index finger to see if they were as wet as they looked. As I touched her mouth, she rolled her head towards me, took my hand and placed it on her chest so I could feel her heart beating.

Paulette always awakened with the most pleasant smile on her face. Now, in her morning-soft eloquent voice, she said, "Mr. Green, I need you to take care of our baby, okay?"

I said to her, "I will, Boo."

"You make sure she does good in school and take her to get her hair done and make sure she gets to Sunday School on time. Ceeze! I'm serious!"

"You know I got you, girl!"

She smiled with a sparkling teardrop on her cheek. I took my hand and slowly wiped away the tear and at the same time told her, "I'll take good care of our child."

Before she faded away into oblivion, her last words were, "I've given you all you need, Mr. Daddy Ceeze Green."

About the Author

Robert H. Young Jr. grew up during the intense years when cities fought crime and blamed blacks for most of it. He pays tribute to his father, Robert Sr., for increasing his awareness of social trends. Encouraged by his parents not to follow the path that led many black youth straight to prison, Robert Jr. studied and played basketball. When he realized he didn't have the skills to enter pro sports, he headed for college.

On the day of graduation from Evergreen State College, Robert Jr. released his first book, *Ghetto Angels*. He was following in the footsteps of his mother, an author of four inspirational books, which inspired Robert to lift himself out of ruts when he fell. Carolyn Vaughn Young told her son: "God has plans to use you as a vessel to empower and inspire those in need of support." *Cobwebbed Eyes* is Robert Jr.'s response.

Robert also names his sister, Terri Dickey, an urban furniture designer and cancer survivor, as one of his Ghetto Angels. In their youth, she helped him practice self-defense the night before he knew bullies would try to take his lunch money. She empowered him to follow God's plan to become a productive citizen and to help others with substance abuse disorders.

Robert Jr.'s life has been threatened many times, and he attributes his survival to the Ghetto Angels who have protected him. He now works as a Substance Abuse Specialist, lives near Washington DC, and is an unconventional father to six children (two adopted), all headed towards a variety of fields of accomplishment.

Made in the USA
Columbia, SC
15 December 2018